The Amber Room

Christopher Matthew

The Amber Room

SINCLAIR-STEVENSON

First published in Great Britain in 1995
by Sinclair–Stevenson
an imprint of Reed Consumer Books Ltd
Michelin House, 81 Fulham Road, London SW3 6RB
and Auckland, Melbourne, Singapore and Toronto

A CIP catalogue record for this book
is available at the British Library
ISBN 1 85619 447 7

Typeset by ROM-Data Corporation, Falmouth, Cornwall
Printed and bound in Great Britain by
Mackays of Chatham PLC, Chatham, Kent

For my family

1

The great palace gleamed grey in the moonlight, like a battleship marooned in a garden. Below, fountains and statues cast long shadows across the white lawns. The night air was warm for early September and the heavens shimmered with stars.

From somewhere away to the south came a succession of dull crumps and heavy rumblings. Lights flashed low in the sky, as if a thunderstorm were on its way. But this was no summer lightning – all sound and fury – that would set the dogs barking and the children gazing out, wide-eyed, between the cracks in their curtains and quickly pass over, leaving the place as serene as before. The tempest that was approaching would rage for three terrible years, bringing with it starvation and destruction on a scale that no one who was present that night could possibly have imagined.

For the great building sleeping in the moonlight was the Catherine Palace in the little town of Pushkin, twenty-five kilometres south of Leningrad. The date was 12 September 1941. Three months earlier, in the early hours of 22 June, the signal 'Dortmund' had been flashed to the commanders of the seven German armies, four panzer groups and three air fleets poised on the Russian frontier and Hitler had unleashed his long-awaited Operation Barbarossa. And now the troops and tanks of Army Group North, under the command of Field Marshal Ritter von Leeb, were at the gates of the town.

Everyone in Pushkin could remember where they had been on that still June evening when they heard the news that their country had been invaded. Many had been taking advantage of the spell of warm weather in the palace grounds. Gregory Pechorin, the Curator and Keeper of the Treasures, had been picnicking beside the lake with his wife, Lisaveta, their son Fedor and his wife Sonia and their two

1

daughters; Gregory's elderly assistant, Olga Marmeladov, had been strolling arm in arm with her sister Dunya between the hothouses and the herbaceous borders; Peter Ilyich Raskolnikov, the new trainee picture restorer, had been lying under the elms in the arms of his childhood sweetheart, Tatiana Sorokin, daughter of Alexander Sorokin, who owned the bookshop on Detskoye Prospekt.

For the residents of Pushkin, the Catherine Palace with its park and gardens was the centre of their world; but its fame spread far beyond the confines of the town. People travelled from all over the world to see it. They would pause briefly to admire the famous Egyptian Gates, designed by the same English architect who had built the Turkish elephant house for the zoo; and stand amazed at the magnificence of Rastrelli's baroque façade and the gold domes of the Church rising at the north end; and admire the white State Staircase and Cameron's classical interior. But really they were there for one reason only. To see that room. The one next to the Picture Gallery. The fabulous room that might have come from the pages of some old Russian romance. The wonder of the modern world that was on every serious traveller's list ...

The air on that June evening in 1941 had been so balmy, the sounds of the summer night so soft, the prospect of war so remote that to the townsfolk of Pushkin the terrible news had seemed as inconsequential as a passing breeze. Now they cowered behind closed shutters as the thunder rumbled and the earth trembled and the tanks and heavy guns of the German 2nd Army Corps pounded the Russian positions on the outskirts.

For a while it seemed as if the lines were holding; but then the rumbling grew louder, the thump of the shells came ever closer. It was only a matter of time ...

At first glance, the palace appeared to be as unaware of the impending catastrophe as a vast whale that glides carelessly through the ocean while the whaling fleet draws ever nearer, harpoon guns at the ready. All two hundred windows that looked out on to the gardens were dark. Or seemed to be. At the left-hand end of the building, on the first floor next to the Picture Gallery, a faint strip of golden light could be seen squeezing out from between carelessly closed shutters. Behind them, in the dull glow of a dozen candles, a handful of people

2

were hard at work taking the panelling down from the walls and packing it away into large wooden cases.

Compared with the other state rooms in the palace – the Great Hall, the Picture Hall, the Kavalerskaya Dining Room – the chamber which was the subject of this frantic activity was small: 22 feet long, 13 feet wide and 15 feet from the inlaid wooden floor to the stucco ceiling. But because the panelling was so delicately wrought and incorporated mirrors and mosaics, and because the panels had been put together like giant jigsaw puzzles and glued on to wooden mountings, the business of dismantling them took far longer than any of them had anticipated.

Gregory Pechorin could not believe that the authorities had given them so little warning. Surely someone must have kept them informed of the rate of the German advance? They must have realised what a task it would be to remove the two hundred panels without damaging them and to ensure that every single one was catalogued. The two men and the woman had been working non-stop for the whole of the previous day and half the night, yet so far they had succeeded in removing only three. But then who told anyone anything in Russia – even when it concerned one of their greatest treasures?

Olga Marmeladov sank on to a rickety chair and held her head in her hands. The tight grey bun on the back of her bowed head shook slowly from side to side.

'It's no use, Gregory Alexandrovich,' she groaned. 'We'll never finish in time.'

The Curator straightened up from one of the cases. The honey-coloured light gave his face a waxy patina.

'Come, come, Olga,' he said. 'This is no time to be talking of defeat. I know you are tired. We all are. But we must do all we can. We must keep going.'

Gregory Alexandrovich Pechorin was a tall man with thin, stooping shoulders and a high-domed head, the hair of which seemed to have missed its sense of direction and emerged in the form of a heavy white beard that hung over his stiff collar and black tie. Many people had told him he looked like the Irish playwright and champion of the people's revolution, George Bernard Shaw. In fact his beard was so large that Olga sometimes used to think that it was sapping his

3

strength, like an overgrown parasite in the branches of a small tree. She felt that, if only it were pruned, his rounded shoulders would spring up broad and square, his stooping back would straighten and hair would once more sprout from the top of his head.

A pair of gold pince-nez glasses perched halfway down his narrow outcrop of a nose, giving him the look of a studious stork, yet his voice was surprisingly deep and powerful.

'Come along now and help me to number these pieces.'

Olga looked up. Her eyes were red-rimmed from dust and fatigue. In the middle of the room two wooden cases stood packed and ready to be removed. A third, half full, stood nearby. She gestured hopelessly in the direction of Peter Raskolnikov and the two workmen, whose faces gleamed gold with sweat in the candlelight as they struggled to prise the jigsaw of pieces from the wooden backings.

'To do the job properly, so that the carvings are not damaged, would take a week at least,' she said. 'We have another twenty-four hours, perhaps less. Any moment now the tanks will be rolling down Komsomol Street and into the palace grounds. We must think of another plan if we are to save the room. Please, Gregory Alexandrovich, I beg you to reconsider, before it is too late ...'

Even as she spoke, the room burst into light, as if it had suddenly caught fire. A split second later, the shutters flew open, there was a great roaring sound mixed with the clatter of shattering glass, and then all the candles blew out.

They lay face down on the floor in the dark for several fearful minutes, listening to the boom of the guns rolling up from the direction of the Great Pond, their hands over their heads, their hearts pounding, convinced that at any moment they and their precious room would be blown to dust and sprinkled over the Gulf of Finland. But nothing happened. The guns boomed on, but no shells came.

Eventually they all scrambled to their feet, brushing slivers of glass from their clothes. One of the workmen took some matches from his pocket and started to light the candles.

'You are right, Olga,' said the Curator. 'Another solution must be found very quickly. Now this is what we will do ...'

* * *

4

As it turned out, Olga Marmeladov was wrong. The Russian defences held out for longer than she had anticipated. It was not until the middle of the afternoon of the second day that the first German tank, with soldiers sitting on the top and sides, nosed its way cautiously past the Triumphal Arch, rumbled along Komsomol Street and drew up, grumbling and squeaking, outside Rastrelli's gilded gates. It rocked gently back and forth on its tracks, then swung the barrel of its gun round until it pointed at the north-east wing. It looked like a great grey beetle, waving its antennae, trying to make up its mind which way to go next.

After a while the engine was switched off. The soldiers slid down and pushed the gates open. Two of them took up guarding positions just inside. A few moments later a German staff Mercedes-Benz approached at speed from the direction of the Egyptian Gates. Sitting in the back was an officer wearing the uniform of an *Oberst*, or colonel, in the Panzer Korps. In the front, next to the driver, was an overweight *Feldwebel* (the German army equivalent of a sergeant) who looked as if in civilian life he specialised in winning pie-eating contests.

As the car swept through the gates, the two soldiers leapt to attention. The car drove fast across the gravel, swung across the courtyard and drew up with a crunch outside the main entrance.

The driver jumped out and ran to open the rear door, but the colonel was already out of the car and taking the front steps two at a time. The sergeant puffed and sweated at his heels. He threw open the front door and marched into the White Vestibule. The clack of his polished jackboots echoed around the walls and up the State Staircase. He had never been in the palace in his life, but he knew it as well as he knew his own home. He had studied every guidebook and every photograph. He knew precisely how many years it had taken Neyelov to build the Marble Bridge and exactly where in Siberia the marble had been carved. He knew that the Agate Rooms were falsely named and how it was that Cameron achieved the right effect by using a combination of jasper and marble. He knew by heart many of the Pushkin poems that were kept in manuscript in what was originally the Church Wing. He longed to see them for himself. But for the moment they could wait. There was something far more important that needed to be done first.

5

'Come along!' he shouted over his shoulder to the sergeant. He sprinted up the State Staircase, turned left at the top and strode briskly through a succession of rooms, pushing the doors open in front of him as he went, until he came to it: the legendary room that he had dreamed about so often …

Or was it? Had he misread the plans? Light streamed in through the broken panes. The colonel stared wildly around.

'What has happened?' he shouted. 'What have they done with it? Are we too late? Where is it?'

The fat sergeant was breathing hard. Sweat ran down his porky neck and into his high collar. He looked around at the dull, pale-green wallpaper. The colonel unbuttoned his tunic, reached into his inside pocket and pulled out a folded piece of paper. He unfolded it, tearing it slightly as he did so. He stared at the neatly drawn room plan of the palace. He held it out in front of him and stood facing one of the windows, trying to get his bearings.

'The White Vestibule's here,' he murmured, stabbing at the paper with a gloved finger. 'And here's the Grand Hall …' He ran his finger along the page. 'And the Green Dining Room … the Blue Chinese Drawing Room … So this has to be it! This *must* be it! But it's not here. Where *is* it?'

He swivelled round, arms raised high, as though praying for a miracle.

'Herr Oberst?' The fat sergeant wasn't absolutely certain he knew what was happening. The colonel said nothing. It was as if the sergeant wasn't even there. He strode across to one of the walls and peered at it closely. He ran his hands over it. Then he bent forward until his face was almost touching it. He sniffed at it. Then he ran his hands over it again. He scratched at it with a fingernail.

'Aha!'

'Sir?'

'What have we here?' The colonel tapped on the wallpaper. It made a dull, slightly hollow sound. He did it again, with a similar result. He straightened up.

'This wallpaper is new,' he said to himself. 'Not only new, but still damp. Feldwebel!'

'Herr Oberst?'

6

'Knife!'

'Yes, Herr Oberst!'

The sergeant reached into the scabbard at his side and drew out a big military knife. He handed it to the colonel, who thrust the point into the wallpaper and gently lifted one corner. It peeled away at once.

'Brilliant,' said the colonel. 'Quite brilliant!'

'Sir?'

Now the colonel began stabbing at the wall with the knife – slowly and methodically at first, but then with increasing frenzy, tearing the paper off in strips and gouging out not plaster, but wood. And clearly new wood at that.

'Cheap plywood!' grunted the colonel. He stabbed at it again and twisted the blade sideways. There was a sharp crack and a large section came away. He wrenched it out and threw it to the floor.

'It's got to be here!' The colonel was shouting now. 'It's *got* to be!'

'What would that be, then, Herr Oberst?'

The colonel pulled again at the jagged edges of the wood. There was another rending sound and this time a huge sheet of plywood came away. The colonel staggered back, panting with the effort. His eyes were wide, his mouth dropped open.

'I was right!' he whispered. 'It *is* here! Look!'

The fat sergeant moved gingerly forward and squinted into the hole the colonel had made. Something yellowish glowed dully within the rough opening.

'I can see you've found it, sir,' he said. 'But what is it?'

'Sergeant,' said the colonel, 'you are looking at one of the greatest treasures in all Russia. Or, at least, a part of it. And very soon it will be one of the greatest treasures in Germany, which is where it really belongs.'

The sergeant tried to appear impressed.

'Well, don't just stand there,' shouted the colonel. 'Let's get the rest of this horrible stuff off.'

An hour later, the parquet floor of amaranth, rosewood and mahogany was knee-deep in shredded wallpaper and splintered plywood and the room glowed in the reflected light from the panelling.

'Funny thing to cover a wall with,' said the sergeant. 'I prefer a nice paper myself. Like the one that was here just now.'

'Three missing,' said the colonel. 'Where have they put them?'

'Three ... Herr Oberst?'

'Three panels are missing.'

The sergeant looked at the empty spaces on the far wall where the officer was pointing. 'Never mind, sir, eh?' he said cheerfully. 'Plenty here to be getting on with.'

'They can't have gone far,' said the colonel. 'Somewhere in the house? Possible, but unlikely. In one of the outbuildings perhaps? The Orangery? The Pavilion? The Grotto? Or have they been a bit cleverer than that? Feldwebel!'

'Herr Oberst?'

'I want you to take a party of men and search the house and grounds. We're looking for a large wooden packing case. Possibly several. They could be anywhere. But I want them found. Now. Do you understand?'

'Perfectly, Herr Oberst. Right away, Herr Oberst.'

The fat sergeant jumped to attention, saluted, turned and waddled away as fast as he could in the direction of the White Vestibule and the door that led out into the garden.

* * *

It was shortly before noon the following day that Heinz Grüber, Obergefreite, 2nd Army Corps, met Fedor Ilyich Zamyotov, Under-Gardener, Catherine Palace. The meeting was a special delight for Heinz, since in civilian life he was a professional nurseryman. The opportunities to look at gardens, meet fellow horticulturists and talk shop had, up till now, been few and far between. When he had learned that he was about to be posted to the Russian Front, he had given up all hope of ever again finding anyone who was remotely interested in flowers and shrubs. Or indeed of seeing any plant life of any note.

He had scarcely been able to believe his luck when he had heard where they were going that afternoon; and when he had been ordered by Feldwebel Werner to search the grounds he had almost begun to believe there might be a God after all. He didn't know much about rooms, but he knew that the Catherine Palace boasted one of the finest examples of formal gardens in Russia.

8

Heinz strolled amid the geometric paths and marble statues, past the Upper and Lower Bath Pavilions, across the Fish Canal and down to the Cascade Ponds and the pyramid where the Empress Catherine buried her dogs. He was so entranced by the sheer size of the place and the variety of plants that he soon forgot what he was supposed to be looking for.

He was on his way back towards the Granite Terrace, when he spotted the crown of Fedor Ilyich's bald brown head over the top of a tall, sweet-smelling box hedge. He approached the hedge and, standing on tiptoe, peered over it.

Fedor Ilyich was leaning on a spade in the middle of a small enclosed area of lawn that the casual visitor would probably never even have suspected was there. He had evidently been planting shrubs and was putting the final, loving touches to a variety that Heinz knew very well.

'Aha,' said Heinz. 'A *ceanothus floribundus*, unless I'm very much mistaken!'

'Hn?' Fedor Ilyich didn't speak a word of German. He didn't need to. He knew well what the corporal was talking about and he flushed furiously under his weather-beaten skin.

'I'm right, aren't I? It is a *ceanothus*?' The corporal smiled eagerly. 'Lovely blue flower?'

Fedor Ilyich stared at him, his eyes wide and unblinking, like a rabbit who suddenly finds himself face to face with a terrier.

'I think you'll find I'm right,' said Heinz. 'May I take a closer look?'

Fedor Ilyich said nothing as Heinz made his way towards the opening in the hedge. His throat was dry and his jaw trembled uncontrollably. But Heinz was far too excited to notice. He peered closely at the shrub.

'Yes,' he said. 'I thought so. That's the *floribundus*, all right. Oh, and I see you've got a nice little *philadelphus* there. *Grandiflorus*, by the look of it. The big white one. Personally, I prefer the *purpureus maculatus*. The white one with the purple stain, you know. Still, everyone to his own ...'

The Russian gardener shrugged his shoulders helplessly. Heinz looked admiringly at the little garden.

'The only thing is ...' he said after a while, 'aren't you planting a little early? It's still only September. They do like the ground a little on the cool side, these shrubs. Especially that *hypericum* over there. And the *berberis polyantha* ...'

Fedor had begun to relax a little. Recognising the Latin names of the plants, despite this man's thick Saxony accent, he smiled and nodded. Perhaps the German soldier was what he seemed: a keen amateur gardener showing a polite interest.

'Funny ...' A little frown came over Heinz's cheerful features. 'You've had this whole lawn up, haven't you? Quite recently, too, by the look of it.' He bent down. 'These are all fresh tufts,' he said. 'That's an odd thing to be doing in September, isn't it? Re-turfing the lawn?' With the toecap of his boot he lifted the corner of one of the turfs. 'Oh dear,' he murmured. 'What *have* you been up to?'

Fedor Ilyich's eyes were now wide with terror.

'You haven't ...?' said Heinz. 'You couldn't have ... Have you? Oh dear ... I am sorry. Really I am.'

It didn't take the six men long to uproot the shrubs and peel off the strips of turf. By the time the first spade strokes went into the bare earth, Fedor Ilyich was in tears. When they hit the first crate, he all but passed out. Heinz had never felt sorrier for anyone in his life.

2

'A man who has recently been killed by a tiger is as unsavoury
a sight as it is possible to imagine.'

Miles Maltby lounged back on his battered leather sofa and sipped
his coffee. He was thirty-nine and six foot two, with the thick neck
and heavy shoulders of a rugby forward. He had on a Tattersall check
shirt, navy-blue v-neck pullover, navy-blue cords and dark-brown
lace-ups. His sole sartorial eccentricity was a pair of dazzling canary-
yellow socks.

'If the victim is lucky, the force of some 900 pounds of bone
and muscle moving at thirty miles an hour will kill him
instantly. But if his neck has not been snapped like a carrot,
his backbone is still intact and his nervous system has not
been paralysed by the shock, then what follows will guarantee him some of the most nightmarish last few moments
imaginable.'

Miles placed his coffee mug on a small side-table, folded his *Daily
Mail* into a more convenient shape and squared his shoulders. Dr
Alan Rawsthorne, author of the best-selling book on tigers, *Burning
Bright*, was not a man who believed in soft-soaping his readers.

'In the wild, a big cat will more often than not tackle an
animal that is bigger than itself, and probably just as strong.
The quickest and surest method of killing is by suffocation.
Therefore the first thing it will do, once it has seized its prey,
is clamp its jaw on to the victim's windpipe. Sometimes, it
will hang on to its throat, bring up its hind legs, claws fully

11

extended, and rip open the stomach and flanks as it fights to gain purchase on the bewildered body. In this case the entire throat will almost certainly be torn away. The area for yards around will be sprayed with blood as it fountains from the gaping hole, the victim's eyes will cloud over and, with a few last muscular spasms, the drama will be over almost as quickly as it began. The noise will abate, the dust will settle and life will continue as if nothing had happened.'

'Strewth,' Miles murmured.

'Of all the big cats, only the jaguar will actively seek out a human victim. Attacks by tigers on humans are rare, even in the wildest jungles of Sumatra or the foothill villages of northern India. In safari parks in the heart of the English countryside they are unheard of. Modern security systems at establishments such as West Keating, scene of yesterday's tragedy, are tightly controlled and the chances of a member of the public accidentally entering a tiger enclosure are virtually nil. Archie Lambourn, the well-known broadcaster and conservationist, who founded West Keating Safari Park in 1971, maintained that the secret of a happy relationship between man and beast is mutual trust, and was frequently photographed lying amongst his 'beauties', as he called them, playing with them, wrestling with them and allowing them to lick him. But a wild animal is always a wild animal and for once his trust was tragically misplaced.'

'Bloody idiot,' said Miles. The consonants were clipped, the vowels drawled. The vocal hallmark of a good regiment.

He turned back to the front page.

WILD LIFE MAN LAMBOURN'S LAST GAMBLE was the splash headline above a fuzzy image of what Miles took to be Archie Lambourn's shapeless cadaver – captured by an enterprising visitor who happened to be giving his brand-new Nikon FG20 with its modest zoom lens a well-timed and, as it turned out, extremely profitable first airing.

The lead story stuck to the basic facts. The Hon. Archie Lambourn ... tragic accident ... world of conservation shocked ...

flamboyant figure who spent his life taking risks ... a risk too far ... etc. etc. But it was early days. The Sunday papers would make a proper meal of it.

Miles looked at his watch: 9.29. He put the newspaper down, got up and went into the tiny kitchen. The door of the fridge hung open. The interior had been emptied, defrosted and meticulously wiped and the draining board was gleaming clean. He washed up the coffee mug, dried it and hung it on a little wooden stand.

He went through the sitting room and into the narrow bathroom. Two towels and a face flannel hung in perfect symmetry from the rail beside the washbasin. He rinsed his teeth and gums with a pink mouthwash and looked at himself in the basin mirror. The eyes that looked back at him were more grey than blue and surrounded by the open, friendly features that pass for English good looks. He bared his teeth at himself, ran a hand over his straight fair hair and crossed into the bedroom.

The double bed had been stripped and the blankets folded with mathematical precision on the bare, gold-patterned mattress, as if ready for company commander's rounds. At the foot of the bed was a bulging, soft-lidded suitcase. Folded on top was a neatly folded sports jacket in brown herringbone with a red over-check. He pulled on the jacket, picked up the suitcase and placed it in the hall. He returned to the sitting room. The thin pile of the light-green carpet bore the rake marks of an old upright vacuum cleaner.

Miles stood for a while and stared out of the window at the sludge browns and greys of south London. He looked at his watch: 9.35. The taxi was late, but not worryingly late. Not yet anyway. He always allowed ten minutes of leeway when travelling. It was one of the many legacies of army life.

He crossed to his desk in the far corner. Ranged along the back, perfectly aligned, were a small Apple Mac, a Hewlett Packard Desk Writer, a telephone, an answering machine with a red light on, and a pewter mug stowed with sharpened pencils. In front was an elderly leather-bound blotting pad with a family crest in faded gold at the top, and an open leather briefcase in which were a wallet of travel documents, passport, traveller's cheques, a green folder marked EIGERHUBEL, a couple of reporter's notebooks, a review copy of a new

13

history of Scotch whisky, a couple of McBain paperbacks, and a guidebook to the Swiss Alps.

Miles folded the newspaper and put it inside the briefcase. He took out the guidebook and, perching on the arm of the sofa, opened it at the chapter headed 'Bernese Oberland'.

At that moment the telephone rang.

'Miles? Neville here. Long time and all that. Look, how are you on tigers?'

'Tigers?'

Neville Short was one features editor he hadn't heard from in more than a year. It was hardly surprising. Miles wasn't really a tabloid man.

'Big animals with stripes,' said Neville.

Miles said, 'Do you mean tigers as in West Keating Safari Park?'

'How did you guess? Thing is, I'm looking for someone to write a background piece on the Lambourn Set for next week.'

'I'm not really that up on the animal world.'

'Never mind the animals. I'm interested in the man and his circle. See if you can track down any of his cronies from the Sixties. There must be some of them around still, if they haven't all gambled themselves into cardboard boxes. Or screwed themselves into early graves. The chap who used to own that night-club, what's his name? And the Earl of Thing … you know … married that model … There was a wife too. Lady Camilla … married that restaurant owner … took to the bottle … Start with the cuttings library here, I would. About twelve hundred words. Fifteen hundred plus expenses. Copy a.s.a.p. OK?'

'Actually, I'm just off to Switzerland,' said Miles. 'In fact I thought you were the taxi people.'

'Switzerland?' said Neville. 'What on earth could there possibly be in Switzerland that's of the remotest interest to anyone?'

*　*　*

'The village of Eigerhubel perches like an alpine Machu Picchu on a shelf of rock 752 metres above the Wintertal Valley in the Bernese Oberland. Rising up 3,583 metres on the other side of the narrow valley is the Blumenhorn, one

14

of the most spectacular peaks in the Alps. It was the scenery which drew the first visitors to Eigerhubel in the 1840s. Over-dressed holidaymakers would climb up the steep mountainside from Wintertal and walk for three miles along a goat track on the cliff edge for no other reason than the sheer pleasure of being there.'

Miles put down the guidebook. He shifted against the upright seat at the back of the black cab and grimaced. He'd learned to live with pain after five years of it. Occasionally some sudden, awkward movement would remind him it was still there, but most of the time he didn't even think about it. He rarely complained. He was lucky to be walking, let alone skiing. This was the third trip he'd been on since the start of the season, and it was still only the middle of January. Davos in early December, Méribel over the New Year, and now a week in Eigerhubel, writing a piece about the forthcoming Diabolo Race and enjoying a little recreational skiing, courtesy of Swiss Chalets plc. Seven days in which he needn't put his hand in his pocket: a week of non-stop pleasure during which all life was complimentary – ski hire, lift passes, long lunches on sunny terraces in mountain restaurants, *glühweins* on the way home, and as many hot chocolates and beers before and after dinner in the bar of the Hôtel des Alpes as he could manage …

Small wonder his office-bound colleagues ground their teeth with envy. Even his old army chums, most of whom managed to wangle a few weeks in the Alps every year, told him he was a lucky bastard.

Miles wished he could enjoy his good fortune as much as everyone assumed he did. But he'd never quite managed it. Guilt, hovering over him like a small dark cloud, was a constant dampener to unalloyed pleasure. Writing light-hearted pieces about ski resorts was not what real journalists did. Real journalists reported wars and famines, and unearthed scandals, and railed against injustice, and wrote colourful background pieces to hard-news items. When a meaty news story came their way, real journalists dropped what they were doing, grabbed a notebook and a taxi, and followed it up. They didn't make excuses and leave. But then real journalists were not at the constant mercy of PR girls.

15

'Hardly man's work, is it?' his elder brother Henry had once remarked. Miles had felt like saying that shooting pheasants four days a week was not exactly back-breaking labour. Trouble was, he agreed with him.

He glowered out of the window at the passing traffic on the M4 and swore under his breath. Why the hell couldn't Neville have phoned a bit later? Then he wouldn't have known a thing about it till he got back. He would still have been furious at missing a good story, but at least it wouldn't have ruined a perfectly good skiing trip as well.

> 'Cautious men shook their heads and muttered into their beards about nine-day wonders. However, one man could recognise a good tourist attraction when he saw one. His name was Anton Brugger and, in the summer of 1845, he committed 100,000 francs to the construction of a 50-room hotel.'

* * *

'Something of a B-Team outing, I fear, old cock,' murmured Peter Franklin as he reached for the Laurent Perrier.

Miles stared gloomily round at the other members of the press party as they took full advantage of Swiss Chalets' hospitality in the airline's business-class lounge. 'A far cry from Méribel,' he said.

'Very much non-vintage all round, I'd say,' said Peter, looking pointedly at the label on the bottle.

As the acknowledged doyen of British ski writers and with two ex-wives and four teenage children to support, Franklin rarely turned down an invitation during the skiing season. His *Great Ski Runs of the World* was still selling well after five years, and thank goodness there were still plenty of sports and leisure editors who valued his facility for the 750-word piece, his encyclopaedic knowledge and his respect for deadlines. Even so, he needed all the material he could get.

Normally, Miles found him a bore, especially when he launched (as he would do, given the slightest encouragement) into his 'when

16

I was a member of the British Army ski team during the Napoleonic Wars' routine. But today, in the absence of any other familiar faces, Franklin's lugubrious, bloodhound features were like a welcome beacon of light to a lost sailor.

'No Antonia, then,' remarked Miles.

'Still in the Rockies, I gather. Vail and Aspen.'

'Lucky girl. Harry Chalmers? No?'

'Last time I spoke to him, he announced that he was getting too old to fart around the winter playgrounds of the rich and would henceforth be farting around the summer ones, starting with the Great Barrier Reef.'

'Bastard … Who's the spotty Herbert with the earrings and the stubble?'

'He's called Damien. He's a features sub.'

'Strangles stories with his bare hands for the *Sunday Express*, by the look of him.'

'Good try. *Romford Gazette*, actually.'

'Oh, quite up-market, then?'

'He works on the sports desk, I gather.'

'What as? Rat-baiting correspondent?'

'He was reading Trollope before you got here. In paperback, mind.'

'Must be a Young Conservative.'

'The girl from the *Roxburgh Herald*'s OK,' said Franklin.

'The blonde?'

'Kirsty McFee.'

'Nice name,' said Miles.

'Her friends call her Fee.'

'Do they indeed?'

For a brief, mad moment, Miles thought about finding a telephone, ringing Neville and telling him there'd been a change of plan – the trip had been cancelled … he'd got the dates wrong – and legging it to the nearest exit. But Maddy Maguire, the Swiss Chalets PR girl, was already beginning to chivvy people away from the champagne and the canapés and out into the hurly-burly of the departure gates. She was like a relentlessly cheerful golden retriever.

'Be right with you,' said Miles.

He waded through the thick pile towards the television set. A man

17

in a Barbour with fair hair and a cruel face was being interviewed on the lunchtime News.

'Charlie Bishop is the manager of West Keating Safari Park. Charlie, your reaction to this violent and inexplicable attack?'

Bishop crinkled his eyes and looked out across the neatly fenced enclosures. The stripes of distant zebras merged with the bare branches of the parkland trees and a couple of giraffes peered superciliously at a party of Smith's Gazelles in the adjoining field. Nearby, a pair of tigers lay beside a fallen tree trunk, eyes half shut, yawning into the tepid sunshine, indifferent to the fate of the man to whom they owed their comfortable and untrammelled existence.

'Great shock and great sadness,' he said finally. 'Mr Lambourn will be a sad loss for conservationists and animal lovers all over the world.'

Did he have any idea how the tragedy had occurred?

'It's too early to say,' he replied. 'Naturally we will be holding an inquiry, but everything points to a freak accident. Tigers are very unpredictable animals.'

Was Mr Lambourn in the habit of entering the tiger enclosure so early in the morning?

'Mr Lambourn was as unpredictable in his habits as the tigers. I cannot say any more at this stage. We shall have to wait for the outcome of the inquiry.'

A tragedy like this inevitably raises questions of security in the minds of the public at large …

'All visitors to West Keating are handed a list of rules and guidelines as they enter at the main gate, together with a fact sheet on every species in the park. They are asked to study these carefully before beginning their tour and to comply with the rules at all times. There should be no cause whatever for concern or anxiety. We have a one-hundred-per-cent safety record here at West Keating. We are very proud of this and we mean to maintain it.'

And what of the future?

'We shall carry on as usual,' Bishop declared emphatically. 'Archie would have wanted it that way.'

Miles felt a hand on his arm.

'Come along,' said Maddy. 'Some of us have got work to do.'

3

It was after three by the time the Swiss Chalets party had cleared customs at Geneva's Cornavin Airport and begun to make their way towards the coach, and nearly four when at long last they were swishing in air-conditioned comfort through the drab outskirts of the city.

Miles stared out of the window. The neat grey buildings stared back, secretive and unsmiling behind their roller-shuttered respectability.

'Just like a cake,' he murmured.

'What?' Franklin's face appeared in the gap between the seats in front of him.

'Switzerland,' said Miles. 'It's like a huge birthday cake that's been left too long in the larder. Beautifully decorated on the outside, lashings of icing sugar, wonderfully tempting, but underneath all sorts of nasty things are going on.'

'They were bloody tricky in the war,' said Franklin, twisting round in his seat. 'I do know that.'

'I always thought they were neutral,' said Miles.

'If you call it "neutral" to line yourself up behind the side you think is going to win, then I suppose, yes, they were.'

'In all the prison-camp books I read when I was a schoolboy, the ones that got away always made for the Swiss border.'

'Later on, yes. When things started swinging our way. There was nothing the Swiss wouldn't do for us then. By the end of 1944, you could hardly land on a Swiss airfield for Allied bombers.'

'Bombers?'

'Wellingtons. Lancasters. Flying Fortresses. Dumped by crews who'd decided enough was enough. Either they were sick of seeing

19

whole German cities flattened, or else the odds against getting shot down were too short for their liking. Whatever the reason, the moment they were safely over the Swiss border, they'd make up some excuse – pretend they'd got lost or run out of fuel or developed engine trouble or something – and down they'd go. There was no way of checking, and the Swiss never let on. But that was much later on. Things were very different before 1941.'

'You mean the Swiss were pro-German?'

'At the beginning. They thought they were on to a winner. It was a good bet at the time. Mind you, there'd been a pro-Nazi movement in Switzerland since the Twenties. They thought National Social-ism would be a good hedge against Communism. The Germans worked hard to promote the idea. Switzerland's a bugger for any army to get through. Always has been. Hence the fact that nobody's ever tried. Every tunnel's mined. There are tank traps hidden under all the main roads. The mountains are riddled with tunnels and caves. Some of them are big enough to be converted into aircraft hangars. Believe it or not, there are actually runways built into the side of some of the mountains. You can be driving along a road up in the Bernese Oberland and suddenly a Mirage jet will come hurtling out of nowhere.'

'So, if the Germans played their cards right ...'

'All manner of interesting possibilities would open up. By 1939 the place was crawling with agents and subversives. The German legation in Berne was nothing more than a cover for the Nazi underground. But what the Swiss hadn't reckoned on was that the Germans might want to invade and occupy them, like they did the Danes and the Dutch.'

'Was it ever on?'

'Invasion? Well, the Swiss thought it was. Trouble was, they'd got wind of the Germans' plans and had been doing deals with the French behind their backs. You can imagine what a shock it was when France threw in the towel. Suddenly the place was streaming with French troops. The Germans never actually invaded, as such, but they often flew across Swiss air space and some of their planes got shot down. Goering wasn't pleased. Neither were the Swiss when they realised they'd backed the wrong horse.'

20

'So they changed in mid-stream, no doubt. Being Swiss.'

'There were still plenty of German spies lurking behind every Alp, but, basically, yes. The Allies certainly had a much easier time of it from then on.'

Miles said, 'You seem to know a lot about it.'

'I'm not that much of an expert. But I lived here for a while. Got to know the score.'

'Me too. Winter of seventy-three, seventy-four. Ski-bumming in Adelweiss.'

'Adelweiss. Seventy-three,' Franklin mused. 'That rings a bell ... Wasn't there a typhoid scare?'

'You're thinking of Zermatt Seventy-one. In Adelweiss we had a murder mystery to get us through the long winter nights. An English chalet girl was found stabbed with a kitchen knife. Probably some Italian waiter who didn't know the meaning of the word No. Unfortunately the Swiss police were far too eager to get a face in the frame. They weren't fussy, as long as it was foreign. It was my bad luck to have been having a thing with the girl at the time. Not the night she was murdered, thank God, but I'd been round there a couple of days previously and stupidly I'd left an old cricket pullover in her room. It didn't take long for the local gendarmerie to find their way to my door. Being a relic from my school days, the thing had my nametape on it.'

'No bloodstains, I hope?'

'Joking. Even so, within two hours of Belinda's body being discovered I was down in the valley in Druon, banged up in a cell with a large man in a grey suit holding a pen in one hand and a typed confession in the other. That didn't seem fair to me, but he couldn't see it my way. I won't bore you with the gory details. All I can say is that anyone who thinks the Swiss are a nice, gentle, civilised sort of people should spend three days in a police cell in the Valais.'

'Three days!'

'I cursed the day I got my cricket colours. Oh, they let me go in the end, but very reluctantly. I'd hate to think what's written down in my file in Berne. In fact, I'm quite surprised they let me in. Arriving among a party of hacks probably helped.'

'It's possible,' said Franklin. 'Mind you, a secret police force is not the sort of thing most people associate with Switzerland. In fact they'd

21

probably laugh at you if you told them this country thrives on a system of spying and denunciation. You have to have lived here to see it in action. It's only a matter of time before they twig *I'm* here, if they haven't already. Sooner or later someone will make a phone call to Berne. Someone who's paid to keep an eye open. Someone in the village. A postman perhaps, a barman … My file will be hauled out and dusted down. A note will be made; an eye kept out.'

'Naughty boy, were you?'

Franklin laughed. 'No such luck. Just an out-of-work army officer teaching riding and fencing in a girls' finishing school and wondering what to do next. And getting in a bit of free skiing while I was about it. Nothing remotely sinister.'

'Nothing could be half as sinister as the country itself,' said Miles.

Now the road had broadened out. Slivers of light showed between the closed shutters of the big houses set amongst the rolling lawns that stretched down to the side of the lake. Beyond them, on the far side, the tips of the mountains of the Chablais were white against the darkening sky.

Miles lay his head back against the seat and sighed. 'That Belinda,' he said.

* * *

Like all the best Swiss family hoteliers, Hans-Otto Planck, the owner of the Hotel des Alpes, had a gift for hospitality that went some way to relaxing taut nerves and stiff limbs after the long and tedious coach journey. Waving the party off to their beds following a late supper, he had predicted clear skies and brilliant sunshine with a confidence that spoke of a lifetime of alpine living. Even so, the rarefied mountain air played havoc with Miles's brain cells. He finally dozed off some time after two, slept fitfully, and woke shortly before eight to discover that, to add to his nocturnal miseries, the weather had taken a turn for the worse. The clouds had rolled up the narrow valley and now the village lay muffled under two feet of new snow and a thick fog. It was like looking into a glass of milk.

Miles would have been perfectly happy wandering around the village, drinking coffee, gossiping with a local or two, getting the feel of the place; and, when Maddy announced cheerfully at breakfast that a couple of ski instructors were standing by to give them an introductory tour of the main ski areas, his heart sank.

He caught Kirsty McFee's eye and pulled a face. She replied with a wide grin and an enthusiastic thumbs-up sign.

Apart from Peter Franklin, the assistant fashion editor from the *Roxburgh Herald* was the only member of the party with whom he felt the slightest affinity. She had a round, smiling face and a nice line in gently ironic humour; she also shared his distaste for Damien from Romford, who had evidently decided that it was his professional duty to insult and irritate Miles at every possible opportunity.

'All talk and tool,' she commented as she clumped beside him down the village street towards the big Schwarzegg cable car. 'And probably rather more of the former than the latter.'

Their boots, ankle tops open under their salopettes, wires loosened against the unfamiliar and unnatural rigidity, thudded awkwardly through the fluffy new snow and squeaked on the hard pack underneath.

Fee glowed in the monochromatic gloom of the alpine fog. Across her forehead was a blue-and-yellow plaited headband. A pair of green-framed sunglasses were slung from her neck by a green and white cord. Her Descente, all-in-one ski suit was a riot of turquoise and coral and pale yellow, and her Salomon 73 ski boots were white, trimmed with mauve. Her lips glowed shocking-pink and clashed horribly with everything. She looked like a one-woman Disneyworld.

Miles glanced approvingly at her Fischer Monotecs with the Tyrolia bindings. He hadn't owned a pair of skis for years, but Eddie Adelbogen, who ran the ski shop, hearing that Miles had once skied for the Army, had lent him a new pair of Rossignol 4SVs. He wanted to know what Miles thought of the narrower side-cut. It was supposed to make the skis turn that much quicker, and the longitudinal flex had been stiffened slightly to make them more stable when carving turns at high speed. He'd even thrown in a pair of Rossignol 4SL Axial Corrective ski poles. Miles had been flattered, and for a few moments quite excited at the prospect, but by the time they left the shop the cloud had descended almost to the village and so had Miles's spirits. It was hardly a day to be trying out new skis.

They clumped on between the overhanging wooden balconies, the tiny, snow-filled gardens, and the logs neatly stacked against the walls like entries in an art competition.

Miles squinted ahead. The ghostly shape of the Schwarzegg cable-car station loomed up at the far end of the street. One of the big yellow 100-passenger cars hummed quietly across the tops of the firs and disappeared inside the building, like a space vehicle docking.

The Rossis' razor-sharp edges were beginning to bite through the light padding of his ski jacket and into his right shoulder. He made to swing them on to the other side, but they swivelled apart into an elongated X and clattered to the ground.

'Nice one, general.' Damien strode by with the arrogant ease of one who spends more time in health clubs than he does in front of the shaving mirror.

'Don't say what you think,' said Fee. 'Just think.'

The swooping flight up in the cable car was enough to turn weak throats dry and nervous stomachs to water. The passengers, un-hygienically sardined between each other's bulky clothing and pungent morning breath, peered through the undergrowth of arms and skis and sticks in the direction of the windows, uncertain if the all-enveloping greyness was due to condensation or thick cloud, and feared the worst.

'According to the ski-lift people,' Maddy announced brightly, 'there's fresh powder and brilliant sunshine up on Totenkopf.'

The instructor assigned to the advanced party, Werner, leaned forward and rubbed a casual glove across the glass, revealing a view as impenetrable as before. His thin brown features remained as impassive as the bushy blond moustache.

Werner's colleague, Heinz, said to Fee, 'You like to ski in the powder?'

'You bet,' she said.

The two men laughed.

Miles yawned. He wondered if Neville had found anyone to do the Lambourn piece.

The waiting area for the Totenkopf cable car was ominously empty. Either the news hadn't got round or, if it had, people hadn't believed it. And peering out at where the twin cables disappeared into the murk, who could blame them? The old red cabin appeared fuzzily out of the mist a few minutes later, like a hologram, but fewer than a dozen people boarded it, amongst them Werner and his small group of four.

Seconds after swinging blindly out into space, they were whooping with joy as the cable car burst through the cloudline into a scene that any picture-postcard photographer would have given his shutter finger for.

Around them, stretching to the farthest horizon, were mountain peaks, brilliant white against the deep blue of the sky. Between them lay baby clouds, white in the middle, soft and grubby round the edges, like cotton wool left too long on a Christmas table display.

'Look …'

Mountains are like actors: capable of assuming many disguises and transforming themselves into a variety of characters. Veiled in newly fallen snow and well lit, a great peak can seem jolly and friendly. Kill the lights, and under a leaden sky the same mountain suddenly assumes an air of looming mystery: menace even. There is one peak, however, which never fails to strike a faint sense of unease in all who see it for the first time, whatever the season and whatever the weather, and it was facing Miles now at the far end of the cable. The Hannibal Lecter of the Alpine world. The Totenkopf. The Death's Head.

It was chillingly well-named. In the rock face under a high-domed peak were two deep hollows, like eye sockets. Below them, the long, looping wires of the cable car disappeared into a gaping mouth under a low, grey building with a row of windows set at regular intervals, like teeth.

'That is Totenkopf, yes?' said Werner. 'The skull.'

'Death's Head,' murmured Miles.

'I think it looks rather nice,' said Fee. 'It's grinning.'

'Skulls always grin. That's because they know something we don't.'

'I think I know what it is.' Fee pointed ahead at what looked like a sheer face, pock-marked with hundreds of tiny bumps. A few tiny shapes were moving between them, like harvest flies on a rumpled bedsheet.

'Crikey,' said Miles.

25

Werner laughed.

'What's that building over there on the right?' Miles pointed to a small building at the side of Totenkopf, at the point where the peak rose up out of the surrounding slope. It looked as if it was attached to the actual rock face, though from that distance and height, and with the amount of snow that had fallen, it was difficult to tell.

'That is the famous Diabolo Club,' said Werner.

'So that's the Diabolo,' Miles murmured. 'I was expecting something … I don't know … bigger … more impressive.'

'It is very exclusive,' Werner declared stoutly.

'And very expensive. The annual subscription was a thousand a year and that was twenty years ago.'

'You've been doing your homework,' said Fee.

'Not really,' said Miles. 'It's just that people used to talk about it when I lived out here in the Seventies. No one knew much about it, mind, except that it was full of Brits and that to get in you either had to be a film star, a member of the aristocracy or a successful property developer. All I remember thinking at the time was that it was just another of those things in life I couldn't afford and probably never would. Like Lloyd's.'

'It is very hard to get in,' said Werner, who had long since lost the thread but was determined not to be left out of the conversation.

'Unlike Lloyd's, where it's very hard to get out,' said Miles.

'Why Eigerhubel, though?' said Fee. 'There are lots of bigger and flashier ski resorts for people with that sort of money.'

'But not with such strong British connections,' said Franklin. 'Remember, it was an Englishman who brought the first winter sports out to Brugger's Hotel. If it hadn't been for Gordon Byng, there might never have been any skiing in Switzerland. Or anywhere else, come to that.'

'Did he start the Diabolo too?'

'Apparently it came about by chance. In 1924 a bunch of ex-army officers climbed up on skins to the old Totenkopf hut, got pissed on schnapps and decided to race each other back to the bottom. Somehow they all got down in one piece and thought it would be fun to do it every year.'

'So the club and the race are one and the same thing?'

26

'They were, before the war, but not now. I doubt if the majority of the members could put a pair of skis on the right way round, let alone get from the top of the mountain to the bottom.'

'The skiers still start from just below the clubhouse,' said Maddy. 'They set off in pairs at thirty-second intervals and go hell for leather six and a half thousand feet down to Wintertal. Fifteen hundred of them. It's quite a sight, I gather. I'm sorry we won't be here to see it.'

'It is the longest downhill race in the world,' Werner said proudly.'Sixteen kilometres. It is in the *Guinness Book of Records*.'

'Must be the only Swiss entry,' Damien sniggered.

'God Almighty …!'

There was a low grumble like distant thunder and the sharp outline of the steep slope to the left of the Totenkopf was blurred behind a dust-like cloud that rose delicately from the surface as hundreds of tons of newly fallen snow, loosened by the unexpectedly hot sun, began to slide down the valley. Below, hopping from one side of the piste to the other, like tiny birds, were several dozen skiers, apparently impervious to the danger just a few hundred feet above them.

'Look out!' somebody at the front of the cabin shouted.

The avalanche was gathering speed in a great white, smoking wave, thirty yards across, taking half the mountainside with it as it went. For a moment it seemed as if there was nothing to stop it sweeping down on to the skiers below. But then suddenly it changed course. There must have been a hidden contour in the rock face, for it swung to the left, rushed over the ridge that joined the summit with a lower peak and plunged, grumbling and foaming like a waterfall, into the safety of the valley behind.

'It is better you stay on the piste,' said Werner.

It didn't surprise Miles when Maddy announced that she would be taking the cable car back down. A steep metal staircase, encrusted with frozen snow, led down from the cable-car platform. The temperature seemed to drop with every step. Outside, at the bottom of the stairs, there was a small flat area, permanently shaded by the over-hanging mass of the cable-car station.

There was just enough room for half a dozen skiers to drop their skis, step into their bindings and make last-minute adjustments to their gloves and goggles before setting off along the path that curved away to the right, bounded on one side by the rock face and on the other by a precipice. From where he stood, it seemed to Miles as if the only thing preventing the unwary from plunging to their deaths was a length of string tied to a series of flimsy poles and hung with little triangular flags advertising a brand of suntan cream. Some of the skiers who had been with them in the cable car pushed off and, with enviable ease, hissed away down the path and out of sight.

Miles bent down and fiddled with his boot clips. He waited until the others had shuffled and side-slipped their way out of sight, then stuck his skis upright in the snow and, using one pole as a walking stick, made his way round to the left along a much narrower path that someone had beaten in the deep snow. After a few moments, the outlines of the Diabolo clubhouse began to appear. It was a simple, one-storey, pine structure, built lengthways against the rock face, though even from twenty yards away it was impossible to tell if it was actually attached. Several feet of new snow had piled up on the sloping roof and hung down over the eaves, like white thatch. Beneath it, a fringe of icicles was dripping on to a broad, sunny terrace. There was a solid wooden door in the middle, flanked on either side by four big picture windows, and there were two more smaller ones at the end facing Miles. As a building it was undistinguished and anyone who didn't know what it was would scarcely give it a second glance.

Miles reached into the inside pocket of his anorak and took out the little Canon Sureshot he always carried with him. He clicked open the lens cover and looked through the viewfinder. He pressed the zoom button.

The building leapt towards him, and so did the skier. He seemed to come from nowhere. One moment Miles was alone in the silence of the high mountains, the next there was a sound of distant shouting and a hard blow against his right shoulder sent the camera flying out of his hand and into the deep snow. Miles had a fleeting impression of a tall, grey-haired figure in a dark-blue anorak with green and yellow bands above the elbows, crouching low, ski poles tucked under his arms. He called after him, but within seconds the man had carved a long controlled turn round the rock face and disappeared from view.

Miles swivelled. A man with white hair and a bright-red pullover was standing on the terrace, pointing and shouting. Holding up both hands and letting them drop in a gesture of innocent helplessness, Miles edged his way forward into the deep snow, hooked the plastic handle of his ski pole through the little strap at the side of the camera and landed it with all the care of an angler with a ten-pound salmon. He dried it off as best he could but the lens was still wet and he slipped it back into his inside pocket.

With a cheery wave to the man on the terrace, Miles set off along the path. He knocked the hard-packed snow from the soles of his boots with his ski poles and stamped his heels into his Salomon bindings. He slid his Rossis backwards and forwards a few times on the squeaky-cold surface to melt the ice that had formed in the sub-zero temperature, took a deep breath and launched himself into the unknown. Moments later, he was standing next to Fee in the sunshine.

'OK?' she grinned.

'Never better,' he said.

'We go,' said Werner. It was more of a command than a question.

'After you,' said Miles politely.

Werner gave a flick of the heels and slid effortlessly round the first bump, or mogul, as it's known in skiing jargon. A handful of neatly executed turns later and he was standing a hundred feet below them, waiting. Now Fee went. Legs slightly bent, body upright, looking straight ahead down the hill, weight moving from ski to ski with an admirable economy of effort, she seemed to dance her way through the steep bumps and hollows, as if her skis were glued to the surface.

Half a dozen creaky turns and a couple of stumbles later, Miles was standing next to them, breathing hard.

The angle of the slope eased a little from there on, and as they followed each other down through the fluffy, yielding powder Miles could feel the rhythm coming back: the control; the balance; the little dig down with the heels that provided the springboard for the next turn; the punch with the lower shoulder as the point of the ski pole stabbed into the snow and the knees compressed like taut springs; then the full extension of the legs as the weight shifted upwards and across, the knees and the hips swivelled and the skis slid effortlessly through the turn; then the quick check with the heels again, ready for the next one …

Gradually the cloud was beginning to lift away from the lower slopes, and by the time they had done the run a second time the entire region was bathed in bright sunshine. Range upon range of glittering peaks stretched away to the west, while ahead of them the rearing masses of the Blumenhorn, the Blaumeise and the Schilt on the far side of the valley seemed so close that Miles felt he had only to put out his hand and touch them.

He was not a man who believed that happiness was an achievable condition. After months of surgery and long stretches in hospital, it meant little more to him than freedom from pain. But today, for the first time in years, with the warm sunshine on his face and perfect snow under his skis, and Fee's elegant figure a few yards ahead, Miles was tempted to believe that, if not happiness, a sense of well-being was possible. He was contented.

But that was before lunch …

4

The party met at noon on the terrace of Pauli's restaurant – a converted cowshed near the Schwarzegg cable-car station – which had a well-deserved reputation for the best *rösti* in the Oberland. It also served a delicious bottle of Johannisberger, and by the time lunch was over a couple of hours later Miles had consumed rather more of it than he had planned. He'd also had more than enough of Damien's views on the shortcomings of the England football team.

'Attaboy, General!' came the raucous and swivel-eyed response from the far end of the table when Miles announced his intention of skiing down the Gun Barrel to the village.

One of the most dramatic sections of the Diabolo course, the run began with a long curved traverse below the Lion's Teeth Ridge before disappearing into a hidden area of small bowls and twisting paths and emerging through a narrow gap between two tall rocks high above the Nixi chair-lift. From there, a steep path led down in a series of sharp hairpin bends and finally met up with the gentle Blumen run – a popular route home for skiers of all levels at the end of the day.

Werner said, 'I think the Gun Barrel is closed now.'

'I'm sure I saw some people on it,' said Miles.

'You must be very careful. With the new snow and the hot sun … It is better you ski with us.'

'I'll be OK,' Miles told him. 'I'll only go if it's open. Anyone coming? Fee?'

'Go on, darling,' Damien told her.

Miles was pleased to see that his face was beginning to turn red, and it wasn't just from the wine. He was also quite relieved when Fee shook her head and pleaded tiredness. He needed some time to himself.

'See you later, then.'

31

He skied the first part of the Schwarzegg fast and straight.

The run was crowded now with skiers in shirtsleeves enjoying the the last of the warm afternoon sun, and Miles picked his way efficiently through the private ski classes as they snaked their way uncertainly after their patient and impeccable instructors.

The main piste dog-legged to the right and opened out into a wide valley. Above, along the left-hand face, ran the path that formed the first part of the Gun Barrel run. There were about half a dozen skiers on it. Running in a parallel line beneath it for about two hundred yards was an orange nylon rope, strung between a series of light poles. Halfway down was a gap. Miles could see there were ski tracks that ran through it and joined up with the path further down. He bent low over his skis and tucked his poles under his armpits. The Rossignols moved well over the softening snow.

He was halfway there when a *pisteur* in an orange jacket with a walkie-talkie tucked into his belt overtook him and headed straight for the gap. Miles assumed he was going through and made no attempt to slow down. But then, just as he got there, he saw that the man had tied the rope across. Miles slewed to a stop.

'*Geschlossen*,' said the man in response to Miles's groans of frustration. He waved a forbidding hand. '*Fermé.*'

'Why?' Miles wanted to know. '*Warum?*' He pointed to the other skiers away in the distance.

'*Nicht gut*,' said the man, impassive in his bushy black beard and atrocious Swiss German accent. '*Zu viel Schnee. Danger d'avalanche. Geschlossen.*' He pointed towards the long queue snaking to the bottom of the Stockli drag lift.

Miles smiled and shrugged. The *pisteur* gave a cursory nod, turned his skis downhill and disappeared into the mêlée.

Miles waited for a couple of minutes. Then he slid forward, lifted the rope, ducked under it and headed off towards the path. No one came after him. No one called out or waved.

Once on the path, he paused for breath. The skiers in front were out of sight by now and there was no one behind him. A couple of mountain crows floated in an aimless circle above. Otherwise he was quite alone on the mountain. It must have been how skiing once was years ago, before the lifts arrived, and all the people ...

Moments later, he was through the Gun Barrel. The path that zigzagged down from the cleft in the rocks was nothing like as dramatic as it appeared from below, but it was steep enough and demanding enough, even for someone of Miles's experience.

He attacked it in a series of short swing turns, carving his way round the sharp hairpins. At first it was easy enough to maintain the rhythm, but after a while the constant pressure on his knees began to tell. His thigh throbbed. There were several moments when he felt like chucking it in and side-slipping his way to the bottom. No one was watching. But he was not a man to resort to half-measures. He kept the elegant little movements going, even though the path was far too narrow in places. Occasionally the rhythm became very ragged and once he missed a turn completely and only just managed to stop himself from pitching over the edge.

Miles was glad to get down in one piece. And yet, as he floated effortlessly over the gentle undulations of the Blumen run and glided between the slow, fumbling beginners, a faint feeling of dissatisfaction came over him. This was probably his last run and he wanted to end it on a high note. He needed one last challenge to complete a perfect day's skiing.

He was halfway down the broad boulevard leading to the bottom of the little Ringeberg drag lift that serves the nursery slopes when he spotted the short cut.

It was steep and unpisted, not more than fifty feet wide, with trees on either side, but terribly tempting. He couldn't possibly come to any harm, Miles reasoned. If he fell awkwardly, or got stuck, he was within easy hailing distance of the nursery slopes, and if he shouted just a little louder there were plenty of people sitting out on the terrace of the Ringeberg Hotel, soaking up *glühwein* in the last warm rays of the setting sun.

He turned his skis to the right and slid gently into the soft snow ...

The avalanche hit him with the speed and unexpectedness of a grenade launched three blocks away: except that an exploding grenade makes a hell of a noise. This made no sound. It caught him in the middle of the back like a truck and threw him forward and down and over.

It was all so quick that at first he didn't even realise what was

33

happening. Even if he'd had time to remember what he had once been taught about releasing his ski bindings, it wouldn't have made any difference. Within seconds, the weight of the snow was on top of him, crushing the breath from his body and rolling him over and over, like the big breaker that had caught him unawares one summer's day in Cornwall when he was a little boy. He experienced the same unreal feeling of helplessness; of being driven further and further below the surface, away from the sunlight and the air, down and down so far that he thought he could never come up again. And the snow was in his nostrils and in his eyes and in his mouth, so that each time he tried to draw breath, he breathed in more snow … until his throat and mouth were full and he couldn't breathe any more and he knew for certain that he was going to die.

What a bloody stupid way to go, he thought.

And then, as suddenly as it had started, it stopped. No more violent movements and wild unnatural contortions, no more gasping for breath and involuntary grunting and roaring in the ears, no more anything. Just stillness and silence. But not the silence that he had experienced up above the Gun Barrel; nor even the stillness that follows the blast of a land mine and the ensuing cacophony of yelled orders and the shouts of panic and the screams of pain and the crackling gunfire that typify an IRA ambush. This was a silence that was palpable … the silence of the grave – but worse, because he was in it … alive … thinking … feeling … frightened. Buried alive. The ultimate nightmare.

For a brief moment after the avalanche stopped moving, panic consumed Miles's whole being. He couldn't breathe … *I've got to get out* … Couldn't see … Couldn't move … *Christ! I'm going to die! … I've got to get out … Now!*

And then the spasm subsided, the moment passed. Self-control took over: the same self-control that had stopped him from rushing blindly, rifle blazing at the hip, bayonet stabbing, into the Argie trench on Mount Tumbledown when his sergeant's brains had exploded into his face and three of his best soldiers were lying in the heather, screaming and trying to hold in what remained of their stomachs; the self-control that had been dinned into him at Sandhurst, and in the jungles of Belize, and in the grey rubble of

Londonderry; the self-control that is as essential a part of every army officer's equipment as his revolver and his mess kit.

He blinked into the grey nothingness around him. If it was still sunny above, there was no sign of it down here in this icy tomb.

It was some time before it dawned on Miles that he *was* breathing: not easily, but enough to sustain life. *There must be some air coming from somewhere.* He rolled his eyes round as far as they would go. He couldn't see any sign of light, so it almost certainly wasn't coming from outside. And then he discovered that, when he moved his head forward an inch or two, there was no snow pressing against his face. He tried again, neck craning forward until it hurt. Still nothing. Miraculously, a small pocket of air had formed in front of his face. He shoved his head hard backwards. The snow behind gave with a gentle crunch, creating another valuable inch of breathing space.

But his head was all he could move. The rest of him, his limbs and trunk, was as firmly packed into the snow as a dead cod in a tray of ice.

Miles was a powerfully built man, with strong shoulders, arms and legs. If he could free his hands, he could start digging the snow away. Then he might stand a chance of working his way out. But it wasn't going to be easy. One hand was caught up behind him in a half-Nelson, and the strap of the ski pole was twisted so tightly round his wrist that he was already beginning to experience pins and needles in his fingers. The other was clenched round the handle of his other ski pole and jammed into his midriff, which was doubled up over his groin. However, by exhaling in shallow, rapid pants he was able to melt a little more snow and give himself a few more precious centimetres of breathing space.

But he couldn't afford to overdo it. If he used up too much energy, the oxygen would soon run out and he would rapidly become confused and lethargic. It would be only a matter of time before he was overwhelmed by a desperate urge to sleep. His eyes would droop, a feeling of warmth and well-being would steal over him and that would be the end of him. Hypothermia would set in and death would quickly follow. He *had* to keep awake if he wanted to stay alive …

Hang on. Stay alive? What am I thinking of? This is bloody ridiculous! There are people skiing past just a few yards away. I could almost reach out and touch them. I'm within spitting distance of the nursery slopes. The sun terrace of the Ringeberg Hotel is just down there beyond the trees. And yet here am I thinking about whether I'm going to live or die. For God's sake, someone must have seen what happened! A puff of powder would have floated up through the trees. Surely it won't be long before help arrives and the snow around me will be bristling with long thin searching poles and cold Alsatian noses will be nuzzling my cheek ...

'Help!' he shouted. 'Someone! Over here! Help!'

But the sounds dissolved into the snow like drops into cotton wool, and his head began to spin with wasted oxygen.

Right, he told himself: *stop, relax, think. Sooner or later, someone's bound to wonder where I am and raise the alarm. A search party will be sent out. When, though? And where will they start looking? If this was some small, freak snow-slip that happened out of sight when no one was around, there's no reason why anyone should think of looking here, of all places. And even if by chance someone does, and supposing they locate me and dig me out, the chances of my being alive are pretty slight: especially once the sun goes down and the temperature drops ...*

If only I could move my legs ... With all that twisting and wrenching and tumbling, the bindings on both skis should have released pretty well straight away; but to judge from the way his left ankle was twisted under him, at least one ski was still firmly attached, holding him down like an anchor embedded in mud. His right leg was stretched out and locked in behind his left knee. He tried twisting his right ankle to left and right. There was a little movement. It was possible the right ski had released. If he could extricate one hand, he might be able to reach down and release the left-hand ski. With his foot free, he should be able to straighten it and unlock his left leg. Then he could start digging his way out. If the avalanche was as small as he suspected, he was probably only a few feet under the surface. It wouldn't take that long to reach the surface. Unless ... A chilling thought occurred to him. *Which way am I facing? Up, down or sideways?* There was no way of telling. The force of the snow had rolled him over so many times he could have been left standing on his head, for all he knew. If he was in anything like an upright position, he had no problems. If not, he could easily end up digging himself into his own grave.

The pressure on his stomach seemed to be increasing by the

36

second. He coughed and spat out the last of the snow from the back of his throat. The spittle rose in a gentle arc in front of his face and fell straight back against his cheek. He spat again. Again the gobbet went up and came down, this time on to his chin. *I must be on my back. That means my legs aren't twisted under me at all. They're above me. Christ, I've got even more work to do than I thought ...*

Working his way morning after morning through his crumbling Penguin edition of Canadian Air Force exercises in his Battersea flat, he could never have known how grateful he would one day be for all those hours of tedium. For in the end it was the combination of physical strength and mental rigour that enabled him slowly, agonisingly slowly, but surely, to extricate the hand that was jammed into his midriff and disentangle it from the twisted pole strap.

With his free hand he was gradually able to work some of the snow away from around his chest, but it was desperately slow work. The day disappears fast in the Alps in January and the temperature drops like a stone. Only his efforts were keeping his blood from freezing in his veins. Every breath he took, however short and shallow, was agony. The oxygen was going as fast as the daylight above. Again and again he was overwhelmed by waves of claustrophobia, yet somehow he managed to keep going. Some inner strength that he didn't even know he possessed drove him on.

He had no idea how long he had been buried or what time it was. He'd left the restaurant at approximately 2.30 so it was probably about three. But when at last he succeeded in moving his trunk forward enough to release his left hand, he was appalled to see by the luminescent hands that it was already four o'clock. *Christ! Surely by now someone must have noticed I'm not back.* Fee, for one. Assuming she was down. They might have stopped off somewhere for a drink. Even if she had raised the alarm she would have directed the ski patrol to the Gun Barrel. No one could possibly guess that within a few hundred yards of where people were sitting over their cakes and hot chocolate, laughing over the day's adventures and looking forward to hot baths, a man was fighting for his life ...

Miles was right about one thing. The Salomon binding on the right-hand ski had done its job. The other must have been set a fraction too hard. The ski was still there and, however much he contorted his body and stretched his fingertips, there was no way that he could exert enough pressure on the heel clip so that the whole thing would click open and allow his boot to come free.

He needed to do something, and quickly. Each breath now was sheer torture. He could feel his eyes drooping with fatigue and lack of air. Voices came and went ... His father's, telling him to pull his bloody finger out ... His brother's, reminding him he'd got a day's shooting coming up at Clumber ... Fee's, speaking to him from only a few inches away, in her soft, West Highland lilt, like the wind ruffling the grass on a perfect summer's day, saying that she was waiting for him ... *Waiting? Where? In the bar? In Skye? In life? God, I'm beginning to hallucinate! Think, man! Think! ... If I'm as close to the surface as I hope ...*

He drew back his right knee as far as it would go and drove his foot straight upwards. A new-born baby couldn't have felt weaker. He drew his foot back again and chunks of snow fell on to his face. He brushed them away and tried again. It was like walking through glue in a nightmare. He drove upwards again and this time he thought the snow yielded. And again. Now he was sure of it. Only an inch or two, but ... He brought his knee back and drove again ... and one more time ... and again ... Each time he felt his heavy ski boot going deeper and deeper in. But still he hadn't broken the surface. Perhaps he was further under than he'd thought. Perhaps this was all a bloody stupid waste of time.

He lay back, tears of frustration pouring down his cheeks and into the corners of his mouth. His strength was almost gone. Almost, but not completely ... He shoved his foot out again ... and again ... and suddenly there was no more resistance. He moved his ankle to left and right. He pushed his foot back and forth. It moved easily. He could feel cold air curling round his exposed ankle and then it came rushing in, bathing his face like a shower of cooling rain after a heatwave. He took great gulps and drew it down into his lungs. Fresh air had never tasted so good. He shouted and laughed and blasphemed, and then, just as he had when the land mine went off under his armoured car in Lurgan and he realised that he was still alive, he closed his eyes and offered up a silent prayer to the Almighty.

* * *

It was another hour and a half before Miles finally struggled out and on to his feet. He was shivering uncontrollably and his legs trembled from the last few minutes of sheer physical effort. He blew on his hands and clapped them hard against his body in the hope of working some circulation back into his veins, but it was no good. If he didn't get indoors soon, he'd die of exposure.

The sky glistened with stars and the frosted branches glowed ghostly grey in the moonlight. Below, the lights of the village twinkled and beckoned. Miles ran his fingers over his head. His hat had long gone and his hair was wet, and curiously sticky.

How he made those last few hundred yards down to the village he never really knew. He tried to stick to the Blumen path, but kept straying off into the soft snow at the side. Again and again he found himself up to his waist. Again and again, cursing and weeping with fatigue, he fought his way out. Once, he couldn't find the piste at all and spent precious minutes half-stumbling, half-falling, through the trees.

What seemed like a lifetime later, he was standing on the firm surface of the nursery slopes, looking down at the lights of the hotel fifty yards below him, and then his knees gave way and he slid and rolled and crawled towards the slatted surface of the sun terrace.

From somewhere above his head there came the sound of clinking glasses and contented laughter. He took a deep breath and heaved himself to his feet. About twenty feet further along the terrace there was a side-door. Holding on to the tables for support, he worked his way towards it. It was unlocked. He found himself in a side-passage. An open doorway led into the hotel lounge. He shuffled through it on rubber legs. The room was beginning to fill up for pre-dinner drinks. A log fire burned in a big open grate. Beer- and wine-glasses glinted in the flickering light. The family round the table nearest to him was playing Scrabble. A middle-aged couple nearby in cotton roll-necks were reading fat paperbacks. Others were scribbling their way through stacks of postcards. A waiter in a short white coat trotted past with a tray laden with drinks. The Scrabble players looked up hopefully. Then they saw Miles.

'I say,' said the father. 'Are you all right?'

Miles grinned. He tried to say he was fine, but no words came out.

He took a couple more steps, the room swam … and he pitched headlong into the middle of the Scrabble board.

'Well, really!' said the mother.

A thin ribbon of blood ran across the word KNICKERS.

'Terribly sorry,' said Miles and passed out.

5

It was 6.15 when the Scrabble-mad Pikeley-Smiths delivered Miles to Dr Grunner's surgery on the old hotel luggage sledge. A large whisky had gone some way to restoring his vigour, but he was still feeling pretty shaky, not to say light-headed.

The door was opened by a nurse in a high-collared white shirt and crisply pressed white trousers. She had a pale, narrow face, with dark eyes set wide apart. She wore no make-up and her straight black hair was pulled back severely across her head and fastened at the nape of her neck with a plain gold clip. She exuded as much warmth as a *Thunderbirds* puppet.

'Surgery is from four to six,' she said.

Simon Pikeley-Smith's ruddy features crinkled into a smile, which in certain circumstances could be winning but on this occasion appeared merely fatuous.

'It is rather an emergency,' he said, with the eagerness of a man selling raffle tickets.

The nurse cast a cursory eye over the back of Miles's head. 'You can go,' she told the Pikeley-Smiths.

'We'll come back later,' they assured her.

'There is no need.'

'We'll ring your hotel later,' the couple promised Miles. They looked like anxious parents leaving their small son at prep school for the first time.

The nurse closed the door firmly behind them. She helped Miles off with his anorak. The collar was stiff with dried blood.

A door led from the entrance lobby into a wide corridor. To the right were two doors, both closed. On the other side was a small waiting room. It had a maroon cord carpet, bentwood furniture and cushions with Black Watch tartan covers. A skeletal man with thinning fair hair and gold, half-moon glasses was skimming a day-old copy of the *Daily Telegraph*. He wore a white polo-neck shirt, black corduroy trousers and black sealskin boots. A blue and red anorak lay on the chair next to him. He looked painfully British.

'Wait here, please,' said the nurse.

She disappeared through the door opposite. Miles sat down.

The man looked up. 'You the chap who was in the avalanche?' he enquired cheerfully.

Miles smiled. ''Fraid so.'

'Bloody hell.'

'It was.'

'Lucky fellow.'

'Yes. How about you?'

'Nothing so dramatic.' He held up his right hand. There was fresh plaster round his wrist and thumb. It disappeared somewhere inside his sleeve. 'Slipped over on the ice.'

'It's easy enough to do. You need good edges,' said Miles.

'I wasn't on skis at the time, actually. I was giving a hand to a pretty girl outside a restaurant. Bloody silly. The Alpenstock. Do you know it?'

'I only arrived yesterday.'

'They've probably cleared the path now.'

'Probably.'

'Bloody silly.'

'I thought the nurse said surgery was finished.'

'I rang,' said the man. 'Told them I needed a note to get a refund on my ski-pass. Doctor's probably doing it now.'

'They're very good about that sort of thing out here.'

'So far, so good.'

The nurse reappeared in the doorway and gestured at Miles. 'Come in, please.'

Miles looked at the man and pulled an apologetic face. 'Sorry.'

The man smiled amiably. 'Your need is greater than mine.'

The surgery was next to Dr Grunner's office. It was like surgeries the world over: a riot of white paint and stainless steel, kidney dishes and sterilising units, enlivened by a couple of large modern prints in

42

clip-frames. In the middle of the room stood a narrow couch covered with a white sheet. At one end was a thin, businesslike pillow. Above it was an adjustable operating light. At the nurse's invitation, Miles sat on the edge of the couch. His legs dangled several inches above the squeaky-clean floor. Through an open door at the far side of the room, he glimpsed a corner of a desk and a reading lamp with a green glass shade.

'So ...'

Dr med. Felix Grunner, MD, Ph.D., looked about sixty-five, but could have been older. He was still a very good-looking man. Tall – six foot three or four – with thick grey hair and Marmite-brown eyes. He wore a dark green pullover over an open-neck shirt, and brown corduroy trousers. He greeted Miles with old-fashioned courtesy but he seemed distracted, as if he had more important things on his mind.

'Lie down on the couch, please. Face down. Make yourself comfortable.' His accent was as unidentifiable as the nurse's. Miles wondered if he came from the Grisons. He knew they had their own language called Romanges, but he'd never actually heard it spoken. Someone once told him it was a distant cousin of Croatian.

For several minutes Dr Gunner and the nurse worked away in silence, cutting the matted hair, dabbing at the wound with a damp swab, while Miles related the events of the afternoon into the thin pillow. As he talked, he felt he was telling a story that had happened to someone else, in another place and long, long ago. It was hard to believe that it was only an hour since he had scrambled out of his icy tomb. It could have been in a previous existence.

Dr Grunner sighed.

'I didn't like the sound of that,' Miles muttered.

'There is a lot of blood. It looks worse than it is.'

'Does it need stitches?'

'One moment, please. Anna ...'

He heard the two of them go into the office and the door closing. From the urgent exchanges that ensued, it sounded as if they were arguing; but the words were muffled and indistinct and Miles made no attempt to follow the discussion. The sooner they got on with it, the better, as far as he was concerned. The debate continued for several more minutes. Eventually, the door opened and the nurse returned.

43

'The doctor thinks you should have stitches,' she said.

'If he says so,' said Miles. He lay there, passive and resigned like an old dog waiting to be put down.

He heard the doctor come in. There were sounds of instruments being arranged in metal bowls and some more hair was cut away.

The doctor murmured, 'I hope this will not be too painful.'

Miles laughed. 'An hour ago I thought I was dead,' he said.

He felt the needle pushing hard against his scalp. 'Ouch,' he said, remembering there was a lady present.

The skin resisted briefly and then the point drove in and through, drawing the stitching behind it. Like sewing a patch on to the heavy sailcloth of his old Drascombe Lugger, he reflected. After a while he lost count of the number of times the needle went in and out. His mind began to float above the pain and wander in a warm sea of inconsequential thoughts.

He wondered if there was more to the relationship between Grunner and Anna than the obvious doctor–nurse one. Maybe she was Frau Grunner? Or his mistress perhaps? They seemed rather oddly matched. But then Elizabeth and he were hardly ideal computer-dating material. In fact they had almost nothing in common. Riding and sex, that was about the extent of it. Otherwise they disagreed on almost everything. Like the two characters in the Fred Astaire song, they'd often talked of calling the whole thing off. But then she'd had the accident and the whole thing had been put on hold. Still was. Always would be, if her neurologist was to be believed. He still had moments – usually at about four o'clock in the morning – when he felt sure he could have done something to prevent it. Told her he didn't want to race her; that he was tired. Anything. But the wildness in her was irresistible. She was always telling him not to be so boring and to let his heart take over sometimes instead of his head. If he'd tried to talk her out of it, she'd only have laughed at him. There was nothing he could do. She might have got away with it if that stupid bloody mare of hers hadn't taken it into her head to twist sideways halfway over the hedge. And if that patch of concrete hadn't been where it was … An inch to the left and she might have come out with nothing more serious than a sprained wrist. An inch to the right and the man outside in the waiting room could have hit his head on

44

a rock and spent the rest of his life as a vegetable. A sprained wrist, a smashed face, a shattered life … He had never prayed so hard for anyone as he had during the six months Elizabeth was in a coma. All he asked was that she should live. Had he known how things would turn out, he would have prayed very differently.

Outwardly she was as beautiful as ever, but what good is beauty when you can't speak and don't know who anyone is or where you are or what you're doing? The last time he'd gone down to see her, she had spread her toast with earth from an indoor azalea and eaten several mouthfuls with evident enjoyment before anyone realised what was happening. He still loved her, though. He always had. So much for suitability …

'These modern skis …' said the nurse.

'Sorry?'

'The runners are so sharp these days. Even on the hired ones. Eddie Adelbogen says the customers complain if the equipment is not perfect, yet most of them are beginners. We put thirty stitches in a girl's leg the other day. It was only her third day on skis.'

'I don't understand. How could I possibly have cut the back of my head with a ski?'

'Many things can happen in an avalanche. Luckily for you, the snow slowed up the bleeding.'

Miles grunted. 'It didn't seem very lucky at the time.'

'Things are often not what they seem,' the doctor murmured.

'Mm.' Miles drifted. It was an hour later when at last the doctor patted him on the shoulder. Miles eased himself slowly and painfully into a sitting position. Everything seemed to ache. He looked around, blinking and trying to focus in the bright light. There was no sign of the nurse.

'Please.' Grunner shepherded Miles towards the office.

The small room was dominated by a businesslike desk. Facing the door, its back to the window, was a high-backed swivel chair. Opposite, there was an upright wooden chair with arms and a leather seat. The doctor gestured towards it. Miles sat down. The doctor crossed the room, opened a cupboard and took out a bottle of Scotch and two glasses. He poured a generous measure and handed it to Miles.

45

'Will you excuse me for a moment?'

A second door led into the corridor. He went out, closing it behind him. Miles hoped the man with the broken wrist hadn't been waiting all this time. He walked across to the window. The Blumenhorn reared up at him, vast and ghostly white. He stared at the mountain for a long time, hypnotised by its sheer size, and then turned abruptly away. His attention wandered to the doctor's desk. He was struck by how very untidy it was. Piles of papers spilled over on to each other; items of medical equipment were scattered around in a haphazard fashion; an ashtray overflowed with dog-ends; a photograph in a plain black frame lay on its side. Miles picked it up and looked at it. It was a simple, no-nonsense family group: father and mother and three children standing beside a large white boat at the side of a lake. A little ketch of some kind, Miles guessed. The children's hair was almost white against the suntanned skin of their faces. The woman in the picture was tiny. She wore a broad grin and her hair in a gamine style. The first wife perhaps? The doctor's hair was dark and he was wearing sunglasses. An old photograph, evidently.

Miles put it back on the desk. Nearby, lying face up, half hidden amongst the paperwork, was another frame, much smaller and in light wood. Inside was a small square of material, black, a little faded here and there and frayed at the edges. Miles glanced quickly around and picked it up. Woven into the middle of it was a Union Jack and under that a single word: ENGLAND. Beneath that was an inscription, beautifully handwritten in Old German script. There was a word that looked a bit like 'global' with a capital G, otherwise it was as comprehensible as Old Martian.

The material was evidently a badge of some sort. From a blazer pocket, perhaps. The kind of thing members of overseas rugger teams wear, or Olympic athletes. Yet there was something odd about it. The word ENGLAND struck an unfamiliar note. And why black? Team blazers are usually blue.

The material looked hard and coarse. A uniform badge perhaps; but not of any regiment that Miles had ever come across, and he'd become quite an expert in regimental history over the years. Some naval outfit possibly? But even so, black ...?

46

Miles peered at it more closely. No clues. Just the outline of the stitching.

He was about to replace it when he realised someone was standing in the doorway of the surgery. It was the nurse. Her gaze was steady and expressionless.

Miles said, 'Oh, you're still here. I just wanted to say thank you for ...'

But she had vanished as quickly as she had appeared. Like a cinematic trick.

'Hallo ...?'

Miles got up and went across to the door. He stood there for a moment, looking round. The surgery was empty. He shrugged and went back into the office just as the doctor came in through the other door.

'I am so sorry to keep you.'

Miles said, 'She hadn't gone, then?'

The doctor looked blank.

'Your nurse. She's still here.'

But the doctor wasn't listening. He was looking at the thing in Miles's hand.

Miles felt himself flush. 'Oh, I'm so sorry,' he said. 'I hope you don't mind. I couldn't help noticing ... being interested in military history ... I didn't mean to pry. It was just that I saw it lying there on your desk and ... well, obviously it's a badge of some sort, but what exactly?'

The doctor walked across to his desk and held out his hand. Miles handed him the frame and sat down. The doctor looked at it for a while in silence.

'It's nothing,' he said. 'A gift from a patient. An old badge, from an English ski team. A gesture of friendship.' He pulled open the top drawer of his desk and tossed the badge in.

'Would I know him?' Miles asked

'I doubt it.'

The subject, like the drawer, was closed.

The doctor looked up and smiled. 'So ... now ... what story shall we make up for your insurance company?'

* * *

47

It was snowing hard as Miles left the doctor's house. Soon the whole village would be transformed into a series of ghostly outlines barely distinguishable beneath a thick white blanket.

Grunner's prescription for post-operative care was a hot bath and a good night's sleep. A second large Scotch while the medical report was being typed out made a pleasant change from antibiotics and painkillers, and was probably far more effective.

Miles pushed his hands deep into his anorak pockets, hunched his shoulders against the snow and headed off up the hill towards the hotel.

* * *

Frau Planck was standing in the hall, looking anxious, when Miles pushed in through the glass front door, brushing the snow from his shoulders and stamping his feet on the mat. She rushed forward and began to help him off with his overcoat.

'I heard,' she said. 'Are you all right? Where have you been? I was worried. Can I get you something? A drink perhaps?'

Miles thanked her and explained that he had just had a whisky with the doctor.

Frau Planck frowned and jerked her considerable chin. 'A whisky? With the doctor?'

'Beats antibiotics.'

Frau Planck shook her head. 'I don't understand,' she said. 'He was here. I was talking with him a few minutes ago.'

'Dr Grunner?'

'There is only one doctor in Eigerhubel. We have a guest with the flu.'

Miles shrugged. 'He must have taken a short cut. He did say he had another patient.'

* * *

Miles sat on a high stool in the Chasse-Neige Bar and stared dully at a large whisky and water. He'd stipulated no ice but it had still come clanking like the Weddell Sea in early spring and the glass was beaded

48

with condensation. He hadn't said anything. Didn't seem any point. Being alive was enough. He ran a finger up the side and flipped droplets of water on to the highly polished surface of the bar. The barman emptied a bag of cashew nuts into a glass bowl. From the far side of the hall came the sounds of a dining room of satisfied skiers in full throat. Miles swallowed a mouthful of the whisky. The taste exploded round his gums. His eyes fixed on the nuts. Three hours ago he'd been thinking about cashews. Amongst other things. The thought that he might never eat another one had really quite upset him. He'd have given anything to be where he was now, sitting at a bar with a large whisky at one hand and a bowlful of dry-roasted nuts at the other. Now that his prayer had been answered, he could take them or leave them. He left them.

'Christ! Miles! Are you all right?' Peter Franklin wove his way across the empty dance floor, arms oustretched, his features wrinkled in an expression of dog-like concern. 'Someone said you'd got caught in an avalanche. Shouldn't you be in bed?'

Miles waved a dismissive hand. 'I'm fine, honestly. I got stuck in a drift, that's all. Couldn't move. Bloody silly. Entirely my fault. Comes of taking short cuts.'

Franklin said, 'We heard you were at the surgery. Maddy and Fee and I came to see if you were all right. A female gauleiter came out, said there was nothing to worry about and told us to piss off. That was the gist of it, anyway.'

'Thanks. It was a kind thought. Where's everyone now?'

'In the dining room doing battle with the five-course regional extravaganza. They do believe in eating early, the Swiss. It's like being in an old people's home. Couldn't face more than the soup and fish myself. Wine's not bad, though. I'll go and fetch Maddy.'

'Please don't bother,' said Miles. 'I can do without all that PR concern.'

'But you're going to eat?'

'I'm not very hungry.'

'Sensible fellow. Someone said something about stitches.'

'Got banged on the back of the head by a loose ski. I'll be fine in the morning.'

'What are you drinking?'

49

'I'm all right, thanks.'

'Sure? In that case, I'll have a large cognac, Josef, if you'll be so good.'

If the barman derived the slightest personal satisfaction from his job, he was keeping it very much to himself. The brandy arrived gracelessly in a small balloon. Franklin raised it in Miles's direction.

'The stiff upper lip and the throwaway line may go down a treat with the girls,' he said, 'but it doesn't cut much ice with me. I know and you know that you were bloody lucky to get away with it today.'

'You're probably right,' said Miles. He took another mouthful of whisky. 'You were in the army ...' he said.

'Aeons ago. Why?'

'Ever come across a regiment whose badge was a Union Jack with the word "England" under it?'

'England?' Franklin frowned.

'My reaction exactly.'

'What makes you ask?'

'I've just seen one. In the doctor's office. It was in a frame. It had an inscription under it in German. I couldn't make out a word of it. It was in that funny old-fashioned script.'

'German, you say?'

'Yes, why?'

'What colour was it?'

'The usual. Red, white and blue.'

'The actual badge, I meant.'

'Black. A little faded but, yes, black. Definitely.'

Franklin sipped at his brandy and pulled a face as he swallowed, as though taking medicine. 'Very odd,' he murmured.

'Grunner said the man who gave it to him had once skied for England years ago. Could it be an old team badge? Olympics perhaps?'

'Grunner?'

'The doctor.'

'Ah.' There was a pause while Franklin lit a cigarette. 'Any rings?'

'Rings?'

'Olympic rings. If it was an Olympic badge, it would surely have the five interlocking rings on it somewhere. Wouldn't it?'

'No, no rings. Just the flag and the one word.'

'England ...' Franklin took another pull at his brandy. 'The Union Jack and England. Very odd. The Union Jack isn't the flag of England. The cross of St George is. The Union Jack stands for Great Britain. In which case why doesn't it say so? Who would make a badge like that and get it wrong?'

'Someone who wasn't English, presumably. Or British. The sort of person who makes cardboard policemen's helmets for the tourists.'

'Could be just another piece of Taiwanese junk.'

'Could be. Sod it. Let's have another drink.' Miles reached into the inside pocket of his anorak. 'Oh, hell.'

'Now what?'

'It's gone.'

'What?'

'My wallet. It was here earlier. In my inside pocket.'

'You sure?'

'Quite sure.'

'It's just that ... well ... you have had rather a shock and ...'

'No, I'm sure I had it with me at the doctor's. I remember checking in case I needed to pay on the spot. I could feel it through the material. It must have fallen out in the waiting room. Funny thing is, I'm certain the pocket was zipped up ...'

'Funny thing, memory,' said Franklin.

'I'll check in my room, just in case.'

'It'll turn up somewhere,' said Franklin.

'If I don't go to bed soon, my toes will.' Miles got off the stool.

'England ...' said Franklin to no one in particular.

''Night.'

The hall was empty. Miles took his key from the porter's desk and crossed quickly to the lift. The dining-room doors were wide open, but everyone was far too busy talking and eating to notice him. The press party were sitting at a long table on the far side of the room. Romford Man was spearing food with one hand. His other was draped over Maddy's shoulder. A cigarette hung from his fingers. She didn't seem to mind; on the contrary. Miles sighed. The lift arrived. He stepped in and punched the fourth-floor button. There was a mirror on the back wall. He peered at himself. The collar of his anorak was stained with dried blood, his hair was dishevelled and there was a

51

bruise under his right eye. He looked like one of the captured Tornado pilots in the Gulf. His head ached and he'd pulled a muscle in his right shoulder. He couldn't have draped his hand round anyone.

The telephone was ringing as he walked into his room.

'Just a thought.' Franklin's voice was slow and slurred. 'Supposing it isn't England at all.'

'What?'

'I mean England the way we pronounce it: as if it started with the letter I. Ingland. Supposing it's England, pronounced the way it's written, as in 'egg'. The way the Germans pronounce it. England.'

'What *are* you burbling about?'

'The SS wore black.'

'The SS? You mean the German SS?'

'There's only ever been one SS,' said Franklin. '*The* SS. The *Schutz*-bloody-*staffel*. Hitler's personal bloody élite.'

'Are you pissed?'

'Probably.'

'Thought so.'

Miles put the phone down. His head was thudding. He went into the bathroom and swallowed a couple of codeine. He flushed them down with a mouthful of duty-free Grouse. He zipped up his anorak, switched out the light and walked out of the room.

*　*　*

It was snowing heavily now. Miles shivered, pushed his hands deep into his anorak pockets and hunched low against the night air. He was outside Eddie Adelbogen's ski shop when he saw someone coming up the hill towards him: a man, head down, boots squeaking on the hard-pack. There was something familiar about him, the way he walked. Werner. Or was it? It looked like him. Same red jacket, same bushy blond moustache. But then he wasn't so sure … In the light of the street lamp, with the collar turned up high at the back of his neck and the bonnet pulled right down over his eyes, and his head ducked low against the cold wind …

'Werner?'

The man never broke step. He didn't even look up. Miles paused

52

and blinked at his retreating back. He frowned, turned and walked on down the hill. It suddenly occurred to him that, like Franklin, he was really rather drunk. What other reason could there be for turning out again into the bitter cold night? Or thinking that because a man was wearing a moustache and a red anorak he must be his ski instructor?

He wanted his wallet back. That was a fact. Loose ends bothered him. He liked to know where everything was. Couldn't sleep otherwise. Probably couldn't sleep anyway. Bloody headache. Shoulder giving him hell. Franklin was right. Wallet'd still be there in the morning. Would the badge, though? Aha! That was it. That was why he was going back. He wanted to have another look at the badge. Who knew? Could be a story in it somewhere. A real story. Not some pissy little travel piece about some pissy little ski resort and where to go for the best hot chocolate. A proper news story. A real piece of investigative journalism. Something to be proud of.

Miles pressed the bell. There was no reply, so he pressed again. Still nothing. He tried the door. It was unlocked. He pushed it open and stepped in. The entrance hall was dark except for a strip of light shafting through a gap in the office door.

'Dr Grunner ...? Hallo ...? Anyone in ...?'

His voice echoed dully down the corridor. He stepped into the hall, his snow boots silent on the cord carpet. He closed the front door behind him and called out again. Still nothing. He knocked on the office door. It swung open.

The doctor was still there, sitting behind his desk, exactly as Miles had last seen him, upright against the high back of the swivel chair. The lower part of his body and the area of desk immediately in front of him were bathed in a pool of light from an old-fashioned reading lamp with a green glass shade. His face was half-hidden in shadow, but Miles could see that he was pleased to see him again. He was looking straight at him and smiling gently.

'Sorry to bother you again so soon ...' Miles began and then saw his wallet lying on the desk. 'Aha ...'

He picked it up and slipped it into his inside pocket. The doctor was still smiling.

'Are you all right?' Miles took a step towards him.

53

As he did so, he sensed rather than heard footsteps coming from the open surgery door behind him. He had a fleeting impression of long, dark hair and a light-coloured anorak, but it was already too late. For the second time in a day, he was caught by a deadly combination of silence, speed and strength.

The forearm that clamped itself across his throat was machine-like in its remorselessness. Miles wanted to retch, but the pressure on his windpipe was such that he couldn't breath in or out. The hands were clasped together in an interlocking grip. The fingers were long and delicate. Miles couldn't understand it. He should have been able to force them apart with one simple movement. He'd practised it enough times. Yet they could have been made of reinforced steel for all his efforts achieved. Their extraordinary strength contrasted strangely with the softness of the breasts that pressed into the small of his back.

His scruples about using physical violence against women were deep-seated, but it soon began to dawn on him that if he didn't do something very quickly his gentlemanly instincts were going to stand him in very poor stead. Once again he seized the forearm with both hands, but he might as well have tried to wrestle a fork-lift truck.

The grip tightened yet further. The doctor was beginning to acquire the characteristics of an out-of-focus snapshot. Miles took his hand away from the arm, stretched both his arms out as far as they would go, clenched his fists tight and, using all his strength, drove his elbows back into the woman's stomach. The only noticeable reaction was a brief grunt and the grip was racked another couple of notches.

Miles noted, with a detachment verging on indifference, that the strength was beginning to ebb out of his body, to be replaced by a languor of the sort that he imagined people experienced when on the threshold of death. Not unlike being in the avalanche.

And then he saw the paper-knife. It lay on the near side of the doctor's desk, half-concealed by a large brown envelope, and just out of reach. He let his body go limp. His arms dropped to his sides, his head lolled, his knees buckled. He felt the grip on his neck slacken, very slightly but it was enough. In that split second, he drove the upper part of his body forward, threw out his right hand and grabbed the knife, blade downwards. While his attacker was still off-balance he drove backwards and upwards. The point went in and stayed there. Miles let go of the handle. There was a high-pitched shout of pain and the pressure on Miles's throat melted away. He fought to draw air into his lungs. Through the pain and tears he was dimly aware of dark hair falling forward and a figure bending over, sobbing, and hands trying to pull out the thing that protruded from the inside of her right thigh.

Miles's instinct was to help her. He tried to speak, but no sound came. He saw her hobbling towards the far door, and then a red curtain rose from his throat into his eyes, and suddenly he was falling headlong down a long black tunnel ...

6

Dear God, he thought, *I'm back on the ward …*

The smell of surgical spirit, the unforgiving hardness of the bed, the brilliance of the overhead light … Miles had lived through enough long, antiseptic days in the Intensive Care Unit of the Royal Victoria in Belfast and woken up after enough operations in Stoke Mandeville to recognise a hospital when he smelt one.

There was a horrible thudding pain behind his eyes and his throat felt as though someone had rammed it full of old golf balls. He tried to swallow but his neck seemed to have been set in concrete. He grimaced furiously with the pain. It all came back to him now. The badge … the doctor … the nurse with the Schwarzenegger arms …

Light bored into his sockets. He narrowed his lids against the unrelenting glare. He was lying on his back on the same couch where Dr Grunner had so recently and painstakingly repaired his scalp. He turned his head towards the office door – or rather he tried to, but nothing happened. He couldn't move. *God, I'm paralysed*, he thought. *The bloody woman's broken my neck.* But then he found he could move his right arm, and, as quickly as it had overwhelmed him, the panic subsided. Very gingerly he explored the back of his head. His hair was stiff and matted with some tacky substance. Glue? Had she added insult to injury by glueing him to the bed? He peered at his hand. It looked as if it had done a day's work in an abattoir. His fingers were sticking together. Using both hands, he gently disentangled his hair from the sheet which had stiffened with congealed blood. It hurt like hell, but at last he was sitting upright, his feet dangling over the side, head thudding, throat pulsing with pain. The door into the waiting room was shut, but the one that connected with the doctor's office was half-open and the desk light was still on. He cocked an ear

56

towards it. Nothing. He looked at his watch. It was 9.15. He wondered how long he'd been unconscious. Certainly long enough for the nurse to get away. But where to? He lowered his feet gingerly to the floor. It was streaked and smeared with blood. A trail led to the door into the corridor. *First things first, though,* he told himself. He edged his way towards the office.

The doctor was still there, still smiling: but not at Miles. He was looking straight at the door opposite.

Miles moved to the side of the desk. 'Doctor ...?'

He leaned forward, and it was then that he saw the hole. It was in the soft area just behind the ear. Small, neat. A rivulet of blood had run down his neck, staining his collar dark brown. It looked as if something very thin and very sharp had been driven up and into his brain. Some sort of medical instrument perhaps? Whoever had done it had known his business. Or hers. Miles's elbow nudged against the doctor's shoulder. He slumped sideways, his head against Miles's midriff. He was still smiling.

Miles wondered why a man would die with a smile on his face. It's either because he's especially glad to be off – and Dr Grunner certainly didn't look like a man who was eager to be leaving this world for the next – or else because he's been caught unawares in mid-pleasantry, and death has come so suddenly and so unexpectedly that he has not even had time to register its imminence.

Given the position of the neck wound, it looked as if the killer must have had an accomplice: someone who was already known to the doctor, and whose appearance had come as a pleasant surprise, distracting him sufficiently to enable the killer to approach from somewhere behind – through the surgery door probably – and slide the instrument, whatever it was, into his neck before he'd even had a chance to know what was happening.

There seemed no obvious motive. No indications of items of value fought over or of life defended. No signs of drawers ransacked or of money hunted for and found. Unless ...

The doctor's right hand was resting on the desk above the top right-hand drawer, fingers outstretched, as though he had been reaching for something. Or putting something away. The drawer was slightly open. Miles bent down and peered inside. There was a pile

57

of loose papers, but no sign of the badge. He pulled the drawer wide open and rummaged through. Nothing. No frame, no badge. But there was something else there, tucked away at the very back. Something hard and round and misshapen. His fingers closed round it ...

It was a little rose. Exquisitely carved from some honey-coloured stone, it seemed to glow in the palm of his hand as though possessed of a warmth of its own. He took it between his thumb and forefinger and, as he held it out under the light of the doctor's desk lamp, it suddenly came to life, lit with an inner fire, bursting with hitherto unimagined lines and shapes and variations of colour. And, in the very middle of it, frozen in a golden glow of eternity, was a tiny, single fly.

Miles gazed at it with the wide-eyed wonder of a small boy in a toy shop. He moved it around, viewing it now from this side, now from that, like an Antwerp diamond-cutter planning where to make the first vital incision.

It was then that he noticed the bloodstains. They started at his wrist and ran the length of the right-hand sleeve of his anorak. There were three of them. One was about three inches long and two inches wide, the others were slightly smaller. The nurse's blood, presumably. From her thigh wound. And then he saw there were more. Smears rather than stains, but unmistakably blood. Just above his waistband. Where the doctor had fallen against him.

'Christ!'

Ever since he'd left his hotel room, Miles had been reacting to events. There'd been no time for thought or analysis. Survival had been all that mattered. But now, seeing the blood on his sleeve, he realised for the first time that he was no longer a puzzled bystander. Suddenly he was a key player in the drama. More: a suspect. Possibly the chief suspect. Never mind that he had never set eyes on the doctor before that evening and had absolutely no reason to lay a finger on him: from the police point of view, his face fitted the frame very nicely. Not only had he let himself into the house, outside surgery hours and without an appointment, on the pretext of looking for his wallet, which he apparently already had, but when he had found the doctor was dead, instead of reporting it he had started snooping about

58

in the office. And, when apprehended by the doctor's nurse, he had fought with her and injured her – quite badly, to judge by the bloodstains. Finally, he had attempted to steal an item of property belonging to the doctor, about which he had dreamed up some ridiculous conspiracy theory. Frankly, it didn't add up to much of a case, but, as grounds for an arrest, it looked very promising indeed. And when Miles's file came through from Berne and they read about his involvement in the chalet-girl murder ...

Away from the house, there was nothing to link him with the doctor's death. All he had to do was go straight back to the hotel and up to his room – there was bound to be a back entrance, an emergency staircase – wash the blood out of his anorak, and go to bed. As far as anyone knew, he had been there since bidding Franklin goodnight in the bar. The nurse knew differently, of course, but she was the last person who'd go to the police.

Miles was putting the stone back in the drawer when he heard them. Footsteps. Soft, regular, moving backwards and forwards across the surgery floor.

He slipped the stone into his anorak pocket and stepped back until he was standing flat against the wall next to the surgery door. The footsteps kept moving. Something caught his eye. It was on a shelf, further along the wall, next to the doorway. A small, light-coloured wooden frame. He edged towards it. By now the footsteps had moved to the far end of the surgery near the window. He stretched his arm out. His first and second fingers closed on the frame in a scissor-like grip. He lifted it and drew it towards him. And then it slipped.

A lunatic with a hammer in the Hall of Mirrors in Versailles could not have made more noise. The frame lay on the floor, face upwards, blank behind the shattered glass. Miles stared back at it. The badge had gone.

At that moment, a huge black figure leapt through the open doorway – body crouched low, eyes staring, lips drawn back over long murderous teeth, roaring like a soul in torment. It caught Miles on the left shoulder and spun him sideways. Somehow he managed to keep on his feet.

He was through the door and halfway across the surgery before the dog had had time to turn and give chase. God knew what sort of breed it was. Judging by its size and build it seemed to have some water buffalo in it. Miles wasn't going to wait to find out.

Bouncing off the operating couch, and to a fanfare of clattering kidney bowls and assorted spatulae, he shot out into the corridor and slammed the door behind him. He was just in time. The frame shook as the creature launched itself against the polished pine.

Miles ran towards the front door and snatched it open. He almost ran straight into them. There were two of them. They wore black leather coats and grey fur hats. The one on the left was fair-haired with a pale face and spots: early twenties, probably. The other was older, about five foot eight and stocky, with grey hair. His face looked as if it had been carved out of the north face of the Schilt. The eyes were as hard as pebbles. Miles had met men like them before: in a small bare room in Druon.

There was a split second during which the thought flashed through Miles's mind that it would be best for all concerned if he gave up there and then. But then he stepped back, slammed the door to, heard it lock, and legged it back down the hall. There was a door at the far end of the corridor. It opened into a small hallway. On the other side of the open-plan stairs, another door, half-glazed, appeared to lead out into the garden. But it was locked and bolted. To Miles's right was a sitting room. By the light of a small table lamp, he could see it was decorated like a mountain chalet. The pine panelling was hung with antique skiing equipment: a pair of long wooden skis with fixed-plate bindings and long leather straps; a pair of snowshoes like real-tennis rackets; a hand-painted toboggan; a couple of crossed ski poles as long as hop poles with leather baskets the size of bicycle wheels.

A pair of French doors opened on to a balcony. A key with a ring in the shape of a ski hung from a nearby hook. It was stiff in the lock but after a panicky few moments of fiddling he managed to turn it. The door swung open. It was still snowing hard. The little garden gleamed in the moonlight, as deep and soft as a granny's blouse. From somewhere inside the house came the sounds of a dull crash and men's voices, shouting. Miles closed the windows behind him, clambered over the balcony rail and launched himself into space.

He hit the snow feet first and, out of sheer habit, dropped his shoulder and rolled. He needn't have bothered. The snow was so deep, he finished up lying on his back, hypnotised by the snowflakes as they floated against his cheeks. At that moment he felt he could happily have lain there all night. But the shouting in the house was getting louder all the time. He scrambled to his feet and stumbled towards the end of the garden. It couldn't have been more than thirty feet from the bottom of the balcony steps to the little picket fence, but the snow was up to his waist and his feet seemed to have acquired lead weights. There was a large tree in the corner. Some sort of fir or pine. Its branches were weighed down with snow, creating a broad curtain. By the time Miles was over the fence and crouching out of sight, he was breathing like a man in the last stages of emphysema.

He sprinted through a gap in the branches, at the back of the house. Through the falling snow he could see the two men outlined against the sitting-room window. One of them threw a switch and the garden was washed in brilliant light. It looked like a snowstorm in a bottle. The French window banged open and the two of them strode out on to the balcony and stood there peering into the far shadows. Schilt Face pointed to the spot where Miles was hiding. It was if he knew he was there. He ran down the steps and started across the garden. The younger man followed him.

Miles glanced quickly around. A network of paths criss-crossed various gardens and there were street lights dotted here and there. A little further along there was a path to the right. He worked out that, if he took that and turned sharp right again, he would find himself on the lower road. The snowplough would probably have been along there by now and it was only a short distance back to the hotel.

Miles ducked his head and, using the fir tree as cover, stumbled towards the little crossroad. The path dropped down steeply between village houses that seemed to be frowning at him under their heavily browed eaves, then swung to the right and disappeared from view.

The two men were already at the bottom of the garden. He could hear their voices, loud and urgent.

Halfway down, he tripped and fell heavily, winding himself and bruising his knee. As he struggled to get to his feet, his hand touched something hard and angular, half-buried beside the gate to one of the houses. It was the tip of a little toboggan. He dug the snow away and hauled it out.

He couldn't remember when he'd last sat on a toboggan. Probably not since the winter of 1966, when there had been snow in the big meadow beside the house in Northumberland from New Year's Day until the end of the holidays, and he and Henry and their friend Milo had spent every last moment of daylight out there on a variety of sledges, perfecting their techniques, building up their speeds and lengthening their runs in a bid to be the first to leap the stream at the bottom. Milo managed it on the last run on the last day of the holidays. But then his was a metal-framed model with runners you could steer with a wooden bar …

There were no fancy extras on this one. Just a piece of rope at the front for pulling it uphill. Steering was by heel power only. He pointed it down the slope, lowered himself on to it and, using his upper body, urged himself forward. Nothing happened. It wouldn't budge. He got off, leaned down, and, grasping the sides with both hands, ran beside it until the ice under the runners had melted and he could feel it sliding smoothly and easily on the new snow. Then he jumped on, stuck his feet straight out in front of him and began to gather speed.

At first the path was fairly smooth and straight, but then suddenly it turned and dropped away sharply. Blinded by the driving snow-flakes, he found it increasingly difficult to maintain a steady course. He began to veer wildly from side to side, ricocheting off walls and fences and bouncing painfully on the uneven surface.

To add to his growing anxiety, there was no sign of the lower road. *Perhaps I've crossed it already without realising. Or has my sense of direction let me down just when I need it? Where the hell am I and how easy will it be to get back to the hotel from where I finish up – wherever that is?*

The path took another sharp turn to the right, and suddenly he was out in the open in what looked like a narrow strip of meadow and heading for … nothing … empty space … the edge of the village and a sheer drop of two thousand feet down the Eigerhubel Cliff to the valley floor, and nothing between him and eternity but a low, rickety-looking wire fence.

Miles drove his heels hard down and tried to steer the toboggan to one side, but the snow was too soft and the soles of his snow boots were too smooth to secure any purchase. The cliff edge was now less than twenty feet away. He took a deep breath and hurled himself sideways. But instead of coming to an abrupt halt, he realised he was rolling head over heels, at high speed and completely out of control, towards the precipice, and there was nothing he could do to stop himself. He had a brief glimpse of the toboggan as it flew past him, hit a bump and cartwheeled over the top of the fence. It hung in the air for a moment, then dropped out of sight. He rolled over once again … and then he hit the fence. The wire gave, there was a cracking sound, the squeak of rusty iron against old wood, then silence.

Miles opened his eyes. He was lying on his right side, staring straight out across the valley at the mass of the Blumenhorn. He closed his eyes, and this time he prayed. It wasn't much of a prayer, but in the circumstances 'Thank God' was the best he could muster.

He opened his eyes again. He couldn't see a thing at first, and then gradually he could make out what looked like tiny fairy lights, strung out in a haphazard pattern against a dark background. He assumed for a moment that he was lying on his back again, looking up at the night sky. But then one or two of the lights started to move and he realised that he wasn't looking up but down. Straight down. The lights were not stars; they were the lights of Wintertal. He was lying face-down less than a couple of feet from the precipice edge, with only the wire of the fence preventing him from following the toboggan to the valley floor. The fence pole beyond his feet seemed to be more or less upright, but the one behind his head was tilting over the edge. The wire was still attached and the bottom was still in the ground, but only just.

Very slowly, Miles rolled over and on to his back. He could feel the sweat running from his armpits down across his ribs. He lay there for a moment, staring up at the sky, then he began to roll on to his left side. Very carefully, very slowly. After he had made four complete rolls, he felt it was safe to get to his feet. As he did so, a thick wedge of snow slipped away from where he had been lying and floated over the edge in a fine mist, leaving behind a patch of bare grass about the size of a ping-pong table.

* * *

He had been right about the lower road. But not about the snow-plough. In the circumstances it seemed churlish to carp. As he trudged up between the cowsheds, he thought that manure had never smelt so sweet.

Eigerhubel had never pretended to be anything other than a family resort. If people wanted late-night action, there was always Verbier or Crans-Montana or St Moritz. In fact almost anywhere was livelier than Eigerhubel. And thank heavens for that, thought Miles, as he plodded along the deserted road. At one point two people stepped out from a side-street straight in front of him; but it was only a pair of lovers, out for a romantic late-night stroll. He hurried past them with his head averted, but he needn't have bothered. If he had walked along the street with Dr Grunner's dead body draped across his shoulders, they probably would not have given him a second glance.

The porter was shovelling snow from the hotel terrace as Miles approached it. Miles ducked his head and walked on past. At the end of the building he turned sharp left up a short flight of steps and into the little Stübli Bar. The place had evidently closed for the night. He walked quickly across to a door on the far side of the bar. A steep flight of stone stairs ended at the back of the hall. The porter was still working outside. Miles ran across the hall to the stairs beside the lift. He took them two at a time and was up and out of sight in seconds. He was badly out of breath and his legs were shaking. He walked up the next three flights. The corridor was deserted. His room was at the far end. He was halfway along when the door of one of the rooms opposite opened. Miles stepped back into the nearest doorway and flattened himself inside the frame just as Damien stepped out. Closing the door, Damien looked quickly up and down the corridor then crossed to the door opposite and knocked on it three times. It was opened by Maddy Maguire. She also looked up and down the corridor. Damien slipped in past her and the door was closed.

Back in his room, Miles locked his door, tore off his anorak, filled the washbasin with cold water and dunked the sleeve in it. He took a tooth-glass from the bathroom and poured himself a large measure from his bottle of duty-free. He swallowed a mouthful, turned out the

64

light and, nursing the glass, walked across to the window. He threw it open and breathed in great lungfuls of cold clean air.

It had stopped snowing and the sky was almost clear. The world seemed to be covered in a layer of phosphorescent paint that gleamed in the moonlight. The sky was thick-carpeted with stars. Typical Switzerland, he thought. Ten out of ten for presentation, but underneath ...

What the hell have I got myself mixed up in? A murder, obviously: but by whom and why? Someone must have removed the badge from the frame some time between 7.45 and 8.45. Why? What was so special about it that it was worth murdering for? If, indeed, that was why the doctor had been killed. Perhaps Peter Franklin was right and it was from an SS uniform, but then every dealer in World War II memorabilia in every city in the world must have drawers full of SS badges. How many of them had a Union Jack on them, though, and the word 'England'? And what did it mean anyway? Had there been some undercover operation by the SS in England for which they had made up this badge specially? Had certain people in England had associations with the SS? Now that really would be something. If there were English people who had been in the SS – fought in it even – worked, God forbid, in the camps ... And if some of them were still alive ... And if the War Crimes Bill was being implemented ... And if someone they knew was in possession of material that could link them with a past that they preferred to keep quiet about, then the game might be worth the candle. That might be a motive for murder.

It was all very intriguing, but it didn't get him very far. Or the police. The badge had gone, and so had he, leaving them with a dead body and an anonymous suspect on the run. The face in the doorway couldn't have meant much to them. Thank God he'd found his wallet when he did.

Miles put his drink down and went into the bathroom. The anorak was lying on a stool, one sleeve soaking in the washbasin. He unzipped the inside pocket and took out the wallet. He went into the bedroom and sat on the edge of the bed. He had another sip of whisky and riffled through the contents. Money, bank card, credit cards, various membership cards, tetanus record ... Everything seemed to be in place. Or was it? Something was missing. Something he always carried with him; that he never gave a second thought to; that was as much a part of his everyday paraphernalia as his wristwatch or his cufflinks. At first he couldn't think what it was and then he remembered. It was the one document that carried his name and his home address. His driver's licence. And then he remembered something else. The little passport-size mug shot he always took in case he needed one for his ski pass. He could have sworn he'd slipped one in at the last moment ...

He was double-checking when he heard them. They were running fast down the street, their boots crunching through the fresh snow, their voices urgent in the stillness of the night air. Hotel guests, perhaps, who'd had a few too many somewhere in the village and were hurrying back so as not to miss the fun in the dining room. Except they didn't run straight in. They stood out there in the street, talking together in low voices, as if debating what to do next. Not guests perhaps, after all ...

Miles went across to the window and looked down. Their heads were lowered, their faces hidden in shadow, but the fur hats were unmistakable and the black leather coats gleamed under the street light. They looked up. The granite features surveyed the front of the building, but only briefly. Moments later they were up the steps and through the front door.

Miles stepped back. He didn't wait to close the window. He went straight across to the bedside table and pulled open the drawer. He took out his passport and traveller's cheques. He grabbed a large Norwegian sweater from the chest of drawers and, grunting with pain, pulled it over his head. He took his plastic duty-free bag into the bathroom, pulled the anorak out of the basin and squeezed as much water as he could out of the sleeve. He rolled it up and bundled it into the bag, emptied the basin and ran both taps. He washed the traces of blood away with his flannel and squeezed it out. Then he snatched his long tweed overcoat from the wardrobe, and headed for the door, pulling it on as he went. At the door he paused, went back into the bedroom, took a sheet of hotel writing paper and quickly scribbled something on it. He folded it, sealed it in an envelope and left.

He stepped out into the corridor. It was empty. He slipped the envelope under the door opposite and ran towards the emergency exit

66

at the far end. He took the grey concrete stairs two at a time, rammed the bar open on the door at the bottom and fell out amongst the dustbins and empty beer crates.

A short flight of steps led up to the road. The street was empty. Miles turned and headed down the hill towards the station.

A little brown-and-cream train was standing at the platform. A handful of passengers was dotted about in the two carriages. They had the contented look of simple citizens, leading simple, untrammelled lives, on their way home after an honest day's work to loving arms and warm beds.

Miles hadn't the first inkling of a plan, but he certainly wasn't going to hang about in Eigerhubel for a second longer than necessary. The two policemen had had a good look at him in the doctor's doorway and they'd have known at once that he wasn't a local. Chances were that by now they had radioed down to the valley for reinforcements. It wouldn't take long to fly a few men up the mountain by helicopter. Meanwhile, they'd already started checking the hotels. It was only a matter of time before they tried the railway station. At nearly ten o'clock at night, this could well be the last train out of Eigerhubel. There was a risk they might have posted some men at Grützi, four miles down the line, where passengers transferred to the funicular for the short ride down to Wintertal, but it was a risk he was going to have to take.

There was a light on in the ticket office. He wondered if they sold tickets on the train. And then he remembered. He pulled his anorak out of the plastic bag and felt in the outside pocket. It was still there. His five-day *abonnement*: the pass that entitled him to travel on all forms of transport in the region – including the local trains.

The hand on the big station clock jerked round to ten. Miles crossed the ticket hall and hurried down the steps in time to see the train moving away. He sprinted along the platform, grabbed the handles on either side of the rear carriage door and hauled himself up on to the metal step only feet before he ran out of platform.

The rear compartment was almost empty. Miles found a window seat looking out over the valley. In the dull glow of the carriage lights he could see the branches of the trees bowed low under their white burden and the snow heaped high at the side of the track, broken

67

here and there by the footmarks of small, unidentifiable mountain creatures.

Tomorrow would be a perfect skiing day. Up at Totenkopf they'd be sitting well back on their heels, their tips pointing upwards, floating down through unbroken powder so light that it would fly over their shoulders. The Ratraks would have been out at dawn on the lower slopes, flattening the piste for the ski-school classes, but even at Schwarzegg there'd still be plenty of good powder – until it began to soften and grow heavy in the midday sun. Then the less experienced would start forcing their turns, pushing their limbs into unnatural positions, pushing their luck. There were always a few nasty twists and sprains at the end of days like that: even a broken leg or two.

Miles reflected that he must have been the last patient ever to have been treated by Dr Grunner. Whether he was the last person he ever saw was another matter. One thing was certain: whether the police found his licence or not, his sudden disappearance guaranteed that, whoever else was in that surgery after he left last night, the name of Miles Maltby would be in every policeman's notebook in the Bernese Oberland. His picture too, probably. Even now some clerk in some basement in Berne was no doubt pulling out his file, dusting it off and preparing to punch his description to computer terminals throughout the country. By the morning, every railway station and airport and frontier post in the land would be watching out for him.

OK, so ... the funicular down to Wintertal, then what? Train to Berne? Zürich? Basle? The airports are obviously not an option. What then? A train to Germany, maybe? Too slow. Too obvious. They'd pick me up at the frontier straight away. What, then? A compliant lorry driver perhaps? Someone on his way home who could do with the company, and the extra money. But who comes through Switzerland? And there's still the matter of the frontier ...

Then he remembered that on the wall inside the door on every Swiss train there's a map of Switzerland. He stood up, turned and walked straight into a grey uniform.

'*Fahrkarten, bitte. Billets, s'il vous plaît.*' The conductor carried a leather satchel and the expression of a man doing a dull, routine job unrelieved by incident or drama. Miles flashed his *abonnement*. The conductor glanced at it, nodded briefly and passed on. Miles walked to the back of the train. He opened the door, stepped through and closed it behind him. He squinted at the map.

Basle. Of course! It's slap on the French–German frontier. It's also on the Rhine, and the Rhine goes all the way to Holland. Arnhem's on the Rhine. But where does the river go after that? Not Amsterdam. Rotterdam? The Hook? It's a hell of a long way, but if I could find a boat going east – a barge, perhaps, with an owner who could find me a small space … somewhere nosy customs officials would never think of looking … someone who wouldn't say no to a thousand Swiss francs …

The train slowed as the lights of Niederwald came into view round a bend in the hill. On one side was the big chair lift that hauled five hundred skiers an hour up to Oberwald and the complex of lifts and runs that made up the Wald skiing area; on the other, the little Nieder Café. A young woman was sitting at a table by the door. As the train approached, she stood up and walked down the steps that led on to the platform. She was wearing a long, dark coat and a dark fur hat. She looked romantic and rather mysterious: Anna Karenina with a touch of the French Lieutenant's Woman. She moved stiffly and awkwardly, as if suffering the effects of some childhood disability.

Miles watched her through the glass of the compartment door as she climbed into the front carriage and found a seat by the window. She took off her hat. Her hair tumbled down, dark against the whiteness of her long, narrow face.

Miles stepped quickly to one side and flattened himself against the carriage wall. No wonder he hadn't recognised her straight away. The last time he'd seen her she'd been wearing an anorak and she'd had a paper-knife sticking out from one leg.

7

Miles remained where he was for the rest of the short journey to Grützi.

A few minutes later, the train rumbled slowly into the big shed that it shared with the old funicular. There was a squeak of brakes, a slight jolt and it stopped. Miles looked at his watch. 10.15 exactly.

The nurse climbed down and limped along the platform with the other passengers. She turned right and disappeared down the steps where the funicular was waiting. Miles remained on the train while they craned off the wooden luggage container and swung it on to the back of the funicular.

The conductor climbed aboard and started checking the seats. Miles walked into the compartment, picked up the plastic bag with his wet anorak and stepped down on to the platform. He reached the top of the funicular steps as the Grützi stationmaster was closing the carriage doors and locking them with a heavy T-shaped key. He could see the fur hat in the third compartment down. He slipped into the top compartment. The stationmaster locked the door, a bell rang and the old wooden carriage jerked into life.

It took seven minutes to reach Wintertal. Again Miles hung back as the nurse limped towards the swing doors that led into the street. He exited in time to see her walking towards a black Peugeot 905 on the far side of the square. A man got out and opened the rear door. They exchanged a few words, she stepped in and a moment later the car drove off down the road towards Grundsee.

Miles walked across to the railway station. The 10.50 to Brugg was standing on Gleis 1, its carriage lights on. Several passengers were already on board, waiting. He bought a white coffee with sugar and

70

a bar of milk chocolate from a dispenser and settled himself into a corner seat. He'd buy his ticket from the conductor later.

The next fifteen minutes were as tense as any he had ever experienced. Every time another passenger boarded – a young man with a beard and walking boots, a railway worker in blue overalls, or an elderly woman carrying a shopping bag – his stomach knotted and his mouth went dry. At any moment he expected to hear a police siren and see men in uniform running along the platform and feel a hand on his shoulder. When the train pulled out on the dot he offered up a silent prayer of thanksgiving.

By the time they got to Brugg twenty minutes later, he had begun to relax a little. The conductor had shown no undue interest in him when he sold him a single to Basle via Berne. No one entered the compartment or left it. The short journey passed off without incident.

He had a ten-minute wait on Brugg station for his connection to Berne. The old spa town exuded warmth and friendliness. The Hotel Regina – home from home for generations of genteel British ramblers – cast a benign glow through the cold night air. It seemed a good omen.

The train pulled into a grey, deserted Berne station at midnight precisely. There wasn't a connection to Basle until first thing in the morning, but there was a café open nearby. Miles slumped on to a leather banquette. A television set up on the wall was showing *Sky News*. He ordered a bowl of onion soup, an entrecôte, medium-rare, with a pile of *frites*, and a bottle of Dôle from the Valais. He had a small black coffee, paid his bill and went back into the station. The waiting room was filled to capacity with assorted drunks, derelicts and back-packers, so Miles found a free bench in the main concourse. Using his anorak as a pillow and his overcoat as an eiderdown, he finally worked himself into a position of tolerable comfort and almost immediately fell asleep.

* * *

'*Wach auf, bitte … Bitte.*'

Someone was shaking his shoulder, not roughly but with some urgency. He opened his eyes straight into the beam of a powerful

71

torch. Shielding his eyes with one hand, he struggled into an upright position.

They wore dark blue caps and business-like expressions. Leather holsters hung from the belts of their dark blue overcoats.

'*Bitte gehen sie.*'

'Sorry?'

'You are English? American?'

'English.'

'It is six o'clock. It is time to work. You must go now. Goodbye.'

Miles began to mumble a dry-mouthed apology, but they had already turned away.

He caught the first available train to Basle. As soon as he arrived he went to the tourist information desk. Asking anybody anything was a risk. On the other hand, following his nose around a strange city was probably a bigger one.

'*Morgen.*' The stolid, middle-aged features were as severe as the neck of her crisp white blouse.

'*Bonjour, madame.*' Miles laid on the Vaudois accent and the charm in equal measure. 'Is there a boat leaving here for Rotterdam?'

'A *boat?*' Her forehead wrinkled in mild puzzlement. 'What kind of boat?'

Miles shrugged. 'I don't know. A boat.'

'There is a daily service,' she said. 'From April until October.' She reached for a timetable.

'April?' he said.

She shrugged. 'There is no service in the winter.'

'Nothing?'

'There is the train,' she said.

'I meant, on the river.'

She took a city map from a wire rack. 'You could try the Dreiländereck.' She opened out the map and drew an arrow on the opposite bank of the river, pointing northwards. 'This is the port. For commerce.'

'Barges?'

'Excuse me?'

'Do they have barges there?'

'Of course.'

72

'Is it possible to travel on a barge?'

She pulled a face. 'It's possible,' she said. 'You want me to ask?' She put a hand out towards the telephone.

'It doesn't matter.'

Miles folded the map, took a little booklet entitled *Basle: Cultural Heart of Switzerland* and headed out into the station concourse. He looked back. She was talking to someone on the telephone.

He quickly crossed the Centralbahnstrasse and turned into an anonymous-looking café. He found a small table at the back and ordered a croissant and *café crème*. He studied the map as he ate. The river swung in a lazy arc northwards through the centre of the town. Five main bridges were marked and there seemed to be a road that ran the length of the river on either bank. The Rheinweg. Miles liked walking.

He finished the croissant, ordered another and a second coffee. He hoped Basle was well provided with men's lavatories. He paid, left a small tip and went out into the street. He looked in every direction, but the only dark blue uniform he could see was on traffic duty. He turned and set off along the Aeschengraben, towards the river.

It was a glorious winter's morning. The air was crisp and clean and the whole place seemed to exude health and goodness and decency. Eigerhubel was another world.

At the Kunstmuseum he turned left down the Rittergasse. The Gothic spires of the cathedral loomed up ahead of him. The stone-work surrounding the twelfth-century Romanesque door glowed in the morning sunshine. The carved figures of various saints regarded him benignly from their little stone niches, as if giving him their tacit blessing. Miles was not a superstitious man, but he touched one of them all the same. One never knew.

He walked on down the Münsterplatz.

He paused on the Dreirosen Bridge and looked back along the river. He had always pictured Basle as a dull, characterless collection of banks and offices and hotel lounges, full of men in grey suits surrounded by spread-sheets: a city of trade fairs and electronics components exhibitions and scientific conferences. The medieval streets and squares and bridges had come as a delightful surprise. The

Rhine, too, with its little ferries bustling from one bank to the other. At any other time, it would have been positively romantic.

One of these days, he thought. *When Elizabeth is well again. If …*

He continued on over the Three Roses Bridge and turned left.

According to his booklet, the Dreiländereck – the Three Countries' Corner – is 'the meeting place for barge people from France, Germany and Switzerland … a boating paradise'. In reality it was a jumble of wharves and cranes and dirt and detritus. Tankers, tugs and barges lay tied up alongside each other.

Large iron gates led into the port area. A fat security guard sat in a lighted booth, smoking a cigarette and thumbing through a newspaper. He reminded Miles of an over-endowed tart he'd once seen displaying her dubious attractions in a window in Amsterdam. She had made as good a job of herself as anyone could, given the raw material she had to work with, but he still hadn't fancied her.

He looked around. *There has to be somewhere nearby where the bargees drink: a bar, a café, a pull-up for bargemen.* He hunched his shoulders and set off down the street.

It didn't take him long to find what he was looking for. It had a plastic sign outside advertising Feldschlösshen beer. Miles peered through the window. Two men were sitting at a table next to an old juke box, reading newspapers and drinking pale beer out of tall glasses. One of them was smoking a hand-rolled cigarette which he held cupped between thumb and forefinger. He looked like a rat dressed up in a thick plaid lumber jacket. The other puffed at a fat, curved pipe. He wore a black donkey jacket and had a bargee's cap stuck over one ear.

Miles took a deep breath and pushed the door open. The place smelt like an unemptied ashtray. The juke box was playing a dull arrangement of 'Memory' sung in German. He went and stood by the bar. The men looked up, stared at him briefly and returned to their papers.

He ordered a beer in muttered, passable German and took it to a table near the door. It was thin and cold, but it wasn't bad. He stared at the poster of Old Basle on the wall opposite, hoping to give an impression of nonchalance. He wished he had a newspaper to read. Anything. He got up and strolled across to the men.

74

'Do either of you speak English?'

The men looked at each other. The man in the cap jerked his chin upwards in a gesture of acknowledgment.

'I am a writer,' said Miles. 'I'm doing an article on the Rhine. I was wondering if you happen to know anyone who's sailing to Holland sometime soon.'

The man removed his cap and scratched his balding scalp. He put the cap back on and looked hard at Miles. 'And you want a free passage to Rotterdam.'

Miles glanced across at the bar, but the barman had disappeared into a back room.

'Don't worry about him,' said the man. 'Other people's problems do not concern him. Besides, he doesn't speak English.'

'I don't have a problem,' said Miles. 'I just ...'

'Please,' said the man with a pained expression. 'I may only be a simple bargee but I am not a fool. Of course you have a problem. Why else would you be here? There is a perfectly good train service, and Basle has an excellent airport.'

'You're right,' said Miles. 'I do have a problem.'

'My name is Bernhard Hoogeveegen,' said the man. 'I am from Utrecht.' He extended a hand the size of a club armchair.

'Miles Maltby. Look ...'

'Later. We shall have plenty of time to talk. Three days. My passenger cabin is not comfortable, I warn you. It is very small. It has a bunk and a mattress. Nothing more. But you are very welcome. I sail at noon.'

As Miles lay awake that night, listening to the big old diesel throbbing in rhythm with the pain at the back of his head, he wondered what the odds were against walking into a Basle bar on a cold January morning and finding that the first person he spoke to was a Dutch bargee, who was married to an Englishwoman, was a fan of everything English, and was leaving for Rotterdam that afternoon.

'I really think I should explain,' Miles had told him as they sat on either side of the little wooden table in the cabin, drinking thimbles-ful of Geneva, chased down with mugs of dark black coffee.

Bernhard set fire to his pipe tobacco and drew the smoke deep into his lungs. He shrugged. 'That is for you to decide,' he said. 'To me it is the same. I like English people. I like to help people who are in trouble. I like you. When the customs officers come on board, you can hide in your cabin. I will put boxes across the door. You will be quite safe.'

Miles laughed. 'I wouldn't want you to think you were harbouring a murderer or anything.'

Bernhard held his palms out and lifted his shoulders.

Miles knew he'd have to tell him the whole story sooner or later. The journalistic imperative demanded it. That, and the hope that, by going through the events of the last couple of days, some semblance of sense might emerge.

The bargee listened in silence. When Miles had finished, he carefully cleaned out his pipe. Equally carefully he refilled it. He pressed the tobacco down with his thumb. 'There were many in the SS who were not German,' he said.

'Oh?'

Bernhard lit his pipe and narrowed his eyes against the smoke.

He shook his head. 'There were many other nationalities. Latvians, Estonians, Bosnians, Croats, Serbs, Hungarians, Romanians … Many had enlisted early in the war, before the tide began to turn against Germany. Most were conscripted but many joined for nationalistic reasons.'

'What's nationalistic about fighting for your enemy?'

'The Germans were their enemies, of course, but for them there was a worse enemy. If you were from a Baltic state, to fight against the Soviet Union was to fight for your national survival. Many more were recruited in the last year of the war. Belgians, French, Danes, Norwegians. By 1945 there were more foreigners in the SS than Germans.'

'Are you sure?'

'Oh, I am sure all right. There were 50,000 Dutchmen alone. My uncle was one. Luckily he was killed fighting in Russia in 1943. If he hadn't been, my father would have killed him. Unfortunately, my mother did not live long enough in Ravensbruck to hear the good news.'

'I'm sorry.'

'Can you imagine? Her only brother?'

76

'But why? What made him do it?'

Bernhard shrugged. 'Idealism? Coercion? Cowardice? Who knows why people do these things?'

'So it is possible there were English in the SS?'

'I don't know. It's possible. I hope I am wrong. But at least I can help you to get back to England and find out for yourself. Cheerio!'

They raised their glasses to each other in a gesture of mutual respect.

* * *

As a soldier, Miles had slept in a variety of unlikely and inhospitable locations. Once, stuck out on a Falkland hillside near Mount Tumbledown in a knifing wind and sub-zero temperature, he had been forced to bivouac next to the rotting carcase of a dead sheep. And in the course of a special operation at Crossmaglen he had spent the night curled up in the boot of an old Volvo that normally carried potatoes. But, for unrelieved discomfort, that first night aboard the *Rosamunde* was in a class of its own.

The German customs men came aboard just after midnight. A dull thud against the side of the barge was followed by muffled German voices and heavy footsteps. Miles thought he heard the sound of a dog barking and then, when someone came to within a few feet of his head, the sweat began to run down his back as he prepared for the inevitable: the tearing away of the concealing bales, the boot against the lock, the torch beam in the face. But Bernhard was far too old a hand to get rattled by a routine search of the hold and the footsteps soon moved away.

It was not until after four that Miles finally fell asleep and, by the time the sun rose over the morning grey of the river on the Tuesday morning and Bernhard appeared in the doorway with a tray of coffee and bread and jam, he was beginning to think there might be something to be said for Swiss police cells after all.

It was a thought that was to recur more than once in the days and nights that followed. The Rhine twists and turns for nearly 600 miles between Basle and Rotterdam and thousands of tourists a year relish every one of them. There are stretches where the scenery is as

77

breathtaking as any in Europe. But, castles and vineyards and cliffs and medieval city architecture notwithstanding, for the traveller whose objective is to pass them and reach the end of his journey as soon as possible, many of those miles can seem as slow and as featureless as Atlantic waves viewed from 40,000 feet. Occasionally, sitting out on deck or in Bernhard's cabin, Miles would pull out a dog-eared red notebook and make a half-hearted stab at some *bons mots*. There had to be a thousand words in it somewhere. He managed two whole pages of scrawled observation and *pensées* at Strasbourg, but from then on his heart just wasn't in it. The cities chugged by at roughly six-hourly intervals, each one viewed with increasing indifference: Karlsruhe, Mannheim, Koblenz, Cologne, Bonn …

Every now and then Bernhard would pass a fellow bargee he knew. Greetings and good-natured abuse would be exchanged in a variety of languages, but by then Miles would have ducked down inside the cabin, so that even the simplest distractions were denied him.

It was shortly after eleven on the Thursday morning when Bernhard, pipe clenched between his teeth, tapped him on the shoulder and pointed down the river. About half a mile ahead, a launch was setting out from the west bank. Even from that distance it had an officious look to it.

'Elten,' he said. 'Dutch border. You should go below now, I think.'

Entombed in his cabin, staring into the blackness and listening to the heavy tread of officialdom on the deck a few inches above his nose, Miles's thoughts wandered back to Eigerhubel. But the images were fading fast, like early Polaroid snaps without the fixing fluid. Kirsty McFee in her skiing outfit, the avalanche, Dr Grunner, the nurse, the man with the face like the north face of the Schilt, the toboggan ride … Unreal, all of it. The only reality was the thud of boots, the sound of voices, the sniffing of dogs, the stench of the mattress …

He must have dozed off because, the next thing he knew, someone was tugging at his arm.

'You must come with me now!' He blinked against the sudden light. He sat up quickly, caught his head a crack against the low ceiling and, cursing, eased himself sideways and slid his feet on to the floor of the hold.

'Come quickly. Now.' Bernhard's voice was harsh and urgent.

Miles stumbled after the hurrying figure, his eyes fixed on the pool of torchlight wavering ahead. From somewhere above he could hear a dog barking again. Mouth dry, heart thudding against his rib cage, he scrambled up the iron ladder into the cabin. He turned. A man was standing there, a hazy shape against the rays of the setting sun. Miles shielded his eyes. The man moved slightly to his left. His hair was the colour and texture of straw and he was built like a dumper truck. He wore a blazer with shiny gold buttons, a pale blue shirt and a tie with a clubbish stripe, light grey trousers and black moccasins. He had a small cheroot in one hand and a thick leather lead in the other, with an Alsatian on the end of it. Miles wondered where he kept his gun. The man smiled and reached into his inside pocket. Miles took a step backwards. The man took out a packet of Benson & Hedges Gold. He opened it and offered it to Miles. Miles shook his head. He didn't smile back. *They always offer you a cigarette first. Gives you a false sense of security. It's one of the things they tell you on the course. The next thing they tell you is to refuse.*

The Alsatian grinned at him. He looked as if he'd recently had his teeth descaled. Miles did not smile back.

'So. This is the famous Mr Maltby.'

8

'I am Ronnie,' he said. He spoke English with a faint American twang.

'Ronnie?'

'Ronald Hoogeveegen. I'm a journalist on the *Utrechts Dagblad*. My friends call me Ronnie. It is a very English name, I think.'

'Very.'

'My father wanted me to sound like an Englishman. Why not? I am half-English.'

'Your father?'

Ronnie jerked his chin in Bernhard's direction.

Bernhard said, 'I telephoned my son last night, while you were asleep. I explained everything. He will drive you to The Hook. There you can take a ferry to Harwich.'

Miles laughed. 'Look, this is very kind of you, but won't they be looking out for me in Holland?'

'Who knows? There are many police in the docks at Rotterdam. It is better if you get off here, I think.'

Miles peered through the cabin window. A river bank lined with buildings. No features that stood out. 'Where are we anyway?'

'Arnhem,' said Ronnie.

'Not a bridge too far,' said Miles.

The road from Arnhem to Rotterdam is straight and flat and Ronnie drove the BMW 520 with minimum effort and maximum speed. An hour after leaving the *Rosamunde* they were bypassing Rotterdam city centre and heading for The Hook. Twenty minutes later, they glimpsed the first crane. Ronnie drove unhesitatingly through the labyrinth of cobbled streets and alleyways. The Hook–Harwich ferry was already tied up at the quayside and looked as if it wasn't planning to stay there much longer. The last of the cars were being driven up into the gaping jaws at the prow. The man who checked the tickets by the passenger gangway was looking anxiously at his watch and talking into his portable phone. Ronnie reached across Miles and opened the glove compartment. He handed him an envelope. Miles tore it open. It was a ticket. Single. To Harwich.

'The less time you spend getting aboard ... You have your passport, I think ...'

Miles started to protest, but Ronnie held up a hand.

'I hope you'd do the same for me,' he said.

'I hope you'll never need me to,' said Miles.

* * *

He handed his dog-eared blue passport to the Dutch immigration officer. The officer thumbed through the pages. His features betrayed as much emotion as a bath sponge.

'You have been in Switzerland.' It was a statement rather than a question and it came like a well-aimed fist in a dark alley.

'What?'

'Your passport was stamped at Geneva Airport on 16 January. Last Saturday.' The man did not look up.

'A short skiing holiday.' Miles tried to keep his voice calm and low, but it was a struggle.

'Which resort?' The voice was casual. He could have been a friend looking through holiday snaps. Always a bad sign in a functionary.

'Adelweiss,' said Miles. 'I stayed with friends.'

'Friends?' The man looked up sharply.

'A chalet party. They took it for a fortnight. I flew out and joined them for a few days.'

'But you didn't fly back.' Again, a statement of fact.

'I couldn't get the return flight I wanted. I had to see some friends in Basle anyway, so I decided to make a round trip of it.'

'You seem to have a lot of friends in Switzerland.'

'Not really.'

'How did you travel from Basle?' He had transferred his gaze to a spot behind Miles's left shoulder. It was as if someone was standing there answering the questions with imperceptible nods and shakes of the head.

'By river.'

'By river?'

'Someone I know has a barge. I'd always wanted to go down the Rhine. I wasn't in a hurry to get home. It's a wonderful trip. Everyone should try it.'

The man flicked through the passport once again. Looking for his colleague's stamp at the border perhaps? But then he turned back to the page with Miles's photograph on it. He studied it for a moment, then lowered his eyes to a spot just below the level of the window.

Miles felt sure he must have something pinned up out of sight. A rogue's gallery: a list of known smugglers, illegal immigrants, undesirables. Perhaps not a photograph. Interpol would hardly have had time to circulate his picture to every entry and departure point in Europe. They wouldn't need to. Just the name would do ...

The man's eyes flicked back and forth, up and down. Miles's mouth was dry and his stomach churned. It was like the Falls Road all over again, the only difference being that those people hadn't worn uniforms; and they had smiled ...

At last the man looked up. He closed the passport slowly and carefully; then, looking straight past Miles's head, he held it out to him. Miles thanked him.

'Sorry about the weather,' said the man.

'Why? Is it going to be rough?'

'The weather in the mountains. You are very pale.'

Miles smiled. 'I wear a lot of cream,' he said. He didn't wait for a reply. He walked through the barrier and across the quayside and up the gangplank and didn't look back.

* * *

The queue at passport control at Harwich was longer and slower-moving than any Miles had encountered in five years of professional travelling. Getting through the formalities at Beijing Airport was an Olympic hundred-metre final by comparison.

Miles was feeling sick, and it wasn't the cafeteria coffee that was to blame. The reason they were moving at a snail's pace was the unusual thoroughness with which the immigration officers were processing every passenger that passed before them. Most modern passports read about as excitingly as the latest edition of VAT notes. Few countries bother to stamp them any more and visas are a rarity. But, to judge from the way this lot were poring through the pages, you would have thought that every passenger had come equipped with a Booker Prize contender.

Harwich was not the most obvious entry point for anyone returning from Switzerland, but the immigration people were bound to have been alerted. There was no way Miles could get round them. He would just have to keep going and hope that, by the time he got to the front, sheer tedium would have driven them to revert to their normal casual behaviour. He made a mumbled excuse and moved to the back of the queue, but it didn't help. The leisurely pace became, if anything, even more leisurely; the examination of each document even more thorough; and Miles's digestive tracts even shakier.

To make matters worse, by the time he reached the passport desk, his heart was thudding so hard that he felt sure everyone in the building must be able to hear it. The official was wearing a light-blue pullover under a Harris tweed jacket, a check shirt and an oatmeal tie. The right-hand arm on his glasses was attached by a small safety pin and his nose hair would have defeated a hedge-trimmer. He worked his way through all 32 pages of Miles's passport in total silence. He finally handed it back to him without comment.

Miles went straight to the nearest newspaper stall and bought copies of all the tabloids plus a *Times* and a *Telegraph*. During the train journey from Harwich to Liverpool Street, he worked his way through them with the care of a man filleting kippers. Even the City pages. But the only mention of Eigerhubel was in the snow reports. He was missing some good skiing.

At Liverpool Street he rang Neville. A girl with a voice like a circular saw informed him that Mr Short was in conference and Miles told her that he'd call back later. No, no message.

He dialled the number again and asked the man at the switchboard to put him through to the cuttings library. The librarian who took the call wanted to know if he was a staff member. Miles told him he was a freelance working on a story for Neville Short in Features and asked if there had been an item recently about a skier disappearing in Switzerland. The man said that it didn't ring a bell but that he'd check. He came back shortly afterwards to say he hadn't had any luck and could he be given some more details. Miles told him it didn't matter and rang off.

He then rang Swiss Chalets and got another whiner. He told her he was trying to contact a friend and someone had said he was on a press trip to Eigerhubel and he was wondering when he might be getting back. The girl told him she'd put him through to the press office. Miles tried to stop her but she was too quick for him, so he replaced the receiver and went to look for a taxi.

9

London was at its January drabbest. All the bright colours – the blues, the greens, the reds – had been washed away by the rain and had run together to make sludgy greys and browns. It was like being in a John Piper exhibition.

'You look as if you could do with a holiday.'

Miles was in no mood for cabby's chit-chat. He'd hardly slept on the long night-crossing to Harwich and his head ached. 'I've just *had* a holiday,' he told him.

'Where d'you go? Wormwood Scrubs?'

'Why? Do I look the criminal type, then?'

'Hard to tell, these days,' said the cabby. 'Mind you, I've got a very suspicious mind. Always have had. My wife reckons if someone says Hallo to me, I think they're lying.'

Miles gave a non-committal grunt.

'You take that bloke up the wossname, safari park.'

'Lambourn?' Miles sat up.

'Nah. Up in East Anglia somewhere.'

'That's right. In Norfolk. West Keating Safari Park. The man who was killed was called Lambourn.'

'Norfolk, Suffolk, it's all the same to me. Flat and full of sugar beet.'

'What about him? Has something happened?'

'There's been the inquest, of course. But then you'd have missed that, being away on holiday.'

'What was the verdict?'

'Death by misadventure. As the Duke of Westminster said to the man who called him Mr Smith, If you believe that, you'll believe anything.'

'Wellington.'

'Do what?'

'It was the Duke of Wellington, not Westminster.'

'I'll take your word for it.'

'So are you saying that Lambourn wasn't killed by a tiger?'

'That's what we're *supposed* to think, right? Ask me, it was done so as to look like an accident. All very natural, if you know what I mean. All very *à la* David Attenborough.'

'So you suspect foul play?'

'Not 'alf,' said the cabby, carving up a woman in an Audi.

'Put it this way. According to the head keeper, the tigers in question had been fed the previous evening, so they were not what you might call ravenous. Why, then, did they attack and kill their owner? Answer, because they didn't. Someone else did and left them to take the rap. Now then, if you want my opinion ...'

Miles said, 'Actually, I've got a bit of a headache.'

'Now there's a funny thing,' said the cabby. 'I'm prone to the odd headache myself. I reckon my brain's too big for my head ...'

Fortunately the traffic was unusually light on the Embankment and he had barely warmed to the subject of brain tumours and how to diagnose them when they had arrived outside Miles's front door.

Prince of Wales Drive is bordered on one side by the Battersea Park and on the other by a sweep of stately mansion blocks whose grand entrances speak of a gracious world of large prosperous families, of chauffeurs and ladies' maids, of uniformed porters and caps tipped with deferential forefingers, of belief in the past and confidence in the future. These days the inhabitants do not quite match up to the buildings, but it's still one of the best free parking lots in London.

As Miles waited for his change, he noticed there was a man standing on the other side of the road, his back against the park railings. He was tall and thin with long dark hair and wore an old fawn mackintosh over ragged-ended jeans. He was studying a London street directory.

'You need a wossname?' said the cabby.

'Sorry?'

'Receipt?'

'Please.'

The cabby took a pad from behind his sun visor. He tore off a blank sheet and handed it through the window. 'Take care of that head of yours,' he said. 'You've only got one, remember.'

'I'll bear that in mind,' said Miles.

The flat was looking as bachelor-prim as ever. Miles wasn't quite as pleased to see it again as he had imagined. He brewed himself a mug of strong coffee, then he went into the bathroom and ran the bath.

He found a sachet of bath oil with the name of a large international hotel chain on it and poured the contents under the tap. He watched the foam rising seductively for a few moments, then he went into the sitting room and drank some of the coffee. The light on the answering machine was flashing. He ran the tape back and then pressed the Start button.

'Hi, Miles.' The voice whined with concern. 'It's Debbie here. Maddy Maguire's secretary. Maddy's terribly worried about you. We all are. We're wondering if you're all right. Maddy asked me to ring you and see if you were there. If you are and you get this message, could you ring me as soon as possible? Hope everything's okay. 'Bye.'

'Miles. It's Neville. Hope the skiing was good. And the other two s's. Give me a bell when you're back. See ya.'

'Mr Maltby? This is the South Side Dental Surgery. Concerning your appointment for 18 January. Perhaps you could telephone us in order to make another appointment at a more convenient date.'

'Miles, what the hell's going on? I've just had Swiss Chalets on the phone. I gather you just pissed off home without a word to anyone. As you can imagine, they're not best pleased, and neither am I. I hope you've got a bloody good explanation, otherwise you can forget writing any more travel pieces for this paper. Oh, sorry. It's Beth, if you hadn't guessed already.'

'Good evening, Mr Maltby. My name's Duncan Ashby. I'm calling on behalf of Alpine Double-Glazing. Our representative will be in your area in the next few days. If you are out when he calls, he will leave his card. Should you wish to call us with any queries regarding the installation of aluminium double-glazed windows, he will be only too happy to make an appointment at your convenience to discuss your double-glazing requirements.'

'Hallo, Miles. It's me. Mother. What on earth have you been doing

87

in *Switzerland* of all places? How you keep body and soul together at all footling around with those newspaper people I can't imagine. Henry's as appalled as I am. Unlike you, he at least makes a point of popping over every Saturday morning for a drink. I know what you're going to say. It's easy for him, with me just down the road in the Dower House, but he's a very busy man. I mean, he shoots four days a week, and he's got the whole estate to look after, but he still manages to find time for his family. You don't even bother to telephone. I think it's the end. And by the way, did you remember Charmian's birthday? I assumed you didn't so I sent a card from you anyway. Do brace up, Miles, for goodness' sake. And *do ring*. Goodbye.'

'Miles, it's Maddy here. We've tried everybody. The newspaper, the police, the airline people, the Swiss Tourist Office, everyone, but you seem to have vanished off the face of the earth. I hope you haven't lost your memory or anything. Anyway, we're all coming back first thing Saturday morning. I'll call you as soon as I can. I do hope everything's all right.'

Miles switched off the machine and dialled the Swiss Chalets' press office. An answering machine informed him that the office was closed, but, if he'd like to leave his name and telephone number, Maddy or Debbie would get back to him as soon as possible. He recorded a message that managed to be laconic, apologetic and reassuring, all at the same time.

He crossed to the window. The curtains were half drawn. The man was still there. But he wasn't looking at his A–Z any more. He was just standing there, with his hands in his pockets. There was nothing particularly odd about it. Men stand in London streets with their hands in their pockets every day of the week, but not very often in Prince of Wales Drive. They get into cars, they stroll in and out of the park through the different gates, they walk up and down, but they rarely just stand there, doing nothing.

Miles returned to the bathroom. The place was beginning to look like a steam room. He leaned on the washbasin and stared at himself in the mirror. There were black rings under his eyes and he seemed to have a used Brillo pad stuck to his jaw. His instinct was to shave it off, but then he thought again. It didn't look much now, but in another few days he might be very glad of it.

He undressed and threw his clothes into a pile in the passage. They stank of stale sweat mixed with Bernhard's pipe smoke. He turned on the cold tap and waited until the water reached a bearable temperature. He placed the coffee on the side of the bath where he could reach it without sitting up, climbed in and lowered himself gently and with much groaning into the foam. He drank several more mouthfuls of the coffee, then he lay back and closed his eyes ...

He had no idea how long he'd slept. The steam had cleared but the water was still warm. It was also bright pink.

Miles sat up. He ran his hands through the last remaining islands of foam. It was a pretty colour. Like pink champagne.

Except he wasn't feeling like Zsa Zsa Gabor.

It didn't take him long to discover where it was coming from. He put his hand up to the back of his head. It felt warm and sticky. A thin red rivulet ran down over one shoulder and dissolved into a pink stain over his heart.

* * *

'Who the hell was responsible for this?'

'What?'

'This travesty on the back of your head.'

Noel Parker was one of Miles's oldest friends. After five years in the Sudan and Ethiopia with the Save the Children Fund, fighting to keep pot-bellied skeletons alive and nearly dying in the process, he had returned to general practice in Wandsworth. Famous as much for his standard surgery wear of baggy trousers and Fair Isle sweaters as for his curly fair hair and melting baby-faced looks, he was the acknowledged expert South of the River in young women's eating disorders and associated psychological problems. Anxious middle-class parents in the Home Counties bought flats for their daughters in the area expressly in the hope that he might be able to squeeze them on to his books. His laid-back manner, his enthusiasm for homoeopathy, and his downright refusal on occasions to prescribe antibiotics and other standard drugs, were legendary, yet he had never lost sight of the good old-fashioned standards of General Practice that his father – a much-loved and much-missed Cumbrian GP – had dinned into him as a boy and during his years at medical school.

'Why? What's wrong with it? I assumed a stitch had slipped or something.'

'Slipped?' said Noel. 'Half of them are barely attached.'

His fingers probed the back of Miles's head. Miles could feel the indignation trembling along them and into his skull.

'Careful. You'll have the whole lot out in a minute.'

'I mean, look at this. And this.'

'How the hell can I look, you silly sod?'

Noel sat down at his desk. 'Sorry,' he said. 'It's not your fault, but I can't abide sloppy workmanship.'

Miles said, 'What's happened exactly? Am I coming apart at the seams? What? Give it to me straight, doc. I can take it.'

'If you want my honest opinion, I think you've been well and truly stitched up. Or rather, you haven't.'

'What *are* you talking about?'

'I suspect that whoever did this job had never put in a medical stitch in his life.'

'A doctor in a Swiss ski resort who doesn't know how to stitch? It's not possible.'

'He wasn't pissed, by any chance, was he?'

'For God's sake, Noel.'

'It's OK.' Noel put a hand on Miles's arm. 'You're not going to bleed to death or anything. Not in my surgery, anyway. I've just had a new carpet laid. Luckily for you, the wound's in a place where nobody can see it. You're going to have a horrible scar. I hope there isn't a history of baldness in your family?'

Miles wasn't really listening. He was too busy trying to recall the events of Sunday evening. 'He was in rather a hurry,' he said. 'But then I did arrive after surgery hours. His nurse left before he'd finished.'

'Left?'

'It was late and he let her off.'

'Bloody cheek ... Did you have medical insurance?'

'I did. I still do. It runs out at midday tomorrow. It is Friday today, isn't it?'

'So he must have written a letter or a report to support your claim?'

90

'He did write something out. I didn't take a lot of notice. I was feeling pretty wonky by then.'

'I'm not surprised. Well, where is it?'

'What?'

'The letter. The doctor's report.'

'I've no idea. At home somewhere, I imagine. Look, are you doing anything this evening? Could we meet for a drink perhaps? There's something I want to talk to you about.'

Noel pulled a face. 'It's not about sex, is it? I couldn't take another conversation about sex. I've had sex up to here.' He gestured at his throat.

'Lucky you,' said Miles. 'No, it's not about sex. It's about … Actually, I'm not sure what it's about. That's why I need to talk to you.'

'I bet it's about sex,' said Noel. 'It always is in the end. OK. Meet me here after surgery. About seven.'

* * *

He knew at once that there had been visitors in his flat. They'd made a neat job of it: no splintered woodwork, just a faint scratch on the brass plate of the Banham; a grubby mark on the door frame that hadn't been there when he'd gone out; a gut feeling that something wasn't quite right.

His first thought was that they must have been professionals, but he changed his mind when he got inside. The place looked like an explosion in an Oxfam warehouse. They'd been through everything: drawers, cupboards, shelves. Every imaginable nook and cranny had been explored, and some that no workaday burglar could ever have thought of. The undersides of drawers, the insides of radios and TV sets, pillows, mattresses: these were some of the more arcane hiding places where a pro who knew what he was after might look. But the ice box in the fridge? A jar of marmalade? The wooden heads of golf clubs? What could they possibly have thought he had that they wanted? Drugs? Jewellery? Microfilm? And who were they anyway?

Miles crossed to the window and peered out from behind the edge

91

of the curtain. There was no sign of the loiterer. He ran downstairs to No. 23 and rang the doorbell. Nothing. He rang again. There was the sound of shuffling footsteps and bronchial wheezing, followed by the rattling of the door chain and the key being turned in the lock. Finally the door opened.

'Hallo?'

Mr Reeves, the caretaker, reminded Miles of the Badger in *Wind in the Willows*. Whatever the time of day, he always looked as if he had been woken from a deep sleep. In the five years he had lived there, Miles had never seen him dressed in anything but a beige cardigan and check woollen bedroom slippers. Peering out irritably from bleary eyes above a soup-strainer moustache and trailing an odour of stale fried cooking, he dared anyone to ask him a favour.

'Sorry to bother you, Mr Reeves,' said Miles. 'Did anyone ask for the key to my flat while I was away?'

The caretaker glared at him. 'They said you'd got lost,' he said.

'A silly misunderstanding,' said Miles.

'They came looking for you here,' said Mr Reeves. 'There were two of them. They said they were Special Branch. They said they wanted to have a look round your flat. It sounded official and above board so I let them have the keys. They said they'd drop them back through the letterbox when they'd finished, but they never did.'

'Were they carrying any form of identification?'

'They showed me their warrant cards. That's what they said they were anyway. I didn't have my reading glasses with me at the time, but they looked to me to be in order. Very official, if you know what I mean. I did point out that by rights no visitors are permitted to enter the flats unaccompanied, but they said there was an exception in the case of the police, so I didn't like to argue. I hope I did the right thing. Everything is in order, I trust?'

'Everything's fine, Mr Reeves. Just checking. Sorry to bother you.'

Grumbling, the caretaker retreated into his malodorous set and closed the door.

Miles returned to the flat and began to pack an overnight bag. After a while he gave up trying to find the right garments: he just grabbed at anything that came to hand – shirts with frayed collars and cuffs he'd meant to throw out years ago, trousers that were a couple of inches too large round the waist, a sports jacket, assorted socks and underwear …

He threw in an old toothbrush and a spare razor, his diary and address book, chequebook, building society passbook, a couple of notebooks and a handful of pencils. He recorded a new message on the answer tape, giving Noel's telephone number as his point of contact. He looked quickly round at what had until recently been his home. Then he turned, walked out of the front door, locked it, and went downstairs. He let himself out through the back door. His elderly Golf was parked in one of the side-streets behind the flats. For once it started first time.

On the way to Noel's surgery, he called in at Vikram's Dry Cleaners to pick up the anorak he'd dropped off earlier. Vikram was the rudest Indian in south London but, when he promised to dry-clean a garment in an hour, even one badly stained with blood, you could be sure he'd be as good as his word. Vikram himself had been called away to an emergency Race Relations Subcommittee (Battersea and Clapham Area) meeting, and his daughter Sharmi had been left in charge of the shop.

'We have got all the stains out,' she told him, wobbling her head with pride.

'Thanks, Sharmi. Caught my hand carrying stuff to the dump.'

Sharmi grinned as she folded the anorak neatly. 'Oh, by the way,' she said, reaching down behind the counter, 'you left something in one of your pockets.' She held out a clenched fist. Miles frowned. 'You don't remember? What a fool I am. I could have kept it and you would never have known.' She opened her hand. Lying on her palm was the rose.

Miles took it from her. He laughed. 'I wondered where that had gone,' he said. 'I picked it up the other day in Portobello Road.'

'It is very beautiful.'

'Yes,' said Miles.

'What is it?'

'I don't know,' he said.

* * *

'Are you *quite* sure he was a doctor?' Noel asked.

The Nightingale wasn't too crowded at 7.15 and the beer was good. Miles sipped at his pint.

'It said so on the brass plate by the door,' he said. 'Dr med. Felix Grunner, plus all the trimmings. He certainly looked like a doctor. He behaved like a doctor. I had no reason to suppose he wasn't.'

'What does a doctor look like?' Noel asked. 'Do I look like a doctor?'

'There are always exceptions.'

'Do I behave like a doctor?' Noel pulled an elderly, concerned face and pretended to peer over the top of a pair of half-moon spectacles ' "Come in, Mr ... er ... What can I do for you? Oh dear, that's a nasty cough you've got ..." Is that your idea of a doctor?'

'He did have half-moon glasses,' Miles said.

'Oh well, that proves it. He must have been a doctor. He was wearing half-moon glasses. QED. Next!'

'The thing is, Noel ...'

'My builder could have made a better job with a staple gun.'

'Noel ...'

'Don't tell me. He put his hand under your balls and asked you to cough.'

'Noel ... There's something I haven't told you.'

'Go on, then,' said Noel. 'Amaze me.'

So Miles did. He talked for a long time. At last, he stopped and slumped back in his chair.

'You'll be needing a bed,' said Noel.

10

Miles stayed at Noel's for the whole of that weekend. Sarah and the children were away at her mother's in Dorset and, with Noel being on duty, he had the little terraced house near Wandsworth Common to himself.

There was a note on the kitchen table when he finally stumped downstairs shortly after eleven on Saturday morning. 'MAKE USE OF ANYTHING AND EVERYTHING. THAT INCLUDES THE TELEPHONE. N.'

Miles made a pot of coffee and a pile of toast. He ate the toast with butter and marmalade, swallowed two codeine, chased them down with three cups of black coffee and felt slightly better.

He went upstairs and had a very hot shower followed by a very cold one. He brushed his teeth, ran a comb cautiously through his hair, put on the least worn of his shirts and the larger of his two pairs of trousers and looked at himself in the mirror. The beard was coming on rather well. The grizzled look suited him. Silver hairs amongst the gold. He dug around in his hold-all and located his address book, a reporter's notebook and a couple of pencils, and went back down to the kitchen. He finished the coffee and perked another pot. Then he picked up the telephone and rang a Cirencester number.

'Lydia, it's Miles. How are you …? Good. How's Elizabeth …?'

In the early days, it had been a serious question to which he expected, and received, a serious answer. Assurances that 'She seems a little brighter today' and 'She went for a short walk in the garden this afternoon' and 'I think she's beginning to recognise us' meant something. They indicated slow but definite progress. Occasionally they heralded a slight deterioration, so that at least there was some purpose to the conversation. But, as it gradually became clear that being able to move and eat and sleep was about the extent of her recovery, the question had become little more than a polite ritual: an item of conversational chit-chat that required as much attention as an enquiry about the weather.

Lady Hollies's reply, though never less than charming, was now always the same. 'She's coming along very well.' To this Miles would reply, 'That is good news.' The formalities over, they would feel free to move on to more practical matters.

'I've just got back from a trip. I thought I'd come down. Is that all right?'

'You really don't need to ask,' said Lady Hollies. 'You know you're welcome at any time. When can we expect you?'

'I've got some research to do first. Tuesday or Wednesday probably. I'll ring nearer the time.'

'Elizabeth will be so pleased to see you.'

'I'm looking forward to seeing her, too.'

'I'll tell her you rang. She'll be thrilled.'

As usual, Miles felt his throat contract and his eyes went blurry. 'Please do.'

He replaced the receiver and sat for a long time staring out of the window at the little garden. It started to rain.

He cleared the table, put the dirty things in the dishwasher and went out and bought a copy of every national newspaper. There was a brief report in each of the broadsheets, except the *Independent*, to the effect that Michael Hugh Johnson, a 21-year-old assistant keeper, of Abingdon, was helping the police with their enquiries in connection with the death of Archie Lambourn, and the *Mail* had run a double-page feature about the 'Lambourn Legend', but there was not a whisper anywhere about the Eigerhubel mystery.

Miles tried Peter Franklin's number, but got a long and laboured message on an answering machine and rang off before the end. Then he went back to bed and slept until Noel came in at six.

* * *

'Well?' said Miles.

'It's unusually light on detail, but then you did say he was in a rush.'

96

The yellow medical report lay amidst the debris of dinner.

'How light? What would you have expected?'

Noel picked it up and stared at it. 'I see about a dozen of these every winter. Only if follow-up treatment is required. No two are the same. Some read like medical textbooks, others just give you the bare outlines of diagnosis and treatment. If you'd come to me as a patient waving this, I would have expected it to tell me a little more than it does. 'Multiple periosteal lacerations of scalp' ... 'ligation of bleeders of occipital branches' ... 'wound lavage with antibiotic solutions' ... something along those lines. 'Cuts on back of head, stitches applied' doesn't sound very professional. Perhaps his English wasn't up to it, although you'd think that in a ski resort which is so popular with the Brits ...'

'And yet you still reckon I'm imagining it all?'

Noel put down the sheet of paper. He picked up his glass and took a large mouthful of whisky. He sucked in his cheeks and swished it round while he considered Miles's question. Then he swallowed.

'Not all,' he said.

'What's that supposed to mean?'

'I *do* believe you were caught in an avalanche ...'

'That's decent of you.'

'And that you cut your head open, and that someone had a go at stitching you up. I also believe that you left Eigerhubel in the middle of the night, and for some reason decided to come home by the longest, slowest, most uncomfortable route possible.'

'But ...?'

'Forget the matter of the stitches for the moment. You say you walked into the doctor's surgery ...'

'Office.'

'Office, surgery, whichever, and there he was, sitting up in his chair, stone dead.'

'Correct.'

'How do you know?'

'How do I know what?'

'That he was dead. How could you tell? Did you check his pulse? Examine his pupils? Test for rigor mortis?'

'Well, no. Of course not. I'm a journalist, not a pathologist.

97

Anyway, I didn't have time to do anything. I told you. This mad woman attacked me.'

'That was before you realised he was dead. You had plenty of time afterwards.'

'You obviously weren't listening to a word I said. Afterwards I was leapt on by the Hound of the Baskervilles. At that stage, I was more concerned with my own life than the doctor's.'

Noel rinsed his mouth with another dose of whisky. 'OK, so let's assume for the moment that he was in fact a doctor and that the reason he made a pig's ear of the stitches was because he was so terrified of something that his hands were shaking like leaves. You think the reason he was killed was because of the badge, right?'

'If it really was an SS insignia. I'll check with the British Olympic Association on Monday, but I'm damned sure the doctor was covering up for something. If it was true that there was some connection between England and the SS, and if for some reason he was planning to blow the whistle on somebody – somebody who had once worn it (who might or might not be the same person who gave it to him) and who had since become very important and was prepared to kill rather than run the risk of exposure and ruin – then, yes, I think it could be a motive.'

'That's quite a lot of ifs,' said Noel.

'The doctor was dead, the nurse had seen me looking at the badge, she tried to kill me – presumably to keep me quiet – she nearly succeeded, I survived, the badge was missing.'

'Thin stuff,' said Noel. 'Pure speculation. Melodrama of the worst kind.'

'There's nothing speculative about it. These are facts.'

'I accept that certain events took place. I'm not so certain about your interpretation. Or your reaction.'

'Overreaction, you mean.'

'If you like, yes,' said Noel. 'You're convinced you're a wanted man, a man on the run, totally innocent yet sought by the police of half a dozen countries. Richard Hannay crossed with *The Fugitive*. Do you honestly think that if the Swiss police really believed you killed one of their citizens – a well-loved village doctor, to boot – they couldn't have picked you up whenever they felt like it?'

Miles said, 'If I'd taken an obvious route out, via one of the big airports ...'

'Basle is not exactly the back of Baluchistan. Rotterdam is not some obscure fishing village in the Outer Hebrides. You travel across half Europe pursued by the international forces of law and order, looking like a parody of an English gent in your big brown overcoat, and yet the immigration people at Harwich wave you through without a second glance. For God's sake, if they'd really wanted to nick you, they'd have known your identity, your mother's maiden name and your hat measurement before you'd even reached the railway station.'

'As a matter of fact, someone was watching the flat when I got back.'

'I hope that made you feel better.'

Miles was losing the argument and he knew it. 'Are you suggesting those two men in Eigerhubel weren't policemen?'

'I've no idea. Did they tell you they were?' said Noel. 'Did they flash their warrant cards? How do you know they were policemen? They could have been anyone. You assumed they were cops. Once you'd got that idea firmly established in your head, you assumed the identity of an internationally wanted criminal.'

'In other words, you think I'm imagining the whole thing.'

'I didn't say that, but I do think you've taken an awful lot for granted. A lively imagination is not always an advantage.'

'Do you think I imagined my flat had been burgled?'

'No.'

'Who do you think was responsible?'

'God knows. Could have been common-or-garden burglars.'

'Burglars don't present themselves at caretakers' front doors, announcing they're from Special Branch and asking if they can borrow the key.'

'It isn't Special Branch's job to go chasing after murder suspects. Anyway, the caretaker wasn't wearing his reading glasses. They could easily have been burglars. I can't think of an easier way of getting into someone's flat.'

'For God's sake, Noel. You haven't seen the mess they made of the place. They were looking for something specific all right.'

Noel said, 'Well, it could hardly have been the badge.'

'Why not?'

'Even *I* can think of better places to hide a badge than a jar of marmalade. Besides, you didn't take the badge.'

'Well, what else could they have been after?'

'Don't ask me. I'm only a doctor. The sort of person you ought to be asking those sort of questions is Robert.'

'Your brother Robert?'

'Why not? He knows about those kind of things.'

'I though he was a civil servant.'

'"Civil servant" is a term of convenience. Sometimes he tells people he's an academic. All I know is, he sits in an office in a large building near Lambeth Bridge and he's something to do with the Security Service, or whatever they call themselves nowadays.'

'You mean he's MI5?'

'Something like that. He doesn't talk about it much, and I don't ask.'

'I had no idea. What does he do exactly?'

'Haven't the foggiest. Goes to meetings, I suppose, writes reports, stares out of the window, drinks disgusting coffee from plastic cups … What else do people do in offices?'

'I wouldn't have thought the intelligence services had a lot of time for this sort of thing. A tame historian might be more useful.'

'Oh, I don't know. Now the War Crimes Bill is on the statute book, there must be a hell of a lot of people turning over stones to see what crawls out. Talk to him anyway. It can't do any harm. If he can't shed any light on the subject, he'll almost certainly know someone who can. After all, these people are far chattier than they used to be. They even publish informative booklets. How to be a spy in six easy lessons. I'll give him a ring for you. You never know.'

'That's the first helpful thing you've said all evening.'

'Wrong,' said Noel. 'The second. The first was when I asked you if you'd like a whisky.'

'If you'd like to be even more helpful …'

Miles pushed his glass towards the bottle. Noel obliged.

11

Miles spent the whole of Sunday in bed. His shoulder was still sore and his head ached like hell, but Noel had given him some painkillers, and the day passed in happy oblivion, interspersed with a series of nonsensical dreams.

He surfaced finally at seven. Noel was out on an emergency call, so he rang Peter Franklin.

'What the hell happened to you, old cock? And where are you now?'

'In London,' said Miles. 'More to the point, what happened after I left?'

'What do you mean?'

'I mean, *what happened after I left?*'

'Well, you didn't miss a lot, I'm bound to say. We found some good fresh powder snow, just round the corner from Schwarzegg. We went to a folklore evening and people dressed in funny clothes blew alpenhorns and threw flags in the air. We went to the Ski Club of Great Britain cocktail party and Damien from Romford behaved badly. The usual sort of things people do on press trips. What else can I tell you?'

Miles said, 'For a start, you could tell me what the police asked you. And what they said about me. And whether they've made any progress with their murder enquiries.'

'Murder? What murder?'

'What do you mean "What murder?" ! Why do you think I disappeared, for God's sake?'

'Haven't a clue. You told me you were going to bed. When you didn't turn up at breakfast the next morning everyone assumed you were feeling the worse for wear and we decided to let sleeping dogs

101

lie. We thought you'd probably catch us up sooner or later. It wasn't until we came in after skiing that we found out what had happened. Your note wasn't very informative, if I may say so. "Domestic crisis". It didn't give us a lot to go on.'

'What did you expect me to say? "The police are after me. They think I killed the doctor. Here's my address and phone number"?'

Peter said, 'Sorry, chum. Not with you. What police? What doctor? What are you talking about?'

'For God's sake, Peter. Who the hell do you think I'm talking about? Dr Crippen? Look, the fact is, I didn't go to bed after I left you in the bar that evening. I went back to the surgery. Partly because I wanted my wallet back, but mainly because I was intrigued by what you said about the badge, and I wanted to have another look at it. Unfortunately, someone had got there first. The doctor was dead. I think the nurse killed him. She certainly tried to kill me. There was a fight and I stuck a knife in her. Then I passed out. When I came round, she'd gone, and so had the badge. Somebody must have called the police. God knows who. The next thing I knew, they were at the door and I was standing there with blood all over me, and now there's a fat file on me in Berne.'

Peter said, 'I don't know what you're on, old cock, but I hope there's a cure for it.'

'I'm serious, Peter,' said Miles. 'I know what it's like to be a murder suspect in Switzerland and I had no intention of going through it again. Why else do you think I legged it? I knew the police would be round to interview you lot in no time and I didn't want to leave any clues or implicate you in any way. On the other hand, I didn't want you to worry about me.'

There was a pause. Then Franklin said, very slowly, 'I haven't the faintest idea what you're talking about. I never clapped eyes on a policeman the whole time I was there. Neither did anyone else, as far as I know. As for the doctor, he was certainly alive and well up to the time we left. I know that because that spotty Herbert from Romford had to go and see him. He pulled an earring on the dance floor or something. Dr Brunner, wasn't that his name?'

'Grunner. Are you sure it was him? It could have been a locum. They'd have had to find someone to replace him straight away.'

102

'I'm sure that was the name. In fact I was there when they rang up from Reception to make the appointment for him. And Maddy went with him. She'd have said something if anything had happened. Anyway, we'd have heard. News travels fast in villages.'

'But it's not possible,' said Miles. 'I was there. In his office. I saw him. He was as dead as mutton.'

Peter coughed. 'Are you sure you didn't dream all this? You'd had a hell of a bang on the head.' He coughed again. 'And a hell of a lot of whisky on top of that.'

'I realise I must have been pretty light-headed that evening, and the whisky probably lightened the load even further, but I know a dead body when I see one. And a Swiss policeman. Damn it, I saw the two of them out of my window in the hotel. They came in as I left. I can't believe they didn't want to ask you some questions.'

Peter said quietly, 'Look, Miles, I don't know what you saw or didn't see. Something, obviously. No one buggers off at nine o'clock at night in the middle of the mountains for no reason. Especially after the sort of day you'd had. All I can tell you is that the police never spoke to us, and when we left Eigerhubel Dr Grunner was still in business.'

'And his nurse?'

'I've no idea. Nor do I terribly care.'

'Well, I do. She tried to kill me. I have a vested interest. OK then, forget the nurse, forget the doctor, forget the police. What about me? Surely someone must have wondered where the hell I'd got to?'

'Not really,' said Franklin. 'Fee fussed around for a couple of days. She was worried you might have been suffering from amnesia. I think she had visions of you ending up as a tramp under the Pont Neuf. Needless to say Damien was delighted and chalked it up as a personal triumph. Maddy made a few phone calls and had a word with the local fuzz. But, as I said to someone, I can't remember who now, it wasn't the first time a journalist had buggered off in the middle of a press trip and it certainly won't be the last.'

* * *

No sooner had he put the phone down than Maddy Maguire rang. She'd called her office the moment she'd got through passport con-

103

trol. Miles couldn't imagine how relieved she had been to hear his voice. Thank God he was alive. She'd been so worried. They all had. How was he feeling? Was he all right? What had happened?

Miles slipped on the verbal sackcloth and ashes and muttered something vague about an unexpected family drama and circumstances beyond his control. He hadn't expected it would be sufficient to mollify her, and he was right.

'You might have rung,' she said sharply. 'We were worried.'

'I would have done if I could,' Miles told her. 'But I'm afraid it wasn't possible. I can't explain now, only apologise.'

'You're all right, that's the main thing.' Her tone was grudging. 'So you didn't speak to the police, then?'

'After a couple of days had gone by and we hadn't heard from you, I called round and told them what had happened, yes.'

'What did they say?'

'They took a few details. Said they'd make some enquiries and they'd be in touch if they heard anything.'

'Nothing else?'

'Such as?'

'They didn't want to interview you?'

'Interview me? Interview me about what?'

'Doesn't matter.'

'You said it, not me. Why should they want to interview me?'

'Honestly, Maddy. Forget it. I'm sorry I mentioned it. All I wanted to know was whether the only time you met them or spoke to them or had any dealings with the Swiss police was in relation to my disappearance. That's all.'

'Yes, why? Look, what's this obsession with the police? Have you been up to something you shouldn't have?'

Miles said, 'These police you met and spoke to: did any of them have a face that looked as if it had been hewn from the north face of the Schilt?'

'You make it sound like the New York Police Department,' said Maddy. 'The Eigerhubel police force consists of a white-haired man with a beard and a sombre youth with spots and glasses. Oh, and an elderly Alsatian called Rudi who has only been kept on because he's very good at sniffing out people in avalanches. Now, would you mind telling me what this is all about?'

'If only I knew,' said Miles. 'Just put it down to shock.'

* * *

On Monday morning, hung over and looking like the down-and-out from cardboard city of Fee's imagination, he made a series of telephone calls. The first was to La Réserve in Walton Street to ask them to deliver a case of claret to Dr Noel Parker. The second was to Pulbrook & Gould to place an order for a huge arrangement of flowers to be waiting for Mrs Sarah Parker's return from the country at 4.30. The third was to the British Olympic Association, who told him he was welcome to make use of their reference library at any time. And finally he rang the Eigerhubel Tourist Office. The voice that answered was deep and ponderous. It was also female. Miss Eigerhubel, 1956.

Miles assumed the voice of a middle-aged country vicar. 'I'm so sorry to bother you. I wonder if you could help me? My family and I came to Eigerhubel two years ago for a fortnight's skiing and in the course of our visit we made friends with the village doctor. Our neighbours are coming out for Easter and we wanted to write a letter of introduction to the doctor, but stupidly we have forgotten his name ...'

'You mean Dr Grunner?' Slow, ruminative, bovine.

'Of course.' The sound of Miles kicking himself could have been heard over the whole of the Bernese Oberland. 'Dr Grunner. How *could* we have forgotten? He is still there, I hope?'

'Yes. Of course.'

'Only somebody told us he hadn't been well. In fact, I think they said they thought he'd died.'

'Dr Grunner? Died? No. He is very young. Only thirty.'

'Perhaps it was his father.'

There was a silence at the other end of the line. Miles pulled a face like a small boy who has asked a favour and is in agony wondering which way the answer is going to go.

'Dr Grunner's father? He is in his shop, I think.'

'So he's not a doctor?'

105

'Mr Grunner? Mr Daniel Grunner? He has a gift shop. His son is the doctor. Dr Felix Grunner.'

'And he's well?'

'Yes. I have already said.'

'Is his nurse called Anna by any chance?'

'Her name is Lisl. But she has been ill. There was a temporary nurse for a short time. I do not know her name.'

'Tall, dark hair, pale face, doesn't smile much?'

'This is the Tourist Board,' said the woman. 'If you like I can give you the number of Dr Grunner's surgery.'

Miles wrote the number down, but he knew he wouldn't be calling it. Not now. Later, perhaps. There were some people he needed to speak to first.

* * *

It was the first time Miles had stepped out of doors since leaving his flat, and now, even in this anonymous crescent of late Victorian villas, with their neat hedges and smug brick façades and little gardens – or perhaps because of it – he felt suddenly vulnerable: as if there were people behind net curtains watching his every move and reporting back to someone ... As he walked towards the Golf, no one stepped out in front of him and flashed a warrant card. No arms seized him from behind and bundled him into a Jaguar with black windows. No men shouted at him to stay where he was or they'd shoot. Yet he could still feel the hairs bristling at the back of his neck. No amount of Noel's cheerful scepticism could defuse the sense of threat that had pursued him since leaving Switzerland.

Even sitting in the driver's seat, turning the key in the ignition and the radio frequency to Classic FM, he couldn't resist a quick glance into the back seat.

The traditional Monday-morning snarl-up at the roundabout by Wandsworth Bridge had cleared, but the traffic down East Hill was still moving desperately sluggishly, and drivers were looking nervously about as if at any moment expecting sniper-fire from the roof of the Alf Gover Cricket School.

Miles was faintly surprised that the British Olympic Association had not managed to find themselves an address that was more in keeping with the spirit of the event to which they were dedicated than the anonymous-looking building in a side-street off the one-way system where he finally tracked them down. The parking was a nightmare. Once he was through the front door, however, all doubts dissolved and the Olympian spirit asserted itself over the humdrum life of the world around it.

Miles sat in Reception, surrounded by Olympic trophies and medals and commemorative plaques going back to the dawn of the modern era. On one wall was a photograph of the British runner, torch in hand, poised to climb the steps and light the Olympic flame that would set in motion the 1948 Games at Wembley Stadium. Behind him, emblazoned on a large board, were the stirring words that embody the Olympic spirit: THE IMPORTANT THING IS NOT WINNING, BUT TAKING PART. THE ESSENTIAL THING IN LIFE IS NOT CONQUERING BUT FIGHTING WELL. Baron de Coubertin.

'How many times a day do I tell myself exactly the same thing?' Miles said to the girl from the press office.'

She said, 'Everyone thinks Coubertin made it up but he didn't. He pinched it from a sermon given by the Bishop of Pennsylvania based on the text "Many are called but few are chosen".'

'St Matthew,' said Miles.

'St Paul,' said the girl and blew her nose. 'Epistle to the Colossians. Anyway, the bishop said, "The honour is not only in winning but also in taking part." The Baron liked the sound of it and adapted it for the Games.'

Miles said, 'I've obviously come to the right place for accurate information.'

She said, 'You're writing an article about Olympic records, is that right?'

'Badges. Olympic badges.'

'Right. I think the best thing would be for me to take you to the library and let you browse at your leisure. You'll find that everything you need is there. Somewhere.'

Miles said, 'I really don't have any leisure. In fact I only have one question. I'm sure you'll know the answer without having to look it up.'

'Go ahead,' she said.

'What did the British Olympic team badge look like in 1948?'

She dabbed at a red patch just under her nose with a damp Kleenex. She thought for a moment. Then she said, 'I tell you what, why don't I take you through to the library? I'm sure you'll be able to find the answer in there somewhere.'

'At my leisure,' said Miles.

'I am trying to help,' she said.

'And don't think I don't appreciate it,' Miles told her.

There was nothing about badges in the organising committee's report on the 1948 games. He tried the British Olympic Association's official report. Again, nothing. He was on the point of giving up when he came across an advertisement for the Kangol Anglo-Basque Beret. 'Kangol is the official choice for all the British teams in the Olympic Games,' it proclaimed, and showed a pleasant-looking young woman wearing a faraway smile and one of the berets in question. On the front was a round badge comprising the five Olympic rings, the Union Jack and the year 1948 in arabic numerals.

'Is it possible that some team members wore different sorts of badges?' Miles asked the press girl.

She said, 'You could try talking to our assistant librarian, Sandy Duncan.'

'Assistant?'

'He was our *chef d'équipe* at the '52 Games,' she said sharply. 'And he was at Wembley in '48. He does know about these things. He's not in today, but I could ring him at home for you.'

The voice that came down the line was faint but full of vigour for a man of over eighty; and when Miles floated the notion of an Olympic badge with the word England on it, he went for the idea like a Scotch terrier on to a rat.

'Never!' he barked. 'England? We never represented England. We represented Great Britain! You must have seen something else.'

'I'm beginning to think I must,' said Miles.

* * *

When Miles gave Robert Parker's secretary his name, she said briskly, 'Oh yes. We were expecting you to call. One moment.'

Robert came on the line straight away. 'Weren't you in Londonderry?' he said.

'Briefly,' said Miles.

'I thought I knew the name.'

'Were you …?'

'I kept a watching brief for a while. I've moved on since.'

Miles said, 'Noel's obviously talked to you.'

'In broad terms.'

'He thinks I've imagined most of it. I'm beginning to think he may be right.'

'Oh?'

'I've just spoken to the tourist office out there. The doctor's fine. Never better. I've no idea who the man was I saw. Did Noel mention something about a badge?'

'Yes.' There was a long pause. Then Robert said, 'Look, this isn't really my area, but I know someone who might be interested. When can we meet?'

'As soon as you like, provided I'm not picked up by the police first.'

'I'll have a word with someone and see what I can find out on that score.'

'Otherwise,' said Miles, 'I'm at your disposal.'

'Let me see. It's Monday today. What about lunch on Wednesday?'

'Perfect. It'll give me some time to do a bit of sleuthing on my own.'

'One o'clock at the Rising Sun?'

'Is that code for something exciting and exotic?' Miles asked.

'No,' said Robert.

* * *

That afternoon, Miles took a taxi to the London Library.

He hung his scarf and overcoat on one of the hooks just inside the double swing doors. An elderly man was sitting hunched on the old leather bench in front of the big window reading a volume that looked almost as down-at-heel as he was. He wore a shapeless tweed jacket,

109

thick grey trousers and sandals with socks: a man in his natural habitat.

An air of hushed industry hung over the hall, punctuated by the occasional muttered exchange from the issue desk as a reader gave his or her name to the assistant behind the counter. At the far end of the room an elderly lady, grey-skirted, twin-setted and permed – an academic, perhaps, or a respected writer of obscure studies of forgotten nineteenth-century novelists, up from the country for a day's research – pulled ancient maroon leather-bound indexes on to a leather-covered shelf and turned the heavy pages with the care and respect of someone about to read the first lesson at Matins. In the middle of the hall, several more readers stood in front of the banks of little drawers that listed books published between 1951 and 1983, pulling them out, flicking through the cards, pushing them back, moving on to the next, totally absorbed in their tasks. They reminded Miles of gamblers working the fruit machines in Las Vegas.

Miles made for one of the computers that listed books published since 1984. He punched up INDEX KEY WORD and tapped in 'WAFFEN'. Only two titles came up: *Hitler's Samurai: The Waffen SS in Action* by Bruce Quarrie, 1984, and *The Waffen-SS Organization, Ideology and Function* by Bernd Wegner, 1990. Both were shelved in the History section under 'European War II'. He jotted down the details in his notebook and went across to the old catalogue cards.

Nothing was indexed under 'Waffen' or 'Nazis'. He tried 'Army, German, History of'. He noted down two possible titles: *The Order of the Death's-head: The Story of Hitler's SS* by Heinz Höhne, tr. 1969, and *The Waffen SS: Hitler's Elite Guard at War, 1939–44* by George H. Stein, 1966, and headed for the glass doors that led to the History section.

As a means of whiling away a cold, grey winter's afternoon, browsing amongst the shelves of the London Library is as pleasant as any. The gentle clank of the metal gratings, the low murmurings of library assistants in helpful conversation with timid readers, the rustle of turning pages … all combine to create a world that is warm and safe and far removed from the harsh realities of life a few yards away in St James's Square.

But today, Miles felt oddly uneasy as he padded his way towards

'European War II'. A sense of menace permeated the book stacks. Was it possible, he wondered, that they could be affected by the nature of certain subjects? Could the deeds described in some books be so appalling that the evil oozed out through the covers: like the stale smell of cooking that worked its way – through the party wall of the basement and the next-door restaurant – into 'Topography'?

He shrugged the idea off as being too fanciful and headed towards the 'STR–Z' shelves with renewed purpose. As he did so, he became aware that someone in 'Science and Miscellaneous' on the floor above was moving in the same direction. In itself there was nothing odd about this. London Library readers often seemed to be shadowing each other, sometimes three floors apart. On many occasions, while hunting for an obscure title in a totally deserted stack, he had found himself shoulder to shoulder with another reader who seemed to be working his way along exactly the same part of the same shelf. But on this occasion he had the disinct impression that whatever the man upstairs was interested in, it was not books.

Miles stopped and the footsteps overhead stopped. He took a couple of paces forward, and the feet above did the same. He glanced up, but there appeared to be no one there. He crossed between the shelves, looking quickly along each stack, trying to locate the sound, but the whole of the floor seemed to be deserted. He returned to the end stack and stood there for a while, scarcely breathing, straining to catch the faintest sound …

He walked very carefully through the open doorway into the rear store. Here the floor was made of thick, opaque green glass and the ceiling was painted iron. Miles's soles squeaked faintly on the smooth surface. There was no corresponding sound from upstairs. He must have been imagining it.

He found the Stein book almost at once. Appropriately enough, it had black end-boards. The introduction started promisingly.

'The real history of the SS begins on 16 January 1929 with Hitler's appointment of 28-year-old Heinrich Himmler as Reichsführer SS. [*That young?* thought Miles. *He always looked so middle-aged.*] At the time, the total strength of the SS was only 280 men. Hitler commissioned his "Ignatius

111

Loyola" (as he called Himmler) to "form of this organization an élite troop of the Party, a troop dependable in every circumstance". Under Himmler's direction the SS, according to its official history, became a formation "composed of the best physically, the most dependable, and the most faithful men in the Nazi movement". By the time Hitler became Chancellor in January 1933, the SS had some 52,000 members. The SA, of which the SS was still nominally a part, numbered in the neighbourhood of 300,000 men.'

Miles leaned against a shelf marked 'Napoleon 111–Zululand.'

'By the end of the year, the SA had grown into an unwieldy organisation of between two and three million members who, under the leadership of Ernst Röhm, were demanding a continuation of the revolution. Hitler, on the other hand, had already decided to stabilize his regime by coming to terms with the Army and the conservative elements in the nation. Tension increased until the summer of 1934, when Hitler was finally persuaded to purge the unruly SA; the SS provided the necessary gunmen and firing squads.'

How simple it sounded, how clean, how clinical. A purge. Like a glass of Alka-Seltzer after too much rich food and drink. Quick, effective, and really not too unpleasant ...

Miles began to skim the contents page. The Formative Years 1933–1939 ... From Verfügungstruppe to Waffen SS 1939–1940 ... Towards a Military Reputation: the Waffen SS in the Western Campaign, 1940 ... The Waffen SS in Russia ... The West European SS: Mobilisation of Foreign Nationals ... Ah, now then ... Myth of a European Army ... The West European SS in 1942 and Thereafter ... Miles's mouth had suddenly gone dry. There was a chair in the front store next to the interconnecting archway. He sat down and held his breath. 'Baltic Legions of the SS ... The Eastern Waffen SS ... Flights of Fancy: the British and Indian Legions ... *Indian*? His fingers scrabbled to page 189.

'In the spring of 1941 the leader of the militant liberation movement, Subhas Chandra Bose, arrived in Germany to

112

seek support for his cause. A short time later the German Army took steps to create an Indian Legion, which was intended to serve as the nucleus of an Indian "army of liberation". '

Did Gandhi know about this? Had he been a party to the visit? And then he came to it.

'Prompted by its success in recruiting former enemy soldiers from the POW camps, the Waffen SS in 1943 decided to establish a British Legion to take part in the European crusade against Bolshevism. A number of British turncoats were available. The most prominent of these ...'

It was so faint as to be almost imperceptible. Leather on metal; metal clicking against metal. The sound of secret footsteps. The same sound that had followed him earlier. The same shoes, moving about, just above him, as light as a ghost.

Miles peered upwards. But he still couldn't see anything. Just a dim, dusty light between dim, dusty books. But there was somebody up there – had been, anyway – following him, watching him, waiting. He was certain of it.

Who, though? Who would know where to locate him in this cobweb of shelves and staircases and passageways and iron grilles? Or know what he was looking for? Unless ... The computer screen ... He had remembered to clear it, hadn't he? ... If not ... There was a plan of the library up on the wall out there in the hall ... If someone had followed him in and been watching him – from behind the catalogue drawers perhaps ... It wouldn't have taken very long to find him ...

There was another faint metallic clank. And then Miles saw him, standing on the far side of the row of shelves about four feet away above his head. Just a pair of light-grey flannels and black shoes at first. But then the man moved slightly to his left. The light caught the black leather of his sleeve. His features were still in shadow. And then he looked down.

Underlit by the neon strip above Miles's head, and without the fur of the hat to soften them, the granite features looked even more

113

rough-hewn than Miles remembered them from their brief encounter in the doctor's house in Eigerhubel. The eyes regarded him unblinkingly and without expression.

There was an iron staircase just to Miles's right. It led down into an apparently deserted 'History Quarto'. Miles called out in a loud voice, 'Excuse me, I wonder if you could help me?' and walked quickly down the stairs. He headed towards the far wall and turned left. At the end, nearest the door, a young library assistant in jeans and open-necked shirt was rearranging books in the section marked 'Abyssinia–Dutch East Indies'.

Miles made straight towards him, paused long enough to murmur, 'There's a man upstairs, in "Science and Miscellaneous", stealing books,' and then turned left again and continued on down into 'Topography'. He could hear footsteps hurrying along the iron gratings three floors above.

There was a heavy green door at the bottom of the stairs. He pushed through and found himself in a narrow passage lined with shelves of old periodicals – *Illustrated London News* bound in dark blue and *The Lady* in brown. At the end of the passage he turned left, past the big grey rolling stacks and down a ramp and through two more doors. To his right was the room where the back numbers of *The Times* were kept – giant volumes, bound in maroon – and to the left, at the back of an open area, were a pair of dull gold-coloured lift doors. Miles ran across and pressed the button. An upward-pointing arrow lit up and ancient machinery ground reluctantly into arthritic action.

A door slammed somewhere behind him and he could hear footsteps coming along the passage. He punched the button furiously three or four times. The grinding noise continued but there was no way of telling if the lift was actually moving. A short flight of bare stone steps led up to a Fire Exit. Miles sprinted to the top but the door was locked. He ran back down again and across to the far side of the room where there was a deep alcove. He made it just as the second of the two doors opened. The footsteps paused uncertainly before moving off into the *Times* room. After a while they came out again, stopped and went back the way they'd come.

Moments later, the lift arrived with a loud creak and the doors wheezed opened. Miles stepped out of the alcove, ran across into the lift and thumbed the button for the ground floor above. Eventually the doors clunked together and the old, scratched, wooden box rumbled into action – though whether it was actually moving, and in what direction, it was impossible to tell, so slow was its progress. There was a jolt and the doors opened into the hall. Miles was about to step out when someone came running through the swing doors at the bottom of the stairs. He stepped back and stabbed hard at the button for the second floor. With agonising slowness, the doors closed again and he resumed the juddering journey upwards.

Again, the jolt and the grating of the doors, and Miles exited into 'Fiction'. He turned sharp left and through a swing door, then right into 'English Literature'. He crossed beside the rear window, went out through the double swing doors and started down the main staircase. He was on the half-landing, between the first and second floors, when he heard the sound of footsteps coming up the stairs. Down a short flight and immediately opposite was the door of the men's lavatory. An elderly reader was standing beside the washbasins, drying his hands on a roller towel as Miles burst in. Miles gave him what he hoped was an apologetic and reassuring smile, but elderly readers are unused to sudden noise and excessive physical activity, especially in the men's lavatory, and the man edged nervously towards the door.

Miles walked straight past him and out through the Fire Exit door that is always kept open except in the coldest weather. He took the iron escape steps two at a time, crossed the adjoining flat roof, then climbed over another short flight of steps across a low wall and out of sight of the Library windows.

There was another Fire Exit door in the wall opposite. It was dark inside. Miles located a light switch. He was in a bare concrete tunnel. He followed the stairs down. At the bottom was another door with a push bar. He slammed his hand against it and exited into Mason's Yard. The yard was empty as he walked quickly out into the roar and bustle and safety of Duke Street.

12

Miles had met several members of the security forces in his time, especially in Northern Ireland. They never advertised the fact, nor did anyone bring the subject up, but it was an accepted fact that in every HQ there were always one or two who were involved in undercover work of some sort. More often than not, they were in uniform. From time to time they would disappear, without warning and without explanation. One young captain he got to know quite well in Derry came back in a body bag, with a hole in the back of his head, in strict accordance with IRA execution rules. But most would return several days later, just as unexpectedly and without a word of explanation. He never thought anything of it. It was just part of the routine. But the people he'd met, whether they'd been in uniform or not, had all been soldiers. Career officers in the security services were a novel experience, and mildly disconcerting.

Quite what he had expected them to look like he couldn't have said, but certainly not like the pair who were occupying the table in the far corner when he walked into the Public Bar of the Rising Sun in Lyle Street, just off Vauxhall Bridge Road.

Robert Parker could have been a prosperous banker. He was short – five seven or eight – and grossly overweight. Small wonder. He waded into his steak-and-kidney pie and chips like a man attempting some sort of eating record. His beer went down his throat like a flash flood down a storm drain. His face – basically a chin with eyes – glowed red and purple. He had straight dark hair, cut short and brushed back over his scalp so flat it looked as if it had been painted on. He wore a navy-blue, double-breasted suit with a broad chalk stripe that fitted where it touched, which was pretty well everywhere. Not only did he not look as if he belonged to the

116

same family as Noel, he didn't appear to be of the same species.

His colleague was small, whey-faced, fair-haired and built like a Christmas-tree fairy. She was probably in her mid-thirties, but looked about twelve. She wore a modicum of make-up and had a habit of suddenly frowning for no particular reason. In conversation her eyes were fixed permanently on the other person's shirt collar. Whether this was some kind of psychological ploy or a relic of childhood shyness it was impossible to tell. Robert introduced her as Anne Crosthwaite. She was drinking mineral water and nibbling at a chicken sandwich. She didn't look the sort who would know much about escaping over roofs from men with faces like the north face of the Schilt.

Indeed, there was nothing in her appearance, or manner, or way of asking questions, or of responding to answers, that gave the slightest hint of her profession. Once or twice she interrupted Miles's long, fluent and detailed account of recent events to press him on particular details: the precise composition of the badge, the exact location of the doctor's death wound, the nature of the burglary in the flat, but otherwise she confined herself to the occasional non-committal nod.

When he had finished, Miles said, 'I get the feeling you don't think a lot of my story.'

She took a tiny sip of water. 'Really?' she said. 'What makes you say that?' Her voice matched her white-mouse-like appearance.

'You don't seem very interested,' said Miles.

'Let's just say I'm a natural sceptic,' said Anne. 'My job is to listen and absorb, not to make instant judgments.'

Miles said, 'I'm sorry I can't show you the badge. I only wish I had it. Someone obviously thinks I have.'

'If that really *is* what they're after.'

'What else?'

She shrugged.

Miles said, 'I realise I haven't got a scrap of evidence to back up my story. But I know what I've seen and I know what I've been told and I know what I've been through. There's got to be more to all of this than just a random sequence of accidents and coincidences.'

'It's possible,' Anne said. 'I doubt it, though. There rarely is. Except

117

to the sort of people who make it their business to read more into everything.'

'What do you mean? What sort of people?'

'Bored housewives. Gossip columnists. Journalists in general.'

Miles flushed. 'I admit the reason I got involved in all this was because I thought it might make a good story. There was no real need for me to go back to the surgery that evening. The wallet was only an excuse. I'm sure it would still have been there the next day. The fact is, I was intrigued by what Peter Franklin had said about the SS, and I couldn't resist having another look. Serves me right, you may say. If I hadn't stuck my nose in, I'd be sitting at home quietly recuperating and thanking God I was still alive. But, given that things turned out the way they did, you must admit that something very odd is going on. If you didn't think that, why did you agree to meet me in the first place?'

Anne said, 'A lot of people come to us with a lot of stories. We encourage it. It's all part of the new policy of desecretisation. There are box numbers people can write to if they hear or see something they think we ought to know about. We even send out little booklets explaining what we do. Sometimes we act on information received – if it involves terrorist activity, for example. Sometimes we pass it on to the appropriate desk officer and he or she will decide whether to do anything about it. More often than not, it gets filed away and that's the end of it. I'm sorry if I don't appear to be as excited by the story of your exploits as you are. But that doesn't mean to say I'm not interested to hear it.'

Miles felt sure that, if only he asked the right questions, he could force her into taking him seriously. To do that he would have to start speaking the right language, hinting at hidden expertise, bandying shop. The right trigger word needed to be released.

'According to a history of the Waffen SS that I read,' he said, 'there's no evidence to show that this British Legion was anything other than a propaganda device on the part of the SS. But supposing vital evidence had been suppressed that proved British troops re-cruited into the SS actually fought for the Germans. And that they were responsible for committing the sort of atrocities for which the SS were notorious – against the Russian partisans, for example. Worse still, supposing some of them were seconded to the death camps. It's unthinkable, I know. But for many people it's unthinkable that British soldiers were members of the SS at all. Yet it's true. What other unthinkable things might have taken place? Things that people who are still alive and perhaps in prominent positions in Britain would do anything to keep suppressed. What's the current state of play on the War Crimes Bill?'

Anne Crosthwaite narrowed her eyes. The movement was so slight as to be almost imperceptible, but Miles felt sure a button had been touched.

He went on. 'I mean, I know it got the Royal Assent – 1991, wasn't it? I also remember that it was pushed through in the face of a lot of serious opposition. Heath was against it. Hailsham thought it was uncivilised. But it got through. So presumably somebody must be doing something about it. But what? Can we expect some prosecutions soon?'

'It's purely a police matter,' she said. 'A War Crimes Unit was set up and is currently investigating several hundred men and women suspected of operations involving the killing of innocent citizens. That and other things.'

'Such as?'

'It's no secret that there are thought to be men living in this country who ordered and carried out the slaughter of Jews in the extermination camps.'

'Have any names been named?'

'One or two. I doubt they'd mean much to the man in the street.'

'The death camps were made up of men in the street. Some of them survived.'

'I'm afraid you're wasting your time,' she said and squeezed the last few dribbles of mineral water into her glass. 'I've told you already, the arrest and prosecution of alleged war criminals under the War Crimes Bill is the responsibility of the Metropolitan Police and the Crown Prosecution Service. If you want further details or feel you have information which might help them in their enquiries, you should get in touch with Scotland Yard. But I'm afraid I can't help you any further. I'm sorry.'

'Is that it then?'

'What do you mean?'

'Shouldn't you say something like "We'll be in touch"?'

'No.'

'But you'll let me know if you find out anything?'

'I very much doubt it,' she said. 'Obviously we're grateful to you for giving up your valuable time, but it's not as if you'd uncovered some plot to blow up the Houses of Parliament, is it?'

Miles flushed angrily. 'I don't know what I've uncovered,' he snapped. 'But I'd have thought the least you could do is to keep me posted.'

'I'll do what I can,' she said, 'but I can't promise anything.'

'Look,' said Miles, 'I may be just another hack to you, but I'm not a child, and at the risk of sounding pompous I think I deserve more than a pint of beer and a pat on the head. After all, it wasn't my idea to get in touch with you people; it was Noel's. He's not sold on the story either, as it happens, but he's a good doctor and he's seen the mess someone's made of the back of my head and, like me, he wonders what I've got caught up in. He thought you might be able to suggest someone I could speak to who might have some ideas and might – though if everybody I contact turns out to be like you, I doubt it – they might *just* be able to give me some clue as to what the hell's going on. If you don't want to help me, say so, but please don't patronise me. I'm not in the mood for it. My head hurts and I'm tired and I'm going home. You know my number. I'll be there later if you think of anything. Thanks for the beer.'

'Thank you for coming,' said Parker. Anne Crosthwaite said nothing.

Miles pushed his chair back and stood up. 'By the way,' he said to her, 'have you got a contact name you can give me at Scotland Yard?'

'The Press Office,' she said.

'Nothing like having an inside track,' said Miles.

* * *

Miles took a cab to a large, shiny white building two miles further down the river. At Reception he told a girl in a white shirt and black skirt that he had an appointment with Neville Short. She dialled a number and was told to send him up. She handed him a badge with 'Visitor' printed on it. 'Fifth floor,' she said, and returned to weightier matters.

Another girl with a very short skirt and very long legs greeted him at the lift door and made polite conversation about the weather as she led him into an open-plan office slightly smaller than Earls Court. It was only three o'clock but the brilliant overhead lighting made it look dark outside. The girl led him towards a corner room. Neville was on the telephone but beckoned him in. Miles smiled at the girl, but his heart wasn't in it. It never was when he was going to see Elizabeth.

Neville was a big cheerful man whose hair should have turned much greyer and who should have clawed his way up the journalistic ladder to a position considerably more elevated than features editor. On the other hand, many of his contemporaries who had were now out on the street in their mid-forties, touting for any freelance work they could get and wondering what went wrong. What went wrong was that, while they were busy enjoying their heydays, newspapers were changing. A different breed of proprietor was taking over. Men in suits with calculators in their briefcases and their heads full of numbers were sitting in chairs once occupied by men with heads full of dreams and hearts full of ideals. Rationalisation was in the air and blood was on the floor, and all too often it flowed from Neville's contemporaries and ex-colleagues. But Neville was a survivor. He had long ago sacrificed his ambitions on the altar behind which he'd kept his head well out of sight. Roughly once every three or four years he'd move on, always being paid that little bit more and being required to do that little bit less.

'Christ, you look like someone who's just stepped out of an air crash,' he said. 'What happened?'

'It's a long story.'

'Don't.' Neville's voice oozed world-weariness.

'It's a good story, mind.'

'Go on, then. Thrill me.'

'Later.'

'Why later?'

'Because I think I've stumbled on to something really big. A real scandal. But I'm not ready to tell you yet. I need more time.'

121

Neville snorted. 'A scandal in a ski resort?'

'That's only the half of it.'

'I can't wait.' His tone was ironic but Miles could see that he was intrigued.

'You'll have to,' said Miles.

'So you're not on for a piece at the moment, then?'

'Depends what it is.'

'I'm still looking for someone to write a thoughtful, colourful, well-researched feature on the life and times of Archie Lambourn.'

'Not still?'

'There've been some developments while you were away.'

'I gather someone's been arrested.'

'One of the young keepers. They had him in for questioning last week. It didn't come to anything. They let him go the next day.'

'Does that mean foul play is suspected?'

'If you went to Norfolk, you'd find out, wouldn't you?'

Miles pulled a face. He wanted to do the piece. He needed to be out of London for a few days. And he needed the money. 'When do you want it? The thing is ...'

'Yesterday suit you?'

'I'll ring you, OK? Only there's something I've got to do first.'

'By stumps this evening, if you wouldn't mind.'

'Stumps it is,' said Miles.

* * *

There was a note lying on the kitchen table when he got back to Noel's. It was from Sarah to say that Robert had called and could Miles ring him back as soon as he came in. She had taken the children to a swimming lesson in Tooting and would be back around seven, and hoped he'd help himself to anything he fancied. Miles took her at her word and helped himself to the telephone.

'Parker.'

'Robert, it's Miles.'

'I thought you weren't feeling well,' he said.

'I decided to take a positive view,' said Miles. 'How about you?'

'Don't mind Anne,' said Parker. 'She's a nice girl at heart. But she

122

had to know how serious you were. It's not quite her field exactly, but she's had a fair amount to do with this Falklands investigation. British troops knocking off Argie prisoners and so on. She's also pretty much *au courant* with the work of the War Crimes Unit. She's taken on board everything you told her and she'll pass it on to the appropriate desk. If you don't hear from her again, please don't take it personally. We rarely deal on a one-to-one basis in our business.'

'God forbid I should ever take anything personally,' said Miles.

'Two other things,' said Parker briskly. 'Good news. Whoever those two were who chased you through Eigerhubel, they definitely weren't policemen. I've had a word with a chum of mine at the Home Office and there's nothing against your name in the Scotland Yard computer you need worry about. Someone reported you missing on the 17th, but that's since been okayed.'

'I'm relieved to hear it.'

'Now then, there is one other thing. Make of it what you will. Obviously anything I tell you is very much off the record, but I hope that, as an old friend of Noel's, I can trust your discretion.'

'Of course,' said Miles, wondering what on earth was coming next.

'What do you know about the Diabolo?' Robert asked him. 'Did you glean anything while you were in Eigerhubel?'

'Only that it was founded in the Twenties by a bunch of English Hoorays and that most people would need to raise a mortgage to pay the membership fee.'

'Nothing about the early days?'

'Only that the club was responsible for establishing the race.'

'Does the name Blackett mean anything to you?'

'Amazons for Ever.'

'What?'

'Nancy and Peggy. The Amazons in the Arthur Ransome books. Their surname was Blackett.'

'Could never get on with Ransome myself. All those boring children in shorts. No, I'm talking about Arthur Blackett. Brigadier Arthur Blackett, late of the Hampshire Yeomanry. Military Cross. Lost an arm at the 2nd Battle of Mons, but skied for Great Britain just after the First War. A gallant officer and gentleman. He was one of the founding members of the Diabolo Club in 1924.'

123

'I knew they were mostly ex-army.'

Parker said, 'He was also one of the first presidents of the British Fascists.'

'A pal of Mosley's, then?'

'Not in those days. In the early Twenties Mosley was very much in the political mainstream. A committed Labour Party man, like Strachey and Lansbury and Morrison. It was years before he became disillusioned and the Blackshirts appeared on the scene.'

Miles said, 'I didn't realise there were fascists in Britain before Mosley.'

'As early as 1923. A hatchet-faced spinster by the name of Rotha Lintern-Orman – an ambulance driver in Serbia during the war and a field-marshal's granddaughter to boot – was weeding her kitchen garden in Somerset when she suddenly decided that the socialists and communists were getting too big for their boots and it was up to her to put a stop to them. So she put an ad in a paper called *The Patriot* calling for recruits for British Fascists to combat the Red Revolution. The Labour Party got in in January 1924 and by the summer there were 100,000 of the buggers: landed gentry, minor industrialists, retired army officers, Anglican clergy, you name it. Rotha soon dropped out of sight and that was when this Blackett fellow took over. You probably won't find his name in any of the books. He was only in charge for a short time. Bigger men came along, but he played his part.'

'You're not suggesting that he was the one who gave the doctor the badge?'

'Good God, no. He died years ago. Before the war. But it seems the club still has a reputation for being slightly to the right of Genghis Khan. But what the badge has to do with anything I've still no idea.'

'Well, thank you for the history lesson,' said Miles. 'It's hardly Official Secrets Act material, but then I didn't imagine it would be.'

'I'm sorry I can't be more specific,' said Parker evenly. 'I'll keep on beavering and let you know if I come up with anything.'

Miles was suddenly irritated. 'I can't believe that a man posing as the village doctor in a well-known Swiss ski resort can be murdered and no one knows anything about it.'

124

Parker said, 'Oh, thanks for reminding me. *Re* people being killed: that chap in Norfolk was a member of the Diabolo.'

'What chap?'

'Ran a safari park somewhere up there. Got eaten by a lion. Same thing happened to the Rector of Stiffkey, you know. Must be an occupational hazard in East Anglia.'

* * *

'Neville?'

'Speaking.'

'Have you drawn stumps yet?'

'Not quite. The light meters are out, though.'

'You haven't farmed this Lambourn story out to anyone yet, I hope?'

'No.'

'Good,' said Miles.

13

'Sorry to be a wet blanket.'

The voice was as deep and rich as melted chocolate. A brisk military undertone lent bite to the delivery and gave notice that the owner did not pronounce upon any subject unless he knew what he was talking about. It was, in short, the voice of a man who has spent a lifetime giving orders and making decisions at a high level.

Like many successful soldiers – Alexander, Horrocks, Montgomery – General Hollies was a physically small man. No more than five six, five seven, in his stockinged feet, his narrow shoulders and narrow frame had the effect of making his already unusually large head look even larger. However, his tailor, who had serviced his sartorial needs for over forty years, had done him as proud as ever. His medium-brown herringbone three-piece was a masterpiece of English cutting, and his plain brown shoes shone like conkers.

Miles turned the chunky tumbler in his fingers. It was plain with a thick base and the side was engraved with a regimental badge. He swallowed the last of the pale whisky. 'I can't pretend I'm not disappointed,' he said.

'Have another drink,' suggested the general.

He didn't bother to wait for a reply. He pulled himself up from the deep chintz of the armchair and took Miles's glass. He walked across to the sofa table and picked up one of the square decanters.

'Look, Miles,' he said, pouring him a generous measure, 'don't misunderstand me. I'm not suggesting that this sort of thing is general knowledge. I don't doubt that, if you went out into the street and buttonholed ten people and told them that British soldiers had served in the SS during the war, nine of them would be as astonished as you are. But frankly, for anyone who knows anything about what really

126

went on in the last war, stories like this are pretty old hat. I speak with some degree of knowledge. Soda?'

'Please.'

The general handed the drink to Miles and threw a couple of oak logs on to the fire. The black labrador on the hearthrug lifted his head, realised that this sudden movement did not herald a walk, and returned to his slumber with a contented groan.

Miles said, 'According to the account I read, it was the son of one of Churchill's ministers, John Amery, who went round the camps doing the recruiting.'

'And was hanged for it afterwards. Bloody good job, too.'

'He didn't appear to do a very good job.'

'The reports were exaggerated at first. The Germans claimed three hundred recruits at one time. But a lot of those were ordered to go along with it by their own officers simply in order to find out what was going on and report back. The Germans invited whoever was interested to spend a couple of weeks in Berlin, in what they called a holiday camp. A lot of them fell for it. Can't altogether blame them, I suppose. Actually it was nothing more than a fairly intensive indoctrination and assessment centre. In the end only about sixty became full members and wore SS uniforms.'

'There was somebody called Brigadier General Parrington.'

'Ah yes. Poor old Parrington. Sad figure. The Germans picked him up in Greece in 1941 and found he was a big fan of Hitler's. They tried to sign him up as the CO of the British Free Corps, as it was known.'

Miles said, 'You seem to know a lot about it.'

'There isn't a lot to know really. I was in Germany at the end of the war, chasing Nazi war criminals, and one of my jobs was to try and round up these turncoat buggers and get them sent back to England for courts martial. It was a hell of a job. They were all over the place. Russia, France, Italy. They picked up Amery in Milan. He had his girlfriend with him. Pretty girl. The whole thing was really rather pathetic. The Germans obviously had visions of an army of erstwhile Mosleyites marching out to the Eastern Front as if it were Cable Street all over again and kicking merry hell out of the Russians. Most of the ones who actually joined up did so only because it meant living in comparatively hygienic conditions and eating some decent

grub for a change. A sorry episode all round, and one best forgotten.'
General Hollies was in one of his expansive moods: relaxed, easy-going, amused.

Miles said, 'So you don't think any of them ever actually fought on the German side?'

'No.' The general let the vowel out in a long, low breath.

'But they did wear SS uniforms?'

'Waffen SS, yes.'

'What difference does that make?'

'The Waffen SS were soldiers, of a sort.'

'Can you remember anything about their uniforms? The sort of insignia they wore, badges and so on?'

'As far as I can remember they had three leopards embroidered on one of their collar patches. There was a Union Jack somewhere. On the sleeve, I think.'

'A Union Jack?'

'Yes. In the shape of a shield, as far as I remember.'

'Anything else? Any words? "England", perhaps?'

'I don't think so.'

'Are you sure?'

'Quite sure. Why?'

'The badge I saw had a square Union Jack and the word "England" underneath it.'

'If anything, they'd have had a separate flash with "*Freikorps*" on it, or possibly "*Britische Freikorps*". But not "England". Doesn't ring a bell with me at all. I think what you saw must have been something quite different. A sports team, just as the doctor said.'

'There couldn't have been another outfit, I suppose? Something you didn't know about?'

'Such as?' A suspicious note had crept into Hollies' voice.

'I don't know,' said Miles. 'I was just wondering ... You said they didn't do any actual fighting, and yet some of them were picked up in Stettin. Perhaps some of them did see action. On the Eastern Front maybe. Or even in the camps ...'

'I think that's most unlikely,' the general snapped. 'There is no evidence that any British soldier was involved in that kind of thing. The fact of the matter is that there were certain British soldiers who joined the SS. It's all very well documented. The whole thing was investigated at the time. The guilty were dealt with accordingly and that's all there is to it. Over and forgotten. If I were you, I'd do the same and find a real story, instead of picking away at old sores.'

'Was Amery the only one to be executed?'

'And Joyce, of course.'

'I meant members of the British Free Corps.'

'No,' said the general. 'No one else.' The voice was calm enough but there was a tell-tale movement at the side of his face as he clenched and unclenched his jaw.

'What happened to the rest, then?'

He shrugged. 'They served various terms of imprisonment,' he said.

'So some of them could still be around?'

'I really wouldn't know.' The general was clearly bored with the whole subject. 'It was all a very long time ago. Now come along, let's go and have some lunch. We mustn't keep the ladies waiting.'

The two men strolled down the picture-lined passage towards the dining room. The general pointed at Miles's chin.

'Not sure I approve of the beaver,' he said, with a wry grin.

Miles smiled shyly. 'I'm not a hundred per cent sold on it myself. It seems to amuse Elizabeth.'

'I'm glad something does.'

When they reached the dining-room door, Miles turned. 'By the way, sir, there was something else I meant to ask you. Does the name Lambourn mean anything to you?'

'Lambourn ... Lambourn ...' The general flicked through his mental card index. 'Well, there's a village in Berkshire, where a lot of racehorse trainers have their stables ...'

'Archie Lambourn. He ran a safari park in Norfolk. Got killed by one of his own tigers. You may have read about it.'

'It rings a bell. Ne'er-do-well, wasn't he?'

'Once upon a time,' said Miles. 'Do you remember when I was telling you about Eigerhubel the other day I mentioned the Diabolo Club?'

'Vaguely,' said the general.

'It was a member of the Diabolo who gave the doctor the badge.'

'Really?'

'I gather the club used to be a right old hotbed of Nazi sympathisers. Possibly still is.'

'I wouldn't know about that,' the general said.

'By coincidence, Lambourn was a member of the club.'

'Well, well.'

'Even more coincidentally, I'm off to Norfolk to write a piece about him for one of the Sundays.'

'Good for you,' said the general. 'When are you going?'

'Tomorrow.'

'Good show,' he said.

After lunch, Miles took Elizabeth for a short walk round the garden. He took her gently by the arm and pointed things out as they went: the branches of the trees in the Near Wood looking like twisted skeletons against the pink sky; the mist rising over the fields; the rooks gathering to roost. There was a faint smile on her face, but she gave no indication that she understood what he was saying, or even that he was there at all. Miles pushed his free hand deep into his pocket and felt something hard and smooth and oddly shaped. For a moment he was puzzled, then he realised what it was. He took it out and held it up against the fading light. The fly, imprisoned in the honey-coloured rose, suddenly took on a very special meaning. He thought of giving it to Elizabeth, trapped inside her own strange prison, but then he changed his mind and put it back in his pocket.

* * *

Miles returned to London that afternoon. He drove straight to Noel's. There was a note from Sarah on the kitchen table to say that she had taken the children to a party and would be back around six. Miles packed his overnight bag and drove to Prince of Wales Drive. He let himself in by the side-entrance. It didn't look as if there were any new marks on the door. He went in but didn't turn any lights on.

He went straight to the window, cursing as he stumbled over assorted items and wishing he'd made some attempt to tidy up before leaving. He pulled the curtain open a few inches and peered out into Prince of Wales Drive. The rush-hour traffic hummed up and down in a non-stop procession of headlights. A few pedestrians were plodding their weary way homeward on both pavements. Everyone and everything was on the move.

Miles decided that, if his uninvited visitors hadn't come back for a second bite by now, they wouldn't be coming at all. He switched on the only table lamp that hadn't had its bulb broken, sat down on the leather sofa and contemplated the shambles that had once been his home. He understood now why people who had been burgled said they didn't want anything to do with the place again.

He was in two minds about going to Norfolk. The money was good and, if he made a half-decent fist of the story, there could be more work where that came from. On the other hand, it was the sort of piece that could turn out to be extremely time-consuming, and, despite all the rushing around, he felt he had only scratched the surface of the SS story. If that was what it was. Indeed, if there was a story at all. He was beginning to wonder.

Perhaps General Hollies had a point. Was there anything to be gained by opening the musty cupboard of the Third Reich and rattling yet more skeletons? Hadn't enough historians of horror been there already and removed every last splinter of bone and fibre of evidence? And anyway what gave him the right to go rooting around in the nastier recesses of history? He had no personal axes to grind. No family scores to settle. It wasn't even as if his father had been killed in the war. His interest was gratuitous and self-serving, his purpose pecuniary and the premise of his investigation shaky, to say the least. The general had been quite specific about the British Free Corps insignia: a Union Jack in the form of a shield. No mention of the word 'England'. He'd been quite certain about it.

On the other hand, he, Miles, had been nearly strangled to death, he'd been pursued across half Europe, he'd had his flat wrecked and he'd been chased round the London Library. If that didn't give him the right to find out why and who was responsible, what did? The Lambourn–Diabolo connection might turn out to be a complete red herring, but if he didn't try and find out he'd never know.

He pushed himself up off the bed and rang West Keating Park. A woman anwered and made an appointment for him to come to the house at three o'clock the following afternoon.

Afer that he rang the Press Office at Scotland Yard. A woman's voice informed him that the War Crimes Unit, headed by Detective Chief Superintendent Bathgate, was currently investigating some three hundred men and women resident in this country who were suspected of war crimes.

Miles enquired if arrests were imminent. She replied that, although progress was being made, no arrests were anticipated in the near future, but that in the event of a major development a press release would be circulated in the usual way.

He asked her if there was any chance he might be able to have a word with Detective Chief Superintendent Bathgate, since he had some relevant information concerning the investigation. She replied that Mr Bathgate was out of the country and it was not known when he would return, but if he'd like to leave his name and telephone number she would make sure his secretary got the message. Miles said he'd leave it and rang off.

Then he rang Neville again.

'Haven't you gone yet?'

'Tomorrow. Meanwhile I have a favour to ask.'

'If it's to do with money, the answer is No.'

'Do you have Paul Weekley's phone number?'

'Weekley?'

'I need to speak to him before I go to Norfolk. I thought if I could mention your name …'

'Whatever do you want to speak to Paul for? He only ever writes about old spies these days.'

'It is important.'

'You know he doesn't work for us any more? He's been freelance for years.'

'Neville, I haven't got a lot of time. If you don't want to give me the number, I can always get it from someone else.'

'Oh all right. Hang on a moment.'

It was a Kensington number. A girl answered and offered to give him a message. Miles said he'd prefer to speak to him in person and mentioned Neville's name. It worked.

Miles didn't tell him everything, but what he told him was enough. An hour later, he was sitting, drinking whisky, with Weekley in the cluttered sitting room of his fourth-floor mansion flat in Earls Court.

132

Paul Weekley was a New Zealander who had made his name as one of the early Insight team on the *Sunday Times* before moving to the big white building in Battersea as chief feature writer. A bestseller on the great spymasters, followed soon afterwards by an authoritative biography of Guy Burgess, made him enough to give up regular employment, since when he had assumed Chapman Pincher's mantle as the doyen of all things to do with espionage and the SIS. Though, by his own admission, he was no expert in the complex and politically sensitive world of Nazi war crimes, his parish was as broad as anyone's.

He was a squat, toadlike figure, with a pasty complexion and flimsy, flyaway hair in need of a good conditioner. But his eyes sparkled behind his large spectacles, he wore a permanently genial expression, and his capacity for Scotch was as boundless as his appetite for a good story. And Miles was a very good storyteller indeed.

Though Weekley was at the receiving end of a constant supply of stories and had no need to poach those of others less established than himself, Miles had played his cards close to his chest on the telephone. But now, encouraged by the man's boyish enthusiasm and relaxed by whisky, his inhibitions quickly melted away. If he was to gain Weekley's trust, he told himself, he was going to have to give him the whole story.

It took some time, but Weekley listened in silence, interrupting only twice: once for a more detailed description of the man with the broken wrist, and again to refill Miles's glass. His first words were as encouraging as a bowl of cold porridge.

'There's nothing new about the British Free Corps,' he said. 'It's very well documented in all the standard textbooks on the SS. I doubt you'll find anyone who thinks it was anything other than a desperate attempt by the Nazis, at a point in the war when things were going badly, to stage a mini propaganda coup. If any serving British troops fought under the SS banner, it was for a pint in the local *bierkeller*. To try and suggest anything else would in my opinion be a waste of time. As to whether any of them carried out guard duties in the extermination camps, again I think you'd be hard put to make a case. If eleven Scotland Yard detectives working full time for two years can't amass enough evidence to arrest one suspect out of three hundred, I don't rate your chances very highly.'

133

'There must be a fair number of faces in the frame by now.'

Weekley shook his head. 'Nothing like as many as you might suppose,' he said. 'There's a man called Marinka. Jan Marinka. Former Lithuanian platoon commander. Lives in Aberdeen. A couple of years ago a newspaper accused him of war crimes. He brought a libel action against them and lost. The judge said he was satisfied Marinka had participated in many operations involving the killing of innocent citizens and had committed war crimes against old men, women and children. The police have been investigating him for years, but nothing's ever come of it. Doubt if it ever will now.'

'Why not?'

'Apparently the police were relying on evidence from former members of Marinka's platoon who are now living in Britain, but the Crown Prosecution Service wouldn't promise them immunity from possible war-crime charges arising from their evidence.'

'Anyone else?'

'There's a man who's supposed to have been responsible for the deaths of dozens of people near Minsk. He was also named by a newspaper. It even managed to produce its own witnesses. But the police haven't even got round to interviewing him yet.'

'And no sign of any arrests?''

'My view, for what it's worth, is that it's unlikely the cases currently under investigation will come to court.'

'Oh?'

'For a police investigation to be launched and then sanctioned by the Crown Prosecution Service, the people who authorise it have to reckon there's a good chance of a successful outcome. In the case of the three hundred or so referred to Scotland Yard for investigation, about a quarter have died already. Nearly all of the ones who are still alive are over seventy. Given that enough evidence was gathered to make a decent case, it would take several more years to get them to court, by which time there could be only a handful left. And frankly the chances of anyone getting a fair trial in this country after fifty years are pretty slim.'

'So what you're saying is ...'

'What I'm giving you,' Weekley interrupted firmly but not impolitely, 'is my personal point of view, based on a limited amount of inside information and a good deal of guesswork. I may be wrong. We may be about to enter a whole new era of men in glass booths. But the vast majority of these sorts of cases depend on evidence of identification, and, knowing from my own experience how fallible people's memories can be after ten years, let alone fifty, I honestly don't think it's on the cards. Remember, the case against Demjanjuk was quashed on appeal because there was, and I quote, "substantial doubt" about correct identification.'

'In other words, I'm wasting my time.'

'Put it this way,' said Weekley: 'I think you may well have stumbled on to something. I don't know what. From what you have told me, I don't think it's a War Crime story. I'm as intrigued by the badge as you are, but if someone as senior as General Hollies – a one-time Deputy Commander NATO Forces in Europe, need I remind you – kicks it into touch, then I think you can probably take it that he knows what he's talking about.'

Miles gave a grim smile and swallowed the rest of his whisky. 'Ah well,' he said. 'It was a good idea while it lasted. Do you think there might be anything in the Diabolo connection?'

Weekley shrugged. 'Loony right-wing groups are nothing new in this country. In 1939, an anti-communist, anti-Semitic Scottish MP called Captain Archibald Ramsay set up a secret society called The Right Club. The membership was rumoured to include all sorts of eminent names and has never been published. It slid into well-deserved obscurity. In 1975, Colonel David Stirling, the founder of the SAS, decided that England was about to plunge into industrial and social chaos, and set up a right-wing organisation called GB75 whose members would step in and keep essential services running in the event of a general strike. At about the same time a recently retired C.-in-C. Allied Forces in Northern Europe, General Sir Walter Walker, founded a similar action committee called Unison. Again, nothing came of it. The Diabolo Club was known to be pro-Nazi in the years before the war, but if it has any *raison d'être* nowadays, aside from dubious exclusivity, I've yet to hear about it.'

As Miles was leaving, Weekley said, 'I'm sorry not to have been more encouraging. The secret world is still riddled with tempting riches. Unfortunately, it does not give them up easily. Each one has to be dug out with one's bare hands. That's what makes the search so endlessly fascinating.'

* * *

Miles spent the remainder of the evening immersed in the secret world of drawers and cupboards, trying to remember what went where and with what and why he'd bothered in the first place.

Before he went to bed, he took the rose from his pocket and placed it on his bedside table, where he could see it last thing at night and when he first woke in the morning. It would remind him of Elizabeth.

14

Miles set off for Norfolk the next morning shortly before ten. It was a crisp, cloudless, January day. The hedgerows were still lightly dusted with frost, a pale-yellow sun shone out of a pale-blue sky and for once the roads were free of traffic cones. The flat was pretty well back to its normal state of bachelor orderliness, the Golf gleamed from the carwash, and Miles realised that for the first time in over a week, he didn't have a headache.

West Keating lies about ten miles inland from Sheringham, in the north corner of the triangle bounded by the A140, the A148 and A1067. Miles took the M11, turned off at Great Chesterford and took the A11 to Norwich. The Ring Road round the City was slow but he soon picked up the A140 to Aylsham. From there he meandered through a cat's cradle of B roads and anonymous Norfolk villages with forgettable names.

West Keating was a pleasant exception. A narrow street lined with undistinguished red-brick cottages suddenly opened out into an extended village green, with pretty houses, washed in pink and yellow, and attractive-looking shops set back behind islands of green divided by little stretches of roadway. Facing down the village at the far end was a handsome Norman church with a fine tower, and nearby, next to a row of little cottages, was a tall pub called The Pocock Arms.

Miles drove into the car park at the back. It was surrounded by old barns. Round a corner he could make out cattle and sheep pens. There was a rear entrance to the Public Bar.

The landlord, a fat man with a grin that was tacked to his face as permanently as his beard, served him a pint of Abbot Ale. Miles was glad to notice there was no fruit machine and no jukebox. There wasn't sawdust on the floor either, but the old oak boards looked original. Two men with caps were sitting at a table by the fire, playing dominoes. One was young with a round, red face; the other could have been any age between fifty and eighty. He was as gnarled as a tree trunk and appeared to have no teeth.

Miles ordered hot game pie with mashed potatoes and vegetables and drank his beer. The landlord polished some glasses.

'Noice day.' It was a singsong accent, the voice rising sharply on the last word as if asking a question.

Miles agreed.

'You gawn far?'

Miles said, 'The safari park.'

'Thought so. From the noospapers, Oi'll be bound.'

'How did you guess?'

'Blast, Oi don't need to do any guessin',' said the landlord.

He laughed and the two men looked up. They exchanged knowing glances. 'Near on everyone who comes in here these days is from the noospapers. Ain't that so, Reuben?'

'Reckon,' the older man said.

'Are you surprised?' Miles asked.

Reuben shrugged and returned to the game.

'What sort of things do they ask?' Miles asked the landlord.

'All manner of things. About Mr Lambourn and his friends, mostly. And about the toigers, o' course.'

'Gossip,' said Reuben. 'That's what they're after gettin'. Scandal. That's all noospapers are interested in. Juicy titbits.'

'It is rather a sensational case, you must admit,' said Miles.

The younger man said, 'He had it comin' to him, you ask me.'

'Oh?'

'You can't go messin' around with them wild animals loike he did and get away with it.'

'Why? What did he do exactly?'

'Used to get in there with 'em and wrestle 'em, loike. You musta seen the pictures, you bein' a journalist. That's how he started off. As a publicity stunt. He always was a bit of a show-off, was Archie. Remember that time he walked down to the village with one of them toigers on a lead, Reuben?'

138

'Brought it in here an' all. Bloody old thing. Told us there was nothin' to worry about as long as we didn't show we was scared. Blast, Oi was ou' that door and home and int' a clean pair of trousers afore the words were out of his mouth.'

'Didn't even stop to finish your beer, did you, Reuben?'

The younger man and the landlord roared with laughter.

'Even if Oi'd stayed, Oi couldn'ta drunk a drop, Oi was shakin' that much.'

They roared with laughter again at the memory of it.

The landlord said, 'And that was only a foo weeks old, too. Oi reckon if he'd brought down one of them grown-up ones, you'da gone in'a ruddy orbit, Reuben.'

'Wanted his ruddy head tested, ask me,' grumbled Reuben.

'He weren't the only one,' said his companion.

The landlord jerked his chin in the direction of the younger man. 'Jimmy used to work up there in the park.'

'Doing what?' Miles asked him.

'Can't remember,' said Jimmy. 'Can't remember nothin' with an empty glass.'

Miles ordered pints all round, gave the landlord a twenty-pound note and told him to keep them coming. Jimmy remembered then. He'd started off doing odd jobs, emptying litter bins, raking the gravel, sweeping up in the cafeteria, anything he was asked, really. After a while he'd started working with the animals a bit, taking the food round to the different enclosures on the trailer, clearing out the zebra and giraffe areas. He'd even gone into the tiger enclosure a couple of times. With one of the keepers, of course. No one went in alone. Except Mr Lambourn. 'He were a law unto himself, were Mr Lambourn.'

'I suppose it was an accident?' Miles tossed the idea casually into the air, but he looked at Jimmy.

Jimmy shrugged. 'You'd have to ask Charlie 'bout that.'

'Charlie?'

'Charlie Bishop. The manager.'

'You don't sound as if you like him very much.'

'He's an arrogant bastard,' said Jimmy. 'Typical German.'

'German? He doesn't sound very German.'

139

'His real name's Bischof. Karl Bischof. His family ran a famous circus in Germany. Him and his father and his brother. His father performed for old Adolf, Oi heard tell.'

'What else did you hear?'

'Mr Lambourn used to have these house parties. Funny old lot, they were. Not the sort of people you'd expect: people loike hisself, with their woives and that.'

'Who, then?'

'There was a professor that used to come. From one of them universities. Oxford, Oi think it was. And a bishop. All sorts.'

'A bishop? What bishop? What was his name?'

Jimmy shook his head. 'Oi never saw any of 'em meself. That was only what Oi was told. Then there was a man that used to floy down from Scotland in his private plane. The one they used to call the Captain. He used to land it on the big field back o' the house.'

'Captain who?'

'Oi never did know his other name.'

'What did they do, these people? Shoot? Ride? Wrestle with the tigers? What?'

'Oi believe they used to talk a lot. But you'll have to ask Charlie. He was always in there. Tellin' them how to do their jobs, Oi daresay. Ruddy foreigners.' He shook his head and swallowed some more beer. 'That's a pity it weren't him that got done by the toigers. They had good reason, the way he treated them. Funny thing, that. They loiked Mr Lambourn. Everyone did. Yet he was the one they killed. Rum, Oi call it.'

The Long Drive from the road up to West Keating House turned out to be modestly named. The woman on the telephone had warned him not to lose heart. There was little danger of that. It was like driving through one's own personal BBC wildlife programme. Wherever Miles looked there were different varieties of deer, enclosures containing giraffes and zebras, distant lions, a small herd of bison …

The house appeared out of the landscape as if by magic. One minute there was nothing but fields and clumps of wood and well-kept parkland; the next, there it was, nestling in a secret valley: a grand building rather than an attractive one, built in Palladian style in yellow brick. It was like Holkham, further round the coast, only

140

smaller, with plain, simple lines, windows surrounded by classical architraves and, in the middle, a double staircase leading up to a main entrance door behind an imposing portico.

Miles brought the Golf to a crunching stop next to a supercilious stone lion. The front door was opened by a pleasant-looking woman of about sixty, wearing grey-rimmed glasses and matching hair.

'I rang yesterday,' Miles told her.

'Mr Bishop is expecting you,' she said. 'He's out in the park somewhere at the moment, but he shouldn't be long.'

She led him across a marble hall and ushered him into the library. She told him it was designed by William Kent and asked him if he'd like tea or coffee. Miles asked for tea and began to offer words of sympathy, but she was not in the mood for idle chatter.

'Please make yourself at home,' she said and marched out, closing the door behind her.

It was an unlikely suggestion, given the proportions of the room. The shelves, surmounted by classical pediments with spaces for bronze busts of Greek goddesses, were stuffed with yards of hand-tooled leather. A heavily muscled individual was manhandling a half-naked woman above the marble fireplace and various *fauteuils* were dotted about with studied casualness. Opposite the bookcases, three huge windows looked out on to an elaborately carved fountain of a naked man in a large helmet about to decapitate a peculiarly unpleasant-looking dragon. Beyond was more parkland, divided up into enclosures in which half the Serengeti appeared to be wandering contentedly. Miles peered in either direction, but he couldn't see any tigers.

In front of the centre window was an ormolu desk with magnificently wrought legs. Eighteenth-century, thought Miles. Probably French. Another trophy from the Grand Tour. But, unlike many such pieces, this one was obviously used for the purpose for which it was created. Or had been, for there was every indication that this was where Archie Lambourn had sat and written his books and, doubtless, looked out of the window and wondered at his creation.

On the right of the desk top was a silver frame, embossed with a regimental crest, containing a photograph of the young, slim, fresh-faced Archie, dressed in the full parade uniform of the Grenadier

Guards and clasping his bearskin as proudly as if he had shot the bear personally. Opposite, another frame, also silver, held a black-and-white studio portrait by Lenare of a young women wearing a dreamy sort of expression, a clinging ball gown and a lot of feathers. Her hands rested demurely on her lap. Miles guessed this was Lady Lambourn in the days of her slim and giddy youth.

Elsewhere, neatly arranged on the desk, were out-of-date copies of the *Daily Mail*, various files, a red lacquer tray full of correspondence, and a silver tankard, with a coat of arms engraved on the side, bristling with newly sharpened pencils. In the middle of the desk was a letter folder in red leather. The covers were closed. Miles ran his fingers over the surface. He tapped on it a couple of times, then turned away and walked across to the bookshelves next to the window that overlooked a formal garden with rose beds and topiary.

He ran his eyes idly over the titles. Many were devoted to the art and architecture of great country houses in East Anglia, and several shelves were taken up with exhaustive series on a variety of subjects: *Ramblings in Rural England* by Lt.-Col. Harry Shipp; *Composers of the 19th Century* by William Dundas; and, the largest collection of all, a twelve-volume series entitled *Great Poets of the World* by Herbert Lomas.

Miles was about to turn away when his attention was caught by a title at eyelevel that seemed rather out of place. It was Edward Whymper's *Scrambles Amongst the Alps*. Miles had a copy himself, a fairly late edition and sadly foxed, but this appeared to be in almost pristine condition. The tooling looked almost untouched. Miles was curious. He reached up to take the book. It seemed to have become jammed. He put a finger over the top of the spine and tipped it backwards. There was a slight resistance, followed by a faint click, and a section of the shelf below slid out, revealing a slim drawer.

Inside was a neat pile of different-coloured files. The top one was green and had the word 'Kananga' written across the middle of it. Miles opened the file. It was filled with press cuttings. The President of Kananga, Ben-Moulassa, was building himself a vast palace in the middle of the Central African jungle: a *folie de grandeur* – Versailles, the Pentagon and the Taj Mahal rolled into one – that threatened the habitat of a rare species called Rigaud's Monkey. It was yet another of those conservation scandals that gets everyone hot under the collar for a few days and is then completely forgotten. Miles pushed the cuttings back into the file. The next two just had initials scribbled on the right-hand corner in pencil: 'WG', and 'AR'. Miles was about to investigate when something much more interesting caught his eye. Across the middle of the next file down, neatly printed in black ink, were the words 'Diabolo Project'.

Miles looked quickly round the room. There was no sign of anything remotely resembling a closed-circuit TV camera. He pulled the file out. Lying underneath it were a number of photographs, of different sizes, most of them black-and-white. Some looked as if they'd been taken several years ago. There were various views of Eigerhubel and the Totenkopf, one of the Diabolo clubhouse, a handful of the Diabolo race in progress, and a couple of group shots.

One showed a group of a dozen or so men in polo-neck ski shirts and chunky pullovers, laughing and holding beer mugs up in a rather drunken toast. On the wall behind them were framed photographs of more groups, but it was what hung over the fireplace that interested Miles: a black figure with an obscene tail and a forked tongue hanging lasciviously from a grinning mouth, brandishing a pair of ski poles. Above the creature's head was crossed a pair of pre-war wooden skis and between the two, on a painted scroll, were inscribed the words: THE DEVIL TAKE THE HINDMOST.

So that's what the inside of the Diabolo Club looks like, thought Miles. *And those are the kind of people who make up the membership.*

For all the mystique that surrounded this stronghold of wealth and self-perpetuation, they were a pretty ordinary-looking bunch. Just like any group of men on a skiing holiday. Miles immediately identified Archie Lambourn. To judge from the photograph of him on the desk, the picture had been taken within the last few years. None of the other faces meant anything to him. Some were a good deal older than the others. There was one, standing to the right of the group, his hand resting on the back of one of the armchairs, who looked particularly frail. Yet, despite his withered frame, his hair and eyebrows were as dark as those of a man of thirty. The lips beneath a golf-club-secretary moustache were drawn back over long teeth, and at first sight he appeared to be joining in the joke as much as anyone. But when Miles looked at it closely, he could see there wasn't an ounce of humour in his face. The eyes were as expressionless as coal. It was the smile of an elderly crocodile.

All of them were looking straight at the lens, except for one – who was half-hidden behind Archie's considerable bulk and had turned his face away at the crucial moment.

The other group photograph had a slightly different cast list and a very different setting. It could have been any front room in any semi-detached villa in any suburb of south London. The miserable little fireplace was surrounded by glazed tiles decorated with birds and flowers. A single light hung from an artificial ceiling rose. In pride of place above the mantelpiece was a reproduction of *The Chinese Girl* by Tchelitchew. *What in God's name were people like these doing in a place like that?* wondered Miles.

He heard footsteps approaching in the hall. He had replaced the photographs and was putting back the files when he saw it. It was on the floor by his feet. It must have slipped out of the file. He bent down and picked it up. He turned it over. It was a badge. Black, with a Union Jack on it, and, underneath, the word ENGLAND.

* * *

'And these here on the right are from Sumatra.'

'They're beautiful.'

'Yes, they are.'

There were two of them. They were sprawled over an old tree trunk, fifty yards or so from the perimeter fence. They treated their admirers to looks of supreme indifference, yawned and closed their eyelids against the pale winter sunshine.

'A male and a female,' murmured Bishop. 'I reared them both myself by hand.'

'Does that mean they're tame?'

'No wild animal can ever be tamed.'

The German accent had been subsumed beneath a smooth mid-Atlantic drawl. He sounded computerised. The looks were more of a giveaway: the fair, tightly curled hair touched with grey, the hatchet jaw, the clean lines, the pale-blue eyes – the outward trappings of an in-built superiority complex.

'Over there is a family of Siberians.' He pointed to the next-door enclosure. The female was lying on her side, comfortably indifferent to her three cubs who were clambering and tumbling over her, biting and snarling and looking adorable. The male, cool and aloof, kept watch from a nearby grassy knoll. 'You can see the fur of the Siberians is longer and not so striped as that of the Sumatrans or the Indians.'

'Domestic bliss,' said Miles with a chuckle.

Bishop was not a chuckler. 'Tigers are at their most dangerous while they have their young with them,' he announced, as if addressing a school outing. 'If you rob a female of her cub, she can be terrible in her rage.'

'Were there cubs in the enclosure where Mr Lambourn was found?'

'No.'

'Wasn't he killed by a Siberian?'

'We have two enclosures of Siberians. In one there are the cubs, but not where he was found.'

'So why do you think he was attacked?'

Bishop shrugged. 'Who knows?'

'Hunger, perhaps?'

'Tigers do not attack humans to eat them. Anyway, our animals are well fed.'

'Why, then?'

'Tigers do not require reasons to do what they do.'

'So any of them could have been responsible?'

Bishop rounded on him. 'Wild animals have no concept of responsibility. We humans have the choice to be responsible or not and, if we do not behave in a responsible manner, we pay the penalty. Animals act only out of instinct. They cannot be blamed for their actions.'

Miles suspected that he was not just talking about the killing. 'It doesn't sound as if there was a lot of love lost between you two.' He let the remark drop carelessly.

'I had no quarrel with him personally,' said Bishop.

'Are you saying someone else did?'

145

'What are you suggesting?' Again, the sudden rounding; the face hard; the eyes as cold as stones.

Like a tiger, Miles thought. 'Nothing,' he replied, trying to keep the tone light. 'It's just that … well, I gather he had some rather odd friends.'

'His private life was his own affair,' said Charlie coldly. 'I was his manager. He was my boss. My employer. I am still the manager of the Safari Park, and it is as the manager that I am speaking to you. If you wish to know more about the death of Mr Lambourn, you can read the coroner's report. If you wish to know more about his life, you can ask his friends. I am happy to show you the park and the animals, but that is all. Is that clear?'

Miles said, 'Look, please don't misunderstand me. I'm not trying to pry. This story has been thrown at me at the last moment. I'm anxious to build up a picture of all the people involved as quickly as I can.'

Bishop gave a non-committal grunt.

They walked on down the asphalt path between the high wire fences of the two enclosures.

'Oh, really, this is too bad.'

Miles turned. Bishop was standing some distance behind him, staring into the Sumatrans' enclosure. 'What is it?'

Bishop pointed. An empty Coca Cola tin was lying just inside the fence. Miles was surprised he hadn't spotted it himself. 'Visitors,' said Bishop, with feeling.

He started back towards the gate. He punched four numbers into a small panel. There was a faint click. He pushed the gate open, stepped through the narrow gap and closed it behind him. The tigers yawned and stretched. Bishop moved quickly and confidently. As he did so, he kept up a soothing monologue in German. He picked up the can and returned to the gate. His eyes never left the animals for a second.

'Please go ahead,' Bishop said, locking the gate. 'I will be with you shortly.'

A keeper was walking along the far side of the next enclosure, in the direction of the house, pushing a hand cart filled with rakes and forks and brooms. Bishop ran after him, the offending can held accusingly in one hand. Miles wouldn't have been in the keeper's shoes for anything. He walked on down the path.

When he first heard the footsteps approaching from behind, he assumed it was Bishop hurrying to catch him up. He turned and smiled ...

The male was about thirty yards behind him ... the female was already halfway through the gate ... *The open gate ... the gate that Bishop had just locked ... I thought he'd locked, anyway ... assumed ... Bishop who knew everything there was to know about big cats ... who never made mistakes ... who was nowhere in sight ... hell's bloody bells ... where was he? ... where was everyone? ... what the hell am I supposed to do? ... not run, anyway ... animals chase people who run ... sheer instinct ... like a dog after a rabbit or a rat ... high wire fences on either side ... a high wire fence at the end ... no way out ... a rat in a cage ... what do rats do when they're cornered? ... turn and face their attackers ... challenge them ... call their bluff ... on the other hand ... perhaps, if I keep moving, very slowly, not panicking, not running, not turning my back ... I might ... Bishop might ... the tiger might not ... with luck ... he's gaining on me all the time ... less than twenty yards away now ...* Miles was still moving too ... *Stop! ... turn! ... look him in the eye ... call his bluff ... face him down ... now! ... do it! ...* He was doing it, but the tiger was still coming towards him ... panting ... grinning ... savouring ... smiling ... *The smile on the face of the tiger ... bloody great teeth ... bloody great paws ... bloody great claws ... muscles bunching ... tigers don't need reasons to do what they do ...* He could almost smell the animal's hot breath ... he closed his eyes ... *Bloody hell! ...*

'Stay right where you are, sir. Don't move an inch.' The voice was low and calm and reassuring. It came from somewhere behind Miles's right shoulder. 'You'll be all right, sir. Whatever you do, stand quite still.'

A child playing a game of Statues could not have stood stiller. But the tiger was playing to different rules. Miles wondered if there'd be much pain. He remembered reading somewhere that the reason gazelles and zebras lie there so passively while predators eat them alive is because they're in such shock they can't feel a thing. He hoped to God the writer knew what he was talking about.

147

And then … It was a sound somewhere between a roar and a hiss.

Miles twisted his head round. There were two men standing there. The older one was wearing brown overalls. He was holding something tucked under one arm. It was black and shiny and cylindrical, about the size of a large mortar shell. White foam was jetting out of the front and piling up on the path a few feet in front of the tiger's head, like a huge mound of whipped cream.

The male tiger paused. He stood there, mouth open, but not grinning any more. Panting. Puzzled. Uncertain. His great head dropped. There was fear in his eyes. And anger. The great head came up. The mouth opened wide. The lips drew back over the teeth. The head tilted slightly. He snarled. Miles could smell the breath. It reeked of death. He snarled again and this time he brought his right paw up and slashed furiously at the insubstantial foam between them.

The fire extinguisher roared again, and again the foam spurted. The tiger gave another snarl, but this time without conviction. The head swayed from side to side. The eyes were wary.

'Keep right where you are, sir. You're doing very well. You ready, Harry?'

Two other men had appeared at the far end of the path. They were both holding rifles. One of them brought the stock up to his shoulder, rested his cheek against the butt and squinted along the barrel. The other stood, feet planted wide, waiting.

'Don't dart them unless you have to,' the man called out. 'Wait and see if they go back on their own.'

The man moved forward. He was ahead of Miles now, holding the extinguisher in two hands like a sub-machine gun. The tiger looked cowed, awkward, sheepish almost. Another, younger, man eased past Miles, holding a pistol.

The first man was speaking to the tiger now as he moved forward. His voice was firm and kind at the same time. Quite suddenly, the tiger turned and loped, as if in slow motion, back along the path. The other did the same. The men followed along behind, gently shepherding them along. When the tigers reached the open gate, they paused, peered at the two men with the rifles, hesitated briefly, then turned their heads and padded back into their enclosure. The first man

148

stepped forward, slammed the gate shut and peered at the panel. He shook his head.

'Can't understand it,' he said.

The younger man stared.

'Well, don't just stand there,' the older man said. 'Go and find Mr Bishop.'

He hurried away towards the outhouses.

'Someone's going to get into hot water for this,' the older man muttered.

But Miles wasn't listening. He was far too busy being violently sick.

15

'It could have been an accident.'

'Don't be bloody ridiculous.' Miles's voice was muffled by the pillow. He turned his head a few inches to the left. 'He's a German, for God's sake. Germans don't make mistakes. You should have seen him. He looked like one of those robots from an Arnold Schwarzenegger movie. All computer technology. If one of the tigers decided to have a go at him, it'd get a shock, I can tell you. Finish up with a mouthful of wires and electrodes, I shouldn't wonder.'

'For God's sake, lie still,' said Noel. 'How do you think I can get these stitches out when you're moving your head all the time?'

'I thought they needed putting in, not taking out.'

'The wound's healed up very well, all things considered. Nearly done. Just a couple more. There's one …'

'Ouch. That hurt. What's so funny, for God's sake?'

'Twenty-four hours ago you were about to be torn apart by a man-eating tiger, and here you are complaining about a tiny stitch being removed.'

'Knowing there are millions of people all over the world dying of horrible diseases doesn't make having a cold any the nicer.'

'OK, Maltby. You asked for it.'

'Ow! That one really hurt. You did that on purpose.'

'Serves you right.'

'Look,' said Noel when he had finished cleaning around the wound and they were sitting on either side of the desk, 'supposing you're right. Supposing it wasn't an accident. What possible reason could this man Bishop have for wanting to kill you?'

'I can only assume he's in on it, too.'

150

'So you don't think he was responsible for killing Archie?'

'I'm beginning to wonder. If he was, I've no idea why. Anyway, I'm pretty sure the Diabolo's a cover for something. I don't know what exactly, but I suspect ...'

'An Old Nazi Comrades' Association? This isn't Paraguay.'

'That's not to say there aren't dozens of elderly men, well-respected members of the community – Justices of the Peace, Deputy Lieutenants, Members of the House of Lords, God knows who – living in style and comfort in big houses up and down the land, surrounded by loving families, men whom nobody would suspect in a million years, who once put on an SS uniform and took an oath and suddenly found themselves faced with an order they couldn't refuse and who have spent the best part of half a century dreading the knock on the door in the night, the blackmailing letter, the chance incident that leads a reporter to start asking questions. Why else do you think the War Crimes Bill was introduced in the first place? Because there are people who know there are war criminals living in this country. Don't you think they don't know their names and where they live and what they did? And don't you think there aren't organisations dedicated to shielding them and hiding their identities?'

'Listen,' said Noel. 'If what you say is true, and for all I know you may well be right, any day now we can expect to have our television viewing enlivened by the sight of some poor old peer being hustled into a car in handcuffs with a blanket over his head.

' "Fancy that!" we'll say. "Who would have thought it of him?" And then the football results will come up and we'll go out and make a cup of tea and never give it another thought. Until the trial, of course, when once again we'll stick our beady little noses into the trough, root happily around in the ullage for a while and then forget all about it again. A number of elderly people will be wheeled out to testify that they were victims of Nazi atrocities, and they'll scream and yell and point at the defendant and say, "That's him, that's the monster, I'd recognise those eyes anywhere." And the jury will believe them, even though it all happened half a century ago and their eyesight's going and their memory's dodgy, and he'll be found guilty and then it will be discovered that he wasn't the man at all; it was a case of mistaken identity, as with Demjanjuk, and then we'll

151

be the ones who feel guilty and thoroughly ashamed of ourselves. And very soon we'll forget all about it anyway.'

'Have you finished?' Miles asked him.

'Not quite,' said Noel. 'We're old friends and I don't believe in preaching to old friends, but I think you should seriously consider your motives in all this. I know that for a long time now you've been looking for a good story and I can understand you thinking that you might have stumbled on the perfect subject. But think about it a bit more: assuming there are major English Nazi war criminals who have never been discovered and that you unmask one of them, then what? You make a name for yourself and pots of money and you get to appear on television a lot and you can't get to your front door for all the mouth-watering offers that come pouring through your letter box, but what have you really achieved? Justice? Or have you merely presented a bloodthirsty public with somebody to crucify? According to Robert, there are about three hundred names that have so far been investigated. How many of those will ever come to trial, let alone be convicted? I suggest that what you'll end up with is a lottery. Any trials that did take place would appeal to people's worst instincts, not to their sense of justice. I honestly think you should reconsider. End of sermon. Sorry, but that's what I think about it. As your friend.'

Miles said, 'People have been trying to kill me, or had you forgotten?'

'You may be right, or it may just look like that. Either way, it seems to me to be another very persuasive argument for giving up, before you really get hurt.'

Miles said, 'What do you mean, give up? I can't give up. How can I give up? I've got a deadline to meet and bills to pay.'

Noel said, 'Miles, you haven't *got* to do *anything*. Anybody could have written this Lambourn story. The reason you took it on was because you discovered he was a member of the Diabolo and you want to find out more about the Diabolo. So don't give me any of that "I'm only a professional journalist earning a living" crap.'

Miles stood up and stared out of the window at the long, scrubby grass and overgrown borders. There was a variegated syringa in one corner that was badly in need of pruning. The lap larch fencing at the end flapped gently in the wind. It was a pity. It could be quite a nice little suburban garden if somebody took time and trouble over it.

He turned and faced his friend. 'Look, Noel, I'm a journalist and for better or worse I earn my living from it, largely because I'm bloody well organised and I give editors what they want and as much as they want it and when they want it. It's true that the vast majority of the stories that I write are self-contained. I turn them over, like a second-hand car dealer. People ring me, tell me what they want, I deliver it, and apart from a modicum of after-sales service – a spot of rewriting, perhaps, extra fact-checking, proofreading – I never give it a second thought. Sometimes I can't even remember what I've written that morning, so little am I involved. But just occasionally a story comes up that's worth more than a mere thousand words deftly arranged on three sides of quarto. An Armstrong-Siddeley of a story in a courtyard of Ford Fiestas. It's in a bit of a mess, parts of it are missing, it won't run properly, it needs work on it. But it's going to be worth it in the end. I'm going to finish up with something that's going to make me more money than all the rest put together; and, more important still, something I can be really proud of. That's the way I feel about this story. Sometimes parts of one story can be used for another. They happen to fit. They're still two separate jobs, but by chance they become part of one bigger story.'

Noel said, 'Ford Fiesta parts don't work on Armstrong-Siddeleys.'

'Fat help you are,' said Miles.

'Thanks very much.'

'Sorry. I didn't really mean it. I don't know how I'd have got through the last few days without you.'

'Please. Spare my blushes.'

Miles stood up.

Noel said, 'Even if there is a plot afoot, and Bishop is in on it, as you say, I still don't understand what reason he had for thinking you were a threat. Unless someone saw you fiddling about in the drawer. And you say there were no cameras in the room.'

'Not that I could see.'

'Perhaps you didn't cover your tracks quite as well as you thought. In which case ...'

'I'm beginning to wonder,' said Miles.

He got up and went across to where his old brown overcoat was hanging on the back of the door. He put his hand into the cavernous inside pocket and produced a quarto-size manilla envelope, folded carefully so that it fitted in without creasing. He opened the end and tipped it upside down over Noel's desk. Out fell two black-and-white photographs and a black badge with a Union Jack on it and, underneath, the word ENGLAND.

Noel looked at them and shook his head. 'You always were pig-headed,' he said.

* * *

'The Lambourn Set? I'll tell you everything you need to know about the Lambourn Set. They were a bunch of s-h-one-t's.'

Lady Camilla Cressage slurred both the s's. It was a wonder she'd even managed to spell the word right. It was ten the next morning when Miles rang the door bell of the flat in the run-down, graffiti-bedaubed tower block in Kentish Town, but her breath was already well seasoned with gin and her eyes were badly out of sync with her head movements. They were heavily ringed with black mascara, which gave her the look of a demented parrot. Her mouth was slashed with red like an open wound and her teeth hadn't seen a dentist for years. And yet beneath the raddled features and bloated body, barely concealed beneath the outsize floral shift, it was still possible to descry a faint trace of the beauty that had held Archie in thrall for ten years – before he finally drove her from his bed, his friends and the world in which she had felt so secure. Her own friends – the few who had remained loyal – had tried to raise her self-esteem by reminding her that at least her second husband had not left her for another woman, but it was little consolation. The only high spirits she could muster these days came from a bottle of Beefeater's.

'And boring little shits, at that,' she added. She wove her way unsteadily across the rucked surface of the floor rug. A length of flowery material in a vaguely Indian design had been thrown over the sagging remains of the only sofa. She flopped on to it, tucked her legs up under her and lit a Silk Cut. She threw the spent match into a saucer full of dog-ends, inhaled furiously, then felt around on the floor

154

and came up with a half-full tumbler of something blue-tinged and warm. Some of it slopped on to her dress, but she didn't appear to notice. She sucked in a mouthful and held it there for a moment before swallowing. She pulled a face as if it were medicine. 'Sure you won't …?' She waved the glass in the air.

Miles smiled faintly and shook his head.

'I don't normally indulge until lunchtime,' she said, 'but knowing you were coming … Remembering the old days … It isn't easy … One needs something, you know?'

Miles nodded sympathetically.

She lowered another mouthful. 'Archie,' she said, narrowing her eyes as if trying to focus on a distant figure only half recognised. She sighed. 'He was a weak man. Very weak. Who wouldn't have been with a mother like that? She broke his balls like she broke his father's before him. She was like one of those pressing machines you see in junk yards. She only had to look at a man and he'd end up as a square lump of metal. She despised men. Used them until she was bored, then chucked them. She was always desperately possessive where Archie was concerned. She'd think nothing of humiliating him in front of his friends, but she wouldn't hear a word against him. If anybody dared to criticise him, she'd turn on them and tear them to bits. And if anybody was stupid enough to try and take him away … She was a killer, that woman. Perhaps that's why he got so keen on tigers. They reminded him of his mother. It was hardly surprising that he grew up not knowing whether he was Arthur or Martha.'

The tee aitches posed problems. It was as if her tongue was too large for her mouth. She drew hard again on her cigarette and stubbed it out, even though it was only half smoked. She immediately lit another. She threw the match at the saucer and missed.

'Fuck,' she said. 'Anyway, luckily – or unluckily, depending on your point of view – he had a lot of money, and a lot of good connections, so he had no trouble surrounding himself with hangers-on. He thought they were his friends – Cunningham-Walker, Eperon, Sayers, that shit Gerald Deighton – but they used him, just as his mother had used him. They took him for everything they could. They laughed at him behind his back, squeezed the juice out of him and moved on to something stronger. Like me, you might say.' She raised her glass in a fumbled toast. 'Of course they were a gift to the gossip columnists. They gambled and played and screwed their way through the Season. One of them only had to break wind and there'd be a paragraph on it somewhere.'

She laughed. It sounded like a horse with croup.

'I was young and I was a fool. I thought I could protect him against those blood-suckers. I loved him. I knew he didn't love me, but I thought I could get him round to the idea one day. But I never stood a chance. Not while the old tigress was still alive. She encouraged him to make an idiot of himself. Promoted it, you might say. And why not? It served as cover for her real intentions.'

'What do you mean?'

'What?' Her eyes swivelled towards him like a pair of fried eggs floating in oil.

'What were her real intentions?'

Camilla frowned at him in disbelief. 'The revival of the BF, of course.'

'The BF?'

'The British Fascists.' The last word had deteriorated into a single shooshing sound. The machine was winding down fast. Miles realised that, if he didn't keep pushing, there was a good chance it might pack up altogether.

'Was Lady Lambourn a Fascist, then? I knew Archie was involved, of course, but ...'

'Archie? Involved? He stood for Parliament, for Christ's sake. For the Vale of Esher.' She wrapped her lips round the words with mock solemnity.

'As a Fascist?'

'Don't be bloody silly,' she said. 'How could anyone stand as a Fascist? "Britain First". That was the name of his so-called party. All two hundred of them. It was his mother's idea. She was behind the whole thing. Completely barking, of course.'

'Was she always that way?'

'They both were. She and that ugly boot who looked like a man. They started the whole thing going, you know.'

'What ugly boot? Who are you talking about?'

'She was called Lintern-Orman. Rotha Lintern-Orman. Can you imagine? Sounds like a bloody anagram. Founder of the first Fascist Organisation in Britain. Thought it up in a cabbage patch. She dressed like a man, too. Rumour had it she wore a sword at rallies. My mother-in-law thought she was the bees' knees. She was in love with her, I reckon. Until Bill Gordon came along.'

'Who's Bill Gordon?'

'He was a friend of Mosley's in the early days. Someone once told me he helped to finance the Black House. I don't know if it's true. Of course Mosley was very rich himself. So was his wife. Cynthia.' She exaggerated the vowels in a crude upper-class parody.

'What's the Black House?' Miles asked.

She gave him a disbelieving frown. 'Christ, you don't know much, you journalists, do you? The Blackshirts' headquarters in Chelsea. It was a kind of Fascist barracks, according to Bill. Bloody great place. Had been a teachers' training college, of all things. Mosley and his people converted it into a thug-training college. Five thousand of them lived there at one time. It wasn't very difficult to get in. Not in the mid-Thirties; not with all that unemployment. They took pretty well anyone who knew how to use his fists. The really hard ones wore jackboots and guarded Mosley. They were the ones who sorted out the hecklers at his meetings.'

'And this man Gordon helped to pay for them?'

'God knows what she saw in him. He certainly didn't see anything in her. He only liked them young. Horrible little man. He was always trying to get his hand up my skirt. One day I poured a jug of hot water in his lap. He gave me a wide berth after that, I can tell you. Didn't stop him leering at me, though. Those great long horse's teeth and those dead eyes. Yeuch!' Camilla shuddered.

'When was this?' Miles asked.

'Sixties sometime. I forget now. Years ago. He had a big place up on the west coast of Scotland in those days. Castle and five thousand acres. Forget the name now. Something Castle. On the Ardman … Ardmark … Ardnam …

'Do you mean the Ardnamurchan Peninsula?'

'Give me a bloody chance. Up there somewhere. You ought to talk to him anyway. If he's still alive. He'll tell you everything you need to know about the Lambourn Set. He was their elder statesman.'

'He must be very old by now.'

'He was always very old,' she said. 'Very old but very rich. It wasn't much of a compensation, but it was something.'

'You haven't got his number by any chance?'

Camilla scrabbled around in a drawer for a while and finally came up with a disintegrating address book. She fumbled for the glasses that swung from a gold-coloured chain round her neck and, after several botched attempts, managed to get them perched on the end of her nose. She thumbed through the book, shaking her head. 'Must have chucked it away,' she said.

Miles reached for his briefcase. 'You must be able to remember the name of the castle?'

She frowned and shook her head again, as if loosening her memory. 'Ended in -aig, I expect,' she said. 'Most places up there do.'

Miles opened the briefcase and took out the badge. He placed it on her knee.

Camilla picked it up and peered at it over the top of her glasses. 'What's this?' she said.

'I hoped you might be able to tell me.'

'Can't imagine why,' she said, and handed it back to him.

'You don't recognise it?' he said and held it up.

'Should I?'

'I found it at Archie's.'

'Found it?'

'Stole it, actually.'

'What the hell for?'

'It was lying on top of these. I assumed it had something to do with them.'

He handed her the photographs. She picked up the top one and moved it backwards and forwards, frowning as she tried to focus on it.

'Stone the crows,' she said under her breath. 'Where did you say you found these?'

'I didn't.'

'Archie would kill you if ...'

'Why? What's so special about them? Who are these people?'

She stabbed a finger at one of them. 'Well, that fat fart there is Johnny Cunningham-Walker. Never did a day's work in his life. Drank like a halibut. Looked like one too. He married Gerald Deighton's sister, Frances. Is Gerald here? Oh yes, there he is. You can see he's a shit. Look at those eyes. You don't get a face like that for nothing. He used to organise orgies at his place in Gloucestershire. And a lot of other things. He was one of life's great fixers. Anything you want, girls, boys, drugs ... Nothing but the best. And there's little Harry Eperon. Poor little bugger. He was completely out of his depth most of the time. But they liked him because he was funny.'

Miles pointed at the little man with the large head that was turned away. 'Do you recognise him?'

'Could be anyone,' she said.

'Where were these pictures taken?'

Camilla looked at them both. 'I've no idea where this is,' she said. 'I presume this one is the famous Diabolo Club. It's in a ski resort in Switzerland ...'

'I know where it is,' said Miles. 'I was in Eigerhubel the other day.'

'Eigerhubel. That's right. That's where it was. Eigerhubel.'

'But surely you must have gone there many times?'

Again, the croaky laugh. 'Good God, no,' she said. 'Wives and girlfriends were not welcome. Boys only. All very hush-hush. God Almighty, there's Mark Sayers. The best-looking man I ever met. Dying of Aids, someone told me. What a waste. Oh God!'

'What is it?' For a moment Miles thought she was about to throw up. The colour had drained from her face completely. She put her hand over her mouth.

'There's Gordon.'

'Which one's he?'

She pointed at the man with the crocodile smile.

'Big moustache, small physique,' Miles mused. 'Looks like the hen-pecked husband in a seaside postcard.'

'Perhaps that's why my mother-in-law liked him. She was the big fat wife, he was her Little Willy.'

'What was his relationship with Archie exactly?'

'Bill? He was his guru. His *éminence grise*.' Again the exaggerated vowels, as if she was embarrassed at being caught out speaking French. 'Archie wouldn't go to the lavatory without consulting him first. He was the father he never had. That was his excuse, anyway.'

'Could he still be alive?'

'People like Bill Gordon don't get born and die like other people. They suddenly appear one day out of the earth, like goblins, grinning and gibbering and putting their hands up young girls' skirts and generally making a bloody nuisance of themselves, and then one day they disappear back into the earth, and all that's left behind is a nasty smell.'

'And you really can't remember the name of the Castle?'

Camilla laughed. It was the laugh of a woman who smoked too much and drank too much and would soon pay the penalty for both. Not so much a laugh as a death rattle. 'Darling,' she said. 'I can't even remember where I live half the time.' She looked around at the dirt and the cigarette ends and the piles of old newspapers and the empty bottles and there were tears in her eyes. 'And that's on the good days,' she said.

16

'Scotland?' Neville's voice squeaked with outrage and disbelief.

'It's not exactly Patagonia,' Miles pointed out.

'Pity,' said Neville. 'You might have got there on a freebie.'

'Surely you can't be worrying about the expense?' Now it was Miles's turn for incredulity. 'This story hasn't cost a penny so far.'

'That's not the point,' Neville grumbled. 'The point is, how do I justify you titting around in Scotland on the off-chance you might get a paragraph out of it?'

'You never had any problems justifying anything in the past,' Miles reminded him. 'Remember the time I sat around in the Beverly Wilshire for three days waiting to interview Mick Jagger, and he was in the next room? I didn't even get a paragraph out of him. Just an invitation to do something that's anatomically impossible.'

'Things have changed. Life's moved on in the last few years. People like me have got to account for every last paperclip these days. Who is this man anyway?'

'He's called Gordon. Captain William Gordon. Lochintoul Castle, Ardnamurchan. He was the elder statesman of the Lambourn Set. He was like a father to Lambourn. Lambourn's ex-wife thinks I should speak to him. So do I.'

'Fine. Speak to him, by all means, but you don't have to go all the way to Scotland to do that. Just pick up the phone.'

'I thought you said you wanted this to be a colour piece,' Miles said. 'The man lives in a castle, for God's sake.'

'Castle schmastle,' said Neville. 'It's bound to be raining when you get there. Make up the colour. You're a writer, aren't you?'

161

Miles was about to remind Neville that he had nearly got himself killed for his sake, but there didn't seem any point.

* * *

A Mrs McCulloch answered the telephone. She sounded prim and elderly. All Morningside and shortbread biscuits.

'I'm afraid the Captain is no' in the castle,' she said, as though responding to an indecent proposition.

Miles said, 'Have you any idea where I might find him? It is rather important.'

She said, 'Of course I know where you might find him. I am his housekeeper. And who might you be, may I ask?'

'I am a friend of Mr Lambourn's.'

'Oh, I see,' she said. 'I was afraid for a moment you might be from one of those London newspapers. And your name is …?'

'Oh, no,' Miles groaned. 'Don't say they've been on to you, too. Do you know, they haven't given me a moment's rest ever since … well, since that terrible day.'

'Aye,' she said, 'it was a terrible day indeed. But to be expected.'

Miles's brain suddenly switched to fast forward, then fast reverse, then back again, all in a matter of a few seconds.

He said warily, 'You mean …?'

'We-e-ll,' she said, in a tone of quiet confidentiality, 'that Mr Lambourn … He was always one for taking risks, but this time he took one too many.'

'Tigers are very unpredictable creatures,' said Miles.

'I wouldn't be knowing about that,' she said. 'But he shouldn't have gone ringing up the newspapers like he did. He'd had his time in the public eye. He should have been content with that.'

Miles's brain was still racing. 'I didn't actually see the piece myself,' he said carelessly. 'I've been away. Which paper was it?'

'I wouldn't know,' she said. 'Nothing appeared anyway.'

'Thank goodness, eh?' said Miles. 'Anyway, look, I mustn't keep you from your work. Where did you say I could find the Captain again?'

'I didn't,' she said. 'But you could try his club.'

'His club ...?'

'Aye.'

'Which ... er ...?' He knew it was a mistake as soon as he said it.

'You said you were a friend of Mr Lambourn's?' Suspicion had crept back into her voice.

'I did.'

'Well then, you'll know where to find the Captain, won't you?'

'Yes, of course.'

Miles replaced the receiver and cursed. Why the hell did he have to go and get himself tied up in that ridiculous charade? Now he was going to have to waste time trying to track Gordon down in London.

What sort of club would a man with a name like Captain Gordon belong to? White's? Brooks's? Boodle's? The Reform? Surely not. No decent men's club would countenance a man who styled himself 'Captain'. No one under the rank of major keeps his rank, and only then if he's been a regular. Even wartime ranks were considered temporary. Only a bounder would call himself Captain Gordon. Or a Fascist debauchee. What sort of club would a Fascist debauchee feel at home in? Take your pick, Noel would probably say.

It was possible, of course, that he was a naval captain.

Miles pulled a *Who's Who* down from the shelf above his desk. Gordon ... There were plenty of them. Two and a half pages' worth. Professors, architects, major-generals, Richard Gordon, the doctor and comic novelist, even a literary agent. There was one William Gordon: soldier and businessman, but he lived in Buckinghamshire. Miles rang Anne Crosthwaite. She was out of the office; back in the morning. Robert Parker was on leave for the rest of the week. Who else might know ...?

'Clubs?' Camilla's voice sounded sharper at ten at night. 'He once took me to some afternoon drinking place off Shaftesbury Avenue. And there was a casino he used to go to somewhere near Edgware Road underground station.'

'I meant a proper club, like the Athenaeum or the Travellers'.'

'I can't imagine a proper club would want a little shit like that as a member. Tell you who would know,' Camilla said brightly. 'Mrs McCulloch. His housekeeper. She's probably dead by now, though.'

163

'No, she's still very much alive. But she's not giving anything away.'

'What do you expect? She's Scottish.'

'She did tell me Archie had approached a newspaper with some story or other. What do you think he might have wanted to reveal to the world?'

She said, 'I can't imagine that anything Archie had to say would be of the remotest interest to anyone. Unless it was about those bloody tigers, of course.'

'Mrs McCulloch implied that it was something he should have kept his trap shut about.'

'Perhaps he was planning to blow the gaffe on the Diabolo,' said Camilla. 'Tell everyone what really goes on in that silly little scout hut in the mountains.'

'Such as?'

'I've no idea. I already told you, I never went there. Women were not welcome.'

Miles got the feeling that, suddenly, neither was he.

* * *

'Nigel? It's Miles Maltby.'

'Miles!'

He would hardly have called Dempster a friend, but he'd sat next to him at the occasional press lunch – the Savoy, the terrace of the House of Lords, Cowdray Park – and found him sympathetic and generous with information. He'd noticed a pile of old *Daily Mails* on Archie's desk in the library, so it seemed a fair bet that that had been the paper he'd rung with his fatal revelation and that, as an old friend and long-time chronicler, Dempster was the man he'd have asked for.

'I did get a message he'd called,' Dempster said. 'I was out at the time. He said he had a story for me and that he'd call back. But then he got eaten by a tiger.'

'You've no idea what the story was?'

'No idea.'

'You don't think it could have had anything to do with the

164

Diabolo. Something to do with their seventy-fifth anniversary perhaps?'

'Could have been,' said Dempster. 'They'll all be going out this year, of course. Even some of the most venerable members.'

'Such as?'

'Gerald Deighton. Harry Eperon. Johnny Cunningham-Walker. That gay don from Oxford, Claud Austin. The ex-Bishop of Tiverton. The self-styled Captain William Gordon of Lochintoul ...'

'Bill Gordon,' said Miles. 'Camilla Cressage mentioned him.'

'What were you talking to Camilla about?'

'I'm doing a piece about the Diabolo. The Lambourn Set came up.'

'Oh, right.'

'She wasn't very complimentary about him.'

'He used to nourish an unhealthy taste for young girls. He's probably a bit past it now. He was always reputed to be the evil genius behind the Lambourn Set.'

'So I gather. Archie's guru, she called him.'

'He was Archie's campaign manager when he stood as National Front candidate for the Vale of Esher.'

'Britain First.'

'Same kind of thing. I knew Archie very well at one time. He was no fool. I never understood how he could have been taken in by that old fraud.'

'What was fraudulent about him?'

'His name, for a start. I don't know what he was christened, but it certainly wasn't William. And his parents weren't called Gordon either. The Scottish laird stuff is as bogus as his army rank.'

'Not a club man, then?'

'He's been a Diabolo member for years.'

'I meant a London club.'

'No decent London club would have him.'

'I rang him at Lochintoul actually. I spoke to his housekeeper. She said I'd find him at his club.'

'He's always cultivated a hunting, shooting and fishing image. You could try somewhere like the Angler's and Sporting.'

'In London?'

'It's in one of those side-streets off the Strand.'

'I've never heard of it,' said Miles.

'It's not in the first eleven,' said Dempster. 'But then neither is he.'

* * *

From the outside it looked like an office building. Grey stone, turn-of-the-century, anonymous. He must have passed it dozens of times, on his way to and from the theatre, to and from time-wasting lunches with chirpy PR girls, to and from awkward meetings with his bank manager. The brass plaque was modest, but then it had a lot to be modest about.

Miles had rung a couple of times during the day, and a gruff voice had told him that the Captain had not been in. He suggested Miles try in the evening. The Captain always looked in around seven.

Prompt as ever, Miles had set out from the flat at 6.15; by 6.40 he had found a parking space in Bedford Street; and by 6.45 he was strolling along Maiden Lane. He turned right down Southampton Street. The club was near the top on the right. Miles climbed the short flight of steps and pushed through the double glass doors. The porter's lodge was just inside on the left. The porter had white hair and a white moustache. He wore a brown uniform with small gold salmon leaping up both lapels.

'May I help you, sir?' There was a military timbre to the voice.

'I was hoping to find Captain Gordon. I rang earlier.'

'Ah yes, sir. I remember. Mr Marlborough, isn't it?'

'Maltby.'

'I'm so sorry, I'm afraid you've missed him, Mr Mowbray. He's just left. You might catch him, if you're quick.'

Miles ran down the steps. A bent figure in an overcoat and bowler hat was heading briskly down the hill on the opposite side of the road in the direction of the Strand, leaning heavily on a rolled umbrella. Miles crossed the road, narrowly avoiding being run over by two men in a white Renault Clio, and hurried after him. As he rounded the corner, the man raised his umbrella and disappeared from view. Miles arrived in the Strand in time to see a taxi negotiating a U-turn through the early-evening traffic. A face was looking out at him from

166

the nearside passenger seat: a face with dark eyebrows and a golf-club-secretary's moustache over long teeth.

The lights changed, there was a gap in the traffic, and the taxi turned and drove off in the direction of Trafalgar Square.

Miles stared wildly around. There were plenty of taxis, moving in both directions, but none with a FOR HIRE light on. It was the worst possible time to be looking. And then one appeared from nowhere, travelling on the opposite side of the road. But now the traffic lights had changed to green and everything was on the move. Miles dodged and skipped his way through the traffic with the speed and daring of a young man in the Pamplona Bull Run. He reached the safety of the far pavement in time to see a man with a brief-case waving an imperious hand. The taxi swung towards him. The man was leaning forward, issuing instructions to the driver through the open window when Miles arrived.

'Would you mind?' Miles said. 'My wife's just gone into labour.'

The man started to protest.

'Hop in,' said the cabby.

'Sorry,' Miles lied.

The man's hands dropped in a gesture of angry resignation.

'Where to?' said the driver.

'Just drive,' said Miles. 'I'll tell you where to go.'

He thought he'd never live to hear himself say it.

* * *

The traffic on the Embankment was as bad as the cabby had ever known it – an observation that he reiterated at approximately two-minute intervals.

'At least you didn't bring her with you,' he said.

'What?'

'I am allergic to pregnant women. Can't help it. It's just one of those things. Like shellfish.'

'I'm sorry to hear that,' said Miles.

'Couple of months ago, this fare flags me. I pull in. He says, "Quick, to the nearest hospital, my wife's about to have a baby." I don't know where she came from. I'll swear she wasn't there when he flagged me.

167

Next thing I know she's sitting in the back of the cab. I says to him, "Look, mate, I'll take you anywhere you want, but if your wife starts giving birth in the back of my cab you'll have to find yourselves another cab, because I can't be doing with it." Know what he says …?'

Miles didn't know and didn't care and didn't listen to the answer. He was concentrating on not losing Gordon's taxi and at the same time giving the cabby the impression he knew where he was going. He couldn't risk discovering at the wrong moment that the man also had an aversion to people asking him to follow other people's taxis.

'Left here …'

They crossed the river via Chelsea Bridge and joined the nightly crawl up Queenstown Road to Clapham Common. They crossed the Common on The Avenue. Gordon's taxi took a right and a right again into Nightingale Lane.

'You'll just be in time to see your new baby off to university, rate we're going,' said the cabby.

Gordon's taxi turned left into Endelsham Road, down through Nightingale Square and out into Chestnut Grove. A few moments later, its right indicator started winking and it pulled over.

'A little further, just up there on the left, beyond that lamppost. That's perfect,' said Miles.

A group of young black men walked by as he got out.

'Cheers,' said the cabby as he handed him his change. 'Have one for me.'

'What?'

'Better still, I'll have one for you.'

Miles waited until his taxi was out of sight, then he turned and walked back down the road in time to see Gordon disappearing through the front door of a terraced villa some thirty yards away. It had aluminium windows and a privet hedge about five foot high with a wrought-iron gate in the middle. There was a light on in the downstairs room at the front. The curtains had been drawn, but not completely, and the light shone through the gap in the middle.

Miles waited in the shadows on the opposite side of the road on the off-chance there might be more visitors, but when after about ten minutes nobody else had turned up he quickly crossed the road. He was glad to see that the gate had been left open. There was a short tiled path and to the left a small front garden consisting of crazy paving round a rose bed. He moved across to the window.

The gap in the curtains was no more than a couple of inches wide, so his view of the room was severely limited, but by squinting through it from different angles he was able to see as much as he needed to. The miserable little fireplace; the tiles with the bird and flower motifs; the artificial ceiling rose ... It was the room in the second photograph. But with one major difference. The picture had been taken when it was in a plain, dreary, unadorned state. Now it was *en fête*. The little walls were hung with bright red banners decorated with swastikas set in white circles. Between the banners were large, unframed portrait shots of great Fascists of the twentieth century: Hitler, Hess, Goebbels ranting, Mussolini puffed up, looking like a cross between a pouting pigeon and a professional wrestler, Mosley with his arrogant little moustache and staring eyes, the brilliant, Jew-hating Joyce with his sticking-out ears and sinister scar that ran from the corner of his mouth to his ear, the legacy of a razor slash acquired while stewarding a Conservative meeting at the Lambeth Baths in 1924 ... A suburban pantheon to Fascism: amateurish and rather absurd, and yet, because of that, curiously chilling.

The Chinese Girl had been removed from above the mantelpiece and replaced by a poster. There was nothing very unusual about it. Every year, tourist offices all over the world produce similarly ide-alised views by the thousand. But this would have caught Miles's attention wherever it had been displayed, advertising as it did the Bernese Oberland and featuring a glorious shot of the Totenkopf.

The picture had been taken in spring or summer, so that the outline of the skull was perfectly clear: the domed forehead, the empty eye sockets, the gaping mouth. The Death's Head. The symbol of the Totenkopfverbände – the most feared of all Himmler's SS divisions – who had not only policed the newly occupied areas, Austria, the Sudetenland, Czechoslovakia, and carried out the executions and deportations, but had also guarded the concentration camps.

Despite the trappings, an air of informality hung over the proceed-ings. There were perhaps two dozen people in the room, of various ages and, it appeared, social backgrounds, dressed in a variety of clothes, from dark suits to pullovers, jeans and open-neck shirts.

Chairs had been arranged in a rough semicircle facing the fireplace, and people were settling into every available space with glasses of wine in their hands, nibbling at little cocktail snacks. It might have been the monthly meeting of the Christian Union.

In front of the fireplace, in the shadow of the mountain, as it were, stood Gordon, chest out, back as straight as he could make it, eyes shining with an almost religious fervour. He was evidently about to give a lecture, for he had a long ruler in one hand and kept looking at something to his right. It was out of Miles's sight line, but he guessed a blackboard easel had been erected and some kind of map or diagram fixed to it. Miles silently cursed all double-glazing salesmen.

He recognised one or two of the people from the photograph. The fat man was there, Cunningham-Walker, dressed in regulation City wear: double-breasted pin-striped suit, striped shirt, gold watch chain. So was his brother-in-law, the Earl of Deighton, in a blazer with big regimental buttons and the dark-blue and maroon striped tie of the Brigade of Guards.

As soon as everyone was seated, Gordon began talking. Miles crouched there in the dark for a long time. If he had been able to see what it was that Gordon was pointing to, he would at least have had something concrete to focus on: something on which to make an assessment, a plan of campaign even. Instead, all he could do was look at those stupid, trusting faces, fixed on that little man with his mad teeth and his gin-and-tonic moustache, like last-ditch invalids at a faith-healing rally. And the more he looked at them, the more angry they made him. Surely there was something he could do. Run down to Balham High Road and grab as many people as he could lay hands on – blacks, Asians, beggars, young professionals, old soldiers – and bring them all back and show them the things that were going on in their midst. Lead them into the room in a charge and wipe the smug expressions off their silly faces. Find a telephone that hadn't been vandalised and ring up Anne Crosthwaite and Scotland Yard and Special Branch and the local police station and report what was going on. Do something. Anything. He could feel the frustration surging inside him, wrenching his stomach, like a bad dose of indigestion.

Ten minutes went by. Questions were asked and answers given. And then the atmosphere in the room changed. As if at a prearranged signal, everyone jumped to their feet. Backs were straightened, jaw-lines hardened, eyes gleamed, and suddenly the room was a forest of stiff-armed salutes. He looked across at Gordon. He also had his right arm raised, but bent at the elbow, the fingers at shoulder level, like a man taking an oath. And on his face there was a smile. A smile without humour and without compassion. The crocodile smile of a thousand newsreels – in Nuremberg, in Cable Street, in Baghdad. The smile of a man with a moustache and a mission ...

'Right, *you!*'

A hand clamped itself on to his right shoulder. It was big and strong and meant business. Miles struggled to get to his feet but he couldn't move. He twisted his head and looked up. The face that looked down at him was young: thirty at the most. The hair was curly and cut short, the shirt was striped and open at the neck, the pullover V-necked and bright red. He had shoulders like a wardrobe.

'What the hell do you think you're doing?' The voice was loud and assured; the accent, public school.

'Who are you?' said Miles.

'I happen to live next door, actually,' he said. 'Chap over the road saw you skulking about and gave me a bell. He said you'd been here for ages. What the hell do you think you're up to?'

Miles said, 'Do you know the people who live here?'

'Not to have drinks with, but we chat from time to time over the fence. Why?'

'But you know their name.'

'Of course. We're neighbours. We're on the Neighbourhood Watch together.'

'Do you happen to know what else they're involved in?'

The man frowned at him. 'What the hell's all this about? I'm the one who should be asking the questions.'

Miles said easily, 'You certainly should. You'd better take a look.' He indicated the gap in the curtain.

'Why should I?'

'Just look,' said Miles.

Still maintaining his hold, the man leaned forward and peered into the room. Seconds later, he stepped back. 'What's so unusual?' he said.

'I'd have thought that was obvious,' said Miles.

'Not to me,' said the man, 'but then I'm only a dimwitted merchant banker.'

Miles looked pointedly at the hand on his shoulder. 'Would you mind?'

The grip relaxed slightly and Miles stood up. He took a step towards the window and looked in. The portraits had gone, Eigerhubel had vanished, *The Chinese Girl* was back over the fireplace, the chairs were ranged round the walls and a drinks party was in progress.

'Well ...?'

Miles managed to bluff his way out of it eventually. He was afraid he might have laid on the incredulous innocence a bit thick: 'This *is* Beechcroft Avenue, isn't it? ... I *thought* I must have got the wrong address ... One of those silly mistakes ... *So* sorry ...' But the man bought it. He said he wouldn't take matters further, and Miles decided to quit while he was ahead. There was nothing to be gained from lengthy explanations. Both of them had seen what they'd seen. End of story.

Miles walked up Chestnut Grove. If his sense of direction was sound, he reckoned he would eventually arrive at Balham High Road. It wasn't ideal taxi country, but there was probably an underground station not far away.

Only one car passed him the whole length of Chestnut Grove. It was a white Renault Clio with two young men in it. Miles never gave it a second glance.

If he had, he might have noticed that, when he got to Balham High Road, the same Renault was parked opposite Balham underground station, and that now only one young man was sitting in it.

17

It was nearly ten by the time Miles had struggled back to Prince of Wales Drive, using a combination of public transport and urban yomping. On the way he called in at the Ming Garden and ordered a quarter of crispy duck, prawns with ginger and a large portion of fried rice, to take away. Then he went to the off-licence and picked out a modest bottle of St Véran. He let himself in by the side-entrance, went straight up to the flat and slumped, exhausted, in front of the television. He ate the prawns, followed by the duck, and drank half the wine. Then he went into the kitchen, found a banana, an apple and a tangerine and sliced them into a glass mixing bowl. He poured half a glass of the burgundy over it and little cream, and ate it out of the bowl. No point in creating extra washing-up. He found a packet of Douwe Egberts at the back of the food cupboard, made himself a jug of strong coffee, poured a couple of fingers of Armagnac into a brandy balloon and sat on the sofa, warming the spirit with his hands and breathing in the mellow fumes. He closed his eyes. Then he stood up, crossed to his desk and picked up Stein's book. He took it back to the sofa and opened it at the chapter entitled 'Mobilisation of Foreign Nationals'.

He thumbed through until he reached the last section – the one covering the recruitment of the British Legion: the 'Flight of Fancy', as the author termed it. 'There is no evidence that it ever attained a status other than that of a propaganda device.' The sentence had resonated in his head a hundred times since he had first read it on that eventful afternoon in 'Hist. European War II'. Evidence? What evidence? Presumably the evidence that survived those last confused, panic-driven days of the war, when the Nazis with the most damning secrets to hide were as busy destroying evidence and covering their tracks as they were trying to organise safe escape routes. The *surviving* evidence, but almost certainly not the only evidence. If men like Amery and Parrington had been such devoted disciples of Hitler and the Nazi cause that they had been prepared to join the SS, why would they not have gone the whole way and played their full part in eliminating the Jews and Communists and homosexuals and mental defectives who were such an ugly blemish on an otherwise beautiful landscape?

Of course there was no actual evidence that any of them had joined the Death's Head division and of course General Hollies would pooh-pooh the very idea. A man in his position could hardly be expected to do otherwise. But what would he say now? A roomful of would-be Nazis, including one who went back a long way; a secret meeting dominated by a picture of a mountain called Totenkopf ... It wasn't evidence. A newspaper lawyer would almost certainly look askance at it. But it was good enough for Miles. As a working basis, anyway.

He picked up the telephone and dialled the Hollies's number. He often rang quite late in the evening; the general was usually up and about. They always talked about Elizabeth. Never the Army, which was really the only other thing they had in common. They would discuss the latest medical assessment, how they thought she was progressing, what her prospects were for the future. Sometimes they just chatted. The old boy seemed to welcome it. This evening, though, he sounded distracted and slightly irritable.

'How was Norfolk?' he enquired.

Miles described the incident with the tigers, but not in any great detail, dismissing it with muttered phrases like 'silly accident' ... 'sort of thing that could happen to anyone' ... 'all's well that ends well ... ' He didn't want to make too much of it and run the risk of upsetting Elizabeth's mother, and possibly Elizabeth herself – though whether any information got through that wall of silence he never really knew.

The general was clearly shocked. A salvo of questions was fired in rapid succession. How? What? Where? When? Miles responded to each one with calm, laconic assurance. Satisfied that he had covered every angle, the general concluded that Miles had been right, and that it was an unfortunate accident with a happy conclusion.

'That badge I was telling you about the other day,' Miles said.

There was a non-committal grunt from the other end of the line.

'I came across another one just like it.'

'Oh?'

'In the library at West Keating. I was waiting for the manager at the time. I was browsing through the shelves and I came across these old photographs, including one of a group of Diabolo members sitting around in the clubhouse. The badge must have been tucked in amongst them somewhere. It fell out on to the floor. It's exactly the same. Same colour, same Union Jack, same "England".'

'Odd coincidence,' said the general.

'Not really,' said Miles. 'The doctor in Switzerland had been given his by a Diabolo member. And Archie Lambourn was a Diabolo member. You must agree, it's quite intriguing.'

'Not to me,' said the general. 'All this is past history as far as I'm concerned. I thought I'd made that clear.'

'You did, sir,' said Miles, 'and I don't want to keep harping on about this, but, with the greatest respect, your judgment is based on something that happened nearly half a century ago. I'm talking about something that's happening now. I don't know what this badge stands for or why, but I'm more and more convinced there's a plot afoot: something to do with Eigerhubel and the Diabolo Club. Possibly tied in with their 75th anniversary celebrations and possibly involving old Nazis. One of the files was marked "Diabolo Project". Unfortunately, I didn't have time to investigate further, but I'm determined to find out what's going on.'

There was silence on the other end of the line.

'Hallo?' said Miles. 'Are you still there, sir?'

'Yes, I'm still here,' he said. 'What can I say? Leaving aside your dubious working methods, I have to say that I have never heard such a load of unadulterated guano in my life. I took you for an intelligent man, Miles, but frankly you'd be better off giving up serious journalism and writing shockers like that fellow, whatsisname.'

'This isn't some wild fantasy I've dreamed up,' Miles said, stung by the general's harsh words. 'I do have evidence.'

'Evidence?' said the general. 'What evidence?'

'The photographs,' said Miles. 'And the badge.'

'A badge which might be anything, and a couple of photographs of skiers enjoying themselves on holiday. You call that evidence?'

'I agree they don't prove anything in themselves, but in the light of what I saw earlier this evening ...'

'Go on.'

So he did. General Hollies listened in silence.

'Well,' he said when Miles had finished. 'What do you want me to say?'

'That perhaps the British Free Corps isn't past history after all.'

'Look, Miles,' said the general. 'It's late and I'm tired. I've already told you what I think, and what I know. I was there when these matters were cleared up. In some cases, I was personally responsible. If you think that, because a bunch of nincompoops choose to spend their evenings in a front room in Balham attempting to recreate some ghastly period of which they have no knowledge and no experience, I am going to start reconsidering judgments that I made nearly fifty years ago, you've got another think coming.'

'As a matter of historical accuracy, I happen to know that one of them was active in the British Fascist movement before the war, and could well have been a member of the British SS.'

'Quite honestly,' said the general, 'I couldn't give a bull's tit. The one thing that has always distinguished the British soldier from any other nationality is his loyalty. You have no business questioning the judgment of a superior officer in a matter of which you know bugger all. Good night.'

The line went dead.

Miles replaced the receiver. He went across to his desk, opened the top drawer, took out the two Diabolo photographs and laid them down side by side. Then he took the badge and placed it equidistantly between them. He stared at them for a long time.

Then he rang an Earls Court number ...

'When can we meet?' There was a quiet, controlled urgency in Paul Weekley's voice.

'Tomorrow sometime. Why?'

'Do you know the Chelsea Arts Club?'

'Of course.'

'Meet me there at 6.30 and bring all the stuff with you.'

176

'What should I do about Anne Crosthwaite?'

'Nothing,' said Weekley. 'Not at this stage anyway.'

There was a knock on the door.

'Who is it?'

'Package for you, Mr Maltby.'

'What sort of package?'

'Special delivery.'

'Is that you, Mr Reeves? Leave it outside, would you? I'll pick it up in a minute.'

'They want you to sign for it.'

'I've got to go,' he told Weekley, and replaced the receiver.

He went across and turned the key in the Banham. He released the catch and began to ease the door open.

'What the …?'

The impact caught him hard on the left shoulder, knocking him off balance. Schilt Face was the first one through, followed by a younger man in a raincoat and tattered jeans and trainers. He had a long, thin face, dark eyes and long, dark hair. He looked like Daniel Day-Lewis.

Schilt Face put his hand against Miles's chest and pushed him backwards into the room. Miles stumbled and fell against the sofa. The man stood there, looking down at him, his hands folded across his groin.

'Shut the door,' he said, without looking round. The accent was as heavy as his shoulders. East European of some sort.

The younger man did as he was told. His eyes darted hither and thither, his tongue flicked back and forth across his lips, his fingers picked at the skin round his right thumb. He looked very unhappy.

'What the hell do you want?' Miles said. 'Who are you anyway? Secret Service? Some neo-Nazi group? What?'

'Where is it?'

'Where's what?'

'You know.'

'Sorry. I don't.'

'We know you took it.'

'Took what, for God's sake? What are you talking about?'

He hoped it wouldn't come to a fight. He'd been inter-regimental

177

middleweight champion three years running and he reckoned he could probably still handle himself pretty well – but only where there were rules and opponents went about things the same way. Trouble was, outside the ring anything could happen. There were no rules and no referee to step in when things got rough and no one's hand was going to get held up at the end.

'From the doctor's surgery. You took it. We want it back.'

'You're wrong,' Miles told him. 'I didn't take it. I would have taken it, but someone had got there first. All they left was a broken frame.'

'Frame?'

'Yes, the frame it had been in when the doctor showed it to me. The one the nurse saw me looking at. With the funny German writing.'

'What German writing? What are you talking about?'

Miles was aware that somewhere behind him Daniel Day-Lewis was padding quietly round the room. He turned his head.

'You're wasting your time,' he told him.

He turned back to the older man. 'It was in a frame, right? A small wooden frame. There was something written underneath in old-fashioned German script. The doctor, or whoever he was, said he'd been given it by an old friend as a memento. He said it was an Olympic skiing badge ...'

'Alex?'

Schilt Face spun round. Daniel was pointing at Miles's bedside table. Schilt Face walked across. He leaned down and carefully, almost reverently, he picked up the rose between thumb and forefinger. He took it across to the window and held it up against the morning light, just as Miles had done that morning in the surgery. He turned it this way and that and sighed. Then he looked at Miles and smiled.

'Thank you,' he said, and gave a little nod. Daniel turned and moved towards the door. Alex was a few steps behind him. If they were expecting Miles to try and stop them, they gave no sign of it. Neither did Miles. He was busy making a series of lightning calculations.

He concluded that Daniel would probably not be much use in a fight and that Alex looked tougher than he really was. Intimidation

178

was a good weapon, especially when combined with surprise. However, when deployed against a trained individual, it needed to be backed up with effective force. Miles reckoned that, if he was right about Daniel, he could probably deal with Alex on his own. At all events, he had no intention of allowing two strangers to come barging into his home uninvited and walk off with something that had become precious to him. Strictly speaking, it didn't belong to him, but he had no reason to suppose that it belonged to them either.

Hands clenched together, shoulders bunched, he stepped forward and caught Alex a clubbing blow on the back of the head. He'd been aiming for a point just below his skull, but at the last moment Alex moved slightly to his left and the blow landed too high to be completely effective. But it was enough to make him stagger, and Miles was able to get in another shot while Alex was still off-balance. He didn't take long to recover, though. With his right arm bent, he swivelled round and drove his elbow upwards, catching Miles on the side of the face. Miles shook his head and stepped back just as Alex crossed with a left, grazing him slightly. Miles realised he'd need to react quicker if he wasn't going to get caught. Alex stumbled and Miles hit him on the nose. It started to bleed. Alex swung again with his right hand. Miles rocked back and let it go by, then stepped in behind it and jabbed him hard in the ribs, twice. Alex grunted with the pain and bent forward. Miles moved in and aimed a jab at his head, but, as he did so, Alex straightened up and his skull caught Miles's chin. Miles's head snapped back and Alex, skull lowered, butted him hard in the stomach. Miles staggered back against the right arm of the sofa and fell sideways on to the floor. Alex reached sideways for the brass lamp on the little table at the other end of the sofa. He yanked at it and the wires flew out of the plug. Holding it like a club, Alex swung a blow at Miles's head. Miles threw himself sideways and the heavy base thudded into the old leather upholstery.

Miles had been right about the younger man. He was no fighter. He stood near the door, moving back and forth, side to side, in an agitated way like a schoolboy watching a needle house match who's bursting for a pee but can't bear to miss a second of play.

Alex moved forward to seize the lamp base and, as he did so, Miles

179

rolled back, brought his right knee back and drove his foot hard into Alex's midriff. Alex staggered backwards and Miles struggled to his feet. Frankly he wasn't enjoying himself a bit. He felt like a highly trained fencer who enters a serious competition, only to find himself up against someone who thinks he's Errol Flynn. He was beginning to have a nasty feeling that things could go either way.

He was on his feet by now and dancing. He put in another couple of quick jabs to Alex's ribs and followed them up with a straight left to the face and a right uppercut. It was classic textbook stuff – except that the textbook recommends the wearing of boxing gloves. Without them, a jaw can be as hard as a brick wall. *Don't break your hand*, Miles told himself. *Don't hit him on the head.* He circled Alex clockwise, hands up, feet shuffling, left foot forward. He tried a classic combination: left jab, left hook, right cross. It worked. Alex's nose was beginning to look red and puffy. Blood ran down his upper lip. A mouse was starting under his left eye. Miles was easily winning on points. As long as they remained on their feet, he could probably continue hitting Alex as often and as hard as he liked. Trouble was, there was no referee to jump in and hold his arm up. Miles dropped his right shoulder and drove his fist into Alex's stomach. Alex grunted. He straightened up and Miles caught him with another straight left. It looked to be a question of which gave out first, Alex's spirit or Miles's fists.

In the end it was Alex who made the decision. He threw his hands up in front of his face in an attempt to ward off Miles's well-aimed punches.

'Go,' he shouted.

Daniel stood there as if nailed to the floor. Alex shouted again. Daniel edged backwards towards the door.

'Go on! Get out! Go!'

Daniel turned and ran. Alex threw one more half-hearted punch in Miles's direction, then ducked away and ran after him. Miles stood there, taking in gulps of air. God, he was unfit. The pain was beginning to seep into his hands as the bruises swelled and spread. He shook them and swore loudly. He walked to the door. He could hear the footsteps running down the stone staircase. He closed the door, double-locked it, put the chain across and went into the

180

bathroom. He filled the washbasin with cold water and dipped his hands into it, uttering little yelps of pain.

He soaked them for a good five minutes, flexing his fingers and rotating his wrists, while he peered at himself in the mirror. A bruise was developing nicely round his right eye where Alex had caught him with his elbow. It was about the only good blow that Alex had landed. A few more like that and Miles could have been in real trouble.

He took a flannel, dunked it in cold water and held it against his eye. It felt good. He went back into the sitting room and poured himself a large drink. The place didn't look too bad, considering. The sofa would need reupholstering, but that was no bad thing. He pulled the lamp out of the stuffing and placed it back on the little table. He sat down and sipped at the whisky. He held the glass up to the light and it was then that he remembered the rose. Alex had been holding it when he first tried to leave. Miles couldn't remember him putting anything in his pocket or throwing it to Daniel. There hadn't been time. So, either he was still holding it or ...

Miles walked round the room. He couldn't see it anywhere. He got down on his hands and knees and looked under the sofa. There was something there. Then he stretched out his arm. His fingers closed over it and he struggled to his feet. He opened his fist and there it was, nestling in his palm: beauty after an evening of ugliness.

He held it up to the light, as he had done a dozen times before. For the first time he noticed that surrounding the insect there were a number of little swirls, as if the creature was struggling to get out. Miles sympathised.

18

At half past nine the following morning, Miles rang Mary Morgan.

For as long as anybody could remember, Mary had run the press office at Eberhardt's – Fine Art Dealers and Auctioneers. Her enduring enthusiasm, charm and unfailing reliability were celebrated wherever freelance men and women of taste met in the world, and rightly so. In the unlikely event of Eberhardt's not being able to boast the world's greatest expert on any given subject, she would cheerfully and unhesitatingly suggest that the enquirer try so-and-so at Christie's or Sotheby's or Bonhams or Phillips. If Grub Street were ever to add canonisation to its long list of duties, Mary Morgan's name would be at the head of the list.

As well as being an honorary saint, Mary was miraculously available. She never seemed to take holidays, or go home early, or even out to lunch. She was always at her desk at nine in the morning and apparently remained there until seven in the evening, come wind, come snow, come bomb scares, come the end of world, probably. On the very rare occasions when she didn't pick up the telephone herself, she would call back within minutes. You could depend on it.

'Press Office.' The voice was deep and rich and reassuring.

'Mary, it's Miles Maltby.'

'Yes, Miles.'

'Amber, Mary.'

'Jolyon Grant-Forbes,' she said. 'Head of Jewellery and Precious Stones. Do you want to come in, or would a phone call do?'

'It's quite a complicated story,' Miles told her.

'I'll get on to Jolyon and call you back.'

Mary Morgan always did what she said she would do.

'What time would suit you?' she said. 'It's now 9.30. Shall we say eleven?'

'Let's,' said Miles.

* * *

Jolyon Grant-Forbes was plump and fortyish and wore a dove-grey suit and a pale blue bow tie with white spots. He had a large, round head like a cheese and a very small face. He had wet, rather blubbery lips and his little eyes were languid behind round-framed glasses. The whole thing was topped off with a small amount of curly fair hair. He sat, neat and prim, at an old-fashioned roll-top desk in a tiny office on the third floor of Eberhardt's main salerooms in Green Street, Mayfair, surrounded by a muddle of reference books, old sales catalogues, transparencies and paperwork of every description. A space had been cleared in the middle of the desk and lying in it was a single droplet of amber. About two inches long and an inch wide at its broadest point, it was paler than the rose and milkier, less transparent, and there was no insect inside it, but it glowed almost as warmly.

Jolyon said, 'How would you like to tackle this? Would you like to ask me questions, or shall I give you my standard lecturette, and then you can get me to fill in the areas which particularly interest you.'

He spoke with a polite, impersonal drawl. Miles wondered if he had a different voice for his friends, but doubted it.

'I think the latter,' said Miles.

'Right. Well. As you probably know, amber is the fossil resin of extinct coniferous trees that flourished along the Baltic coast forty million years ago or more. The amber deposit forms a seam two or three feet deep below the clay of the sea bed. This gets ploughed up by the jagged bottoms of icebergs and the chunks get caught up in seaweed, which is in turn ripped out by storms and dragged inshore. In the old days fishermen used to wade out into the sea and pull in the flotsam with things that looked like large shrimping nets and then pick it over in search of amber.

'It was thanks to amber that the Baltics first became wealthy. The early tribes used it for trade and barter and it travelled all over the world. Amber has been found at Mycenae and in the tombs of some

183

of the Pharaohs. The treasure of Tutankhamun, for example, includes an amber necklace. When Homer describes the electron on the Greek warriors' shields, he probably meant amber. He was certainly the first one to dub the Baltic shore "the Amber Coast".

'As you might imagine, amber is the stuff of legend. According to Greek myth, it was the congealed tears of the sister of Phaethon which were turned to trees while she was weeping for his death. A Lithuanian legend tells of a queen of the Baltic named Jurate who lived in an underwater palace made out of amber. She was about to be married to the God of Water, Patrimpas, but she fell madly in love with a mortal fisherman called Kastytis and used to visit him in his hut at sunset every night for a year. One day, the God of Thunder, Perkunas, got to hear about it and in a rage hurled down bolts of lightning. One of them killed Jurate and shattered her amber palace into ten thousand pieces. He then punished Kastytis by tying him to a rock on the sea bed, and they say that when the west wind blows you can still hear him moaning for his lost love and when the wind dies down the shore is littered with fragments of Jurate's palace.'

Jolyon laughed. 'But I'm sure this isn't the sort of thing you want to hear. You probably want to know how much amber is worth, what it fetches at auction and so on.'

'I want to know everything you can tell me,' Miles told him.

'OK,' said Jolyon. 'Well, stop me when you've had enough. On a more practical note, amber has been worn ever since the Stone Age, that's to say around 9,000 BC, both as an ornament and as a cure for countless illnesses, including asthma, rheumatism and various internal disorders. In Roman times women wore amber amulets as a protection against witchcraft. The German name for amber, by the way, is *bernstein*. This derives from the Low German word *bernen*, to burn, and dates back to the Middle Ages when powdered amber was much prized in Germany as an aromatic incense. There are various materials resembling amber, notably the reddish Burmite, from Burma, but, as I've already explained, the principal source of classic amber is along the shores of the Samland coast of what used to be East Prussia, near what used to be called Königsberg but is now Kaliningrad.

'Basically there are two sorts of amber: sea amber, which is washed up on to the shore by the action of the sea and can drift for miles. You can sometimes pick up amber as far away as the Suffolk coast. And then there's pit amber, which is mined in open pits from deposits of glauconite sand, or 'blue earth', as it's known. I've got a booklet with all this in it. I'll give you a copy before you go.'

Miles put down his notebook and pencil and smiled with relief.

'Amber comes in a variety of colours and consistencies, from transparent to translucent. It's normally yellow or brown, but can be reddish or whitish. Some amber is clear, some is turbid with gas bubbles – or bastard, as it's known in the business – and some of it can look just like goose fat. The Germans call that *flohmig*. If the pieces are too small to be gems in their own right, there is a process, invented in Vienna, whereby they can be welded together under a pressure of 120,000 pounds a square inch. You can usually tell pressed amber – or ambroid – because of the differing margins of clarity and the fact that bubbles are elongated due to the flow under pressure, but in some cases this is difficult to detect except under long-wave ultra-violet light. Cloudy amber can be clarified by heating it in rape seed oil which penetrates the air spaces that cause cloudiness. However, this can have the effect of producing crack marks which look rather like nasturtium leaves. Amber workers call them "sun spangles". Is this the sort of thing you want to know? There's yards more of it. I can go on all day if you want.'

'Tell me about the flies,' said Miles.

'Ah yes. The flies in amber. Well, these are simply insects that got caught up in the resin as it dripped down. A clear piece of amber with a perfect insect entombed inside is highly prized over one that has more mundane inclusions such as moss or lichen or pine needles. Not least because it provides proof that what you're buying is the real thing. You'd be surprised how realistic some imitation amber can be. Glass imitations tend to be cold to the touch, whereas amber feels warm. Even so, an expert can be taken in. But obviously if the insect is too large, like a moth or a beetle, and the tomb is too clear, then that's usually a dead giveaway. Insects that have been caught in genuine resin tended to struggle, and their death throes produced swirls in the viscous resin which is still clear all these millions of years later. I'm not going too fast for you, I hope?'

185

'Absolutely not,' said Miles. 'Now, you say that a piece of amber with an insect in it is more valuable than one without ...'

'I said it *can* be. It depends on the insect.'

'How much can one expect to pay for a good piece of carved amber with an insect in it?'

Jolyon laughed. 'How long is a piece of string? Mounted or plain?'

'Plain.'

'Could be several hundred pounds.'

'Not a fortune, then?'

'As I say, it depends.' A hint of testiness had entered Jolyon's voice.

Miles reached into his coat pocket. 'A piece like this, for example.'

He placed the rose on the desk. Jolyon's manner changed abruptly. Inasmuch as a barrel of lard can be said to stiffen, he stiffened. His eyes almost filled the round frames of his glasses. He leaned forward and very gently took the rose between the finger and thumb of his right hand. With his other hand, his eyes still fixed on the rose, he fumbled for the switch on the desk lamp. He eventually located it and flicked it on. He held the rose up against the light and turned it round, gazing into it from every possible angle, eyes shining, mouth ajar. Finally he looked at Miles.

'May I ask where you acquired this?'

Miles shrugged. 'Someone gave it to me. A friend. Why?'

'It's very unusual,' he murmured. 'You don't happen to know where your friend acquired it, I suppose?'

Miles shook his head. 'Unusual in what way exactly?' he asked him.

Jolyon continued to turn the stone against the light, emitting the occasional sigh and grunt of approval. Finally he said, 'The subject matter in itself is not that extraordinary. Being a resin and therefore much softer than stone, amber lends itself to all sorts of shapes and designs. Flowers, fruit, fish, animals. But the workmanship here is quite remarkable. I have rarely seen such attention to detail. Look at the delicate way the carver has produced the individual petals. They're so precise and yet so natural. The sepals are beautifully defined. Even the stamens have been picked out. Fascinating ...'

'How would you rate the fly?' Miles asked him.

'As perfect as any I have ever seen,' he murmured. 'Excellent death throes. The swirls are quite charming.'

186

'I'm glad he did his duty,' said Miles. 'Or is it a she?'

Jolyon was not in the market for pleasantries. 'It's also a very clear piece,' he said. 'Lovely honey colour.' He rubbed a thumb over the surface. 'It's been around for a long time, by the feel of it.'

'Seventy million years is a long time in anybody's book.'

'I meant in its present form,' he said. 'I should guess this was carved three hundred years ago, maybe more. And you say you have no idea how it came into your friend's possession?' He emphasised the word 'friend', as if it were a euphemism.

'None,' Miles said. 'Perhaps you could seek a second opinion.'

'I *am* a second opinion,' said Jolyon tartly.

'Sorry. It's just that I want to know exactly how valuable it is.'

'I'm not absolutely clear why you have come to see me,' he said. 'As I understood it from Mary Morgan, you are researching an article on amber for a newspaper. Is that right or have I got it wrong? Are you here for quite a different reason?'

Miles said, 'If you mean did I worm my way in under false pretences, the answer is yes, I did. It is true that I am gathering material for a feature. But not about amber. It may finish up that way, but that's not what it was about when I started. Recent events lead me to think that amber – or, at least, this particular piece of amber – is a more important ingredient in the story than I had supposed. I'm sorry I can't be more specific at this stage. I'm not sure I know what's going on myself. All I need to know at this point is what this piece of amber is and why two men I've never met in my life before should be so desperate to get their hands on it.'

'You mean, someone's tried to steal it from you?'

'It's rather more complicated than that, but, basically, yes.'

'How interesting.' He pronounced all four syllables.

Jolyon held up the stone and subjected it to another long and detailed scrutiny. Occasionally he emitted a non-committal hum; once he murmured, 'I wonder,' but did not elaborate. After what seemed to Miles like hours, he put the stone down and steepled his fingers under his nose.

'To be perfectly honest with you,' he said at last, 'I have no idea what this particular piece would fetch at auction. Any figure I give you would be misleading, for the simple reason that I think what you've got here is a part, and only a tiny part, of something else. I don't know for certain what that something else is, but if it's what I *think* it might be, then it could be worth any figure anyone wants to put on it. I'm talking now about the complete artefact. The rose itself is only valuable inasmuch as it could lead whoever possesses it *to* that artefact.'

Miles frowned. 'What is this artefact exactly?'

Jolyon lowered his hands from his face and held them up, palm outwards, against his chest. 'I'm only saying that I *think* I know what it might be. I go no further than that.' His face was very solemn. 'If I am right, it could turn out to be one of the greatest discoveries since Howard Carter opened up Tutankhamun's tomb in 1924.'

'Heavens,' said Miles.

Jolyon said, 'I may be quite wrong, of course. Believe it or not, even at Eberhardt's we sometimes make mistakes.'

'I promise I won't hold you to anything,' Miles told him. 'Tell me what you think it *might* be.'

'Frankly, I would rather ...'

'For God's sake, two men forced their way into my flat last night and tried to make off with it. Luckily, they didn't succeed.'

'Good God,' said Jolyon. 'Who were they?'

'It doesn't matter who they were: it's what they were after that concerns me.'

'Look,' said Jolyon. 'Before any of us go jumping to any conclusions we might regret, there is someone I think you should go and talk to first. She is not a professional expert, but she knows more about this subject than anyone alive. As I say, I may be quite wrong and she may send you off with a flea in your ear. But if I'm right, and I think I am, she will have a story to tell you that is bigger and better than anything you could possibly be working on.'

'She?'

'She lives in Chelsea. I could easily give her a call.'

* * *

Weekley was sitting alone at a corner table in the Arts Club bar when Miles arrived. In front of him was an open bottle of white burgundy

188

and two glasses. One already had wine in it. As Miles entered, Weekley filled the other glass and topped up his own. There wasn't much small talk: they were both keen to get down to business.

Miles's glass was nearly empty when Weekley finally looked up from the photographs.

'Well?'

Weekley sat back and drank some wine. 'Well,' he said. 'By themselves, they don't tell me anything very much. But then I spend a lot of my time staring at jigsaw pieces that don't fit together and for which I don't have the rest of the puzzle; and, even if I did, I could easily find they're not part of the same puzzle anyway. Another problem posed by loose pieces is not knowing what part of the puzzle they fit into, so it's almost impossible to assess their comparative importance. For instance, are we looking here at the features of the central character, or merely a bit of background landscape? As individual pieces in a puzzle, they pose more questions than they answer. Take the badge, for example. If this man Gordon lives in the West Highlands, why does it have "England" under the flag and not "Britain"? I'd also like to know who the figure is in the Diabolo Club picture; the one who concealed himself behind Lambourn when the shutter was activated. It's obvious that he did it deliberately, but why? What did he have to hide that his fellow Diabolicals didn't?'

'His face, presumably.'

'But why? The club is full of distinguished members and several of them are in the picture, apparently quite happy to have their presence recorded. What's so special about him that he feels the need to pull away at the last moment?'

'There's something vaguely familiar about him,' said Miles. 'The outline of his head, the set of his shoulders, something ...'

'Having said which,' said Weekley, 'all we're talking about here is a couple of perfectly innocuous group photographs of members of a well-known skiing club relaxing and enjoying themselves.'

'Except that one of them happens to have been taken in a front room in Balham where these same innocuous members were to be seen only a few hours ago taking part in a mini-Nazi rally. That alone would surely warrant a call to Miss Crosthwaite. Never mind the duplicate badge, the files and the curious events at West Keating.'

Weekley pulled a face.

Miles leaned forward. 'The activities of political groups operating against the national interest: isn't that what the security services are there to monitor?' he persisted.

'I'm sorry to play the killjoy,' said Weekley, 'but the fact of the matter is that this country is seething with small, fervent groups meeting in front rooms, and back rooms for all I know, bent on action for or against some perceived iniquity or other: a stretch of motorway through an area of outstanding natural beauty; the use of animals for scientific experiments; racial discrimination; the council tax; VAT on books; cuts in the National Health Service; factory farming; the power of the left; the power of the right; the closure of this; the opening of that ... Quite honestly, the security services do not have the time or the resources or the will to investigate every pressure group in the land, well-meaning or otherwise.'

Miles interrupted: 'If I may say so, I think that the very real possibility of a pro-Nazi faction harbouring a British war criminal here in London is a rather more serious matter than whether or not a rare species of grass is under threat from a new motorway.'

Weekley's genial features hardened suddenly. 'Look,' he said. 'There are neo-fascist organisations busying themselves all over Europe. If it isn't Schoenhuber and his Republicans bashing up immigrant workers in Dresden, or pro-Franco demonstrations in Madrid, it's the National Front stirring it up in the East End of London, and Alessandra Mussolini and her lot gaining ground in Naples. Luckily, in the absence of major financial resources, it's all pretty marginal stuff. So far, anyway. Quite honestly, people like Anne Crosthwaite have got all their time cut out keeping tabs on the IRA without worrying whether some clapped-out old Mosleyite haranguing a dozen disciples in a front room in Balham might or might not be hatching a Hitlerian plot in a ski hut in the Swiss Alps.'

'Is that the way you see it?'

'I have no picture at all at this stage: just a ball of different-coloured threads with dozens of ends. Nor does she, mind. But then her job is only to pick up the bits and pieces and make the ball: ours is to unravel it and try to marry up all the little ends and make one long multi-coloured narrative thread. It's a totally different discipline.'

'I'm not sure if I've got the stamina for this job,' said Miles. 'I feel like a hundred-metres runner who's blundered into a five-thousand-metre steeplechase.'

'The trouble is,' said Weekley, 'you're trying to tackle every obstacle at once. Take one jump at a time. Try and find out exactly what this badge is.'

Miles picked up his wine and held it against the light. He swirled the pale-yellow liquid round in the glass. 'To tell you the truth,' he said, 'I'm beginning to wonder if the badge is what these people have been after all along.'

19

The next morning, Miles walked to Chelsea. It was a cold, crystalline day. The grass in Battersea Park was still white with hoar frost and the pale sun glinted off the river as he crossed Albert Bridge. The only blot on this otherwise perfect landscape was the prospect of having to share the morning with Jolyon Grant-Forbes.

He had tried every low trick he knew in his efforts to put him off. He'd even gone so far as to say that he really couldn't interview people when there was a third person in the room. But Jolyon was not a man who was easily fobbed off with cheap psychological ploys. He made it quite clear that Mrs Rogers was his discovery and he wasn't about to let some pushy hack have her all to himself: not even for an hour. Miles, on the other hand, prided himself that he had never suffered the slightest twinge of professional jealousy. He believed in giving credit where credit was due. If it weren't for Jolyon, the name of Mrs Rogers would never have swum into his ken. And yet, for some unaccountable reason, the thought that Joylon was going to be there too, fat and smug and proprietorial, irritated him.

He crossed the Embankment, cut down Cheyne Walk, in front of the Eight Bells, then turned right up Cheyne Row, and right again into Glebe Place.

The number of the house was not advertised, but he recognised the wooden door from Jolyon's description. There was a modern entryphone set into the wall just to the right. He jabbed the button. A man's voice answered. Jolyon, the perfect host. Miles lowered his mouth to the grille. 'It's Miles Maltby.'

The lock buzzed irritably. Miles pushed the door open and stepped through. He found himself at the side of a small cottage overlooking a walled garden about thirty foot square with a lawn and beds and climbing plants. A number of trees had been strategically planted: a red maple, a *gleditschia*, a prunus of some sort. They didn't look much now, but in the summer they would provide a screen against the outside world and create an oasis of green tranquillity. If Miles had stepped through the looking glass, he could not have been more surprised.

From the gate, snuggled beneath an arbour covered with creepers, a flagged path led to a small terrace. A rose clambered over the front door. Miles went to grasp the rusty knocker and, as he did so, the door was opened – not by Jolyon, but by a short stocky figure with close-cropped white hair and a face like a chubby von Stroheim. He was dressed in a white shirt and black tie, with a black waistcoat and a green apron over black trousers.

'Mrs Rogers is expecting me,' said Miles.

The man gave an odd, stiff little bow, stepped to one side and gestured him in. 'Please.' The voice was deep, the accent foreign. It carried echoes of a distant birth.

The small hallway had a stone-flagged floor over which someone had thrown a couple of thin, faded prayer rugs. On the left-hand wall was a half-length mirror in a chipped gilt frame. Below it, a narrow table was piled high with opened envelopes, old newspapers and discarded bills. A narrow passageway led towards the kitchen at the back. A staircase with a threadbare red carpet started almost opposite the front door. To the right of that was an open door.

Miles looked warily around him.

'Is that Mr Maltby?'

The voice was low and husky, the enunciation clear and precise. Upper middle class 1940s, thought Miles. Rather sexy.

'I'm a bit late, I'm afraid,' Miles called out as he struggled to remove his coat. 'It was such a beautiful day I decided to walk across the park. Unfortunately, I lost track of time.'

The man took the coat, stepped forward and gave the door a push.

'Never mind. You're here now.'

The door swung open. She was standing just inside: tall, five nine or ten, wafer-thin, hair as white and fine as a baby's over narrow, fine-boned features faintly etched with tiny lines, eyes as blue as a summer's afternoon and slightly mocking. She had been very beautiful and still was. She was dressed from head to foot in jumble sale best: a shapeless beige cardigan over a long, brown woollen frock, grey lisle stockings, brown lace-up walking shoes. Unaccountably they did nothing to detract from her looks. Clutched in one hand, between long thin fingers, was an ivory cigarette holder. Something was smouldering in it. It was untipped and fiercely pungent. It could even have been tobacco.

'Come along in. Jolyon rang. Something's come up. He'll try and get along later. So it's just us. I hope you don't mind. Pierre has made us some coffee. We might have a little mid-morning something to go with it. Do you like Calvados? I've found one in Waitrose that's not at all bad. Pierre, would you be so kind?'

The major-domo turned and headed off towards the kitchen.

'Pierre,' she said, lowering her voice confidentially, 'was our chauffeur when we first lived in Paris. When my husband died, I asked him to stay on. Now he does everything for me: cooks, shops, cleans the house, does the garden. He even drives me still. A Honda is not quite the same thing as a Cadillac, but he enjoys it, and I cannot drive. I don't know how I could manage without him.'

'So you haven't always lived here?' Miles said.

'Now come and sit down,' she said. 'Make yourself comfortable. I never feel one can discuss anything properly unless one is sitting comfortably, don't you agree?'

She turned and moved with infinite slowness in the direction of a high-backed armchair upholstered in a faded tapestry material. Miles hurried forward to help but she waved him away and lowered herself slowly between its ample arms and gestured towards a handsome wooden chair on the other side of the fireplace. The arms curled round and ended in the shape of eagles' heads. Across the back was another elaborately carved decoration incorporating leaves, a hollow shell and a coronet. The seat was piled high with books. Miles placed them carefully on the floor and sat down.

The room looked like a cross between an antique shop and a theatrical props store. The dark-red walls were hung with portraits of solemn nineteenth-century figures in heavy gilt frames of various shapes and sizes, interspersed with family photographs, ads torn from

194

glossy magazines, and posters advertising art exhibitions. Every table, every sideboard, every chair was crammed with bits and pieces. An exquisite Sèvres parrot jostled for space with a plaster Alsatian of fairground quality with one ear missing. A clock mounted in blue-and-white porcelain stood alongside an out-of-date calendar advertising a local off-licence. A pen-and-ink portrait miniature of a baby in a bonnet was half-concealed behind a snapshot of a cat in a broken black frame. And everywhere there were books: on shelves, under shelves, beside shelves, on the sofa, on chairs, under chairs, on the floor, in the fireplace. And where there weren't books there were newspapers and magazines and periodicals and old theatre programmes: piles of them, everywhere.

'Are you warm enough?' She indicated the single bar that glowed in the heavy old electric fire. Miles said he was fine but he was secretly glad he'd had some brisk exercise. After a while, Pierre returned with a bottle and two tiny glasses on a silver tray. While he poured the coffee and the Calvados, Mrs Rogers studiously removed the remains of her cigarette, crushed it into a full ashtray, took another from a battered silver case, screwed it into the holder and set fire to it with a well-thumbed Zippo. It was like watching a film in slow motion.

She held the case out to him. 'Gasper?'

Miles smiled and shook his head.

Pierre fussed over her like a mother hen with a sluggardly chick, but suddenly she lost patience with him and brushed him away with a series of quick hand movements, like a schoolmistress who has had enough of a small boy's constant questions.

She waited until he had left the room, then she said, 'Now then. Jolyon tells me you have something to show me.'

Miles said, 'This is entirely his idea. He said that if you didn't know what it was, nobody would.'

'Always the *claqueur*,' she said. 'I like Jolyon. If he were five stone thinner and I were fifty years younger, I might even fall for that line he shoots. Who knows, he might even take a shine to me. He makes enough fuss of me. But I don't altogether trust him. He loves amber, and he knows a lot about it, but he's first and foremost a dealer. He flirts with me and flatters me because he thinks that one day I might let him sell some of my bits and pieces. I know why he wants me to see this piece. You have brought it, I hope?'

It didn't show up in the shorter sentences, but, listening to her talking at length, Miles detected that the accent was not entirely English. The occasional over-stressed vowel, the slightly rolled 'r', the authentic pronunciation of *claqueur*: little things.

Miles reached into his jacket pocket. His fingers closed round the shape that was by now so familiar to his touch that he could hardly remember a time when it hadn't been a part of his life. He took it out and placed it on the little sofa table next to her.

Mrs Rogers clenched the holder between her teeth and picked up the rose. She held it up against the light and uttered a barely audible sigh. It was the sound of one who arrives home after a long, hard journey.

'Ah yes,' she breathed as she turned it hither and thither. 'Yes … Yes …' Still gazing into it, she said, 'Jolyon tells me somebody gave this to you. A friend.'

'Yes.' Miles wondered what else Jolyon had told her.

'And your friend didn't tell you how he came by it? Or is it she?'

'He. No, he didn't.'

'So you have no idea what it might be?'

'No.'

'That I *do* believe,' she said quietly.

'Meaning?'

'Exactly what I say,' she said. 'I don't believe it was given to you by a friend, but I do believe you have no idea what it is.'

Miles leaned forward, placed his elbows on his knees and bent his head over clasped hands in an attitude of silent prayer. He stayed like that for some time, then he sat up.

'Mrs Rogers,' he said, 'the circumstances in which this object, gem, treasure, whatever it is, came into my possession were very extraordinary. I still can't fully explain them. All I know is that the man who had it before me is dead. I think he was murdered. I think I know why, and I think I know who did it. It was pure chance that I happened to turn up very soon after he was killed. Even so, the suspicion fell on me. The evidence against me was purely circumstantial, but it was none the less damning for that. I had no alternative but to make a run for it. I'm still not sure why I finished up with the rose at all. I found it by chance while I was looking for something else. I happened to be holding the rose when I did my bunk. I could have put it back where I found it. I certainly should have. In my anxiety to escape, I must have slipped it into my pocket. Anyway, I forgot all about it, until I got back to England. The reason I have been so cagey about it is that ever since that extraordinary evening my life seems to have been constantly under threat. At first I thought I knew why. Now I'm not so sure. Something happened a couple of evenings ago which makes me think that taking the rose was more than coincidental.'

If Jolyon had mentioned Alex and his friend's visit, she gave no hint of it. 'I see,' she said. Her face was solemn. Her eyes were fixed on him now, unwavering and unblinking. All trace of mockery had vanished. For the first time Miles had the feeling he was talking to someone who understood what he was saying: someone to whom it really mattered, even more than it did to him, and in a quite different way.

Miles looked into her eyes. And then an extraordinary thing happened. All he was aware of at the time was that the old lady sitting in front of him was suddenly transformed. Her wrinkled skin became smooth, her white hair turned black, her eyes were young and dark and full of hope. It was as if someone had pulled off a real life cinematic effect specially for his benefit; or, perhaps, as if a pair of special glasses had been slipped on to his nose which cut out all the characteristics of old age, enabling him to see the eternally youthful spirit that lay beneath, hidden for ever to ordinary eyes. Thinking about it afterwards, he wondered if perhaps she had hypnotised him for a few moments. However it happened, Miles was certain of one thing: that the person he saw in that brief moment was the same person as the one sitting in front of him. He had, literally, seen into her soul. But then the moment passed. The picture faded, the haze came over the sun, and the old lady was back. Only her eyes hadn't changed. They were still dark and intense.

'Do you?' Miles said. 'See, I mean?'

She said, 'When you have been lied to as many times and for as many years as I have, you know the truth when you see it.'

'See it?'

'I can see it in your eyes. I can also see it in this stone.' She held it up again and allowed the light to flood through. 'For years the Natural History Museum here in London claimed to possess the oldest insect in the world. For three hundred million years it had been entombed in a piece of amber. It made a wonderful story. Children would stand and stare at it with their mouths open. They couldn't believe it. Three hundred million years old! It was better than anything Steven Spielberg could invent. And then one day, not long ago, someone decided, for reasons best known to himself, to carry out some tests on the insect, using the very latest scientific techniques. And do you know what he discovered? It wasn't three hundred million years old at all. It wasn't even three hundred years old. Someone in 1859 had created a piece of artificial amber and taken an insect and put it inside and taken so much care to make it look the real thing that no one could believe it wasn't.'

'How can you be so sure that this piece is real? Or are you? Are you telling me this is a brilliant fake as well?'

Mrs Rogers smiled. 'I've just told you. When you've lived with as many lies as I have ...'

'OK. So what is it, then?'

The mocking look had re-entered her eyes. She held up one hand, palm outwards. 'Patience,' she said. 'One thing at a time. Now then. You see that little clock on the mantelpiece. Open the back of it and you'll find a key inside. It doesn't fit the clock, it actually fits the right-hand top drawer of my desk. Open the drawer, and inside you'll find a pocket file full of drawings. If you would be kind enough to bring them over to me here in the light ...'

The drawings were on sheets of graph paper which, when spread out, measured approximately eighteen inches by twelve. They appeared to be architect's designs for decorative work on panelling and door frames and friezes. They were extraordinarily elaborate in concept and precise in detail. There were pages of them. Mrs Rogers discarded at least half before she found what she was looking for: a cartouche, heavily decorated and surmounted by swags of flowers and fruit.

She laid the drawing out on her knee and reached for the rose. She moved it along the line of swags, pausing frequently to compare it

198

with this flower and with that and cursing mildly when they didn't match. And then she found what she was looking for: a single rose, tucked between a lily and a peony. She laid the stone next to it, reached out to the side-table and took a large, ivory-handled magnifying glass. For fully five minutes she peered at the drawing and then at the stone and then back at the drawing, comparing every twist of every sepal, every curl of every petal. Miles stood by her chair, bending low, his head close to hers. He didn't need a magnifying glass. To him it was quite clear that they were identical.

At last Mrs Rogers put down the glass and sat back. 'That's it,' she murmured. 'I knew it. I *knew* it.' Her voice rose triumphantly. She held the rose up, clasping it by the tips of her fingers as if giving it a human mount. She looked at Miles and there were tears in her eyes.

'My dear boy,' she said. 'You have found the Amber Room.'

20

The name rang a bell, but only a very faint one. The Amber Room. Something to do with a palace in Russia. Near St Petersburg. Hadn't it been stolen during the war? That was it. He'd read an article about it, only a year or so ago. It had disappeared, but someone thought he knew where it was. Boris Yeltsin, was it?

Mrs Rogers lit her umpteenth cigarette of the morning and lay back in her chair, her eyes mocking, her lips twitching with amusement at his fumblings.

'People are always claiming to know what became of it,' she said. 'Yet nobody has found it. There are as many theories as people who propound them. Some say it was hidden down a mine shaft in the old East Germany; others that it lies in a ship's cargo hold at the bottom of Königsberg Harbour; others that it is buried in the rubble on which the town of Kaliningrad was built after the war. The legend is as potent as it ever was.'

Miles frowned. 'So where does this rose come from?'

Mrs Rogers said calmly, 'I don't know.'

'But you think it's part of the Amber Room?'

'I think so,' she said.

'Where was this room originally?'

'In order to answer that,' she said, 'I will have to go back nearly three centuries. And you will need to go back to your chair.'

While Miles poured more coffee and Calvados, Mrs Rogers lit another cigarette.

'From earliest times, kings and emperors have decorated rooms in all manner of substances – beautifully carved wood, gold, silver, marble, even precious jewels. Yet only one king had ever conceived the idea of panelling a room entirely in amber. In 1705, the Emperor

200

Frederick Wilhelm II of Prussia ordered that his study in his palace of Montbijou in Königsberg on the Baltic coast should be lined in this rare and unlikely material.

'As you probably know, the source of true amber is the low-lying southern shore of the Baltic, most of which in those days belonged to Prussia. Six tons of rich, honey-coloured amber were used to create the room. German and Danish craftsmen worked for four years cutting the two hundred individual panels, carving them, polishing them, assembling them. The job was completed in 1709, but within a few years the Emperor had tired of them and in 1716 he had the whole thing dismantled and sent to Tsar Peter the Great as a token of gratitude and friendship. The two countries had recently signed an alliance against their common enemy, Sweden.'

'Some gift,' said Miles.

'Evidently the Tsar was not as delighted by it as the Emperor had hoped. He never so much as unpacked the room. For years it lay in storage and it was not until after his death in 1725 that the crates were opened and the panels and decorations were used to line a room in the Winter Palace in St Petersburg. Thirty years later his daughter, the Empress Elizabeth, had the room dismantled and taken to the Catherine Palace at Tsarskoe Selo; what is now Pushkin. In order that the room should fit the larger space, the Italian architect, Bartolomeo Rastrelli, added tall, gilt-framed mirrors and Florentine mosaics depicting landscape scenes, and there it remained for two centuries, a source of wonder and pilgrimage for curious visitors and, for a handful of collectors, the object of a desire so obsessive that it bordered on the insane. One British ambassador to St Petersburg called it the Eighth Wonder of the World. You can get some idea from these drawings. Of course these are not Rastrelli's original drawings. They are nineteenth-century copies, but they are very good copies. If they had had a photocopier a hundred and fifty years ago, it could not be more accurate.'

Miles picked up the rose and looked at it. 'This is a beautiful piece,' he said. 'I can see why people are fascinated by amber. Obsessed, even. But a whole room of it! Rather indigestible, I'd have thought.'

'Taste doesn't really come into it,' she said. 'It was a phenomenon. Not everyone would choose to have the Taj Mahal in their back garden, but that doesn't stop them travelling halfway round the world to look at it.'

'It's exactly the sort of thing the Nazis would have gone for, of course. Grandiose, theatrical and worth a fortune.'

'That's true, but of course the real reason they wanted it was because they believed it was rightfully theirs. It was part of their national heritage, as they say these days.'

'The German equivalent of the Elgin Marbles,' Miles murmured.

'Except that the Amber Room had not been requisitioned. It had been given away. They considered that the Emperor's gesture had been a foolish error of judgment which it was their duty to correct.'

'So they just marched in and removed it?'

'In the late summer of '41. As the German army advanced towards the palace, the Soviet curators realised what the fate of the room was likely to be, so they tried to dismantle it. The idea was to transport the whole thing to a place of safety. But the task was far too delicate and they ran out of time. They managed to get three or four of the panels packed into wooden crates and buried in the palace grounds. But the Germans soon found them.'

'What did they do with the rest of it?'

'The only thing possible. They covered it with plywood and wallpaper and hoped for the best. But it was no good. The Germans knew what they were looking for, and they weren't going to go away without it. It would have been more than their life was worth. The order to retrieve it and restore it to its rightful home had come from Hitler himself.'

'So it wasn't taken to Berlin?'

'No. The Gauleiter of East Prussia, a man by the name of Walter Koch, was ordered personally to take it to Königsberg and reassemble it where it belonged: in the Montbijou Palace.'

'So then what happened to it?'

'It remained there for the rest of the war. But by the beginning of 1945 the tide had turned on the Eastern Front. The Russian army was on the point of capturing Königsberg. The curator of the local museum, an art historian called Dr Alfred Rohde, received an order at the highest level that the panels were to be taken down, put into crates and loaded on to a convoy of lorries, provided by Walter

Koch, and driven away to a place of safety.' Mrs Rogers paused.

'And?'

'That was it. The Amber Room has never been seen again.'

'Never?'

'All sorts of theories have been put forward. There was a rumour that it was loaded aboard the freighter *Wilhelm Gustloff*. It was the last ship to leave Königsberg Harbour and it never made it. It was torpedoed by a Russian submarine and went down with five thousand refugees on board. Then a Czech eyewitness appeared from nowhere and claimed that the room had arrived in Czechoslovakia in May 1945 on a special train, guarded by SS soldiers under the command of the famous – or should I say notorious? – Otto Skorzeny.'

'Who was he?'

'Skorzeny? He was the SS officer Hitler sent to Italy in 1943 to rescue Mussolini from prison. Anyway, according to this so-called eyewitness, the crates were unloaded at a small town just inside the Czech frontier and taken to the "Wolf's Lair". That was the name given by the Germans to the secret underground bunker used by Field Marshal von Schörner who commanded the million men who were still holding out in the last few days of the war. But we know that the Wolf's Lair was blown up shortly before von Schörner surrendered, so that theory doesn't look any too dusty.'

'What did this man Rohde have to say about it?'

'Not much. The Russians finally ran him to earth in the ruins of Königsberg and summoned him to attend a Commission of Enquiry that had been set up under a Russian art historian named Barsov. Dr Barsov. On the morning he was due to appear, Rohde and his wife were both found dead in their home.'

'Suicide?'

'According to the death certificate signed by one Dr Erdmann, they'd both died from dysentery. The Russians went to interrogate the doctor, but he had disappeared and was never heard of again. It was only then that they discovered he had been a prominent member of the local Nazi party.'

'And Walter Koch? Did he disappear along with everyone else?'

'He tried to make a run for it, but he was caught by the British. They found he was high on the list of Poland's war criminals, so they handed him over to the Polish authorities, who sentenced him to death.'

'Another dead end. Sorry. Bad joke. Not intentional.'

'Not quite. The Russians were convinced Koch knew where the room was, so they persuaded the Polish authorities to postpone the execution. He languished in prison for twenty years until his daughter managed to get an assurance that his life would be spared, whereupon Koch agreed to make a statement to the Russian Commission of Enquiry. It didn't add up to much. He told them that the room had been bricked up in some underground cellar in the outskirts of Königsberg, but he couldn't remember exactly where. That, at least, rang true. The city was so devastated by the Russian army that the authorities bulldozed the ruins and built a whole new city on top of the rubble and renamed it Kaliningrad. A lot of people believe that the room is still there, buried under the concrete.'

'But you're not one of them,' Miles said.

'If you mean, do I think it's lost for ever, the answer is, no, I don't. In war, things disappear. People disappear. Often for no apparent reason and without trace. Like Raoul Wallenberg. They say the Russians took him, but why should they have done? He was a good man. He had done nothing but good. He was on the side of the Allies. Perhaps he had information about the Germans that the Russians wanted, but why did they keep him? Many people swore they had run across him in various prison camps. Yet the Russians have always denied they ever had him. It is a mystery. Perhaps there will never be an answer. In which case we shall have to accept that Raoul Wallenberg was just another casualty of war. Just like one of those hundreds of thousands of young soldiers who slid into the mud at Ypres and the Somme or were blown into pieces too small to recognise. "Known to God".

'For many years after the war we often received information about the room. People wrote to us to say that they knew where it was. That they had seen it in packing cases, in its original form, in a house, in a cellar, at the top of a tower, at the bottom of a mine. It was in Weimar, it was in Prague, it was in a palace in Lhasa, it was in a monastery in Tashkent, it was at the bottom of the sea. Most of the leads were too preposterous to be worth pursuing. And too expensive.

My family was rich once, but not now. Some stories we investigated, but they all turned out to be lies. Why do people bother to lie about such things? Does it give them pleasure to know we are disappointed and cast down? I do not understand.

'After thirty years of deceit and disappointment, we agreed that we couldn't go on any longer raising our hopes only to have them dashed. We told ourselves that the room was just another casualty of war. Its fate just one of those many unexplained mysteries, its whereabouts known only to God. But then, two years ago, we received information that once again revived our hopes. It wasn't much. A throwaway sentence discovered in a long-forgotten correspondence by someone who was looking for something completely different. But then I have never underestimated the value of luck. I have had more than my fair share of it. It is luck that I am here in London, that I found this house, that I am alive at all ...'

She was beginning to ramble. Miles sympathised. He'd been more or less lost from the moment he'd arrived. Why was this old lady so passionate about the fate of the Amber Room? Was she a collector? An art historian? Was Jolyon a party to this wild-goose chase? Or was it just family? If so, what family? And what was this chance information they had received that had so heartened them? Had his own unexpected contribution confirmed them in their new line of enquiry? Indeed, how much had he contributed? An amber ornament which appeared to correspond with part of the original design. What did that prove? At best, that a tiny piece of it had come to light: at worst, that it was sheer coincidence. And yet the old lady had seemed to be in no doubt about it. 'You have found the Amber Room,' she had declared. Where was it, then? Not in Eigerhubel, anyway. It was like one of those telephone calls where you don't quite catch the caller's name, but you keep going in the desperate hope that he or she will let drop a hint, but the person doesn't, and you have been talking for far too long to come out with it and ask who you're talking to.

There was a knock at the door and Pierre entered. Mrs Rogers looked up enquiringly.

Pierre murmured, 'Forgive me for interrupting, Your Imperial Highness, but will you be wanting any more coffee?'

'Thank you, Pierre,' she said. 'I think not.'

He bowed and left the room.

'Mrs Rogers ...' Miles began.

'Please don't be embarrassed,' she said. 'That really is my name. Irina Rogers. My late husband was Alec Rogers. He was a diplomat. Brussels, Belgrade, Paris. My family's name was Romanov. The surname may be familiar to you. My father was first cousin to Tsar Nicholas II. When I was a child, I spent all my holidays with his family. Olga, Tatiana, Maria, Anastasia; they were my closest friends. Their main home was the Alexander Palace at Tsarskoe Selo. My Aunt Alexandra, the Tsarina, loved England and she made the palace look like an English country mansion. The only difference was that it was looked after by four beautifully dressed Negro guards. The Alexander Palace was very near to the Catherine Palace, where the Amber Room was. We sometimes drove there for a picnic in the gardens. We always made a point of visiting the room before leaving. Once or twice we stayed in the royal hunting lodge at Spala in Poland, but in the summer holidays we usually went to the Black Sea. They had a wonderful palace there at Livadiya. We played together, we bathed together, we slept together. So you see, I am even older than you thought. Ninety-two last month, and I feel every second of it sometimes. Not today, though. Today I am fifteen years old again. Playing with my cousins. My poor cousins ...

'When the Revolution came, it was term time and I was away at school, far from St Petersburg. My father sent my mother and my younger sister Natasha ahead to Paris, then he came to fetch me. Luckily he had a friend who was very high up in the railway and he persuaded him to smuggle me over the frontier in a guard's van. It was a terrible journey and I was very frightened, but in the end I arrived in Paris and met up with my mother and Natasha. My father did not come with me. He said he had some important matters to attend to and that he would join us later, but he never did. We heard later that he had been taken by the Bolsheviks and shot.'

She was suddenly silent. Her shoulders slumped, her head dropped. Then she seemed to pull herself together and she sat upright. Her eyes were damp. She shrugged and gave a little smile. 'It was a long time ago.' She reached for the old silver cigarette case. 'Nothing like

206

a gasper for raising morale,' she said, screwing the cigarette into the holder and lighting up.

'Are you a Grand Duchess?' said Miles.

She gave a low, throaty chuckle. 'I never think about it. Pierre likes to keep it going, though. I haven't the heart to say anything.'

Miles said, 'That answers a lot of questions. But I still don't understand how you can be so definite about the Room. You said just now that I'd found it. I haven't. All I've found is a small piece of amber in the shape of a rose. Nothing more.'

She wagged a finger at him. 'You take me too literally,' she said. 'To receive information that the Amber Room still exists is one thing. But to see a part of it with one's own eyes, and to hold it in one's hand …' She shook her head as if trying to clear it of emotions and make room for words. 'You see, my dear boy, the Amber Room was *our* room. It was a gift to our family. A gift is a gift. It belongs to us. For fifty years we have been searching for it and this' – she held the rose between her fingers – 'is the first time any of us have seen any part of it. I always knew deep down that it had survived somewhere, somehow. And you have just given me the proof I have been waiting for for all these years. You have found the Amber Room. I'm sure of it.'

Miles said, 'I have one other question. This sentence in this letter that this researcher came across. What did it say exactly?'

'The letter was written in 1950 by an art historian called Walter Grobius to a friend called van Berkel. On the face of it, it was perfectly unremarkable. A bread-and-butter letter thanking him for a book he had sent him. A book on stage design. It seemed that the chapter on Restoration Comedy had been of particular interest to him and he commented that no room-set for a play like *School for Scandal* could be elaborately decorated enough for his liking. And then he went on, and these were his exact words: "Talking of which, you will be glad to know that the world's most theatrical room is still safe and well and that I visit it every day and think of you." '

'He could be talking about any room,' Miles pointed out. 'There's no mention of the word "amber".'

Mrs Rogers drew deeply on her cigarette. She said, 'I forgot to mention a couple of things. Walter Grobius was a Swiss who had strong connections with pre-war German industry, and from 1939 to 1941 van Berkel was German vice-consul in Berne.'

Miles said, 'And I forgot to mention something. I found the rose in Switzerland.'

'Ah.' Mrs Rogers nodded slowly several times. 'I wondered.'

* * *

There was a message on the answering machine from Jolyon Grant-Forbes when he got back, wondering how it had gone. All very casual. Miles rang him back straight away. It seemed only polite.

'Sorry I couldn't make it,' Jolyon said. 'They sprang a heads-of-department meeting on us. How did you get on with Mrs R?'

Miles told him. Given the dramatic nature of the morning's events, he received the news with surprising nonchalance.

'I suspected as much,' he said breezily. 'It's good to have it confirmed.'

'Elation is hardly the same thing as confirmation,' said Miles. 'It could be wishful thinking on her part. Given the circumstances.'

Miles wasn't sure how much Jolyon knew about Irina's past life, or indeed how much she wanted him to know. She hadn't made any comments that suggested she had any feelings about him one way or the other; but, from the little she had said, he had the impression that their relationship was purely professional and that she was quite happy it should remain that way. His oblique afterthought produced no obvious reaction, so he assumed he had taken the correct line.

Jolyon said, 'But I thought you said she compared it with the original designs.'

'It certainly looked very similar to my untutored eye,' said Miles. 'She seemed utterly convinced.'

'No one is more knowledgeable about the room than she.'

'Except Paul Olsen.'

'Olsen?' The voice was suddenly sharp, suspicious.

'Yes. Why? Do you know him?'

'I know who he is.'

'She wants him to see it. She's asked me to take the rose to Copenhagen. She'd like me to go at once. Obviously, I'd be happy to do what I can to help, and of course it's a fascinating story, but I am rather busy at the moment, and frankly, with the best will in the world ...'

'Did she say why she wanted Olsen to see it? He is a very respected dealer in amber, and there are many people I would approach for expert advice and comment. But in this case I would have thought she knew far more about the Amber Room than he does.'

Miles said, 'It's not authentication she's after; it's information. Seeing the rose on its own like that, she's worried in case the Room has been broken up and is being sold piecemeal. She wants to know if any other pieces like that have passed through his hands.'

'I hadn't thought of that,' Jolyon admitted.

Miles didn't believe him. People like Jolyon don't get to be the head of their department by not thinking. Nor, for that matter, by taking a polite, dispassionate interest in other people's property. Eberhardt's, for all their smooth accents and expensive tailoring, are not art historians. Although they might like to give journalists that impression. They are dealers. Their job is to get their hands on the best-possible objects and the richest-possible customers and marry the two together. It was unlikely that in this case Jolyon had someone standing by, fingers drumming on chequebook. It was quite clear that, whatever his suspicions concerning the whereabouts of the Amber Room, the first real sniff he'd had of it had been that morning.

Miles said, 'I asked you this morning what you thought my rose was worth. You said that if it was what you thought it was, the value of the whole thing was inestimable. Now that your suspicions have been confirmed, would you be prepared to make a stab at an estimate?'

Jolyon said, 'The amber alone, as amber, could be worth anything up to a hundred million. That's a figure that could be estimated, just as one could estimate the value of the individual stones and materials in the Crown Jewels. But there's no way anyone could estimate the value of the Crown Jewels. They are literally priceless.'

'Are you seriously comparing the Amber Room with the Crown Jewels?' Miles asked him.

Jolyon said, 'In its day, the Amber Room was one of the greatest treasures in the world. If it has survived, and all the pieces are in one place, and they are all original, then I would say it is still one of the

209

greatest treasures in the world. Like the Crown Jewels. If it could be reassembled and put back in the Catherine Palace, it would be a huge feather in Boris Yeltsin's cap. The way things are going in Russia right now he could do with one. In terms of tourism alone it could bring in millions in much-needed foreign currency. My guess is that it would be a tourist attraction to rival any in the world today.'

'And if Mrs Rogers' worst fears are realised, and the whole thing has been broken up into small pieces?'

'As pieces, they'd be worth what any other nicely carved pieces of old amber with insects in them are worth. A few hundred, a few thousand perhaps. It would depend on the size and quality of the item.'

'But people would pay over the odds for the chance of owning part of the legendary Amber Room, surely?'

'If it could be authenticated. But how on earth could anyone prove it? Obviously a person or organisation selling it off piecemeal could make a fortune, but it would be a drop in the ocean compared with the complete item.'

'So the sooner I get to see Paul Olsen the better.'

'At least you might have some idea what you're dealing with.'

'And who.'

'I don't understand.'

'I thought you said he's one of the most respected dealers in the world.'

'One of them.'

'No prizes for guessing who the other is.'

An easy, self-deprecating laugh floated down the line. 'It goes without saying that I shall be interested to know what he has to say. What steps you take as a result is, of course, entirely up to you.'

'Of course,' said Miles, and smiled as he put down the phone.

* * *

'What do you mean, another story? You haven't delivered this one yet.' Neville's voice combined the schoolmaster and the schoolboy: finger wagging and complaining simultaneously.

'I feel like a man dying of thirst in the desert, convinced that not a single drop of liquid is ever going to pass his throat again, and then suddenly from nowhere appears this bar, stocked with every drink imaginable. The choice is so wide that he simply doesn't know where to begin. Do you know what I mean?'

'No.'

'The romance of Fleet Street,' said Miles.

'Fleet Street's history, sunshine,' said Neville.

'So's Archie Lambourn,' said Miles. 'A fortnight ago he was the flavour of the week; today he's budgie-cage lining. There's nothing more to be said about him that hasn't been said already. The corpse of the Lambourn Set has been exhumed in every tabloid, and in most of the broadsheets too. The few remaining scraps of rotting flesh have been picked over, the bones have been rearranged in every conceivable combination and there's nothing there. It stinks as much as it ever did, but it's the same smell.'

Neville said, 'Well, put a clothes peg on your nose and keep picking. Have you been to Norfolk? Interviewed the staff? Talked to the locals?'

'Done that,' said Miles. 'Got the T-shirt. Literally. Got a tiger on it. Sumatran male.'

'And?'

'Nothing,' he lied.

'Wasn't there a wife? Lady something-or-other?'

'There was, and is. Camilla. She lives in an alcoholic haze in a council tip in Kentish Town. She thinks they were all shits.'

'Well, there you are.'

'What do you mean, there I am? There I am *where*?'

'I mean, there's your story.'

'You can't be serious. Talk about scraping the barrel!'

'Not at all. Now all you have to do is find the shits and interview them. "Where are they now?" Always a winner.'

'Neville,' said Miles putting on his mock stern voice, 'yours is meant to be a serious broadsheet newspaper. An opinion former. The vade-mecum for the chattering classes.'

'Exactly,' said Neville. 'Well, get on and get them chattering, then.'

* * *

211

Miles put the telephone down. 'Damn and blast,' he said. He got up and went over to the window. The setting sun cast a pale-yellow glow over the park. 'Damn and blast,' he said again, slowly and with feeling.

Once, in the course of a press trip to California, a group of carefully selected hacks had been taken to a disused prison on the edge of the Mojave Desert that had recently been refurbished and transmogrified into a tourist attraction and visitors' centre. The star draw was the electric chair. If the chatty guide was to be believed, it was still wired up. This information was let drop only after a few of the journalists had been invited to try the chair for size. Harry Chalmers was in it at the time. He had looked down at his hands, then up at the metal cap hovering above his head. 'Life,' he'd remarked, 'is all a matter of timing.'

It wasn't that Miles didn't want to write the Lambourn piece. The Lambourn Set was clearly integral to the whole Eigerhubel–Diabolo–English SS saga in which he appeared, to an extent that he was still unable to work out, to be a player. The further he delved into it, the more the pieces would fall into shape and the clearer the picture would be. Then he really would have a story worth writing. But, to get what he wanted, he would need to play his cards very close to his chest. To fritter valuable material on a half-baked feature now would be tantamount to chucking away the whole story. It could also be very dangerous. He didn't mind having a little excitement injected into his humdrum existence from time to time, but he was no fearless investigator. He didn't have the physique to cope with savage dogs and men wielding iron bars; he wasn't paid well enough, either.

But how to explain all this to a man like Neville Short? Short by name, Short by nature, that was Neville's problem. The whole of life for him was divided up into easy-bite portions. 'Make it short.' That was his motto. Short articles, short delivery dates, short payments. 'Writers write to fill the space available', that was Neville's Law. To him, three thousand words was a book. 'Neville, I've discovered that British soldiers served in the SS during the war and I strongly suspect that some of them committed atrocities. They may even have worked in the concentration camps. But I need more time to assemble the evidence. When I do, it could be the biggest story since Eichmann.' 'Yes, yes, very interesting,' Neville would reply. 'Could you do me eight hundred words on the enduring popularity of the Barbour jacket, by this time tomorrow?'

He still wanted to do the Lambourn story, but not now. Not like this. Not now that the Amber Room had entered his life. And the Grand Duchess Irina.

If anyone had told him that, at the age of thirty-eight, he would fall for a woman of over ninety, he would have invited them to take a running jump. Now that he had, he couldn't imagine why he had thought the prospect so repellent. Presumably because in his mind the words 'fall for' had always implied a brisk physical follow-up, the sooner, the better. And therefore the very idea of a relationship with a very much older woman that was anything other than grandmotherly automatically placed him in the category of a mentally disturbed rapist. But of course his feelings for Irina (as he now knew her) were nothing of the sort. She had been a very beautiful and a very sexy woman, and those qualities, though faded, lingered, like a trace of expensive scent. She knew it and she was still quite capable of deploying them to her advantage.

But that was only a part of it. From the very first moment he and Elizabeth had met, he had felt – and so had she – that they were picking up on a friendship established long ago and in another place. In another life perhaps? And now it had happened again. He would never have believed it possible. But then, twenty-four hours ago, he had never heard of the Amber Room.

21

Flight 806 to Copenhagen swooped low over the sea and touched down at Kastrup Airport at 5.23 p.m., two minutes ahead of schedule.

Miles peered through the window. The shore of the Köge Bugt was sprinkled with lights; the bay below was iron-grey in the fading light. He dry-washed his face and yawned. He was beginning to wish he'd taken the morning flight, but he'd never have made it. There had been far too many things to squeeze into far too short a time. Booking his ticket, depositing the badge and the photographs with the bank and cobbling together fifteen hundred workmanlike words on the Lambourn Set from a wadge of assorted cuttings, garnered at admirably short notice by Big Betty in the reference library.

It was hardly the best piece he had ever written, but it was a long way from being the worst. Nevertheless, he waited until the last possible moment before faxing it through. He wasn't going to risk having Neville ringing him up with footling changes.

Travelling with only a small overnight bag, he was through the Green channel and out into the cool, clean, silvery elegance of the transit area in a matter of minutes.

He was looking for the sign to the city-centre bus link when he spotted the man coming towards him. Miles recognised him at once by the white, polo-neck ski shirt. He was carrying a black leather briefcase in his right hand.

He was about to walk past when Miles called out, 'Did you get your refund?'

The man stopped and looked blankly at him. 'I'm sorry?'

'Eigerhubel. The doctor's surgery. You were waiting for a letter to get your lift-pass money refunded.'

Recognition dawned on the man's thin features. 'Oh, of course.

The chap in the avalanche. What an extraordinary coincidence! What are you doing here?'

'Business,' said Miles. 'You?'

'Me too,' the man said, 'and yes, I did get my money back. How about you? You were in there a hell of a long time.'

'I'm sorry. I hope you didn't wait. The back of my head was in a worse mess than I realised. Must have caught it with the edge of a ski.'

'Bad luck,' the man said. He looked around, as if anxious to be on his way. 'Actually, I realised something must have happened. I waited for a while but then I decided to come back the next day.'

'So you never saw him?'

'The doctor? Not that evening, no. Of course I'd seen him the previous afternoon. When he put the plaster on.'

'So you couldn't have known.'

'Known what?'

'That he wasn't the real doctor.'

'Sorry?'

'I mean, the man I saw. The man who stitched my head. Tried to, anyway. He wasn't the real doctor.'

'Not the real doctor?' he said. 'I don't know what you mean. He seemed perfectly pukka to me. Made a damned good job of this, anyway.' He held up his left wrist. The plaster gleamed white in the glittering lights of the airport shops. It might have been put on that morning.

'Of course,' said Miles. 'I realise now. You only saw the real doctor. No reason why you should have seen the other one.'

'What other one? What are you talking about?'

Miles frowned. 'You mean, you didn't know?'

The man glanced at his watch. 'Look, I really must dash. Big meeting in Copenhagen. Jolly good to see you again. Glad the head's better.'

Miles said, 'Why don't we share a taxi? We could talk.'

'Love to have done,' said the man, 'but someone's picking me up, actually. Another time, perhaps.' And, with a quick smile and a nod, he turned and headed off into the crowd.

'Damn,' said Miles.

215

He changed some English currency into *kroner* and made for the exit. There was a taxi rank outside. Half a dozen people were waiting in a queue. At the front was the man with the broken wrist. A taxi nudged forward. The man bent forward and gave instructions to the driver, climbed in and the car swept away, leaving a faint trail of exhaust hanging in the air.

'Miserable sod,' muttered Miles and joined the back of the queue.

Miles had picked the Admiral Hotel out of a little guide to Copenhagen for no other reason than that he liked the sound of it. The notion of a converted warehouse fitted in with his policy of trying, whenever possible and certainly when visiting a place for the first time, to avoid the anonymous trappings of international luxury in favour of a hotel that in some way expressed the spirit of the place. With its large, beamy rooms the Admiral more than fulfilled his hopes, and the discovery that his room overlooked the stately square of the Amalienborg Palace was an unexpected bonus.

He showered, put on a fresh shirt, helped himself to a Scotch and water from the minibar and sat down with a street map he'd picked up at Reception.

Paul Olsen's workshop was in Klosterstraede, just off Strøget, the city's main walking street that started life nine hundred years ago as a footpath and now winds its way through three quarters of a mile of book stores and cafés and fashion boutiques and four different street names from Kongens Nytorv to Radhuspladsen, the Town Hall Square. His meeting with Olsen was scheduled for ten o'clock the following morning.

He swallowed another mouthful of whisky, reached into his pocket and, and for the umpteenth time, took out the rose. He held it up against the bedside light. Every time he looked at it, he seemed to see something different: another shade of colour, a variation in the pattern of the tiny bubbles ... Every day the stone seemed to draw him further and further inwards, teasing him, hinting at its secret, yet never quite revealing it ...

This evening, there was a sinister look to the fly that he hadn't noticed before. The legs seemed less helpless and delicate and more grasping and predatory, almost as if the amber had softened momentarily, allowing the creature to wake briefly from its three centuries of slumber and shift its position slightly before freezing it back to sleep.

Miles shivered slightly and swallowed some more whisky.

Amongst the other cuttings that Betty had sent over was from *The Times* in the late Eighties, speculating on the present whereabouts of the Amber Room. There wasn't much in it that he hadn't already learned from Irina, but there was one paragraph ... He hadn't given it much thought at the time, but now, looking at that fly ... He located it in a file at the bottom of his overnight bag.

> 'Following ex-Gauleiter Walter Koch's statement to the Soviet Commission of Enquiry hinting at the possibility that the Amber Room was languishing in a bunker near Königsberg, a number of journalists – most of them West Germans – decided to instigate their own personal hunts for the room. Within a very short time, four of them had died or been killed in mysterious circumstances. One fell down the shaft of a disused salt mine at Bad Assee in East Germany, two others were victims of hit-and-run drivers – one on the Czech border, the other in Berlin – and the fourth, a highly experienced deep-sea diver, was drowned while diving near a submerged wreck off the Baltic coast.'

'Cheap fiction,' said Miles out loud. He closed his fist round the rose and jammed it into his jacket pocket. Then he folded the cutting, replaced the file, finished his drink and took the lift down to the lobby.

'*Goddag.*' The girl at reception was called Britt. She had perfect teeth surrounded by an enormous smile and was almost embarrassingly helpful.

The Tivoli Gardens are closed for the winter, she told him, but she could recommend a very nice restaurant, very elegant, not too far away, near Kongens Nytorv, where he could have a very nice meal, not too expensive. It was called the Kommandanten. She took a fresh street map and marked the exact location on Adelgade. Would she like him to ring and book a table? For one? At eight? She was really very pretty and for a moment Miles considered asking her to make

217

that for two. But in the end he just nodded his assent and smiled. She looked as if she'd just come on duty anyway.

It was a clear brilliant night and a cold wind was whipping in across the Inderhavnen, the stretch of waterway that divides Copenhagen's city centre from Christianshavn. Miles pulled up the collar of his old brown overcoat and pushed his hands deep into the cavernous pockets as he strode along Toldbodgade. He turned right into Amalienborg Square. The identical, mansion-like palaces that take up four of the eight sides were bright with lights. Despite their bearskin hats, the soldiers guarding each palace must have been feeling the cold, though they showed no signs of it.

Four roads converge at right angles on the courtyard and Miles took the one to his left, Amaliegade. At the end he turned right into Sankt Annae Plads, then left down Bredgade and into Kongens Nytorv – the King's New Square. The Hotel d'Angleterre glowed majestically on the far side, but it was too cold for serious sightseeing. He'd have time for that in the morning. Meanwhile, he was starving.

He liked the look of the Kommandanten the moment he walked in. The beams and blue-painted doorways set off the stylishly minimalist furniture and the simple table settings a treat.

The *maître d'hôtel* had short fair hair, a matching beard and designer glasses. If Miles had been royalty he could not have been given a more enthusiastic welcome. In fact he was shown to a table next to a large portrait of Queen Margrethe. It had a bright-green background made even greener by a strong spotlight.

'Nice picture,' said Miles as the *maître d'hotel* eased the anorexic chair under his thighs and a waiter flourished a snowy napkin.

'That is our Queen.'

'Excellent likeness,' said Miles.

'It is by Andy Warhol.'

'One queen by another,' said Miles.

'May I get you an aperitif?'

'Scotch, please.'

'Of course.' He relayed the order to the waiter. 'Enjoy your meal,' he told Miles and swept off.

Within moments he was back. 'There is a telephone call for you,' he said.

218

Even the telephone booth qualified for a major feature in *World of Interiors*.

'This is Paul Olsen.' The manner was brusque, but there was a tremble in the voice.

'How nice to hear from you,' said Miles conversationally. 'How on earth did you track me down here?'

'I am very sorry. I cannot see you tomorrow.'

'Can't see me? I don't understand ...'

'It is impossible,' he said. 'I am very busy. You must go home.'

'Go home? What do you mean, go home? Why? Has something happened?'

'I am sorry. I cannot explain.'

'Why not? I've come all this way to see you. I think the least you owe me is an explanation.'

'Please go home. Goodbye.'

'Does Mrs Rogers know about this?'

'Goodbye.'

The *maître d'hôtel* was greeting a party of four when Miles exited from the booth. 'Is everything all right?' He seemed genuinely concerned.

Miles said, 'Yes, thank you. I mean, no, it isn't. I don't know. I have to go and see someone. He lives quite near. I shan't be very long. Can you possibly keep the table for me?

'Of course.' The *maître d'hôtel* gave a little bow. 'It is yours for the evening.'

Miles half-walked, half-ran down Strøget. All the big names were there: Georg Jensen, Illums Bolighus, Bang & Olufsen ... Glittering windows, the best of Danish. But the crowds had long since escaped indoors into the warmth.

Klosterstraede was just off to the right, about two-thirds of the way along, near Helligåndskirken. No. 23 was a tall thin house: three storeys high, well proportioned, eighteenth-century. A light was burning on the first floor. Miles was on the opposite side of the street and about to cross, when the front door opened. He took a step back into a nearby doorway. The ground floor of No. 23 was in darkness. A shadowy shape was standing just inside. A fur-hatted head came out and looked quickly up and down the street. There was no one in sight. The figure stepped out, closed the door and strode off in the direction of Strøget, long dark overcoat swinging around high leather boots, heels clacking on the pavement. Anna Karenina with a hint of the French Lieutenant's Woman ...

Miles waited until the footsteps had faded, then he crossed the road and rang the bell. There was no response. He stepped back and looked up at the lighted window. No signs of life. He stepped forward and pressed the bell again. That was when he saw the damage. There wasn't much to see: a few indentations around the lock, a small split in the white wooden frame. Professional stuff. Miles turned the handle. The door swung open easily. He stepped into the darkened hallway. Light flooded out across the landing and washed the top half of the narrow staircase.

Miles called out Olsen's name a couple of times, but there was no reply. He started to climb the stairs ...

The room ran from the front of the building to the back and doubled as an office and workshop. At the far end there was a desk; at the front, overlooking the street, a workbench with knives, a polishing machine and assorted items of amber: rough chunks, polished gems, lumps of mutton fat, clear droplets ... In the middle was Olsen's head, white hair brushed back across the crown, face turned to one side, the wound clearly displayed under the bright light of the work lamp: small, neat, surgical, a thin dribble of blood, just under the right ear. Miles recognised it only too well. The only difference between Olsen and the doctor was that Olsen wasn't smiling when he died. But then he wouldn't have known Anna.

Miles's brain whirled. For a long time he had been convinced it was the badge they were after. It made sense. It was the only obvious thing missing from the surgery. It matched the one he'd found at West Keating. Everything pointed to some sort of Nazi-inspired conspiracy based on Eigerhubel and the Diabolo Club. But then Alex and his long-haired friend had come in search of something quite different and he'd started to have doubts. Now, with Olsen's death, it was beginning to look as if he was going to have to start all over again.

It was possible, of course, that the two deaths were unconnected. Having a sharp instrument shoved up into your brain could be a more

220

common cause of death than he'd realised. Perhaps the presence of amber in both cases was an astonishing coincidence. And perhaps by yet another extraordinary quirk of fate it would turn out that he, Miles, was the rightful heir to the throne of Russia, and that by this time next year he'd have given up freelance journalism and be living in idle luxury in Palm Beach. Perhaps the bang on the head had been worse than anyone had realised and he was fated to spend the rest of his life wandering the world in a state of mild hallucination, forever caught up in a convoluted adventure story to which there was never any conclusion, only more questions. All he knew was that, whatever the hell he'd got involved in, he wasn't going to be panicked into running away for a second time. At least, not until he'd found out why Olsen had been so anxious to cancel their meeting.

Miles ran down to the hall. The lock on the front door was still in one piece. He pushed down the catch and returned to the workshop. He switched off the work lamp and crossed to the window. He flattened himself to one side and peered down into the street. It looked as deserted as before. He closed the curtains and sat down at the desk. He swiched on the thin, angular reading lamp. It looked like a praying mantis. Miles stared at the top of the desk. He didn't know where to begin or what he was looking for. Some clue that might explain why Olsen had changed his mind. A message of some sort, perhaps? Something. Anything.

There were papers everywhere, bills, letters, leaflets, but nothing obvious, nothing that leapt out at him. No scribbled messages. No impressions on a notepad. No notepad. Miles covered his hand with his handkerchief and tried the drawers. They were all locked. There was a grey metal filing cabinet next to the desk, but he didn't even bother to open it. What was the point? Even if he succeeded in forcing it open, he had no idea what he was looking for. There was nothing to do except go back to the hotel and ring Irina.

He ran downstairs and unlocked the door. Klosterstraede was deserted. He closed the door quietly behind him, gave the handle a quick wipe with his handkerchief, then walked away towards the bright lights of Strøget. He didn't look back.

Fifteen minutes later he was in the lobby of the Admiral. Britt was still there behind the desk. So was her smile. Naturally she wanted to know if he had enjoyed his meal. He told her it had been memorable and asked for his key. He was still smiling as he headed towards the lifts, even though he couldn't quite remember what he'd done with Irina's telephone number. He wondered if all hotel receptionists in Denmark had the same effect.

The lift doors were opening when the man caught him by the arm.

'Mr Maltby?'

'Yes?' His stomach churned.

'May I have a word with you?'

He seemed rather old for a policeman. 'Who are you?' said Miles.

'May I offer you a drink?'

'On duty?'

'Please.' The man held an inviting arm out in the direction of the bar. He wore a short tweed overcoat with a fur collar. In one hand he carried a briefcase and in the other something that was either a fur hat or a dead rabbit. Such hair as he had was cut short. His eyes were bright behind his tiny, wire-framed spectacles. He looked like a monk on the razzle.

They sat down. He ordered a whisky for Miles and an Old Danish for himself. 'My name is Haraldsen,' he said. 'Harald Haraldsen. I am a friend of Paul Olsen.'

'Oh?'

Haraldsen handed Miles his business card. 'As you can see, I am the Chairman of the Copenhagen Association of Jewellers. Paul is our Life President.'

'Is?'

'It is an honorary position.'

'Ah.' So he didn't know.

The drinks arrived.

'Skål,' said Haraldsen, raising his glass and giving a funny little bow from the waist.

'Good health,' said Miles and nodded.

They sipped their drinks in an awkward silence.

After a while, Haraldsen said, 'We were due to meet tomorrow morning. But Paul rang me earlier this evening. He said you are leaving very early.'

'Did he explain why?' Miles enquired.

'An unexpected change of plan.'

'Something like that,' said Miles.

'He said you are writing an article for an English newspaper about amber.'

'That's right.'

'We are famous for our amber in Copenhagen,' said Haraldsen.

'So I understand.'

Haraldsen gave a nervous cough. He sipped some more of his Old Danish. He looked up. 'Paul tells me you have brought a piece of amber with you. Something very unusual.'

'I do have an item, yes.'

'If you would like, I could …'

'Actually, the item doesn't belong to me.'

Haraldsen looked solemn. 'Paul and I have been friends for sixty years. Of course, if you feel …'

Miles shrugged. 'I'm sure the owner won't mind,' he said. He looked quickly around. Everyone else in the bar appeared to be engrossed in their own conversations. He took the rose from his pocket and placed it in Haraldsen's open palm.

'O-o-o-oh.' It was not so much a word as a breath. Long, low, filled with wonder.

While he examined it, Miles finished his drink.

'What do you think?' he asked Haraldsen.

'Think?' said Haraldsen. 'I can't think. I can only look, and feel. I never thought I'd live to see such a piece again.'

'Why? Have you seen something like it before?'

'Yes, but it was a copy.'

'A copy of this?'

'Perhaps. I can't be sure. I would need the two side by side to compare. It was more than a year ago.'

'But like this?'

'Yes.'

'Where did you see it? Here in Copenhagen?'

'In Sweden. In Malmö. At a trade fair. A man came to our stand. He wanted to know what I thought.'

'Why?'

Haraldsen shrugged.

'What was his reaction when you told him it was a copy?'

'He was happy.'

'Happy?'

'It was a good imitation,' said Haraldsen. 'Very good. Most people would never have known. It was very clear. Homogeneous in appearance. The colour was good. The bubbles were not elongated, which is a sure sign of pressed amber. There was a good insect, not too big. Everything looked perfect, but I had my suspicions. Perhaps because it was too perfect. Under long-wave ultra-violet light the shapes of the original individual fragments could clearly be seen.'

'He must have said something.'

'He smiled and thanked me and walked away into the crowd.'

'You don't remember what nationality he was?'

'We spoke in English.'

Miles took a deep breath. His heart suddenly started to race. 'The person who owns this piece thinks it might be part of the Amber Room,' he said, in what he hoped sounded a casual tone of voice.

'Oh?'

'You don't sound impressed.'

Haraldsen shrugged. 'In our business we hear many stories.'

'I'm sure you do. However ...'

'There is a strong rumour that the Russians are very soon to make an announcement.'

'An announcement? What about?'

'They will say that the Room never left Russia after the war. That it has been recovered and is now being restored and will soon be put back where it belongs.'

Miles stared at him. 'In Pushkin, you mean?'

'In the Catherine Palace, yes.'

'Good God! Is this true?'

Haraldsen pulled a face. 'Who knows?'

'But where did this rumour come from?'

'About five years ago a colleague told me he had heard of its existence, but he could give no details. I thought no more about it. Then came the break-up of the Soviet Union. In the last year, various members of our Association have started mentioning it again. One or two seem convinced the story is authentic.'

224

'But not you.'

'May I buy you another drink?' Haraldsen said.

'Not for me, thanks,' said Miles. What he really needed was food. He wondered if his drink was still waiting for him at the Kommandanten.

'Let me tell you something,' Haraldsen said. 'Natural deposits of amber are very rare these days. Most is only good for industrial use. We have to take what we can. But in 1984 something very strange happened. There was suddenly a flood of good amber. Prices became depressed. We complained to the Danish Ministry of Trade. They were as mystified as we were. There was nothing they could do. But in November of 1984 and January of 1985, the Danish customs at the ferry terminal in Copenhagen discovered more than 150 kilos of high-quality amber. It was hidden in two cars, in specially designed panels. The drivers were arrested and sent to prison.'

'Where did they get it from?'

'It seems,' said Haraldsen, warming to his task, 'that they stole it from somewhere on the coast of Latvia between Kolka and Riga, then brought it by car to Gdansk in Poland and then by ferry to Copenhagen.'

'Why Latvia?'

'Riga has for centuries been the centre for amber craftsmen.' 'You mean that two men in a car upset the entire amber market?'

Haraldsen nodded. He seemed embarrassed, as if he had been personally responsible. 'But then suddenly, when the price of amber was at its lowest, everything changed. Overnight, all the amber that was stockpiled here in Copenhagen disappeared. The supplies dried up. Good amber is rare and the price is high again.'

'What do you mean, disappeared?'

'Someone bought it.'

'All of it?'

'Several tons. He got a good bargain.'

'He?'

'A man called Kirilov. Anatoly Kirilov. He is Russia's leading craftsman in amber.'

'Where does this Kirilov work?'

'In Riga,' said Haraldsen.

225

'Where it had come from in the first place,' said Miles.

'Yes,' said Haraldsen.

Miles leant foward. 'How easy is it to get to Riga from here?' he said.

22

He hadn't the heart to telephone Irina that night, or the energy. It was after eleven when Haraldsen left the hotel. By then, Miles was not only tired and hungry, he was also pretty drunk. It was something that seemed to happen to him a lot in very cold places. Besides, late at night is not the time to be delivering bad news, or receiving it.

He rang room service and ordered a pot of coffee and an open sandwich. He could have eaten three. He lay awake for over an hour and when he finally managed to doze off, he slept badly and had a nightmare about finding Noel lying flat out on the couch in his surgery with a small hole behind his ear. He woke up to find it was nearly eight o'clock. He got up, ran a bath and called London. Pierre took the call. Of course Her Imperial Highness was awake. She had woken at five, as usual. He would pass the telephone to Her Imperial Highness straight away.

'How are you getting on?' The tones were as slow and measured as if she were putting in a grocery order at Harrods.

Miles hesitated, but only for a moment. 'I've got some bad news, I'm afraid.'

'To do with Paul?' It was as though she'd been expecting it.

'He rang. I was in a restaurant. He said he couldn't meet me. He was too busy and I was to go home. He wouldn't explain. He sounded odd. Very strained. As if he didn't really mean it. As if somebody else had told him to put me off. I decided to go round anyway. The restaurant wasn't far from his house. Someone had got there before me.'

'Oh dear.'

'There was nothing I could do for him. I've seen the method used

227

before. It's quick, neat and instantaneous. It also allows no margin for error. I'm so sorry.'

'Paul and I were friends for half a century,' she said quietly. 'Did you call the police?'

'No. I'm afraid I couldn't face it. But I think I know who did it. The same person who killed the man in Switzerland.'

'How do you know?'

'I saw her. She left just before I got there.'

'Her?'

'I'm pretty sure. Tell me, when you spoke to him the other day, how did he sound?'

'He was very excited, of course. He did say one thing that I didn't quite understand.'

'Oh?'

'He mentioned a name. It sounded like Molotov.'

'Molotov? Like the cocktail?'

'Something like that. He said he wouldn't like to be in Molotov's shoes. Words to that effect.'

'The name wasn't Kirilov by any chance?'

'That's it. Kirilov.'

'Haraldsen mentioned that name last night.'

'Haraldsen? Not Harald Haraldsen?'

'Yes, why? Do you know him?' Miles asked.

'I met him once or twice with Paul. He is a good friend. Was, I should say.' There was a pause. Then, 'Where did you meet him?'

'He came to the hotel. He said Paul had asked him to contact me.'

'What did he want?'

'First, to see the rose. As he was a friend of Paul's, I showed it to him.'

'What was his reaction?'

'He was obviously impressed. I asked him if he'd seen anything like it. He said, yes: four or five years ago. But it was a copy. A good copy, but a copy all the same. At about that time, apparently, the market was being flooded with amber smuggled in from Latvia, or at least that was the assumption. Prices hit rock bottom and suddenly the Russians started buying it all back.'

'Did he say why?'

228

'He's heard a rumour that the Russians have found the Amber Room, or at least large parts of it, and that they've been restoring it for the last two years, and that's why they needed so much amber. This man Kirilov is in charge of the restoration. He's supposed to be one of Russia's leading craftsmen. Haraldsen says they're going to make an announcement about it. Very soon, he thinks.'

There was a long silence.

'Are you still there?' Miles asked.

'Yes,' she said. 'I'm still here.' Her voice was low.

'I'm flying to Riga today,' he told her briskly. 'I'll report back if I find out anything. If this man Kirilov is as well-known as Haraldsen said, it shouldn't be very difficult to find him.'

'I'm afraid you'll be wasting your time,' Irina told him.

'What do you mean?' Miles said. 'How do you know?'

'I know.'

'A single chance sentence in an obscure letter and you're sold?' said Miles. 'Surely you're made of more rigorous stuff?'

'I know you mean well,' she said soothingly, 'and I appreciate everything you have done. But you are very new to all this. You are also a journalist. You become quickly enthusiastic about subjects and immediately knowledgeable. Soon you will forget everything you ever knew about the Amber Room. For me this has been the work of half a century. The room for me is not just a story: it is part of my life. I have not seen it since I was a young girl, but I know every inch of it as well as I know my own room, and I know the Russians. They would give anything to have it back.'

'Perhaps they have,' said Miles.

'I think it very unlikely,' said Irina. 'This is nothing new. Every few years they announce to the world that they know where it is buried and that they are about to dig it up. But nothing ever comes of it. It is just a propaganda exercise, to boost their morale and to distract people like you.'

'I ...'

'Look here: two years ago, when Boris Yeltsin was in Germany, he told a group of politicians that he knew for certain it was buried under an old Soviet military base near Gotha and publicly asked their permission to dig it up. Yeltsin! What does he know about it? He is a politician. All right, go to Riga if you must. The old city is very beautiful. The Latvians are nice people. You will find plenty to write about, but you will not find the Amber Room. I can assure you of that.'

'You may be right,' said Miles. 'There may be nothing in it. But you are forgetting one thing. Paul Olsen is dead. I think he was killed because someone knew about our meeting and guessed he was going to tell me about Kirilov and the Russians. Someone warned him and that's why he didn't want to risk meeting me in person. So he sent Haraldsen instead. Thank God he did.'

'Whoever killed Paul may not know about Haraldsen, but he ...'

'She.'

'He ... she ... knows about you. You're as much at risk as Paul was. You're mad to even think of going to Riga. You've done everything you can. Come home, now.'

'I'm not giving up now,' Miles said. 'Paul Olsen died because of me. I'm going to find out why. I'll call you in a couple of days.'

'Don't blame me if you get hurt,' Irina told him.

'I won't,' said Miles. 'I promise.'

'You're very stubborn,' she said.

'That makes two of us,' said Miles.

* * *

The SAS midday flight from Copenhagen to Riga lifted off on time. Miles adjusted the angle of his seat, let his head drop back, closed his eyes and sighed deeply.

His first plan had been to go by boat and train, and, with Britt's enthusiastic assistance, he had spent a breathy twenty minutes thumbing through maps and timetables in an attempt to plot a route.

It could have been done. Catamaran from Copenhagen to Malmö. Train from Malmö to Ystad. Car ferry to Swinuoujscie in Poland. Train to Gdynia. Overnight in the Novotel in nearby Gdansk – 'reconstructed old town destroyed during war, worth a visit', if Britt's guidebook to Poland was to be believed. Then up at crack of dawn to catch the train for the seven-hour journey to Kaliningrad. The rest of that day plodding round Kaliningrad trying, and almost certainly

230

failing, to identify possible sites for the last resting place of the Amber Room. Then by overnight train to Riga, via Sovetsk and Klaipeda, arriving at 07.55 the following morning: or not, remembering previous experiences on Russian railways.

He had been tempted. It was the sort of journey that reeked of romantic promise. In the event, it would almost certainly turn out to be two days of hard seats, crowded compartments, bad food, miserable hotel rooms, unreliable connections, colourless scenery, frustration, irritation and exhaustion.

He was sorry to disappoint Britt after all her efforts, but was going to need all the energy he could muster. He had no idea what he was going to find in Kirilov's workshop. Or where to start looking. Irina had good reason to be concerned. Three men had died in the past trying to track down the Amber Room. Now two more had been killed. As long as the rose remained in his pocket, his life was also at risk. 'Don't blame me if you get hurt,' Irina had said. If he did, he had only himself to blame.

He looked out of the window. They were crossing the coast somewhere between Malmö and Skanör. Even from 30,000 feet the quiltwork patterns of the farms of southern Sweden were clearly defined. Dotted here and there, like models on a military ground plan, were clumps of buildings – barns, cowsheds, farmhouses. He wondered what it felt like to be totally content: to live a humdrum existence untrammelled by thoughts of fame and reputation and ambition; a life of few troughs and fewer peaks. Like his brother in Northumberland, or even Noel in Battersea. The quiet life could be his if he wanted it, starting straight away. He could spend a couple of nice days in Riga, visit a few churches, look round a few museums, see the sights, eat the food. There'd be a good thousand words in it. More, if he recycled them. He didn't have to go putting himself at risk. It wasn't wartime. He wasn't in the army now. He could step out of the game and return to the touchline any time he wanted, and no one would think the worse of him. No one would even know. Except himself. That was the trouble. Stubborn and foolish? Yes, possibly. He'd soon find out.

At passport control, Miles picked up another unusual stamp and walked through the Green customs channel. No one wanted to know what he was bringing into the country. God knows what would have happened if they had. There was an information desk on the ground floor. Using a mixture of German, English and sign language, he booked a room at the Hotel de Rome. Rebuilt since the war, it had four stars, a sauna and car-rental service, and it was centrally located, on the edge of the Old Town near Rifleman's Square. He changed a couple of 50-dollar traveller's cheques into 62 *lati* and went outside.

It was like stepping into a black-and-white photograph. The snow was piled high at the sides of the roads, and from the looming darkness of the sky it looked as if there was plenty more to come. It was only the middle of the day but it seemed more like late afternoon. Miles had expected it would be cold, but not so cold that it took his breath away. It was like breathing in ammonia. A vicious wind whipped round the airport buildings, numbing his nose and ears and bringing tears to his eyes. An electronic sign alternately flashed the time and the temperature: 13.50/ −10C.

There was a bus waiting to take passengers to the city centre, but this wasn't the moment for economies. The taxi rank was well stocked with light-green, state-owned Volgas, and a smattering of private Volvos and Mercedes. At the front of the rank was a well-maintained but elderly white SL120. The driver wasn't in the first flush either. He wore a black leather cap and looked like W. H. Auden.

'Twenty *lati*,' he said. His English was as rotten as his teeth.

'Ten,' said Miles, extending the fingers of both hands.

The driver shrugged and jerked a thumb in the direction of the back seat. Miles wondered if anyone ever paid the twenty.

'Hotel de Rome,' he said.

The iguana features nodded briefly. The Mercedes nosed out into the grey gloom of the Latvian afternoon.

'Is it always as dark as this?' Miles enquired.

The driver shrugged his incomprehension.

Miles stared out of the window at the bleak, featureless landscape. He tried to remember what he knew about Riga. It didn't amount to much. Old Hanseatic port. Popular crusading country for the Livonian knights, who wore white tunics and buckets on their heads with crosses on them and raped and burnt and pillaged in the name

232

of Christianity. The birthplace of the *Untermensch.* The Bournemouth of the Soviet Union – the 'near abroad' where old KGB generals went to retire, weighed down with their medals and their memories. Or so he'd been told by Noel, who'd once been there on a camping holiday. He also remembered a line he'd read somewhere. 'The only reason the Latvians don't hate the Germans is because they hate the Russians more.'

'American?'

'English.'

'Ah.' The leather cap nodded gloomily. So much for a big tip.

The outskirts of Riga sprawled endlessly like the outskirts of all big cities. The tower blocks of successive Stalinist housing estates seemed to rise organically from the earth, their grey, featureless façades illuminated by powerful spotlights beamed downwards from the roofs. Grim reminders of what had once been. Was it really only four years ago?

It made the contrast with the Old Town of Riga that much more striking. For all their brutal tastes, the Russians had preserved the ancient architecture. Miles was reminded of Prague. The narrow, winding streets, the tall, flat-fronted medieval houses with their shuttered windows, the secret courtyards, the dim street lights, the ancient cobbles … He wondered if, like Prague, it was all façade; and if, behind the photo opportunities, the place was like Miss Havisham's wedding cake: crumbling, cobwebbed, rat-ridden.

Two-thirty and it was almost dark when the Mercedes drew up in front of the Hotel de Rome. The driver didn't bother to get out but Miles gave him an extra couple of *lati* anyway. It was impossible to tell if he was pleased.

Miles ducked his head against the whipping wind and the whirling snowflakes and ran the few yards from the taxi into the hotel lobby. Even so, his ears were tingling as he signed the register and waved his American Express card. A half-remembered statistic flashed through his brain. Thirty per cent of a man's body heat is lost through his head. Or was it more? Fifty, perhaps? He needed to buy himself a good fur hat.

His room was on the fifth floor with a view over Kaļķu Street and the clock from the old Laima chocolate factory. Away to the left was

233

the Latvian Rifleman's Square with its ugly monument to the heroic local unit Lenin chose as his personal guard. Beyond it was the Oktobra Bridge and the River Daugava. In the other direction, beyond the Opera House and barely visible through the gloom, was Riga's Statue of Liberty, known to everyone as Milda – an elegant lady holding aloft the three gold stars representing the three regions of Latvia. It was beneath her arms that the citizenry automatically gathered for the first ever anti-Soviet demonstration in 1987.

Miles stood and watched the people battling their way along the pavement, shoulders bowed against the wind and snow. The whole city seemed to be wrapped in furry mystery. After a while he went across and took his overnight bag and tossed it on to the bed. He unzipped it, felt around and took out a rolled-up sock. He unrolled it. The amber rose fell out into his palm. He looked at it for a moment, then he closed his hand over it and went to put it in his jacket pocket; but at the last moment he changed his mind, rolled it up again in the sock, put the sock back in the bottom of the bag, zipped up the bag and put it in a cupboard.

He sat on the bed. There was a Riga telephone directory in the drawer of the bedside table. It listed seven Kirilovs. Four of them were obviously private numbers. The others were in capital letters and looked like businesses. The alphabet was Latin but there was nothing that looked remotely like the word 'amber'.

Miles pulled his tweed jacket on over his cashmere pullover, tucked the directory under his arm and took the lift to the lobby.

The head concierge was busy with another guest. His young assistant smiled politely while Miles riffled through the pages and hung up his key. Miles showed him the names and stabbed at them with his forefinger.

'Amber?'

The young man looked blank.

'Amber.' Miles repeated. 'Kirilov? Makes amber? You know. Yellow stone. Jewellery.'

The young man shook his head and frowned. Miles mimed a necklace. The young man's face lit up.

'Ah,' he said. 'Restaurant.'

He pointed to a door on the other side of the lifts. At that moment there was a loud ping. Miles looked round as one of the lift doors slid open. A man stepped out into the lobby. He wore a grey-fox-fur hat and a matching fur coat down to the ankles. The hat came well down over his eyebrows, like a guardsman's bearskin, and the coat had a high collar, turned up all round, which concealed much of the lower part of his face. But there was no mistaking the granite features and the pebble-hard eyes. Or the bruise under his eye where Miles had caught him with the straight left.

23

Miles quickly turned away and pretended to be examining the directory. The clerk was saying something in German, but Miles wasn't listening. He glanced round. Alex strode across the lobby. He hadn't cut much of a figure in the flat, but now the furs lent him style and stature. Authority even. The doorman leapt forward the moment he saw him coming.

But Alex held up a hand and moved across to where a clutch of armchairs stood in a circle round a low coffee table. A young woman was sitting in one of them, her back to the room, flipping through a magazine. Alex stood in front of her and held out a hand. She took it and stood up.

'Anna,' Miles murmured.

They walked arm in arm through the big glass doors and paused. Alex said something to the doorman, who moved forward and beckoned. A black stretch Russian Zil with smoked windows slid into view. The doorman leaned forward and opened the rear passenger door. Anna stooped and climbed in. Alex slipped something into the doorman's hand. The doorman saluted. Alex climbed in after her, the doorman closed the door carefully after them, gave another salute and the big car glided silently out of sight.

Miles ran across the lobby and out on to the front step. The limo was easing its nose out into the traffic, left-hand indicator flashing, as he came through the front doors. There was heavy traffic coming down the street towards the Oktobra Bridge. No one was going to stop and let a Russian car push out in front of them. The Zil would have to wait until the lights changed at the intersection with Aspazijas Boulevard, just beyond the hotel.

'Do you know where they're going?' Miles called out to the doorman.

The doorman jerked an enquiring chin.

'That car.' Miles pointed at the limo. 'Where is it going?'

The doorman put his hands out, palms upwards, and lifted his shoulders.

'Forget it,' Miles told him.

A line of taxis was parked at one end of the forecourt. More Volgas, with a sprinkling of Mercedes and Audis. A dark-blue BMW 520 stood at the head of the rank. Miles ran across, pulled open the passenger door and climbed in. The driver didn't even turn round. His small eyes regarded Miles in the rear-view mirror with sullen indifference. The traffic lights had changed, the stream of cars had temporarily dried up and the limo pulled out and drove down Kalku Street towards the river.

Miles pointed in the direction of the vanishing rear lights. 'That car. Could you follow it, please?'

He made a flapping movement with the back of his hands. At the sound of the English words, a gleam of cunning crept over the driver's pointed, ratlike features. Miles reached into his inside pocket and pulled out his wallet. He snatched a handful of dollar bills, pushed them past the unusually protruding ears and waved them under the long nose. It twitched faintly.

'Go,' he repeated. 'Now!'

The driver nodded briefly once, floored the accelerator and, to a faint squeal of tyres, spun the wheel and shot into Kaļķu Street. The traffic lights had changed by now and he only just managed to squeeze in before the leading phalanx came level with the hotel entrance. Horns were sounded, lights were flashed. The driver waved a contemptuous hand. The BMW gathered speed. It needed to. The limo was already a couple of hundred yards ahead. There were other cars behind it and, if they didn't keep up, they would quickly lose them.

'Right! Right!' shouted Miles. The limo had swung into Škūnu Street and was heading towards a large cobbled square.

'Dom,' said the driver, pointing to his left.

'What?'

'Cathedral. Very beautiful.'

'Very,' said Miles.

They crossed the square and exited down Pils Street. A large shape loomed ahead.

'Riga Castle,' said the driver.

'Ah yes,' said Miles.

'Very big.'

'So I see.'

At the little square just below it, the limo turned right again and dived down Mazā Pils Street and into the narrow cobbled lanes of the Old City. It pulled up outside a row of tall, flat-faced buildings with small shuttered windows and wooden doors, rounded at the top, set flush into the brightly coloured stucco.

Miles's driver was obviously beginning to enjoy himself. He seemed to know just how far to hold back, when to slow down, when to speed up and, when the limo stopped, how far away to park so that they could have a good view without arousing suspicion. Miles wondered if he watched a lot of American police series.

'I wait here,' said the driver.

'Good thinking,' said Miles.

For what seemed an age, but was probably only a minute at most, nothing happened. No doors opened. No one got out or in. Miles asked the driver what his name was. He said it was Josef.

Then one half of one of the wooden doors opened. An elderly man in a dark suit came out, looked quickly up and down the street, then turned and nodded at someone inside the house. A very tall man in a dark coat and a black fur hat came out. The elderly man hurried forward and opened the rear door of the car. The tall man climbed in, the door was closed behind him and the car slid away, leaving a faint grey trail of exhaust in the cold night air. Like a big black slug, Miles thought. Josef fell in behind without a word.

They turned right and right again, past the Castle, then left and over Vanšu Bridge. There was a signpost on the far side: Jurmala 5 km.

'Jurmala,' said Josef. 'Seaside. Very nice.'

'I bet,' said Miles.

'Big houses,' said Josef. 'Many Russian generals.'

'The Bournemouth of the Soviet Union,' said Miles.

He peered out of the window. There were yellow street lights down either side of the road. They seemed to be heading into the suburbs. Where the hell were they going? And what was *she* doing here, for God's sake?

'Anna,' he murmured to himself.

'Amber?' said Josef brightly. 'You like amber?'

'What?'

'Very much amber at Jurmala. Very beautiful. You like?'

'What amber?' Miles said. 'Where?'

'Beach,' said Josef.

'People find amber on the beach?'

'Big storm. Much amber.'

'Of course. And workshops? Do they have amber workshops at Jurmala? Make jewellery? Necklaces?'

Josef pulled a doubtful face. 'Is possible,' he said.

'You haven't heard any stories about amber?' said Miles.

Josef shook his head. Miles had lost him.

The limo turned left about a hundred yards ahead, and headed off into an industrial estate – a giant, grey Legoland of looming concrete factory buildings, characterless warehouses, wide intersecting roads and harsh neon lights. The place was buzzing with activity. Light streamed out from windows at all levels. Men in cheap fur hats, ear flaps hanging loose, buzzed back and forth in fork-lift trucks. Giant articulated lorries lumbered in and out of various entrances, brakes hissing, bodywork clanking. A car moved out of the parking area in front of one of the long, low, brilliantly lit office complexes that cowered beside the concrete monoliths. There was less danger of the BMW being spotted here than in the middle of Riga.

The Zil swept contemptuously through the middle of it all. For a moment Miles wondered if it was going to drive straight out the other side, but then, on the outer perimeter of the estate, it turned left off the main road and drew up in front of a pair of high metal gates. Behind them, surrounded by a broad concrete strip, was a long red-brick building. There were large metal-framed windows along both sides with lights on in all of them.

The area was ringed by a wire fence supported by concrete pillars and guarded at regular intervals by powerful floodlights. Beside the gate was a security kiosk. A man scurried out and unlocked the gates.

He swung them open and the car slipped through and vanished behind the main building. The man closed the gates again and locked them. High-tech stuff. Another man, with a beefy-looking dog on a short leash, approached the gate along the perimeter fence and greeted the gate man. They chatted briefly and the dog-handler continued on his beat. The gate man disappeared inside his shed.

Josef maintained his speed and drove past the building. Twenty yards further on there was a road to the right.

'Turn here,' said Miles.

It was a cul-de-sac with a little roundabout at the end. Josef eased the BMW through 360 degrees, drove slowly back and pulled up near the end of the road.

Miles pointed across at a wooden sign just outside the gates. 'What does that say?'

Josef repeated the name in the sign.

'I can see that,' said Miles. 'But what does it mean?'

Josef struggled to find the word. 'Light,' he said finally.

'Light? Light what?'

Josef indicated a nearby street lamp, cupped his fingers together and made a downwards gesture.

'Light bulbs?' said Miles.

Josef's face lit up. 'Bulbs. Yes. Lights.'

'Light bulbs?' said Miles. 'What would they want with light bulbs?'

Josef shrugged a face at him in the rear-view mirror. Miles wondered what Josef was thinking. That he'd picked up a madman, probably. He couldn't blame him. A man comes rushing out of the Hotel de Rome at 3.30 on a freezing January afternoon, dressed only in a sports jacket and grey flannel trousers, jumps into the back of his car, waves a handful of notes under his nose and tells him to follow some big black car. No word of explanation; no word of Latvian either. They drive halfway round Riga and end up in a side-road in an industrial park in the middle of nowhere, staring at a light-bulb factory. If Miles were Josef, he'd have reckoned the man was barking and that the sooner he got rid of him, cut his losses and got the hell back to Riga, the happier he'd be.

There was only one way Miles was going to get any answers but, if he set off on a recce, what were the chances of finding Josef there when he got back? What were the chances of his getting back, come to that? Grey flannel trousers and a sports jacket, albeit with a cashmere pullover underneath, are hardly ideal clothes in which to be doing anything in the depths of a Baltic winter, never mind walking up and down trying to figure out a way of getting through or over or round a twenty-foot-high wire fence.

On the other hand, he wasn't going to achieve anything by sitting there in the back of the car thinking about it. He reached into his inside pocket and closed his fingers round the wad of dollar bills.

'Russian,' said Josef suddenly.

'What?'

Josef jerked his head in the direction of the building. 'Light bulbs,' he said. 'Russian.' And he turned his head and mimed spitting into the front passenger seat.

'Russian?' said Miles. 'Still?'

'Comecon,' said Josef. 'Moscow. No more. Finished.'

He didn't elaborate. Couldn't, probably. But Miles understood enough. Comecon was the Soviet equivalent of the Department of Trade and Industry. In the old days this must have been one of countless factories making countless light bulbs on countless industrial estates from Warsaw to Vladivostok. Perhaps they were still turning them out. Comecon might have collapsed into a black hole, but people still needed light. But what of the factories that had been made redundant? There must have been plenty of entrepreneurs in all the old Soviet states who couldn't wait for the Russians to leave so that they could begin the task of establishing their own personal versions of a free market economy. And not just ex-Soviets either.

Whether Josef meant that this particular factory was finished or the whole Comecon regime it was impossible to tell. It seemed unlikely that he could spot a redundant light-bulb factory in the dark at a hundred yards. But that didn't matter. It was up to Miles to find out. The important thing was that Josef was a Latvian, and, like all good Latvians, he hated the Russians. And the car they'd been following was a Russian car. From which it followed that the people in it were probably Russians. In which case, the chances were that Josef was on Miles's side.

'Russians,' said Miles as contemptuously as he could and pushed a twenty-dollar bill into Josef's hand. 'Go round,' he told him and made a circular gesture towards the factory.

Josef nodded enthusiastically, eased the BMW forward and turned left up the main road. There was a road to the right at the far end of the factory. Miles cursed. He was hoping there might be a back entrance. On the other hand, the wire didn't look so forbidding close to. It was certainly no more demanding than the grappling nets officer cadets scramble up and down at Sandhurst every day of the week. Moreover, the central floodlight was out of commission and most of the area was in shadow.

'Stop here,' said Miles.

He peered out into the semi-darkness. There was no sign of the dog-handler. Probably indoors somewhere, sitting by a stove drinking schnapps, if he'd got any sense.

'Have you got any gloves?' he asked Josef. He mimed a pair.

Josef's face creased apologetically.

'I don't know how you lot manage to live so long,' Miles told him. 'I suppose a set of thermal underwear's out of the question? Never mind, forget it. You stay here, OK? I go there. Look. Come back. Soon. You stay. Don't go. Stay.'

Josef grinned and nodded.

'Russians,' Miles said, and mimed another spit.

Miles opened the car door and stepped out. The cold hit him in the face like a wet flannel after a long sauna and he gasped with the suddenness of it. His nose and ears were numb in seconds. It took longer to penetrate his clothing, but not much. By the time he'd reached the wire he was beginning to shiver. The thermometer had dropped at least ten degrees since lunchtime and, with a piercing wind upping the chill factor by a further fifteen to twenty degrees, Miles reckoned the ambient temperature was somewhere around the minus 40 mark. He blew into his cupped hands and looked up. The fence looked as high and sheer as the north face of the Eiger. But the wire was of a thicker gauge than he'd thought, and it definitely wasn't electrified. It wouldn't be too bad once he got going. Speed and rhythm: that was the trick. Opposite hands and feet. Like crawling.

He put his left foot into one of the lower meshes, reached upwards with his right hand and seized a crosspiece about thirty inches above his head and slightly to his right. The wire scorched his skin. He didn't feel any discomfort, just a feeling of tackiness, as if he were taking a lump of ice out of the deepfreeze. He was going to have to move even faster than he'd thought.

'OK,' he told himself. 'Go for it.'

It was not an evening for breaking records. He wasn't fit enough for that. Even so, he was at the top by the count of ten, and standing in the frozen grass on the far side before he got to thirty – breathing hard, though not as hard as he'd imagined.

He glanced down at his hands. His palms were criss-crossed with thin red lines. But there was no pain. He looked back towards the car. Josef was sitting there grinning and giving him the thumbs-up sign. He returned the gesture and set off towards the left side of the building. The windows were a little above head height. By standing on tiptoe, Miles was just able to peer in. There wasn't much to see. A large warehouse area filled with hundreds of unmarked wooden packing cases. Bordering the walls was an iron gangway with two sets of iron steps leading up to it on either side. A man was walking amongst the cases with a clipboard and pencil, apparently carrying out an inventory. Of light bulbs, perhaps? Though Miles would have expected something as utilitarian as light bulbs to be transported in something rather less expensive than wood.

At the far end of the warehouse area there was a wall with a set of double sliding doors in the middle. Miles moved slowly along the side of the building. About two-thirds of the way down there was a door, half glazed. The limousine was parked just outside. It gleamed wickedly in the light.

Miles was starting to shiver. Any body warmth he might have built up from his exertions on the fence had already drained away. He pulled his jacket tighter round his body but it wasn't much protection against the vicious wind. He tried not to think about it.

He stood on tiptoe and looked through one of the windows into a huge workshop. Some two dozen men and women, dressed in brown overalls, were bent over lines of workbenches beneath crude fluorescent lights, sorting, cutting, shaping, polishing, checking for quality. An air of urgency pervaded the room, yet at the same time each

243

person was totally absorbed in his or her task. But then this was no run-of-the-mill production line and these were no semi-skilled manual workers turning out anything as humdrum as light bulbs. They were craftsmen and -women, every one of them, and they were working in one of the oldest and most fascinating materials in the world: amber. Even the hideous overhead light could not drown out its warm glow.

There was no gangway in this part of the building, but at the far end, iron stairs led up to a landing. Behind it was a row of glass-fronted offices from which the local Comecon-employed managers once surveyed the ranks of workers below and make mental notes, should any of them appear not to be producing quite as many bulbs as the next person.

There were four figures now framed in the middle window: Alex and Anna in rich furs and attitudes of polite attention, like dutiful minor royalty on a visit; the tall man they'd picked up in the Castle district – grey-haired, hawk-faced, slightly stooping in his close-fitting black overcoat; and a short, jolly-looking man in a white coat, with a bushy white beard and wire-rimmed half-moons, who was doing all the talking. Kirilov perhaps? He looked like Santa Claus explaining his latest line in soft toys to a group of visiting wholesalers. Miles stretched and strained, but the focus of their interest remained just outside his line of vision.

The talk came to an end. Santa took a step back and ushered his guests towards the door. They paused on the landing while their host called down to a man in a brown coat who in turn hurried to a nearby bench and spoke to a couple of young men. They put down the pieces they were working on, got up and crossed to the near side of the room. For a moment or two they were out of sight; then they reappeared, carrying a panel of pale coloured wood, about three foot square. They held it upright between them, like porters at Sotheby's bringing in the next lot for auction. The three visitors nodded approvingly. Santa beamed. He held out an arm, inviting them to take a closer look. They descended the stairs and walked up to the object. For a long time they stood there, admiring it. Then they stepped back. Santa issued an instruction and the porters shuffled away. Miles swore under his breath. But then the party moved towards him and turned their backs. The porters stopped and swivelled round.

Miles drew in his breath sharply and held it. It was obviously part of a much larger section – a single roundel containing an urn overflowing with flowers, all in low relief, and framed by a pair of elaborate, matching curlicues. The pale, honey-yellow amber blazed beneath the neon light. Miles's breath was white in the night air, like a glimpse of a ghost.

24

The four of them stood there for a long time, discussing the panel. Occasionally one of them would step forward to examine a particular piece of carving and this would lead to further debate.

Even from that distance, the amber seemed to exude a warmth that was almost tangible, so that for a while, despite spasmodic shivering, Miles forgot how cold he was. But, when Santa dismissed the porters with a wave of the hand and Miles was faced again with the plain wood of the backing, the effect was as dramatic as if somebody had doused a fire with a bucket of water. The cold closed over him like the hand of death, paralysing every inch of exposed flesh, probing every last cranny of clothing, clawing at his chest and stomach and thighs, piercing his innermost organs with icy fingers. His whole trunk ached as the muscles fought to contain the last vestiges of warmth.

He stepped away from the window and threw his arms round his body as hard as he could, again and again, desperately trying to force some blood into his fingers and life into his aching bones. He remembered reading that, during the war, anyone on the Arctic convoys who fell into the sea lost consciousness after about twenty minutes and was dead in little more than an hour. He wondered how the northernmost waters of the Atlantic compare with a winter's night in Latvia. He hoped to God Josef was still there. He turned and started to run back along the side of the building. He had taken only a couple of steps when the side-door behind him opened and voices flooded out along with the light. He stopped and looked wildly for some sort of cover. There was nothing. There was no point in flattening himself against the wall. His shape would stand out at once under the perimeter lights. There was no alternative but to keep running towards the end of the building and hope to God that he made it before they came out.

God was on his side. Miles looked back. The first one to come out was the driver. He hurried to the back of the car and opened the boot. Then Santa appeared, shepherding the two porters as they moved gingerly sideways, carrying the amber panel between them. They laid it flat inside the boot and covered it with a rug. When Santa was satisfied, he dismissed them. The driver closed the boot and went to open the rear passenger door. The tall man now emerged, closely followed by Alex and Anna. The driver stood to attention beside the rear door as they ducked into the car's cavernous interior. He closed the door behind them with a dull thud and hurried round to the driver's side. Soon afterwards, white smoke dribbled from the exhaust. The car slid forward, turned right and disappeared from view.

It was about fifty yards from the back wall of the building to the fence. Miles covered it in a time that would have done credit to a good club sprinter. Panting, he reached for the wire, but to his horror, he realised that his fingers refused to hold it. The order had gone out from the brain all right, but the hands were now so cold and devoid of feeling that they were incapable of obeying it. He glared at them as they lay across the wire, utterly impotent, willing them to work. Gradually they began to move, until at last they were sufficiently hooked to give him some purchase. He placed one foot on the wire and pulled down with both hands.

The next few seconds were some of the most frightening he had ever experienced as he fumbled and stumbled his way up the fence. By the time he threw his legs over the top, the beams from the limo's headlights had already swung in a slow arc away to his left. Moments later, he hit the grass at the base of the wire. There was a patch of shadow to his right. He made it just as the car swooped past the end of the road, heading south. He looked around. There wasn't another vehicle in sight. He swore once, very loudly, jerking his head and body forward in his fury. As if responding to a doorman's whistle, a pair of headlights stabbed the darkness away to his right and turned towards him. He stood there, cold and exposed and frightened, shielding his eyes against the glare. The car pulled up next to him and the driver's window slid open.

247

'We go?'

Miles was still blinking. 'Josef?'

'I wait, you see?'

'I never doubted it for a second,' said Miles.

It took a good ten minutes for the adrenalin to stop pumping and the blood to take over. With the gradual return of circulation came the pain: just a light tingling at first, but then, as the palm reddened and swelled, a burning and a throbbing which, though not intolerable, was uncomfortable enough for him to curse out loud and squeeze his hands together for comfort between his knees. He felt like a schoolboy who has just received six of the best with a stiff ruler.

They followed the rear lights of the limousine to the edge of the industrial estate. Josef maintained a steady distance between them of between a hundred and two hundred yards. They came to the main Riga–Jurmala road and they turned left.

'Now what?' Miles murmured.

'Seaside,' said Josef. 'Jurmala. Very nice.'

The road was as heavy with traffic as it was with potholes.

'I'll take your word for it,' said Miles.

The word 'jurmala' in Latvian actually means 'seaside'. It is the name given to the most famous resort in the Baltics – a narrow five-mile strip of land, pressed against the sea by Latvia's second largest river, the Lielupe, and comprising sand dunes and wild grasses and pine forests. Tucked away in the trees, and often invisible from the road, are large Edwardian villas, mostly built of wood, their ninety-year-old stained-glass windows and fancy duckboards still intact. These were where the old Soviet generals came – or were sent – to live out their days in elegant retirement, pottering around in their big gardens, easing the aches in their creaking bones in the mud and peat and mineral waters of the local spas, and strolling along the deserted beaches and through the echoing woods, looking for amber. Riga's last local Communist Party boss, a man named Voss, had a seaside home in Jurmala. He loved it so much he had the road diverted and a suspension bridge built, so he could get there even quicker.

Josef's English being so sketchy, Miles might have missed some of the finer details of the story. But his drift was plain enough, and the

248

fleeting glimpses he was able to catch of the area in the light of passing headlights were enough to confirm it.

They drove on through the forest, staying well back from the limousine, even allowing other cars to get between them, but never letting it out of their sight. And then suddenly the rear lights burned bright, the right-hand indicator flashed and the car pulled off to the right.

'Go past,' said Miles. Josef hesitated. 'Keep going!' Miles's voice rose urgently. 'Go!'

Josef muttered something in Latvian and toed the accelerator. They drove past in time to see the lights of the limousine disappearing up a long drive between tall pine trees. A pair of high, wrought-iron gates were closing automatically behind it.

Josef drove on past a metal fence that was not as high as the one at the factory but was considerably more forbidding, being topped with two strands of barbed wire which angled outwards like a projection on a rock face. After a couple of hundred yards, the fence took a right angle and headed off alongside a narrow side-road that led towards the sea.

'Go down here,' Miles told Josef.

The trees loomed on either side. Through them, away to the right, Miles could see the outlines of a big house. Lights were on in all the windows. The headlights of the limousine flickered towards it through the tree trunks like a very old film.

When the BMW came parallel with the house, the road ran out in a small parking lot surrounded by a low concrete kerb. A couple of clearly defined paths led up into the sand dunes beyond. Josef switched off the engine. The marram grass on the tops of the dunes swayed, the sky was brilliant with stars. The wind had stiffened and with it the temperature. Miles lowered the window an inch. The cold air knifed through the gap and he quickly wound it up again. The wind roared round the car, like a wild animal trying to find a way in.

He looked to his right. The big house seemed to be perched almost on the edge of the dunes, directly overlooking the beach. If the fence ran the whole way round the property and across the front of it as well, that was the end of the adventure for the evening. His venture at the factory had been foolhardy enough and there was no way he was going to tackle a barbed-wire overhang in those temperatures. His hands were in agony as it was. At the same time, there was no way he was going to give up just because he didn't like the look of it. If there was any chance at all of having a look at what was going on in the house, he was going to take it.

He did a quick calculation. Two hundred yards from the car park to the corner of the house: a minute's hard running in sand and scrub – say two: five to six minutes of recce-ing – given that he could get near the house: two minutes back to the car. If he kept moving, he should be able to keep up his body temperature sufficiently. He should make it. He looked at his watch: 7.15.

'Ten minutes,' he told Josef. He pointed at the face and held up both hands. 'Ten. You stay here, OK?'

Josef shook his head. This time there was fear in his eyes. 'No ten minutes. Bad people. Very cold. We go.'

'No, Josef,' Miles said. 'I go. You stay.' And he got out of the car.

The going in the dunes was tougher than he'd expected. One moment he was moving well over short, flat grass, the next he was floundering through soft sand that gave way beneath his feet or tripping over treacherous tufts of coarse marram. Even so, he was standing on the area of beach in front of the house in under two minutes. For about a hundred feet the fence gave way to a six-foot-high stretch of brick wall, divided in the middle by a solid wooden gate. He tried the handle but it was locked. There was a gap of an inch or so where the gate was hinged to the wall. By putting his face close to the wood, Miles could see that the house was further back than he'd thought – on a terrace reached by a flight of a dozen stone steps above a formal garden of paths and flower beds. It was a solid, square house built on three floors in a style reminiscent of a French manor house, with a symmetrical central section to which extensions had been added at a later date. The one to the left was tall and thin with a copper mansard roof but its counterpart was altogether more substantial, with tall French windows leading directly on to the terrace. It looked as if it might once have been a ballroom. The lights from the hall flooded through the windows on either side of the main door, but the main reception rooms on the ground floor, including the big room, were concealed behind tall shutters.

250

The garden was mostly in shadow, with plenty of shrubs for cover. In seconds Miles had climbed over the gate and was moving fast in a crouching run along the paths and between the flower beds.

At the steps, he turned right and ran below the wall and round to the side of the house. Another flight of stone stairs led up on to the terrace that surrounded the house on three sides. He took them two at a time and flattened himself against the side wall. The wind hissed through the pines. He edged round in front of the French windows. The shutters fitted perfectly. He cursed and looked at his watch: 7.18. Just one more minute. Was it his imagination or was there a sliver of light coming through the next window? He moved towards it ...

The dog came from nowhere, and without warning. No barking, no snarling, no heavy breathing, no sound of any kind. One minute there was nothing; the next, something slightly smaller than a JCB had launched itself out of the darkness. Miles stood no chance. It caught him in the small of the back with the force of a demolition ball and suddenly he was face down with his mouth full of frozen earth. He smelt hot fetid breath and felt saliva dripping on to his neck. His stomach crawled as he waited for the teeth to go in.

There was a dull roaring sound in his head and a great weight was pressing down on his back. He could hardly breathe. Again he felt the hot breath on his neck. And then, as if from somewhere far out at sea, came the sound of a whistle so high-pitched it was almost nonexistent. Then:

'Dolf!'

The stench of the dog's breath faded. The weight was lifted from his back. His relief was short-lived. A hand reached down and grabbed him by the hair, wrenching his head backwards. He arched his neck and upper back. If he hadn't, his neck would have snapped. The hand went on pulling. He put his hands below his chest and pushed. His trunk rose a few inches from the frozen ground in a desperate press-up. He brought his knees up into a semi-crouching position. The fingers tightened their grip. Half pulled, half scrambling, he struggled to his feet.

The hand let go of his hair. Miles turned. The owner of it looked like a Russian weightlifter. Not an amateur who works out for fun, but a man who lifts for his country, and wins medals at it. He wore a

251

grey double-breasted overcoat and a black fur hat. He was the size of a dray horse, with a face to match. One gloved hand held a short lead. Dolf was attached to the other end. The creature looked at Miles and licked its lips. Miles didn't recognise the breed, but in England it would have been detained under the Dangerous Dogs Act. By a detachment of the SAS, probably. The lifter reached into his pocket and gave the animal a titbit. Somebody's hand, Miles wouldn't wonder.

Miles looked at the man. He had two choices: fox him with a dazzling display of fancy footwork and follow it up with a straight left to the jaw, or give up without a struggle. He didn't do a lot of thinking. He raised his hands in an attitude of surrender. The man jerked his head towards the house. Miles turned right and started walking.

The hall was two floors high with a gallery on four sides and doors off. It had a highly polished parquet floor with a copper grille in the middle: a relic from an out-of-date heating system.

A door on the left opened as the weightlifter pushed Miles ahead of him. Alex and Anna came out first. The tall man was a few paces behind them. In his elegant charcoal-grey suit, he looked even more like a distinguished financier. The sort of man who teaches Ivy League high-fliers, advises presidents, writes best-sellers and amasses a fortune, all at the same time. Close to, the thin cheeks and narrow outcrop of a nose were even more hawklike. Heavy brows overhung grey, close-set eyes, underscored with deep lines. They could have been the result of a lifetime of laughter, though he wasn't doing a lot of it at that moment. No one looked to be in much of a laughing mood.

There was a brief exchange between Alex and the weightlifter. Anna looked at Miles, but with no sign of recognition. He noticed she was limping slightly. He was genuinely sorry about that. Alex had a shifty look. He had good reason to be. If he'd done his job properly, Miles wouldn't have been there.

'How's the black eye, Alex?' he said.

Alex scowled. 'What the hell are you doing here?'

'I might ask you the same question,' said Miles.

'You are out of your depth,' said Alex.

'I know,' said Miles.

'You should have left well alone when you had the chance. You are a fool.'

'But dogged with it,' said Miles cheerfully. '*Noli concedere.*'

'What?'

'It's the family motto,' Miles told him. 'Roughly translated, it means, "If someone comes barging into your home uninvited, barge into theirs." '

Alex sneered. 'We have a saying in our family, too. "Don't take what doesn't belong to you." '

'That didn't stop *you*,' Miles reminded him.

'Where is it?'

'Where's what?'

Alex walked forward and ran his hands over Miles's jacket pockets. He stepped back. 'You know what I'm talking about,' he said.

'Tell you what,' said Miles. 'Give us a clue. Animal, vegetable or mineral?'

Alex hit him hard in the stomach. Miles grunted and bent double.

'That's enough.' The voice was deep; the accent East Coast American; the tone one of quiet authority.

Alex stood there, breathing hard. A muscle pulsed along his jawline.

'Do you know this man?' The tall man was looking straight at Miles but the question was directed at Alex.

'This is Maltby,' said Alex.

'Maltby?'

'The man who took the rose.'

'Ah yes. Mr Maltby. The journalist and amateur sleuth. What's he doing here?'

'Pushing his nose into other people's business,' said Alex. 'Like all journalists.'

'When people break into my home and try to kill me, it's very much my business,' Miles said, returning the tall man's gaze.

'How did he find us?'

'God knows,' said Alex.

'Unfortunately, God isn't here to ask. Anna? Any ideas?'

He moved to her side and put an arm round her shoulder. His eyes looked into hers. His voice was gentle. She looked straight ahead at Miles. Her face was very pale; her eyes quite expressionless.

'I have never seen him before in my life,' she said dully.

Miles searched her face in vain for some hint of irony. Perhaps she really thought she hadn't. After all, their first meeting had hardly been conducive to familiarity.

The tall man nodded. 'How extraordinary,' he said, his hand massaging the back of her neck. 'Perhaps he just happened to be in the neighbourhood and thought he'd look us up. What do you think?'

Neither of them replied.

'Well?' The anger was quiet and well controlled.

Miles addressed the tall man: 'I don't know who you are, or how you know who I am, or what this is all about, but I'll tell you exactly how I found you. It was pure accident. I am an English journalist. I happen to be writing a story for my newspaper about amber. I was told the best person to speak to was here in Riga. Someone called Anatoly Kirilov. I gathered he's the world's greatest amber craftsman, so I came out to interview him. I hadn't got his address and I was in the lobby of the Hotel de Rome looking him up in the local telephone directory when I happened to spot Alex here. Since we share an interest in amber, I decided to follow him on the off-chance he might lead me to Kirilov. You're not Kirilov by any chance, I suppose?'

The tall man stood there, his hands crossed in front of him, nodding. And then he struck.

The hand moved with the speed and ferocity of a mamba and caught Miles hard across the side of the face. He staggered and there was a taste of blood in his mouth.

He gave a short laugh. 'Obviously not,' he said.

'Who told you about Kirilov?' They were the first words the tall man had directed at Miles.

Miles shrugged. 'Some antique dealer, I think. I can't remember now. I've spoken to so many people in the course of my research.'

'I'll ask you again. Who told you to come and look for Kirilov?'

Miles gave a light laugh. 'Journalists never reveal their sources,' he said.

The man looked past his shoulder and gave a barely perceptible nod. Miles was aware of a sudden movement behind him, and a sickening pain ripped through him as the weightlifter's hand chopped into his kidneys. He went down on his knees, retching and gasping for breath.

'I'm sorry?'

'So you should be,' groaned Miles.

The weightlifter's boot caught him under the ribs. A red film rose in front of Miles's eyes and he went over on to his side. There were footsteps on the parquet and a shoe appeared next to his face. Black, half-brogue, hand-lasted.

'Would you mind repeating that?' the tall man said softly. 'I didn't quite catch what you said.'

'I didn't say anything,' said Miles, coughing.

'Oh dear,' sighed the tall man. 'I was afraid of that.'

Miles looked up as the weightlifter drew back his foot.

'Wait.' Anna took a step forward. The weightlifter paused. She said, 'It is not important who told him, surely. In a week our task will be completed. By that time he'll be gone and no one will be the wiser.'

'That depends,' said the tall man.

'On what?'

'On whether anyone else has seen the rose.' He looked down at Miles. 'Where is it by the way?'

'I really don't know what you're talking about,' gasped Miles. 'What rose?'

'Stefan!'

'No, wait.' Anna moved close to the tall man. She stood looking up at him like a child begging a favour from a stern father. 'Listen. Perhaps we're making too much of this rose. After all, what is one small piece of amber compared with what we've got? Even if all the experts in Europe said it was genuine, do you honestly think anyone's going to listen to them?'

'Not if there really *is* only one piece,' said the tall man, staring ahead over the top of her head.

'Surely you do not believe ...?'

He put his hand out and touched her cheek. 'Sweetheart, it's not a matter of what I believe or do not believe. If the room exists ...' His voice was all gentle, all persuasive.

'But the man who saw it, or said he saw it, is dead.'

The tall man smiled indulgently. 'But the rose isn't.'

'If we kill the man who knows where it is ...'

'And if there are others?'

'It's a risk we have to take,' she said.

Waves of pain surged through Miles's body. He had never known anything as bad: not even in those early days in the Royal Victoria. The brain was working well, though. The pain seemed to sharpen it. *Unless it's the imminent prospect of dying. Good old Dr Johnson. Talked an awful lot of balls most of the time. The original pub bore. Got it right occasionally. I doubt they'll hang me, though. Something sharp poked up behind the ear is more their style. Either way, I'm bloody well not going without first finding out why. I've nothing to lose. Neither have they. Even if I tell them where the rose is, it won't help. That Anna. I guessed she was a hard-faced bitch the first time I saw her. People don't get faces like hers for nothing. That was one thing Dr Johnson never thought of saying. But then people like this tall man hadn't been invented in his day.*

'Am I going to be let in on the secret?' Miles asked. He tried to get up, but the weightlifter placed a foot in the middle of his back and pinned him to the parquet.

The tall man said, 'Stefan!' and made a dismissive gesture with the back of his hand.

The foot was removed: reluctantly, Miles felt. He struggled, un-aided, to his feet. He felt terrible. His kidneys throbbed like hell and the pain in his rib snagged sharply, taking his breath away every time he inhaled. It felt as if it was broken.

'Why not?' said the tall man. 'Since you've come this far. My name's Smith, by the way. But you can call me John, if you like.'

'You can call me Mr Maltby,' said Miles.

'Come along then, Mr Maltby.' Smith took Miles gently by the arm and led him across the hall towards the door they had come out of earlier. He opened the door. 'Now,' he said. 'What do you think of that?'

There, glowing in the dark of the Baltic winter, was the Amber Room. All 4,300 square feet of it, give or take a couple of panels. The Eighth Wonder of the World.

Miles stood in the doorway for a long time, speechless with awe, while his eyes tried to assimilate the sheer size and scale of the thing. The swags of flowers and fruit, the minutely carved decorations, the jigsaw-like precision of the amber pieces. The panels were surrounded by cartouches of gilded *boiserie* in the style of Louis Quinze and divided by tall, narrow, gilt-framed mirrors. The centres of four of them were further adorned with landscapes, executed in Florentine mosaics of coloured, polished stones, set in frames of gilded bronze.

It was one of the most beautiful things Miles had ever seen and one of the most grotesque. It was like a nightmare of the sort you sometimes get after eating an over-rich dinner. It was like a miser's dream of heaven. It was like nothing else in the world.

'It's incredible,' Miles breathed. 'Unreal.'

'I thought you might appreciate it,' said Smith. 'Mr Kirilov and his team of craftsmen will be most gratified. After all, as the first member of the public, as it were, to have seen it, your judgment is of special value. In a few weeks' time, the whole world will know the answer to one of the great mysteries of modern times. Possibly of all times. The fabulous Amber Room, whose whereabouts has been the inspiration for so many stories for nearly half a century, never left the Baltics at all. The front pages of every newspaper in the world will carry pictures of it. Millions of words will be written about it. Television companies will spend the equivalent of their annual budgets in the fight to be the first to tell the true story of the discovery of the greatest treasure since Howard Carter uncovered Tutankhamun's tomb in 1924. It will be one of the biggest days in the history of modern Russia. Sadly, you yourself will not be alive to join us in the celebrations, but I hope this exclusive sneak preview will make up for your disappointment.'

'That depends,' said Miles. 'Is it real?'

'Is it or isn't it?' said Smith. 'Genuine or fake? Fact or fiction? What does it matter? Can you tell the difference between a real Picasso and an Emil de Hory? I bet you can't. Would you really know if you were sitting on a genuine Chippendale or a very good reproduction? And would you honestly care even if you did?'

'It would depend on whether the person who sat me on it tried to

257

pass it off as the real thing. There is a difference between an imitation and a fake. It's the difference of intention.'

'And what would you say if, by passing a good imitation off as the genuine article, you were able to shore up an entire economy, free an entire population from starvation, and save a nation from a right wing dictatorship that has the potential to out-Nazi the Nazis? What would your considered view be on that?'

'So it *is* a fake,' said Miles. He looked round at the walls. 'It's incredible. It's brilliant. But it's still a fake.'

'What the hell do you care?' said Smith. 'You're not a Russian. You don't know what it's like to queue all day for bread in sub-zero temperatures and get there to find it's all sold out. To live in an atmosphere of permanent insecurity, not knowing where your next meal ticket's coming from, or your next meal. To be cold and frightened and sick and demoralised.'

'And you do, I suppose?'

'Not personally, no. But I've spent enough time in Russia to know just how bad things are and how much worse they could get if people like me don't do something about it.'

'And who the hell are you?'

'Just a businessman,' said Smith, casually.

Miles laughed. 'What's that supposed to mean?'

'It means whatever you want it to mean. In my case it means someone who gets things done.'

'And never mind how.'

The tall man shrugged philosophically. 'Our methods may not be to everyone's taste, but who cares if a few rules are broken as long as the majority reap the benefit? *Pro bono publico*, that's my motto. What's yours?'

'I've already told you.'

'Listen,' said Smith. 'I'm not alone in this. There are many others like me who realised years ago the mess everyone was going to get into when Communism failed. And, when it duly did, we were the ones who were ready to step in with the expertise and the materials and the funding they're all going to need if they are to survive the next few years. No one else. Not the politicians, that's for sure.'

Miles laughed. 'You're not going to try and tell me this is going to do anything for the Russian economy.' He gestured round at the room. 'God knows what your interest is, but it's Lombard Street to a clockwork orange that it won't be the wellbeing of the Russian people.'

Smith leaned very close to Miles and murmured into his ear, 'Well, that's just where you're wrong, old man. The wellbeing of the Russian people is exactly what I'm interested in. Me and Mr Yeltsin. A big propaganda coup right now would go a long way to restoring his standing with the Russian people and their morale. Not to mention renewed respect from the West. It would also bring in a fortune in hard currency. Put the Amber Room back in the Catherine Palace, exactly as it was in the summer of 1941 before the Germans stole it, and Russia would have a tourist attraction to rival the Taj Mahal, the Great Wall of China, and the Tower of London. Oh yes, old man, I have the interest of the Russian people very much at heart. Ten years I've been working on this, and if you think I'm going to allow some pipsqueak of a journalist to ruin it all now for the sake of some crummy little story, you can think again.'

'Wow,' said Miles. 'I've heard a lot of reasons for having my stories killed. One or two have been genuinely compelling. But I've never heard one quite as unarguable as this. What can I say? In the circumstances, I have no alternative but to kill the story. But if I do, will you still kill me?'

Smith put a hand on Miles's shoulder. It looked like a well-manicured chicken's claw. 'I like you, Maltby,' he said softly. 'Your heart's in the right place. I'd like to believe you. But I have this problem, see? I just don't believe a single word any journalist ever utters. And I'm afraid that includes you. So, the answer to your question is Yes. I'm sorry, but we're talking *pro bono publico* here.'

Miles beckoned him closer. He looked past him at Alex and Anna. 'What if I told you,' he murmured, 'that the rose was phoney all along? You can have it if you like. I'm sure you can fit it in somewhere. Call it my contribution to democracy.'

'I don't believe you,' said Smith. 'Not that it matters. As my young friend said, who'd give a damn one way or the other? What's one piece of amber compared with a whole room?'

'Oh, it matters,' said Miles. 'And you know it. Or, rather, it would

259

matter if it was real. If it could be proved to be a genuine piece from the original room, and if other pieces like it were to turn up in the same place, a lot of people would give a great deal more than a damn. Not least, Mr Yeltsin and his friends. How much has this thing cost them? OK, so you were able to manipulate the amber market for a while and buy tons of the stuff at a depressed price, but even so … Millions? Billions? How many people could that have fed and clothed over the years? If it got out that the newly uncovered Amber Room was a fake, and that the Russian government had colluded with it at the expense of the people, there'd be a third Russian revolution. Vladimir Jhirinovsky would be swept into power overnight, the Soviet Empire would be restored in less than a week and God help us all. On the other hand, if I'm right and the rose is a copy, you have nothing to fear.'

'Except you,' said Smith. 'You'd write the story anyway. So would I in your place. So would anyone. I wouldn't blame you. It's a great story. Perhaps one of the greatest stories never told.'

Miles said, 'I didn't come here alone, you know. A colleague is waiting for me in a car nearby. If I don't return by a prearranged time, he has orders to contact the police.'

The American smiled. 'He needn't bother. I just rang the police myself to tell them we had an intruder on the premises. They asked if we needed any help, but I told them we could handle it.'

Miles heard what Smith was saying, but it wasn't sinking in. Here he was, being informed, calmly and dispassionately, by a man calling himself a businessman but who was almost certainly Mafia, that he was about to be murdered. There was nothing he, Miles, could say that would alter that decision, and in the next hour or so – possibly within the next few minutes – he would be taken outside and killed: quickly and painlessly if he was lucky, but there was no guarantee. He heard it and he understood it and yet he simply couldn't take it seriously. An air of unreality hung over the proceedings. The dream-like quality of the room itself added to his sense of detachment. But there was something else. Something that had dug itself deep into his soul. A sense of invulnerability, engendered by an existence in which things didn't go wrong; a conviction that ugly reality had no part in a life of smooth perfection so carefully created and nurtured by countless hoteliers and tour operators and public relations executives. And if it by some remote chance ever did – if the car wasn't waiting at the airport, or the hotel room wasn't quite up to the expected standard, or the wine did not quite live up to its promise – then a brisk telephone call to the PR man ensured that something would be done about it. Fast.

Ordinary tourists got murdered in Florida. Sex-crazed punters contracted Aids in Bangkok; not journalists. Journalists are observers, not players. Things don't happen to them: they hear about them from others and write them down *as if* they had happened to them. A freelance who hears a good story about an unsolved mystery and tries to turn an honest bob by working it up into a feature does not expect to be attacked by a savage dog, beaten up by a tame gorilla and told he is dead meat. If he is, he explains that it was all a silly misunderstanding, and that a call to the local Tourist Board will clear the air and he'll be on his way, no hard feelings.

'Look, Mr Smith,' said Miles, adopting a conciliatory tone of voice, 'I think we've got our wires crossed somewhere along the line. If I could just call my editor in London, he'd explain …'

'Frankly,' said Smith, 'I don't have the time.' And he turned and walked from the room. Alex followed him, smirking. He paused briefly to murmur something to Stefan. For the first time Anna looked Miles in the face. There was triumph in her eyes. Then she, too, turned away.

Miles was still watching her when he felt Stefan push him hard in the back. He stumbled into the hall. The man pushed him again. Miles whirled round, fists raised, shoulder muscles bunched, eyes blazing. The man smiled, stepped forward, shook his head and wagged the forefinger of his left hand in front of Miles's nose. With his other hand, he hit Miles in the solar plexus. He didn't hit him very hard: he didn't need to. Miles doubled up and gasped for breath. When he stood upright, his hands had been tied.

Stefan jerked his chin in the direction of the front door. Miles complied. He didn't protest. What was the point? After all, he was going to wake up in a moment …

As they were going out through the front door, Alex emerged from the opposite side of the hall and handed a bottle of water to

Stefan. Then he smiled at Miles and gave a polite little bow – for all the world as if he were taking leave of a house guest after a country weekend.

The cold had sliced through Miles's jacket, his cashmere pullover and his Viyella shirt before they'd got halfway along the terrace.

By the time they started down the stone steps to the formal garden, he was shivering uncontrollably. By the fence, his hands and face had lost all feeling, and his mind all hope.

The wire was stretched between metal poles three or four inches in diameter: roughly the circumference of a man's grip. Stefan signalled to him to stop and then held the bottle of water towards him, as if offering him a drink. Miles nodded. He was grateful. His throat was taut and dry. And, who knew, if he could get his hands on that bottle ...

Stefan grinned and began to unscrew the top. Again he seemed to be offering it. Miles put his hands out to take it. At the last minute Stefan tipped the bottle and poured the contents over them, like a server assisting at a high altar. Miles stared at his hands, as if hynotised. Already he could feel the water congealing over the joints. Stefan took a step forward and seized Miles by both wrists. He forced him towards the fence. Miles put up a token show of resistance, but Stefan's strength was awesome. As Miles felt his hands being drawn nearer and nearer to the metal posts, he suddenly realised what was about to happen.

Laurence Olivier once described how, during rehearsals for *Oedipus Rex*, he had tried to find a sound that would express the king's feelings on discovering that he had murdered his father and married his mother. Over the weeks he tried many different sounds, but none of them quite summoned up the intensity of pain and fury and despair that he was searching for. And then he remembered reading that the way the trappers in the Arctic catch ermine in the middle of winter is by putting salt on the rocks. The animal goes to lick the salt and its tongue is instantly and irrevocably frozen to the rock. No record exists of ermine screaming into the frozen void, but in those who witnessed Olivier's performance there lingers a memory of one of the most chilling sounds on earth.

Miles started screaming before either hand had touched the pole.

That was because he hoped the sound might carry along the beach and into Josef's car. Some hope. It took less than five seconds for the wet skin to be welded to the metal. The next time he screamed, it was for the same reason as the ermine.

25

Stefan pressed Miles's hands hard against the pole. He held them there for several minutes, a couple of feet or so above Miles's head – roughly where he would have grabbed if he'd been trying to climb the fence. Miles was a strong man, but with his hands pinned he was virtually immobilised and, hard as he fought, his struggles were as pathetic as those of an angry baby in the hands of an experienced nanny. Stefan smiled indulgently at Miles's efforts and only when he was quite satisfied that the skin was welded to the metal did he step away.

Miles moved his left foot backwards a few inches in the hope of gaining a little purchase. Almost at once the dog snarled and rushed forward. Miles could feel its hot breath on the back of his leg.

'Dolf!'

The dog shuffled reluctantly out of range. Stefan pulled a length of thick cord from his jacket pocket and quickly and efficiently secured it round Miles's ankles, so that he was now incapable of any useful movement. Stefan gave the knots one last tug, then stepped back and regarded Miles with the professional air of a gamekeeper who has bagged a particularly troublesome fox and has just strung the corpse up on his game pole as a warning to others. He nodded with satisfaction.

'For Christ's sake!' Miles shouted. 'What the hell do you think you're going to achieve by all this?'

Stefan pointed to where Miles's hands were clamped round the pole. He shook his head. He pointed at the top of the fence and shook it again. Then he made a pillow out of his hands and rested his cheek on it and mimed tears.

The sub-text was clear enough. A phone call to the police would explain that an intruder had been found in the grounds. In trying to make his escape via the fence, he had grabbed at one of the metal supports with his bare hands and become frozen fast. Unable for some reason to extricate himself (the ropes would be removed later), his body core temperature had dropped rapidly, causing unconsciousness and death by hypothermia. An unfortunate accident, but what can people expect if they will insist on going out in such low temperatures, dressed in such unsuitable clothing?

'For Christ's sake, Stefan! No! No!' Miles shook his head, but he knew he was wasting his energies.

Stefan gave him one last grin. Then he raised his hand, wiggled his fingers at him and walked off towards the house. Dolf turned away with evident reluctance and trotted obediently after his master across the frozen grass.

Miles uttered a string of quiet expletives in time with Stefan's tread until man and dog had disappeared from view round the side of the house. Then self-control took over and he began to consider his options. It was a lifetime since he'd last consulted his survival manual – not since that terrible, never-ending night he was stuck out with his platoon on Mount Tumbledown – but he could remember enough to know that he wasn't going to die quickly. Even in temperatures approaching 50° below, it could be three hours before he lost consciousness and four before his vital organs packed up altogether. His hands were a different matter. Another hour and they'd be in a very bad way: longer and they'd be out of action for a week or more. And since frostbite would already have put paid to a certain amount of skin tissue, and since all feeling had gone, he had nothing to lose by tearing them off before the damage went too deep: nothing, that is, except the strips of skin that would inevitably be left attached to the metal.

It sounded easy enough: an intake of breath, a couple of sharp tugs, a second or two of resistance, a brief moment of disgust, a few frustrating minutes while he fumbled to untie the knots, and he'd be over the gate and away ... But Stefan, for all his oafishness, had good reason to be proud of his handiwork. He'd done this sort of thing before, and he'd made quite sure there was no way Miles could work up any leverage on his hands from that position: certainly not tied together at the wrists like that. And even if, by some burst of superhuman willpower and strength, he were to succeed in wrenching himself away, his fingers would probably be incapable of any movement at all, let alone unravelling knots.

This could be one dream he was never going to wake from.

Miles wondered whose idea it had been to dispose of him in this vicious way. Smith, presumably, though the Mafia were not known for wasting a lot of unnecessary time when disposing of their enemies. A single bullet in the back of the neck was about the extent of their imagination. Someone else, then. Anna perhaps? To judge by that last look she gave him, she was capable of any amount of cruelty. Clearly she held a special place in Smith's affections; she could well have been the one who'd dropped the notion into his mind. Presumably Stefan would have reported back to Smith by now. They were probably all, at this very minute, watching him from one of the windows, laughing and joking, and taking bets on how long it would be before he slumped.

The wind was getting up by the second. It moaned through the pines like a wraith in torment. Miles wasn't feeling any too good himself. He shivered in great shuddering waves of pain and despair. *I am dying, very, very slowly, and the stupid thing is I'm doing absolutely nothing to prevent it: just standing here like a naughty schoolboy in a corner, long after everyone's gone home, because no one's remembered to tell me I can go. Bloody silly. I'm a grown man. I can go home whenever I want. What's to stop me? All I have to do is ... what? ... something ... anything, rather than stand here, freezing to death, while the strength and the willpower drain out of me along with the last vestiges of warmth. Perhaps if I was to stretch up and then let myself go ... Let the knees buckle and the body drop. The skin area is far too small to support 200 pounds of dead weight. It'll come away as easily as peeling a stamp from an envelope ...*

Miles hopped forward on both feet until his toes were touching the base of the pole. He breathed quickly in and out several times like a weightlifter about to go for a snatch and lift, then raised himself on to his toes. Or, rather, he tried to. It wasn't easy. All feeling had left his feet and they were reluctant to obey orders. But slowly and with a great deal of cursing he began to inch upwards until the pressure on his arms eased, his elbows flexed and his calf muscles ached. Now all he had to do was let go and …

'Wait!'

His heels dropped, his elbows straightened, his knees held firm, and the skin of his hands tautened against the metal. Breathing hard, he turned his head.

She was ten or twelve feet away, a fuzzy black outline against the dim light from the house, her face invisible amid the furs. She stood there for a moment, perfectly still, then the outline changed as she reached inside her coat. When her gloved hand came out it was holding something: something metallic that glinted dully in the moonlight. She moved towards him like the Angel of Death.

Miles gave a short laugh. 'Come to put me out of my misery?' he said. 'Pay me back for stabbing you in the leg?' He could barely get his lips round the syllables and the words were slurred. 'I'm surprised,' he mumbled. 'I thought all this was your idea. Or have you just come to gloat? Curiosity got the better of you, perhaps? Well, I'm sorry to disappoint you, but you're a little early. Come back in an hour. I should be in a really bad way by then. You might even catch me in the last stages of consciousness. You never know your luck.'

'Please don't talk,' she said. 'Just do as I say. Trust me.'

'Why the hell should I trust you? You've already tried to kill me once. You've killed two other people to my certain knowledge. I wouldn't trust you if you were the last person on earth.'

'I *am* the last person on earth as far as you are concerned,' she said quietly. 'And you are going to *have* to trust me if you want to live.'

'You're English.'

'So?'

'You weren't English in Eigerhubel.'

'I was in disguise in Eigerhubel.'

'Oh, for God's sake.' Miles spat the words out. 'If you're going to finish me off, finish me off, but please don't talk balls.'

Miles was interested, in a detached sort of way, to find that, when it came to it, he felt none of the things he thought he'd feel: fear, self-pity, regret. He was sorry he wouldn't be seeing Elizabeth again. He hoped she wouldn't be upset. Irina, too. And his mother, of course, though she'd still have her beloved Henry. And poor old Josef.

Presumably he was halfway back to Riga by now, cursing and telling himself you can never trust foreigners. The way things had turned out, Miles wished he'd given him something up front. Enough to cover his expenses, anyway. Otherwise all he felt was relief. He was going to die sooner or later anyway: better to do so with a quick blackout than a long, slow fade.

'Keep still.'

The voice was deep and low and came from very near his left ear, accompanied by a faint hint of something expensive by Saint-Laurent that he couldn't quite place. He swivelled his head. She was standing very close to him. Her eyes were huge and dark against the whiteness of her skin. They were concentrated on the thing she was holding. He looked down. He could see now that it wasn't a gun, as he had supposed, but a small thermos flask. She was trying to unscrew the top and having trouble with it.

'What the hell's that?' Miles asked. 'Hot soup? "The prisoner consumed a healthy cream of mushroom before he died"? Or is it oxtail? Very nourishing in the cold weather, oxtail.'

Anna grunted with the effort, and then sighed as the top came loose. She removed it completely and put it in her pocket, then pressed herself up against him and, placing her left hand on his shoulder and holding the steaming flask in her right, stood on tiptoe and stretched until the lip was just above the level of his hands.

'The moment you feel the slightest movement, pull,' she murmured. 'You're bound to lose some skin. There's nothing I can do about it.'

Miles said, 'What's going on? I thought you were one of them.'

'You thought wrong.'

'But ...'

'I haven't got time to explain now,' she said.

'What about Eigerhubel? And Copenhagen?'

'Appearances can be deceptive.'

'At least tell me who you are.'

'Later,' she said. 'I'll tell you everything later.'

'Give me one good reason why I should trust you,' he said.

'Because you have no alternative,' she said.

She tipped the flask and warm water began to run down the pole.

268

Most of it trickled over the backs of his hands, but a certain amount made its way between palms and metal. Miles began to tug at his hands.

'Wait,' she murmured. 'Not yet.'

The water continued to dribble from the flask. Within seconds of touching the pole it was beginning to freeze.

'Terrific,' said Miles. 'It's not going to work. It's not bloody going to work.' His voice rose.

'Ssh. Patience.' She poured a little more. 'Anything?'

Miles gave another tug. This time there was definite play. Not a lot, but enough perhaps, if only he ...

'Wait,' she said. 'Once more ...' The flask was almost upright now. 'Can you ...?'

'As you say, I don't have much choice.'

As the last few drips ran down the pole, he rose slightly on his toes, closed his eyes and let his knees give way. For a moment he hung there by his arms.

'Bloody hell,' he gasped.

And then he fell. He never felt a thing. A faint sensation, as of dried glue being peeled from a finger, and the next thing he knew he was lying face down on the frozen grass and Anna was leaning over him.

'Stay there for a moment.'

She took a small kitchen knife from her pocket and started to saw through the rope that bound his ankles. It had hardened with the frost but she worked hard and fast and he was soon able to work his feet free.

'Can you stand?' She put the knife back into her pocket.

'What about these?' Miles indicated his wrists.

'Later,' she said. 'There isn't time. We must go at once.'

'We?'

'Please. You must get up. Hurry. We don't have much time.'

She put both arms round his upper chest and pulled upwards. He struggled to his feet on the second attempt. He stood there feeling weak and shaky, as if he had just climbed out of bed after a bad dose of flu.

'Put one arm on my shoulder,' she said.

He did as he was told. Looking like a pair of losers in a three-legged race, they hobbled towards the garden gate.

'I'll never be able to climb over *that*,' Miles said.

She reached into her coat pocket and produced a large iron key. The hinges were rusty from the salt sea air, but the gate opened easily enough.

'Come on.'

Anna seized him round the waist and the two of them set off through the dunes in the direction of the car park. Miles staggered along beside her, stumbling in the soft sand, his limbs driven more by instinct than by conscious effort. A couple of times he fell, but somehow he managed to get to his feet and to keep moving.

The car park was deserted. He probably wouldn't have waited either, in Josef's place. Even so, it was a bitter blow.

'Hell.'

'What?'

'Josef. The chap who drove me out here. I said I'd only be ten minutes, but I was hoping he might have hung on for a bit.'

'Never mind,' she said. 'Let's head for the main road. We should be able to thumb a lift.'

'*Joking!* In this weather?'

'Have you got any other ideas?'

'We could try swimming,' said Miles. 'It couldn't be colder.'

'It's a busy main road,' she said. 'We'll pick up a lift in no time.'

'Hallo ...'

A pair of headlights had turned off at the T-junction and were coming down the road towards them.

'Quick.' Anna seized Miles by the arm and pulled him to the far side of the road, but that was fenced as well and the two of them stood there watching the lights coming closer, feeling appallingly vulnerable.

'What's a car doing at the beach at this time of night?'

The headlights were on full beam. Miles shaded his eyes against the glare. The driver flicked them down and up several times, as if signalling a message to lost souls at sea. The car drew level and stopped. The window was wound down and a long, pointed nose protruded, like a mole sniffing the air.

'Ten minutes, yes?' One little eye winked in Anna's direction and chuckled.

'Sorry, Josef,' said Miles. 'Got rather held up. Keep the engine running.'

Josef was still chuckling as he jumped out and opened the back door. Then he looked more closely at Miles and stopped chuckling. It took some time for the two of them to get him into the back seat. Every limb and muscle ached with stiffness, and his hands were so numb and immobile as to be virtually unusable.

'Where to?' said Josef.

'Hotel de Rome,' Miles mumbled.

'Are you mad?' Anna said.

'But I've left all my things there,' Miles protested.

'You can send for them later,' she said.

'But I need some warm clothes,' he insisted. 'I wouldn't say no to a hot bath either.'

'We're in hot enough water as it is. When they find out what's happened, they'll go mad. The hotel's one of the first places they'll look. If they discovered we'd been there and gone, they'd cover all the obvious escape routes: the airport, the harbour, the railway station ... They have people everywhere.' She took out the knife.

'Where to, then?'

'We'll go north,' she said. 'It's only an hour and half to the Estonian border. We can be in Tallinn in four. We'll catch the first ferry to Helsinki tomorrow morning. We could be back in London in time for lunch.' The blade sliced through the wrist cords.

'We?' he asked, for the second time that evening.

'You don't think I'm going to stay here, do you?' she said. 'Besides, how far do you think you're going to get without me? Those hands are going to need proper medical attention if you don't want to lose the use of them for good.'

'You certainly know the way to a man's heart,' said Miles.

'Have you got any money?'

'A little. Fifty *lati* and a couple of hundred dollars. And an American Express card.'

'Good. We can probably change the Latvian money at the Estonian border. I've got some dollars too.'

'How about visas?'

'Not these days. But you'll need your passport.'

Miles waved a hand in the direction of his jacket pocket and grinned. 'Naturally.'

'You haven't?' she said, and she laughed with delight and disbelief. It wasn't exactly Garbo in *Ninotchka* but, as firsts go, it was quite an event. 'I was sure you'd have left it at the hotel.'

'Never travel in strange countries without it.'

Josef's eyes were anxious in the rear-view mirror.

'We want to go to Tallinn,' Miles told him. 'Can you drive us?'

The eyes widened. 'Tallinn?' he said. 'Estonia?'

'Is it possible?'

'Is possible, but ...'

'But what? No passport? What?'

'I have passport,' he said, patting his chest. 'New Latvian passport. Is good. But Tallinn ...' He pulled a doubtful face.

Anna reached into a pocket and produced a sheaf of ten- and twenty-dollar bills. She leaned forward and spoke to him in fast and fluent Russian. The effect was electrifying. 'OK,' he shouted and stamped on the accelerator. The tyres squealed with excitement as he shot forward into the car park, threw the BMW round 360 degrees and set off towards the main road.

'What did you say?' Miles asked.

'The things that mattered,' she replied.

Anna peered out of the window. The house was pale through the pine trees. Like a stage set for *The Three Sisters*. 'Look.'

The area of garden between the garden door and the beach was suddenly washed in powerful floodlight. Figures were running out of the house and across the terrace. Below them the wire fence gleamed.

Josef had seen them too. The car slowed perceptibly.

'Keep going!' Miles shouted at Josef.

The car bounded towards the T-junction and juddered to a halt.

Headlights were beaming past in both directions. Josef stared left and right. His eyes had doubled in size.

Now lights had come on at the back of the house. A large dog was zigzagging through the trees, pursued by a man with a torch and the beams from the headlights of the limousine as the nose swung round and headed down the drive towards the main road. If they got a move on they'd be past the front gate before the limo got there. Miles looked to his right. A heavy stream of headlights was bearing down on them fast.

'Left! Left!' Miles shouted.

Josef saw the lights and hesitated.

'Go!' Miles yelled. 'Now! Go, go, go!'

They made it, just. The automatic gates were swinging open as the BMW headed the procession towards Riga, and by the time the limo nosed out into the traffic they were half a mile up the road. They watched through the rear window as the limo turned right and then right again towards the beach.

Only when they were safely out of Jurmala did Anna switch on the passenger light and turn her attention to Miles's hands. They were in a dreadful state. With the return of circulation had come the pain and with the pain came the swelling, so that his fingers were beginning to look like half-cooked sausages. As for his palms, if he had held them on the rings of an electric stove the effect could not have been more disastrous. Where the skin had been torn away there were great red weals that oozed a mixture of straw-coloured liquid and blood.

She rested them, palms upwards, in her own cool hands, but the slightest movement or pressure had him crying out.

Anna spoke to Josef again in Russian. Her tone was urgent; Josef's, reassuring.

'I told him we need morphine,' she translated. 'And bandages and plastic bags to keep out infection. He says he knows a pharmacy which is open till midnight. His cousin is the dispenser. It's about ten minutes' drive from here. Do you think you can hang on?'

The pain was coming in great waves now. His face was grey. He felt sick. He nodded and closed his eyes.

'How are we going to get morphine?' he muttered after a few minutes.

'I always carry my nurse's card with me,' she said.

'Are you as good a nurse as you are an actress?'

'Better.'

'In that case I'll hang on,' he said.

The speedometer needle trembled on 100 kph. The road was as

full of bends as it was of potholes and about as ideal for overtaking as the Sea of Tranquillity. Only Josef appeared not to have noticed. Miles wondered if they gritted the roads in Latvia. Not that he'd have minded if the whole of Latvia had been one long stretch of black ice. The way he was feeling, a head-on would have been a blessed relief. He dozed fitfully, his head bouncing against the back of the seat. His brain was churning with questions. *Who is this woman? Who are those people? What was she doing with them? Why was she in Switzerland? She's killed two men already: who's to say she won't kill me? Perhaps she's lying and she was one of them all along. Smith had second thoughts about leaving me to die in the garden and sent her out to finish me off. With a shot of morphine perhaps? Who knows? Who cares? Let her. At least it gives me an excuse not to write the piece for Neville. Knowing Neville, he'll tell me I'm being unprofessional and to get on with it. Except Neville is dead too. Someone poked something sharp up into his brain. She did. Is that how she's going to kill me? A hypodermic needle behind the ear? That's the way it's done ...*

Miles opened his eyes. Anna was looking at him. Her eyes were huge and dark. *I've seen those eyes before somewhere. But where? In Switzerland, of course. No, not there. Somewhere else. Copenhagen? But it had been dark ...* 'I saw you coming out,' he mumbled. 'I was in the street. You walked out of the house. I waited until you'd gone and then I went in. He was dead. Like the doctor. A needle in the brain. Like me.'

'Don't talk,' she said. 'We're nearly there.'

Miles nodded and closed his eyes.

The pharmacy was in a terrace of shops set back behind a row of plane trees.

'We shan't be long.'

Anna got out and followed Josef into the shop. They were back in no time. Anna was carrying a large white paper bag.

'Useful people, cousins,' she said as she settled into the seat beside him. 'We should all have more of them.'

While Josef drove slowly down a dark side-turning, she put the paper bag between them and took out two plastic bags, both sealed. One contained a disposable hypodermic, the other a small glass phial with a rubber top. Anna tore open the bags. She pushed the needle

274

through the rubber and carefully drew out an amount of clear liquid. She held the hypodermic up against the passenger light and pressed the plunger. A thin jet fountained on to the floor.

'We'll never get your jacket off,' she said. 'I'll have to inject into your thigh.' She moved a hand towards his belt.

After a moment or two of pure farce, they managed between them to pull his trousers down to his knees. Anna reached into the bag again and came up with a cotton-wool ball and a little bottle of surgical spirit. Holding the hypodermic between her teeth, she soaked the cotton wool and wiped it over a small area of skin. She fountained the liquid for a second time and, before he knew it, the needle was in and so was the morphine.

'You'll feel dopey,' she said. 'Don't worry. It's quite normal.'

She leaned forward and kissed him gently on the cheek. He smiled, then everything went black.

26

Miles awoke to find he was back in the Army. More precisely, he was in his old room at Warminster. One or two things had been changed since he was there in 1982, before the Falklands thing had blown up, along with a dozen of his best men and a couple of old friends from Sandhurst days. His mahogany chest of drawers had been replaced with something white and shiny, with gold handles. The curtains were different, too. Gone was the orange-and-brown pattern: in its place, a riot of fruit and flowers in blues and greens and pinks. They looked quite pretty with the morning sun shining through. The bed was the same, though. What his mother described as 'firm' and he called 'hard'. He wondered what time it was, and why he wasn't wearing pyjamas.

'Jimson!'

Where is the bloody man? Been out on the beer last night, no doubt. The tea will be undrinkable. Harry Holden-Taylor swears Jimson pees into it.

'Jimson!'

Hang on though, Harry's dead. Picked off by an Argie sniper on Tumbledown. And Jimson's running a pub near Marlborough. Where the bloody hell am I? What's going on?

Miles rolled over on to his back and pushed himself up. Or, rather, he tried to. The pain shot up both arms and he cried out and fell back on the pillow. He pulled his hands out from under the sheet. They were bandaged and plastic bags had been tied over the tops and secured round the wrists with elastic bands.

What the bloody hell …?

And then he remembered. The needle going in. And Anna's eyes. And darkness closing in on him. And the sensation of plunging into a bottomless well …

'Anna?'

Miles struggled, groaning and cursing, until he was almost in a sitting position, his back against the headboard. He looked around. He could see now that he was in a hotel room. *But where, for God's sake?*

He pulled the sheet back and lowered his feet to the carpet. He was wearing just his shirt and underpants. He stood up and went across to the window. By holding the material between the bent knuckles of both hands, he managed to draw back one curtain. Pale sunlight trickled through the double glazing. He put his face very close to the glass, screwed up his eyes and squinted out.

The hotel was as high as the London Hilton and he was on about the twentieth floor. Directly below and slightly to the left was a large park, its skeletal trees and mangy grass dusted with a light sprinkling of snow. Beyond it, less than half a mile away, perched on a low hill, was one of the most beautiful collection of medieval buildings he had ever seen. A glorious jumble of ancient stone and elegantly painted façades; of churches and towers, merchants' houses and fortification walls, interwoven with narrow cobbled streets and fine squares and secret alleyways. And beyond that, circling the town in a wide arc, was the sea – misty and mysterious in the pale grey light. Miles was enchanted. He stood there for a long time, drinking in the view, and then the telephone rang. By sheer force of will he managed to hook the fingers of his right hand round the receiver.

'Mr Miles?'

It was a female voice: young, with a Scandinavian lilt to it.

'Yes?'

'Would you like we send you breakfast?'

He looked at his watch: 9.15. It occurred to Miles that he hadn't eaten for twenty-four hours. 'Thank you,' he said. 'By the way, where am I?'

'Tallinn.'

'Tallinn?'

'It is the capital of Estonia.'

'It's very beautiful.'

'You're welcome.'

Miles dropped the receiver on to the cradle. There was an envelope lying beside it, with his name on it. He tore it open with his teeth. Inside there were two hundred dollars in notes wrapped in a letter. He sat on the edge of the bed and smoothed the letter open. The handwriting was big and bold.

You are in Room 2002 in the Hotel Viru in Tallinn. It is all paid for. Sorry I could not stay with you, but my plans have changed. I suggest you take the 11 o' clock ferry to Helsinki, then the 16.05 or 16.50 to Heathrow. Alternatively, the 16.25 from Tallinn via Stockholm. Everyone takes credit cards but I have left you some dollars, in case. Keep your hands well covered and see your doctor immediately on return. Josef sends best wishes. Good luck. A.

Breakfast took a quarter of an hour to arrive. Miles was glad. He needed every second of it to get dressed. He would never have believed it possible it could take quite so long. Thank God he didn't have to shave. The simple act of pulling up his trousers had suddenly become as fiddly and frustrating as building a Tornado out of Airfix.

A thin girl with grey eyes and a pale, unsmiling face brought in the breakfast tray. A pot of coffee, rolls, butter, jam. She placed it carefully on the top of the chest of drawers. Miles smiled and thanked her, but her expression remained unchanged. She glanced at his bandaged hands and hurried to the door, as if afraid of catching something. There was a hint of Elizabeth in her blank solemnity.

Miles ate a couple of the rolls, without butter or jam, and drank two cups of coffee. The white linen tray cloth was stained skewbald by the time he'd finished, and he was beginning to feel almost human again. He picked up the cup between both hands, crossed to the window and sipped as he stared out at the old buildings again.

So ... Her plans had changed. And not a moment too soon. The way things had been going, the less he had to do with her, the better his chances of enjoying a long and happy life. He still had no idea who she was, or what she was up to. From the events of the previous twelve hours, it seemed that the two of them were roughly on the same side. But he wouldn't have bet on it. There was no guarantee that the next time he brushed up against her the needle would finish up only in his leg. As for what Smith might do if ever he caught up with him …

Not that Miles posed a serious threat to their plans. The notion of the Russians forging an entire Amber Room was preposterous enough, but, with the only possible item of evidence lying in a sock at the bottom of an overnight bag in a cupboard in a Riga hotel room, not even the most sensation-seeking tabloid would be prepared to listen to him.

Whether Smith saw it that way was another matter. He didn't look the sort to leave any loose ends lying around.

Nor was Miles. He had promised to report back to Irina the moment he came up with anything, and that was exactly what he was going to do. Heaven knew where he'd go from there. First things first, though …

His coffee was getting cold. He threw it into the basin and poured himself a fresh cup. He ate another roll and washed it down with the rest of the coffee, checked his jacket pockets for his passport and wallet, then went down to Reception.

A chubby-faced man with round glasses, staring eyes and a ginger beard was on duty. He looked like a deranged gnome.

'Excuse me. Do you speak English?'

'So-so.' He wobbled his hand.

'There was a girl here. Tall, dark hair, wearing a fur coat and hat.'

The man's eyes lit up behind the glasses. 'Girl? You want a girl?'

'No, no,' said Miles. 'You don't understand. I came here with a girl. She went away very early. Did you see her?'

'Your girlfriend? Ppphhhttt?' He made a running gesture with his two front fingers.

Miles sighed. 'Yes. If you like. Ppphhhttt. Did you see her?'

The gnome nodded.

'Did she say where she was going?'

'You are going?'

Miles smiled. 'Yes,' he said. 'I'm going. Goodbye.'

A bitterly cold wind blew down Viru Street. Miles longed for his big overcoat. He wondered if he'd ever see it again. Or England. Or anything vaguely familiar. If Neville Short had suddenly hove into view, he would have thrown his arms round him and kissed him on

279

both cheeks for the sheer joy of encountering something he recognised.

A taxi nudged forward hopefully across the hotel forecourt.

Miles squeezed in.

'You take dollars?' Miles enquired.

'Dollars, OK,' said the driver. 'You go Old Town?'

'No,' said Miles, 'I go London town.'

'Airport?'

Miles flipped a mental coin. 'No,' he said. 'Port.'

* * *

The *Georg Otz* sailed at 11.00. The bar had a country-and-western feeling to it. Miles sat at a table, drinking Heineken and watching old episodes of *Dallas* on satellite television, occasionally getting up for a stroll to the little tourist shop to buy chocolate and to stare glumly at the revolving racks of Jeffrey Archer paperbacks.

The crossing took four hours. It's only fifty-three miles from Tallinn to Helsinki and the hydrofoil does it in half the time, but in the winter months only first thing in the morning and last thing at night. The old steamer zigzagged its slow, stately way from marker to marker across the Gulf of Finland. Miles was quite content. He had bought a packet of painkillers at the port. He had no idea what they consisted of, but, speeded through the system by the Heineken, they had a pleasantly numbing effect and he wished he'd bought a caseful. He was sorry not to have seen more of the town, but his relief at being out of the Baltic States overcame any lingering regrets. Mistrust had been his principal reason for not risking Estonian Airlines.

Helsinki harbour was majestic. The domes of the Cathedral glowed in the winter twilight above the handsome waterside architecture.

Miles caught the 16.50 British Airways flight and three hours later was bowling down the M4 in a black cab.

'Been anywhere interesting?' the cabby enquired.

'Latvia and Estonia,' said Miles.

'I've always wanted to go to Africa myself,' he said. 'Only, my wife has a dodgy tummy. Stick her within a fourpenny bus ride of foreign food and she's got the trots. Know what I mean?'

280

Rain spattered against the windows. Miles smiled. He'd never been so glad to be back in England in his life.

* * *

After five gloomy minutes with Mr Reeves, Miles was beginning to think that the desk clerk at the Viru Hotel had been positively sparkling.

'Need I remind you,' the caretaker said, 'that, in the event of a resident mislaying his front-door key, a new lock must be fitted at the resident's expense within forty-eight hours unless proof can be furnished that the errant key in question has been recovered by or returned to the resident in question?'

'No,' said Miles, and firmly closed the door.

There were only two messages on the answering machine. One was from his mother demanding to know if he was ever to call her, he'd always been a selfish little beast, wasn't it about time he pulled his socks up. The other was from Irina, asking him to telephone her the moment he got in. Nothing from Neville. Miles rang Noel's surgery.

'He's just this moment walked in,' said his receptionist.

Noel came on the line at once.

'You're not going to believe this,' Miles told him.

* * *

He didn't. Miles never expected he would. If it hadn't been for his hands, he wasn't sure he'd have believed it himself.

Noel dressed them with fresh bandages and told him there would be no long-lasting damage. With plenty of sleep, he said, Miles would be back to normal in a few days. 'I'll give you some pills. Take a couple when you get home. They should knock you out for twenty-four hours. What's your next plan? The South Pole and back, in the nude?'

Miles laughed. 'All I wanted was a good story, and I've finished up in a remake of *Raiders of the Lost Ark*, but with a far less believable storyline and a fraction of the budget. I don't blame you for making fun of me. I've made a complete idiot of myself. What's more, I seem

281

to have ended up more or less where I started. I've been half suffocated in an avalanche, I've been half strangled and rescued from certain death by a murderess who looks like Anna Karenina ...'

'With a hint of the French Lieutenant's Woman.'

' ... As you say, with a hint of the French Lieutenant's Woman. I've been Switzerland's number one murder suspect. I've been chased halfway across Europe by men posing as policemen. I've been burgled, mugged in my own flat, attacked by a Sumatran tiger, bewitched by a ninety-year-old Russian Grand Duchess who knew Anastasia, nearly frozen to death on a wire fence in Latvia, injected with God knows what by who knows who – and, do you know, I have no more idea what the hell's going on than I did three weeks ago.'

'That's not quite true,' said Noel, mildly.

'Oh?'

'You may not have a story, but even you must be beginning to suspect that you might, just might, have the makings of a real journalist.'

'Thank you, Noel,' said Miles. 'You've made my weekend.'

* * *

He was dreaming that he was in the garden in Jurmala. It was still dark. He seemed to have been there for hours, yet oddly enough he wasn't at all cold. The temperature must have dropped dramatically. He could hear the telephone ringing up at the house. Why hadn't anyone answered it? Had they all left? Did they know it was for him and couldn't be bothered? It could be something important. He had to get there before they rang off. But he couldn't move. His hands were still stuck to the fence. He sweated as he struggled to wrench them free, but the harder he pulled, the more firmly they became welded to the metal. He gave one last depairing tug and his right hand came away. He held it out and stared at it in horror. The skin was undamaged but his fingers were still attached to the metal pole. He yelled out at the top of his voice, 'No!' And then he woke up.

The telephone was still ringing. He fumbled in the darkness. There was a thud and a tinkle as it fell to the floor. Miles swore. Where was he? He reached out again and his fingers came into contact with

282

something else. A bedside lamp. He found a switch. He squinted into the sudden glare from the hundred-watt bulb. He was in his own bed. Whatever time was it? What day? He rolled over and picked up the receiver.

'Hallo?'

'Oh, you *are* there. I've been trying you all day.'

He might have just popped out for a pint of milk, for all the urgency in Irina's voice.

'I've been asleep,' Miles grunted. He tried to focus on his watch. 'What time is it?

'Seven o'clock.'

'Morning or evening?'

'Sunday evening.'

'Sunday? Good God!'

'Are you all right?'

'I don't know,' said Miles. 'I'll let you know in the morning.'

'I was hoping you could come over this evening.'

'What, now?'

'It's important.'

'Can't it wait till tomorrow?'

'I'm afraid not.'

'Are you sure?'

'Quite sure.'

The rain was flecked with tiny shards of snow as Miles climbed out of the cab in Glebe Place. A man answered the entryphone. It wasn't Pierre.

'Jolyon!'

The pin-striped bulk filled the doorway. He smiled and extended a hand like a flipper's seal. Then he saw the bandages and transformed the gesture into one of bonhomous welcome. 'Come on in,' he said. 'How are you feeling?'

'Exhausted,' said Miles. 'And confused.'

'All will be revealed,' he said, and waved Miles through into the sitting room.

Mrs Rogers was sitting upright in her high-backed armchair, a lighted cigarette drooping from the old ivory holder. A large black shawl was draped over her thin shoulders and both bars of the electric fire had been turned on. She turned as he entered the room. There was no hint of mockery in her eyes now: only concern. Miles returned her gaze with a lukewarm smile.

'Hallo, Miles.'

The voice came from behind him and to his left. He spun round.

Irina said, 'You know my granddaughter, Anna, of course.'

A faint smile flickered over the lips and there was laughter in the huge, dark eyes. Miles stared at her. He opened his mouth to say something, but nothing emerged. She moved forward, placed her hands on his shoulders and kissed him on the cheek. It was as if a butterfly had brushed against his face. She stepped away and took his hands lightly in hers. 'How are they?' she said.

'Not bad.'

'How was the breakfast?' she said.

'Fine. Fresh rolls, good coffee.' He spoke in a low monotone, as if hypnotised.

'I'm glad,' she said. 'And Estonian Airlines?'

'No idea,' he said. 'I went to Helsinki. What happened to you?'

'I went back.'

'Back?'

'To Riga.'

'To Riga? Whatever for?'

'Well, I knew you had the rose with you in Copenhagen ...'

'How ...?'

She looked across at Irina. Miles nodded slowly.

'You had obviously brought it with you to Riga,' she went on. 'As you didn't have it with you in Jurmala, I guessed you must have left it behind at your hotel.'

'You went back to the hotel?'

'My first thought was to get us as far away from Jurmala as possible. Especially since you were in such a bad way. Everything was going to plan. Josef drove to Tallinn in four hours. But then it suddenly occurred to me they might guess where the rose was, too. It wouldn't have taken much to find out where you were staying. Josef told me he'd picked you up at the Hotel de Rome and I rang them. No one had been asking for you, but I didn't dare risk it. I had to get to the rose before they did.

284

'Josef helped me to get you into bed and then we drove back to Riga. We got to the hotel at about six. I was wondering how I was going to talk my way into your room, but it turned out that another of Josef's cousins is the assistant night concierge. I waited outside in the car. He was gone for ages. I was just beginning to get worried when Stefan turned up. I couldn't believe it. There was nothing I could do. At that moment I saw Josef coming out, carrying the bag. I nearly died. But then I realised that Stefan had never seen Josef in his life. He actually smiled and held the door open for him. Then Josef drove me to the airport. There was a flight leaving in the next half-hour. I managed to squeeze on to it. Only having the one bag ...'

She pointed towards the door. The bag was sitting just inside. Miles's big old overcoat was folded neatly on top.

He said, 'Now that *was* worth going back for. Did you find ...?'

Irina put her hand into her cardigan pocket and took out the rose. 'Honestly,' she said. 'Yellow socks. What next?'

'It seems we all have our little secrets,' said Miles, looking meaningfully at Anna.

'I was going to tell you,' she said. 'There was a lot going on at the time, though. If you remember. Perhaps you don't.'

Miles turned to Irina. 'What else haven't you told me?'

Irina's face was solemn. 'Come and sit down, both of you.' She gestured towards various chairs. 'Jolyon, would you be so kind as to make some coffee?'

'Of course.' He rolled towards the door like a loose balloon. Miles and Anna sat next to each other, facing Irina across the fireplace.

'Why ...?' Miles began.

Irina held up a hand. 'You are very tired,' she said kindly. 'You are also confused and probably angry. I don't blame you. I would be the same, in your place. You feel I have not been totally honest with you, and you're right. I am sure you have many questions you wish to ask. First, let me explain. Anna is the daughter of my youngest son, Dmitri.'

The two women exchanged glances.

'I had three sons. My eldest, Michael, was killed fighting on the Eastern Front in 1945. My second, Sergius, died of cancer in 1964. Dmitri is ... was ...' She fell silent and stared at the floor.

285

Anna got up and sat on the arm of her grandmother's chair. She took her hand and held it gently between her own.

'Our family have been searching for the Amber Room ever since it disappeared at the end of the war,' said Anna. 'The Soviet Government have always claimed that the Room was theirs. They argue that the ownership passed to them in 1917 in the same way that when Henry VII picked the crown of England out of the thornbush at Bosworth he assumed the sovereignty that went with it. We've never accepted this. We say that the Bolsheviks usurped the authority of the ruling family at the time of the Revolution. The legal line of descent is through our family. They have no right to anything that was in our ownership before then. And that includes the Amber Room. It was one of the greatest jewels in our family crown and when my uncle Sergius died my father gave up his teaching job in Paris and continued the search. For the last year I have been helping him.'

'I don't understand. I thought you were a nurse.'

'I was. I am. I ...'

Irina looked up. 'A year ago, Dmitri had begun to believe that the Room would never be found. We'd had so many setbacks and pursued so many false trails. He was almost ready to give up. But I was sure the Room still existed. And then, just before Christmas, I received an anonymous letter, typed on plain paper and posted in Norwich. The writer claimed to know that the Room had been taken to Switzerland at the end of the war and that it had been there ever since.'

'Where in Switzerland?'

'The writer did not reveal its exact location; only that it was somewhere in the Bernese Oberland. Normally I would have treated such information with great scepticism, but then I remembered that researcher's letter in 1950 and those lines about the world's most theatrical room.'

'What was his name again? The Swiss businessman?'

'Walter Grobius.'

'Grobius. Yes. And his friend had been in the German Consulate in Berne.'

'Van Berkel.'

286

'But surely Switzerland must have cropped up dozens of times in the course of your researches?'

'That's true,' said Irina. 'Except that the person who wrote this letter said that if we wanted proof he knew where we could find it.'

'He?'

'It sounded like a he.'

'And did he tell you what this proof was?'

'Not exactly.'

'What do you mean, "not exactly"?'

'There were clues. We didn't realise they were clues at first. They didn't make any sense at all. We put it down to a quirky sense of humour.'

'What sort of things?'

'There was something about "eyes that cannot see".'

'Go on.'

'And the letter finished up: "Good running and the devil take the hindmost." '

'The motto of the Diabolo Club,' Miles murmured. 'And of course "running" is an expression that describes the way skis move across the surface of the snow.'

Anna said, 'We guessed it was something of the sort, but at the time it was sheer gibberish.'

'So it was the reference to the Diabolo that led you to Eigerhubel?'

'It meant nothing to us at the time. My father was in Interlaken and he saw a poster advertising Eigerhubel, and he remembered the line about the eyes that cannot see.'

'The Totenkopf.'

'Exactly.'

Miles remembered a small front room in Balham, and a man with a moustache and long teeth with his hand raised in the Nazi salute. He shivered.

Irina said, 'Are you all right?'

'It's nothing. I'm fine. Honestly.'

'You look as if you've seen a ghost,' said Anna.

'Ghosts,' said Miles. 'But go on with the story. Where were you when your father went to Switzerland?'

287

'New York, Moscow, Riga.'

'Riga?'

'Wherever John Smith was.'

The thought of Smith's dry old hand crawling across Anna's shoulder made him shudder again. 'What on earth were you doing with a man like that? I can't believe there was anything going on between you.'

'He would have liked it if there had been,' she said dully.

'What, then?'

She glanced across at her grandmother, as though seeking help. But Irina was busy attempting to fit a fresh and unusually obstructive cigarette into her holder. Anna gave a quick, humourless smile and sighed. 'I met him through Alex.'

'Alex?'

'Alex was originally in charge of overseeing the construction of the new Amber Room. The bogus one. The one you saw at Jurmala. He's a Russian. One of the new entrepreneurial breed who have crawled out of the woodwork into the sunlight of the new free enterprise society.'

'He's a crook, you mean?'

She laughed. 'Yes, I suppose you could say he's a crook. He prefers to think of himself as a businessman.'

'Businessman as in Smith?'

'That sort of thing. In fact the work on the new room started back in the mid-Eighties, in the bad old days of concrete-faced Communism. The Russians were desperate to discover it, in quotes, before anyone else did, and they knew the only way they could do that was by making a replica and hoping no one would notice. It cost them billions of roubles. In fact at one point good amber became so scarce and so expensive, they very nearly gave up. But then Smith appeared on the scene. He'd been moving freely in and out of the Soviet Union since the Sixties. Import–export. Concrete, optical instruments, furs, jewellery, you name it. He manipulated the amber market to the Soviets' advantage and single-handedly saved the project. He was besotted with me. The idea that I might have been an infiltrator never occurred to him. Even now he probably can't believe it. Somehow, God knows how, he got to hear a rumour that the real room might have been found in Switzerland. I persuaded him to send me to investigate.'

'How did you meet Alex?'

'I was hoping you wouldn't ask.'

'You don't have to tell me if you don't want.'

Anna took in a deep breath. 'You might as well know. I met him through my brother.'

'Your brother? How did *he* know him?'

'He is ... Alex and he are ... friends, lovers, whatever. There. Now you know. I tried to talk Andrew out of it. It was like talking to a brick wall. In the end I thought, If you can't win him, use him.'

'What does he look like, your brother?'

'Tall, thin, dark. Romantic-looking. Early thirties.'

'A bit like Daniel Day-Lewis?'

'Very.'

'I've met him,' said Miles. 'He came to my flat. They both did. They were looking for the amber rose. He was out of his depth.'

'I know,' she said. 'I only hope my father never knew the truth.'

'Knew? You talk as if ...'

'When I arrived in Eigerhubel, my father was staying with a local carpenter, Willi Graf. He had a spare room, so I moved in too. He'd been there nearly a week. He'd gone up to the Totenkopf every day in the hope that someone would contact him, or that he'd discover something, but nothing had happened. He'd come up with nothing and it was making him ill. He wasn't a young man, after all. I was having a drink in the Hotel des Alpes one night and I happened to meet the doctor. We got talking and he told me that his nurse had arranged to spend a few days in Zürich with her parents and he was desperate to find a temp. What better place to discover what's going on in a village than in the doctor's surgery? I could keep nosing about and my father could have a few days' rest back in England. It was a perfect arrangement. I got the job. Two days later, someone told me about the Diabolo Club. As soon as I heard what the club motto was, I rang my father, who took the next plane out. Somehow he wangled an invitation into the clubhouse. The rose was lying in a place of honour, on the mantelpiece. He slipped it into his pocket, made an excuse and left.'

'Good God,' said Miles.

'What? What is it?'

'I saw him. I saw your father. I was up there. The morning of the day I had my accident. I was looking at the clubhouse and he collided with me. Almost knocked me flying. He must have just taken the rose. He was in a terrible hurry. He didn't stop.'

'He was,' said Anna. 'Unfortunately, I was on duty all that day. There were a lot of accidents. Twisted knees, sprained wrists, breakages. There always are after a heavy fall of snow. People take one look at the fresh powder and get completely carried away. Trouble is, most of them aren't up to it. They only know how to bash up and down flat pistes. My father looked into the surgery several times, but there wasn't a moment when we could be alone.

'Things eased off towards the evening. Dr Grunner went off on his rounds. I told him I'd stay late, in case of emergencies. My father waited outside until he was sure the place was empty, and then he came in. He was frozen, poor chap. He was about to show me the rose when an Englishman turned up with his wrist in plaster. Apparently Dr Grunner and I had set it a couple of days previously and he'd come for a doctor's letter so he could get a refund on his ski-lift pass. I couldn't remember anything about it but I hadn't got time to argue. I stuck him in the waiting room and went back to my father, and then you arrived ...'

'My God,' said Miles, his voice dropping to a whisper. 'So that was your father!'

'Can you imagine the state we were in?' she said. 'It was obvious you were quite badly hurt. We had to do something. He was certain his every move was being watched. I'd never done any stitching, but I'd seen it done enough times. At first I thought of doing it myself, but that might have looked odd. He said he'd do it, if I talked him through it. That's why there was so much chat. Luckily you don't speak Russian. God knows how he did it.'

'He didn't,' said Miles. 'Most of the stitches fell out when I got home.'

'Oh God!' she said and clapped her hand over her mouth. 'I'm so sorry. We tried our best. And no sooner had we patched you up than I tried to kill you.'

'You nearly succeeded, too. Who trained you?'

'Mr Caswell.'

'Who?'

'My instructor at night class.'

'He's good. So are you.'

'I'd gone next door for a moment. I heard someone moving about and saw you by the desk. Your back was turned. I assumed you were his killer. I'm sorry.'

Miles smiled sheepishly. 'Don't apologise. I gave nearly as good as I got.' He raised his bandaged hands. 'Anyway, you've more than made up for it.'

Anna nodded slowly. 'If only I could have saved him, too. I was only out of the room for a moment. I was desperate to go to the loo. I came back into the office and … He was smiling at me. I smiled back. We'd got through it together. It was such a relief. It never occurred to me that he … that he …'

Her eyes glistened and tears ran down her thin cheeks.

'Darling,' said Irina. She took Anna's head in her arms and rocked her, whispering little words of comfort, in Russian, like a *babushka* with a baby.

Miles went across and laid a bandaged hand on Anna's arm. She put her other hand gently over it, and the three of them wept together.

27

There was a faint cough from the direction of the hall and Jolyon entered clutching an old papier-mâché tray with a huge white china coffeepot on it and three cups and saucers so small and delicate they might have belonged to a doll's house. He held the tray at chest height and carried it across the room with all the gravity of an overweight Jeeves. He placed it carefully on the table next to Irina and stepped back, evidently pleased with his achievement.

'Thank you, Jolyon,' said Irina. She peered pointedly at the Lilliputian cups. 'You didn't manage to find the mugs, then?'

Jolyon gave a painful smile and carefully poured out three tiny cupfuls of very dark coffee. 'I must go,' he said. 'Big jewellery sale tomorrow. I need to be on top form.' He gave Miles an awkward little wave and bent low over Irina's hand. She made no attempt to hide her distaste. Anna stood up and saw him to the door.

'One does miss Pierre on his evenings off,' Irina said loudly.

Miles raised an eyebrow and sipped his coffee. He leaned forward. 'When I mentioned Switzerland the other day,' he said quietly, 'did you know then ...?'

'That Dmitri was dead?' said Irina. 'No, not then. Later.' Her voice was low and level. 'I knew he'd been out there, of course. He stayed here for the two days when he came back. When Anna rang and told us about the Diabolo Club, it seemed like the answer to our prayers. I never dreamed when I kissed my son goodbye that it would end the way it did. I heard nothing for two weeks. Not till Anna came here yesterday. I didn't expect to. Most of the time I never know where she is anyway. I just pray for her and wait for news.'

There was the sound of the front door being closed and Anna came back into the room. 'Really, Ina,' she said, 'do you have be quite so beastly to Jolyon?'

'I don't know what you mean,' she said.

Anna sighed and turned to Miles. 'The thing is, Jolyon and I were lovers for a while.'

'Don't remind me!' Irina interjected.

Anna looked at Miles and rolled her eyes skywards. 'He was quite good-looking in those days, believe it or not. He only started putting on weight after we split up. I'm still very fond of him. Unfortunately, he's still madly in love with me.'

'Cupboard love,' said Irina. 'He's only got eyes for objects. Ours, mainly.'

'I really can't be bothered to argue,' said Anna. She took a cup of coffee and sat on the other side of the fire.

Miles waited for a moment. Then he said, 'What did you do when you realised your father was dead?'

'I didn't know what to do,' she said. 'I was in a state of total shock. I couldn't believe it. I sat there in the office for a long time with him, not doing anything, just being with him, talking to him, trying to take in what had happened. I couldn't think of anything else … the rose … nothing. I don't know how long I was there. Perhaps an hour. Then I went into the house to find something to drink. Then you turned up. I thought … Well, that was the trouble; I didn't think …'

'I don't blame you. What happened after you laid me out?'

'All I could think about was getting away. I knew Smith had sent Alex to keep an eye on me. He'd rung up earlier that afternoon from Berne to say he was on his way. If he'd turned up while I was there, I was going to have an awful lot of explaining to do. I also needed to do something about my leg. As it turned out, it was only a flesh wound, but it was bleeding badly and hurt like hell. I patched it up as best I could and left. I took Dr Grunner's little pick-up and drove down the walkers' path to Niederwald and waited for the train in the café.'

'I saw you.'

'Saw me where?'

'I was on the train. I was trying to get away as well. Alex and another man found me in the surgery. I thought they were the police. There I was, covered in blood, and the man I took to be the doctor dead in the next room. I wasn't going to wait around and explain. So I made a run for it.'

Anna gave a puzzled frown. 'I never saw you on the train,' she said. 'Where were you?'

'Keeping well out of your way,' said Miles. 'I thought you'd killed him.'

'I don't blame *you*,' she said. 'I've never killed anyone in my life, but the way I was feeling that evening ...'

Miles nodded sympathetically. 'Anyway, I followed you down on the funicular, and then you got into a car and drove away. He looked like a friend.'

'Just a local taxi man. He drove me to Zürich. I found a little hotel and caught the first flight to Paris the next morning.'

'Paris?'

'I've got friends there,' she said. 'I stayed with them until I felt fit enough. Then I went back to Jurmala. I couldn't bring myself to phone Ina and tell her what had happened. Besides, now that I knew there was a real chance the original Room existed, I thought I could persuade the Russians to delay their announcement. Then I could go back to Switzerland and try and find what my father had tried so hard to find.'

'So who did kill him?'

She shook her head. 'Someone who knew that he was on to the real Room and didn't want him telling anyone.'

'Perhaps Alex had turned up without you realising it. It's possible. You could have been busy with a patient at the time. He could have waited somewhere, out of sight, and when you finally left the room ...'

'If it had been him, he'd have taken the rose and gone. Why would he have come back later looking for it? Besides, it wasn't his style. Alex is a thug. The man who killed my father was a technician. An artist. Certainly someone with medical knowledge. And possibly medical equipment.'

'He had plenty to choose from. Needles, scalpels, probes. You can see why I jumped to the wrong conclusion. Was anything missing?'

'I've no idea. I had other things on my mind. He must have worked very fast. I never saw anyone.'

294

'Wait a minute.' Miles's voice rose suddenly. 'Of course you saw someone. I saw him too. But he was so ordinary and unobtrusive that neither of us gave him a moment's thought.'

'You don't mean that man …?'

'Exactly. With the broken wrist. The man sitting quietly outside, waiting for someone to sign his certificate. The man who was so ordinary and unobtrusive that although you had helped to deal with the injury only two days earlier, you couldn't remember a thing about it. The man who made so little impression on me that until this moment I had forgotten that I saw him a couple of weeks later at Copenhagen Airport.'

'What?'

'I don't think he really remembered me. Anyway, we exchanged a few words. Just small talk. He said he was there on business. I suggested sharing a taxi into Copenhagen, but he said he couldn't because someone was meeting him. Then I went outside and saw him getting into an ordinary taxi on his own. I thought then there was something odd about him. It niggled me for a while, but then I had better things to think about and I completely forgot about him: until now.'

'But he was just some skier. He was on holiday. Why would he want to kill my father?'

'Perhaps he wasn't just a skier after all. Perhaps he hadn't –' Miles stopped. His eyes stared straight ahead and his mouth dropped open.

'What is it?'

He turned and looked at her. 'I've just remembered what it was. I knew there was something about him that wasn't quite right.'

'Not wanting to share a taxi, you mean?'

'The plaster was on the wrong wrist.'

'What do you mean, the wrong wrist?'

'I've got an eye for trivial detail,' Miles explained, 'and when I spoke to him in the doctor's waiting room that evening, I do remember noticing it was his right wrist that was plastered, and hoping he wasn't right-handed.'

'So?'

'When I bumped into him at the airport, it was his left wrist that was in plaster. He held it up and showed me. Said what a good job the doctor had made of it. I remember thinking how new it looked, considering he'd had it on a fortnight. He must have just had it done.'

Anna frowned and pulled a face. 'I don't understand.'

'You told me that when he came in that afternoon for the doctor's letter, you couldn't remember having treated him, even though it had happened only the previous day. Of course you couldn't, because you never did. Because he never broke his wrist. If he had, he'd never have been able to carry a large briefcase with that hand without even a surgical bandage to support it.'

'But why on earth would anyone pretend to have a broken wrist?'

'So he'd have an excuse to wear a plaster.'

'But why …?'

'A couple of years ago, a girl was stopped in the Green channel at Heathrow by a customs officer. She had a plaster cast on one leg. She said she'd broken it skiing in Italy. By coincidence, the customs officer's daughter was out there skiing in the same resort. She'd rung up to say the snow conditions were poor but the weather was brilliant. Hot sunshine every day. Yet this girl hadn't a trace of a suntan. He was suspicious. He called her over and started asking some questions. They found a pound of top-grade heroin hidden in her plaster cast.'

'You mean …?'

'I don't know what this man used to kill your father, but I bet he smuggled it in in that plaster. It probably wasn't even a real plaster: just a made-up thing with a hinge at the back that he could slip on and off whenever he wanted.'

'And you think he killed Paul too?' said Anna.

'Why not? The method was identical. You saw for yourself.'

'How do you know?'

'Because I saw you coming out of Olsen's house.'

'You saw me?'

'He sounded so peculiar on the telephone, so I went round. I was on the other side of the street and when I saw it was you I stepped back into a doorway. I still had you down as a murderer. When I saw Olsen lying there dead with a hole behind his ear, I naturally assumed you'd killed him too. And when I first saw you in Jurmala I was sure of it. Your eyes … If looks could have killed.'

Anna shrugged. 'That's a year at Drama School for you.'

'What were you doing in Copenhagen anyway?'

'Jolyon contacted me in Riga. He said Ina was sending you to see Paul and that you were bringing the rose with you. He was afraid Paul might tell you about the amber shipments and Kirilov and what the Russians were up to, and that you wouldn't be able to resist rushing to Riga, and that might put me at risk. I said I'd go straight to Copenhagen and talk to Paul. I didn't get there quick enough.'

'So who rang Paul to tell him to put me off? Jolyon?'

'I did,' said Irina calmly.

'You?'

'Jolyon rang me and told me what he'd done. I knew Paul wouldn't take any notice of someone he didn't know, so I rang him. He wasn't there. I left a message on his answering machine. I didn't want to go into details. I just said that there was a problem and that he was to ring the Hotel Admiral and put you off.'

Her cigarette was almost down to the cork tip. She regarded it for a few seconds, then pinched it out with all the ferocity of a gardener dealing with a slug.

'Damned answering machines!' she said. 'If only I could have spoken to him in person.'

And she stubbed the cigarette furiously into the ashtray, again and again.

* * *

Lying in bed in the small hours, staring at the ceiling, too tired to sleep, Miles wondered why Anna and her grandmother were still talking to him, since he had been responsible, albeit unwittingly, for the death of two fine men, both dear to their hearts, in the space of as many weeks. In addition, he had put Anna's life at serious risk. Never mind that she could never return to Riga: would she be safe anywhere from now on? Smith couldn't possibly allow her to live, knowing what she knew. It was a wonder he hadn't caught up with her already.

God what a mess, and all for the sake of some piddling newspaper article. And not even a commissioned article, at that. And as if he were not already well and truly racked with guilt, it now looked as if all his efforts had been totally misguided. The story he had been pursuing so assiduously and for the sake of which he had wasted good people's time, and lives, was not about English Nazi war criminals at all. Whatever it was the badge represented, it bore little relation to the events now unfolding. Like *Alice's Adventures in Wonderland*, his life had suddenly taken a curious and illogical turn. He had started off in one story and finished up in another.

And yet clearly there were connections between the two. Several. The fact remained that between the time Miles left the surgery and returned an hour later, someone had removed the badge. The man with the broken wrist perhaps – though why was still a matter for speculation. And then there was the coincidence of finding a replica hidden away in a secret drawer in Archie's library. Archie had been a prominent member of the Diabolo Club, like his old friend and mentor, Bill Gordon, and both had been in their time enthusiastic fellow travellers of the extreme right. Anna's father had said that the badge had been a gift from a member of the Diabolo Club. It was probably the first thing that came into his head. Nevertheless it was from the Diabolo Club that he had taken the rose ...

There was another connection, too. Walter Grobius. The mysterious figure whose name some unknown researcher had chanced upon in a letter written over forty years ago. The Swiss art historian with his connections with pre-war German industry and his interest in stage design and his friendship with the one-time German vice-consul in Berne. The man who had assured his friend that the world's most theatrical room was safe and well and that he visited it every day. Did he still visit it every day? If so, where? Was it still safe and sound? Was *he*?

These were questions which none of them could have answered that evening. But there was another ... If only he had dared to ask it.

* * *

Noel's morning surgery was from nine to eleven but he was usually out of the house and on his rounds by half past seven. To be on the safe side, Miles rang him at seven.

'A safe house?' Noel burst out laughing. 'You've been spending too much time talking to my brother and his friends. All this secret-service talk is going to your head.'

'You may laugh,' said Miles, 'but you saw what they did to my hands. These people don't mess about. It won't take them long to trace her to Chelsea, and when they do ... I just thought ... If she could stay with you for a few days ... If it's not too much of an imposition. I don't know what Sarah ...'

'Hang on. Sarah! ... Sarah! ...'

There were sounds of footsteps on the stairs, children squawking, Sarah shouting. Miles was tempted to put the phone down.

Then Noel came on again. 'When were you thinking of?'

'As soon as possible. It would only be for a few days. Until ...' Until when? Miles had no idea.

'Sarah's taking the children to her mother's this afternoon. Can your friend wait till this evening?'

'I'm sure she can,' said Miles.

* * *

'You've just missed her.'

'Damn,' said Miles. 'When will she be back?'

'I've no idea,' said Irina. 'She had already gone by the time I got up.'

'Did you hear anything? Any unusual noises? Doors being pushed open? Voices? Sounds of a struggle?'

'Heavens, no,' said Irina, astonished at the idea. 'Why do you ask?'

'It's just that ... It's nothing. Forget it. Just my imagination running away with me.'

'There was a scribbled note.'

'What did it say?'

'To expect her when I saw her.'

'Nothing else?'

'Nothing else.'

'She didn't say where she was going?'

'I've just told you.'

'You have a habit of internally editing certain things.'

'Put it this way, I don't think she's gone for a walk in Battersea Park.'

'Where, then?'

'I told you before, I never know where she is half the time and she doesn't tell me. I just pray to God that she'll come back safe and well. I suggest you do the same.'

'I couldn't possibly just sit at home and hope for the best,' Miles protested. 'Not after what we went through in Latvia. They'll be looking for her everywhere. There must be something I can do.'

Irina gave a little cough. 'I know how you must be feeling,' she said. 'You're a soldier. You have been trained to act. Your instinct is to *do* something. But action is not always helpful. There are some people who operate at their best when they are alone. For them, companionship, however well intentioned and however practical, can prove more of a hindrance than a help. Need I say more?'

Miles understood only too well. Twice he had blundered in on her in his well-meaning, gung-ho way, and on both occasions he had merely succeeded in putting both their lives at risk.

'Point taken,' he said.

'I'm glad,' she said. 'For all our sakes.'

There was a silence. Miles expected to hear a click at the other end, but nothing happened. It was as if neither of them wanted to break the chain of thought between them.

It was Miles who spoke in the end. 'I wanted to ask you both something last night, but we'd all been through enough as it was. This may not be the moment either, but I'm going to say it anyway. After I got back to England from Eigerhubel, I rang one of the people who'd been on the skiing trip with me. It was quite obvious that he knew nothing about anyone being murdered. I know from my own experience how much trouble the Swiss go to to cover up any unpleasantness, especially if it occurs in a place which depends for its survival on the tourists. So I can understand the local authorities drawing a heavy veil over Dmitri's death. But who took charge of the arrangements afterwards? Anna was in Paris, Andrew was chasing around with Alex. You knew nothing about it. Was there a funeral? Will there be one?'

There was another silence. Miles feared for a moment that he might have overstepped the mark. But after a while Irina's voice came on again, as calm and level as ever.

'I'm glad you didn't mention it last night,' she said. 'Anna still blames herself, you know. After you left last night, I tried to persuade her that she had nothing to reproach herself for, but it was no use. I have never seen anyone cry as much as she cried. 'I should have stayed with him,' she kept saying. 'He was alone, I should have stayed with him.' She was inconsolable and will remain so until she has said goodbye to him, in the proper way. Perhaps then the pain will begin to ease.'

'Thank you, Irina,' said Miles. 'You have told me what I wanted to know.'

'Oh dear. I was afraid of that,' she said.

* * *

'Switzerland?' said Noel.

'I'm certain of it.'

'I hope you're not thinking of following her out there.'

'No fear. I've learned my lesson, thank you.'

'That didn't stop you chasing her out to Latvia.'

'I didn't *chase* her out to Latvia, as you put it. She happened to be there already. Had I known that, I might have thought twice about it.'

'Well, you can certainly think twice about it now. There's no way you're going to be tearing around in the mountains with hands like yours.'

'I've told you. I'm not going. So you can stop banging on about it.'

'I won't mention it again.'

'Good. *I* certainly won't.'

'Good.'

'By the way, how much longer do I have to go on wearing these dressings?'

'Miles ...'

'Just wondered.'

* * *

301

'The man you want to speak to is called Peter Franklin,' said Paul Weekley.

'What?'

'He was posted to Berne at the end of the war, ostensibly as British Military Attaché but in fact working for British Intelligence as part of an enormous investigation by the allied intelligence services into Nazi collaboration throughout Europe. He probably knows more about the Swiss and their dealings with the Nazis than anyone alive. He'll almost certainly be able to tell you about this man Grobius. And if he can't, he'll know who can.'

'Franklin,' said Miles in a low voice.

'There may be others, but I've made enquiries in all the right places since you called, and I'm pretty sure Franklin's your man.'

'But I know him,' said Miles. 'He's a skiing writer. A bit *passé* now, but still one of the best.'

'Extraordinary coincidence,' said Weekley.

'More extraordinary still, he was with me in Eigerhubel. In fact he was the one who suggested the badge might be something to do with the SS. That was the main reason I went back to the surgery. And yet, when I spoke to him about it later, back in England, he claimed to know nothing about it. He said that, what with the bang on the head and too much whisky, I must have imagined the whole thing.'

'Someone may have got in touch with him out there after you left and told him to put you off the scent.'

'Like *who*?'

Weekley shrugged. 'Police … Security Services … who knows?'

'If he's been frightened off once, who's to say he won't play dumb again?'

'Mention the name Schmid. Peter Schmid. Press Attaché at the Swiss Embassy here in London. He was the man who gave me Franklin's name.'

'You really think that might have the desired effect?'

'Try it and see.'

'By the way,' said Miles, 'I think I ought to tell you that since we last met, this story of mine has taken an extraordinary turn.'

'These sort of stories usually do,' said Weekley.

'It's all a bit of a muddle still.'

'It generally is.'

'I started out convinced I was searching for a British Nazi war criminal, but now I'm not so sure. I think I'm on to something far more sensational.'

'Good God. What?'

'I need to talk to Franklin first.'

'Well, before you abandon your original line of enquiry, listen to this. I've been doing some work on mass executions and other atrocities committed by SS troops on Allied prisoners in the field during the last war. There were many more than perhaps people realise, and several of the SS commanders who were responsible are still alive and free and enjoying comfortable and peaceful retirement. The trouble is, in the nature of these things, there are few survivors and, apart from a tiny handful, those who might have given evidence have died or are untraceable. And anyway, after fifty years, memory becomes stretched beyond the limits of reliability. However, I pressed on undeterred and shortly after we last spoke I came across a case that immediately set my whiskers twitching. In June 1944, following the D-Day landings, fifty-five unarmed British prisoners-of-war, some of them badly wounded, were massacred by members of an unnamed Waffen Grenadier-division near the town of Isigny. The prisoners were herded into a field and machine-gunned by a group of half a dozen SS soldiers. Those that were not killed in the first burst fell to the ground and lay there while the soldiers continued to fire into them. After about five minutes, the order was given to the machine guns to stop, and the soldiers went through the piles of dead and living, shooting anyone who moved in the head. One British soldier survived even though he had been hit several times. According to his testimony, the officer in charge of the division shouted his orders in English, and, as the soldiers were laughing and joking together and firing into the crowd, they were also speaking English.'

'That's incredible,' Miles breathed. 'I wonder if he's still alive. The English soldier, I mean. If so, I ought to try and find him and talk to him.'

'I don't know,' said Weekley. 'But in April 1945, men from the same division under the same commander carried out another massacre on the outskirts of Königsberg on the Prussian coast.'

'Did you say Königsberg?'

'Yes. Why?'

'Go on.'

'According to the account I read – and remember, these accounts are all based on hearsay – a group of Russian soldiers consisting of two officers and about twenty men was leaving the city in a convoy of half a dozen trucks when it was stopped by a group in SS uniforms. They were quite surprised to find German troops so near to Königsberg, since by that stage the city had been pretty well flattened after days of heavy bombardment by Russian artillery. They were even more surprised when the officer in charge and his men spoke to them in English. Assuming them to be British soldiers working under cover, they climbed down from the trucks and were promptly lined up and machine-gunned. Most died instantly. Again, those who were still alive were shot in the back of the head. By a miracle, one of the officers survived. Being face downwards with several bodies lying on top of him and blood everywhere, he was able to give a realistic enough impression of being dead. Finally the shooting stopped, the SS men got into the trucks and drove away. He was later found by Russian soldiers and reported the incident to the War Crimes Investigation Unit in Potsdam.'

'Is there any record of what they were carrying in the trucks?'

'No,' said Weekley. 'No one seemed to know, or bothered to ask.'

'I think I do.'

'Oh?'

'I may be wrong. Anyway, please go on.'

'The Russian was in a very bad way and spent weeks in hospital, so it was two or three months before he got round to telling anyone. It was complete chaos, as you can imagine. By the time he did, the SS officer had been captured and charged with the Isigny massacre. He was tried before a British Military Court at Dachau, found guilty and condemned to death. He appealed against the sentence and it was then revealed that he was a member of the British Free Corps. Since everyone knew the British Free Corps was purely a propaganda exercise and that none of them ever saw action, it was adjudged by the court of appeal that there had been a clear case of mistaken identity and the charges against him were dismissed.'

'So he was never charged with the Königsberg massacre?'

'Not as far as I can see.'

'What was this man's name?'

'Wilhelm Gruber.'

'Gruber? What was a man with a German name doing in the British Free Corps?'

'It almost certainly wasn't his real name,' said Weekley. 'But then, all members of the British Free Corps went under assumed names. Anyway, there's no record of a Wilhelm Gruber being in command of any SS division at that time.'

'And you say this particular division had no name?'

'Apparently not.'

'There must have been some identifying insignia on the collar patch.'

'There's no mention of it in the document I saw. But I've seen the transcript of Gruber's appeal trial at which the British survivor gave evidence. It seems that at the first trial he had forgotten to mention one very important fact, namely that embroidered on the lower left arm of all the SS uniforms was a very unusual badge.'

'Don't tell me.'

Weekley nodded. 'It was black, with a Union Jack and the word "England" underneath.'

'Not quite the British Free Corps, then.'

'Near enough for the appeal-court judges.'

'So that's why General Hollies didn't recognise the badge when I mentioned it. This was obviously some special unit which may or may not have been recruited from the Free Corps and never officially existed.'

'They may have called themselves the "England" Division, but there would have been no record of it; and the moment Germany surrendered, the badges would have been removed, never to be seen again.'

'Until a fortnight ago.'

'Seems there might have been more to your original story than you thought,' Weekley said.

'Looks like it.'

'You said you knew what was in the trucks.'

'I'm only guessing, but if I'm right … Just one more question. What was the name of the Russian officer?'

'Well, that's another strange thing. Unlike Gruber, he did have an English name. Rogers. Sergius Rogers. Seems the other officer, the one who was killed, was his brother. Michael. If only we could find Sergius. I wonder if he's still alive.'

'No,' said Miles. 'He died of cancer in 1964.'

28

As Miles had predicted, Peter Franklin put on his old-buffer, no-good-asking-me-I-can't-remember-a-thing act when he telephoned him later that morning.

'You're not still banging on about that bloody badge, are you?' he said.

'Forget the badge,' said Miles. 'I'm much more interested in a man called Grobius. Walter Grobius.'

'Sounds like some medieval Dutch astronomer. No one I've ever heard of. Should I have done?'

'Peter Schmid thinks so.'

'Schmid?' The tone changed abruptly. 'Have you been talking to Schmid? What's he been telling you?'

'I didn't speak to him myself. A colleague got in touch with him on my behalf. He told him I was interested in this man Walter Grobius. He said you were the man to speak to and that I was to mention his name.'

'OK.' Miles could almost hear Franklin's shoulders dropping in resignation. 'What do you want to know?'

'Can we meet? I owe you a drink anyway.'

'Oh well, in that case … how about six o'clock at the Ski Club of Great Britain?'

They met in the hall. Franklin was dressed exactly as he had been when Miles had last seen him in the bar of the Hotel des Alpes in Eigerhubel: sports jacket with patched sleeves, dark-blue roll-neck jumper, cavalry twills, plain brown lace-ups.

'You look even worse than when I last saw you,' Franklin told him. 'Why the bandages?'

'Accident with a stove,' Miles lied airily. 'You look rather better.'

307

'We were both the worse for wear that evening,' agreed Peter and waved him in the direction of the bar.

'For rather different reasons,' said Miles.

Franklin laughed. 'Well, I can promise you, I have been keeping myself pure and unsullied by alcohol ever since you telephoned. If I was going to have to start plunging the old paw into the sludge of memory, I reckoned I'd need to be reasonably *sur la balle*, as they say.'

The large room was almost deserted except for a couple of elderly male members who had taken up positions at tables near the window. One had his nose in a copy of *Ski Survey*, the other was gazing out at the skeletal treescape of Eaton Square.

'Here suit you?' Franklin pointed at a corner seat to the left-hand side of the door.

'Fine.'

'Whisky and soda?'

'Let me,' said Miles.

'Sorry, cock,' Franklin told him. 'No can do. You're a guest.'

'Actually,' said Miles, 'I'm a member.'

'No excuse,' said Franklin, and headed for the bar.

Known to generations of Ski Club members as D'Eggers Bar, the walls are hung with pre-war, Fougasse-like cartoons of skiers getting into the silly sort of muddles skiers are traditionally supposed to get into – all the work of the man after whom the room was named, Alan D'Egville.

Franklin returned with a large Scotch and a glass of white wine.

'Did you ever sort out that business of the doctor?' he asked.

'Simple case of mistaken identity,' Miles told him. 'You were right. The knock on the head plus the whisky must have sent me doolally.'

'Sent you packing, too. More's the pity. I could have done with some civilised company. Romford was never my spiritual home.'

'Sorry.'

'Sort of thing that can happen to the best of us. So, no murder, then?'

'I must have imagined it.'

'And the badge, or whatever it was?'

'I'm still working on it.'

'What makes you think I can help?'

308

'Because it was you who put me on to this thing in the first place. If you hadn't mentioned the SS that night in the hotel I would never have gone back to the surgery and I would never … well, my life wouldn't have taken the dramatic turn it did.'

Peter grunted into his wine. 'Bit of an exaggeration,' he muttered.

'Come on, Peter,' said Miles impatiently. 'Drop the silly-old-fart performance. It may have fooled me that night in the Chasse-Neige bar, but not any more.'

'Don't know what you mean,' he mumbled.

'When I first mentioned the badge to you, you appeared to be as baffled as I was. I fell for it. Maybe you didn't know exactly what it was, but I think you had a damned good idea. The first thing that came into your head when I mentioned the badge was black was that it was something to do with the SS. Perhaps you didn't mean it to slip out: *in vino veritas* and all that. The Olympic skiing team was an inspired cover-up. I thought it was odd when I rang you at home and you pretended you couldn't remember a thing about it, but now I know that you spent time dealing with Nazi collaborators I don't believe a word of it. You knew all along, didn't you?'

Franklin took another sip of his wine and stared out of the window. The lights of the cars sped silently up and down Eaton Square. 'Being a spook, even for a short time, becomes a habit that you never quite throw off. I know women who worked as cipher clerks at Bletchley during the war, gathering information, decoding enemy messages and so on, and to this day they would never dream of telling anyone what they did. Not even their families. You're quite right. The moment you mentioned the badge, I guessed what it might have been. OK, so I blurted out something about the SS. What the hell. The war's been over for nearly fifty years. But I still wished I'd kept my trap shut. Especially now I know where it led you.'

'The man who showed me the badge was dead by the time I got back.'

'I believe that, too,' said Franklin. 'I knew nothing about it, though. As you know, the Swiss have made an art form out of the cover-up.'

'I know now who he was and why he was killed. One of these days I'll tell you the whole story. I'd tell you now, except I haven't got to the end of it yet.'

'And Walter Grobius features in this story?'

'Yes, but I don't quite know where. Or why. I know he's Swiss and an art historian – or was, anyway – that he had pre-war connections with German industry, and was friends with a man named Gustav van Berkel. What I'd like to know is what he got up to in the war.'

Franklin sipped at his wine. 'Have you got all night?' he said.

'Start with his pre-war activities.'

'OK. Walter Grobius. Born in Sweden in 1914. Father a banker, mother the youngest daughter of a big landowning family. Lots of money sloshing around. Houses in Sweden, Geneva, London, Antibes, New York, you name it. Walter joins the family bank. Travels widely in Europe. Meets Oswald Mosley through a shared interest in fencing and is seduced by him into joining the British Union of Fascists.'

'Now there's a coincidence.'

'Coincidence?'

'I know someone else who got very pally with Mosley at about that time.'

'A lot did,' said Franklin.

'Never mind. Please go on.'

'Where was I? Ah yes. 1933. In 1934 he meets Werner Stich of Meier Industries, one of Germany's biggest steel-making companies. Stich has just embraced Nazism in the biggest possible way and is about to turn over part of his factory in Düsseldorf to the manufacture of small arms. He persuades Grobius that the future of Europe lies with Hitler, and Grobius bankrolls Meier Industries to the tune of several million marks. In 1935 Grobius joins the Nazi party himself and the following year moves to Switzerland, where he acquires a huge estate called Monte Cino on a mountain-top overlooking Lake Lugano. The following year he acquires Swiss citizenship and establishes a branch of the family bank in Bellinzona, though effectively it is his own personal bank. In 1939 he is approached by the German High Command, who see the bank as a perfect way to channel secret funds to pay for their intelligence networks throughout the world. It's estimated that between 1939 and 1942 more than two million Swiss francs passed through Grobius's bank. You can imagine how much that would work out at in modern currency. It's only a matter of time before he's contacted by Gustav van Berkel, a Dutchman by birth though not by inclination, who is the German Vice-Consul in Berne, though in reality he is a member of the German Intelligence Service. As I think I told you before, the Swiss were very pro-German in those early days – before they began to twig that perhaps the Germans weren't going to win after all. The German legation in Berne was crawling with spies, many of them courtesy of Grobius & Company.'

'So, basically, he was a paymaster.'

'Up till 1942, yes. But then suddenly he disappeared from view. His movements between 1942 and 1945 are very hard to follow in any detail. He covered his tracks brilliantly. But then he had been trained by some of the best agents in Germany, not least Gustav van Berkel. There seems little doubt that he had become more and more caught up in the German Intelligence Service. We don't know what date he actually joined, but there were rumours that he was seen in Berlin in December 1942 and again in March 1943 and on both occasions he was in the company of Admiral Canaris, who was Germany's leading spymaster at the time, though later his name was linked with various conspiracies to murder Hitler.

'The next time Grobius surfaced was in the spring of 1944, at Hildesheim, where the SS had set up a training camp for British prisoners-of-war who had been recruited to the SS by John Amery and others in the late summer of the previous year. It's not quite clear what Grobius was doing there. He didn't appear to take part in any training, but by all accounts he spent a lot of time socialising with some of the more aggressive elements. And then suddenly he disappeared again, along with several of the *Britische Freikorps*, as they were known.

'By the time the war ended, he was back in Switzerland, running the bank and adding to his famous collection of Chinese porcelain at his estate at Monte Cino. He was arrested by the Swiss authorities and charged with "irregular financial dealings". His Swiss citizenship was taken away and he stood to serve a long sentence in prison. However, it all came to nothing when he offered his entire Chinese collection to the Munch Museum in Lucerne. Whether this deal was engineered by the Swiss themselves is not entirely clear. Few things are in Switzerland. They were already embarrassed enough by the fact that a Swiss citizen had collaborated with the Germany army and any further revelations would have been most unwelcome. Anyway, within a year the charges had been dropped, but his Swiss citizenship was never renewed. He sold Monte Cino and moved to the United States. In the early 1960s he came back to Britain and bought a pile somewhere up in the wilds of Scotland. The security services still keep an eye on him, but he's an old man now – a curious relic from a bygone age, and about as harmless as a stuffed coelacanth.

'Oh, by the way, I forgot to mention. He changed his name when he went to America.'

Miles said, 'It wouldn't have been the first time. From 1944 to 1945, he was known as Wilhelm Gruber.'

'The last I heard of him he was calling himself Bill Gordon. He's probably dead by now. Bloody good thing, too.'

Miles said, 'Sorry to disappoint you, but he's very much alive. The last time I saw him he was strutting around and giving Nazi salutes in a front room in south London. I peeked through the curtains. It was quite a mini-Nuremberg.'

'Good God, he must be eighty if he's a day. Silly old bugger.'

'Silly old buggers have a habit of being taken seriously.'

'What on earth has he possibly got to be serious about?'

'I don't know,' said Miles. 'But in pride of place amongst the Nazi flags and pictures of Hitler was a poster of the Totenkopf at Eigerhubel.' He swallowed his whisky and pointed at Franklin's empty glass. 'Another?'

'Definitely,' said Franklin.

* * *

'Globus, you say?' The general bent over the fire and poked at it in a desultory fashion.

'Grobius. Walter Grobius.'

'Grobius. Extraordinary name,' the general murmured. 'Sounds like one of those chaps who always seemed to be sticking their oar in when Caesar was trying to divide Gaul into three parts. Friend of Labienus, probably.'

'You might have known him better as Wilhelm Gruber,' said Miles.

312

The general stopped poking and stared into the flames. 'Gruber. No. Can't help you, I'm afraid. Who is this man?'

'Grobius – or Gruber, as he called himself in those days – was tried by a military court at Dachau for the murder of fifty British prisoners-of-war in Normandy in 1944. He was in command of a detachment of SS infantrymen at the time. An odd thing for a Swiss citizen of Swedish birth to be doing, you might think. Even odder was the fact that the men under his command were all English.'

The general stood upright. He held the poker, point upwards, as if it were a sword. 'Miles,' he said, 'I thought I'd made it quite clear on the last two occasions you brought this subject up that there is absolutely no evidence that the British Free Corps was anything more than a propaganda exercise on Hitler's part. None of them ever saw action, and they certainly never committed any atrocities. I should know, for God's sake. I was there when all these investigations were going on. Now can we please drop the subject once and for all, or we really are going to part brass rags. What's more, we're going to be in trouble with the girls. Have another drink and let's talk about something else.'

He launched one last sabre attack on the fire, leaned the poker against the carved wooden surround and headed towards the drinks table.

* * *

After lunch, Elizabeth walked arm in arm with Miles across the forecourt. When they came to the car, he took her face in his hands and kissed her gently on both cheeks. She looked intently at him. He thought he detected a hint of fear in her eyes, but it must have been his imagination. As he drove away she was still standing there, gazing after him, as if a spell had been cast on her.

* * *

He made a number of telephone calls when he got back to London later that afternoon. The first was to an Argyll number. The voice that answered sounded like thick, lumpy porridge.

313

'Lochintoul Castle.'

'May I ask who I'm speaking to?' Miles enquired politely.

'This is Ferguson. I'm in charge.'

Miles asked if could speak to Mrs McCulloch.

'Mrs McCulloch's no' here.'

'Actually,' said Miles, 'it was the Captain I really wanted to speak to.'

'He's no' here either. There's no one at home.'

'It's important that I speak to the Captain. Can you tell me where I might find him?'

'He's no' here,' Ferguson repeated. 'He's off in Switzerland.'

'Oh, of course,' said Miles. 'I'd quite forgotten. He's in Eigerhubel, isn't he?'

'Aye, mebbe. Can I tell him who called?'

'It doesn't matter,' said Miles, and replaced the receiver.

He then rang Maddy Maguire, who told him he had to be joking: there was no way she or anyone else could find him a room anywhere in the region during the Diabolo Weekend, but for old times' sake she'd see what she could do and call him back.

He then called the British Embassy in Berne. The young man in the consular Section was polite but hesitant. Was Miles a relative of the deceased? he enquired. A close friend of the family, Miles told him. In that case, said the young man, he must be aware that Mr Rogers had died in suspicious circumstances and that the police were currently investigating the matter. Miles said that he was well acquainted with the situation and that, as he understood it, the body had now been released for burial and the deceased's daughter was even now in Switzerland making the arrangements. Unfortunately he had, for various reasons, been unable to contact her and was anxious to know if the funeral was going ahead, and if so where and when.

'I see,' said the man from the Embassy. 'And you say you're a close friend of the family?' He emphasised the word 'close'.

'I know this must sound odd to you,' said Miles, 'but the thing is ...'

'Perhaps if I might take your name and some details ...?'

The last thing Miles wanted was for his name to pop up on some bureaucrat's computer in Berne. He said casually, 'Look, there's no

314

reason why I should expect you to do my legwork for me. I'll keep chasing her. She may well ring me. Sorry to have bothered you.' And he rang off.

Afterwards he wondered why he had bothered. It took the woman at International Directory Enquiries less than three minutes to discover that the nearest undertaker to Eigerhubel was Urs Stäger in Brugg. Five minutes later, Miles had the information he needed and was ringing the bank to order Swiss francs and traveller's cheques.

He was laying out his skiing clothes when Maddy called with the news that she had booked him a single room in the Hotel Gummi in Wintertal. Swiss Villas had used it a couple of times. It wasn't the Hotel des Alpes, or anything like it, but it was clean and comfortable and cheap and, most important of all, it was available.

'You're a genius,' Miles told her.

'And you've got a cheek, Maltby,' she replied.

'I owe you one,' he said.

'Several,' she said.

29

The Hotel Gummi was two-star to the point of spartan and lacking in any charming grace notes, but Miles's room was bright and warm and new-pin clean, and, as Herr Müller was at pains to remind him, probably the last available room in the entire region. He doubted that at five o'clock on the Thursday afternoon of the Diabolo Weekend it was possible to find so much as a dog kennel.

Miles said it was about time he had some luck. Herr Müller said the Diabolo deserved some good luck too. Conditions for the race had been very poor for some years: seventy centimetres of snow on the lower slopes before Christmas, a couple of light falls in January and nothing worth speaking of after that until the beginning of March. For the last three years, they had had to stop the race at Niederwald. This year, though, it had snowed continuously for the last three days. The wooded paths below Grützi were well covered and on Saturday they would be able to ski all the way from Totenkopf down to Wintertal.

Miles said that was good news.

'You have come for the race?' Herr Müller enquired.

'What else?' said Miles.

He unpacked and went out for a meal. It was snowing hard and, from the glimpse he caught of himself in the hall mirror of the Café Alpenrose, he looked as if he was suffering a terminal attack of dandruff.

He ordered a steak with *rösti* and a green salad and a half-carafe of chewy red Dôle du Valais. He followed that up with a piece of Emmental the size of a brick, which he helped down with another glass of Dôle, and, to ensure that it didn't hang heavy on his stomach, he drank two glasses of Poire William with his coffee.

Snow was still falling as he trudged back to the Gummi. This was the first time he had been in the Alps in winter without the prospect of any skiing. It was an odd feeling. Like sitting on a beach in Barbados in a three-piece suit. He flexed his hands inside his pigskin gloves. They were still sore and the palms sticky with pus. He remembered someone telling him that wounds heal much more slowly in the mountains.

He stood for a moment in the middle of the square and looked around, breathing in the silence. There wasn't another living soul to be seen. The main railway station was deserted at this hour, grey and sinister under the harsh lights, like a scene from an old Cold War spy movie. The door of a pub on the opposite side of the road banged open and a crowd of half a dozen young Germans charged out, shouting and laughing. A snowball fight soon got under way. For a short while the square was loud with squeals and yells; then the youths chased one another up the street, and soon the sounds were swallowed up in the muffling whiteness as the snow continued to fall, like feathers after a pillow fight.

Miles smiled. Despite everything, he was glad to be back. He zipped his anorak tighter round his neck, lowered his head and set off toward the Gummi.

From somewhere away to his left came the whining, clinking sound of heavy wires taking the strain as the funicular made its way down the invisible mountainside, followed by a hiss and a clunk as it arrived at the buffers. A few moments later, the first of the passengers appeared in the doorway, adjusted their hats and gloves, and set off briskly into the night. Locals, by the look of them; on their way home after a long day's dusting and sweeping and carrying trays and washing dirty dishes. But no tall, dark-haired figures in fur hats and long overcoats. No one to set the heart racing. Not tonight.

Herr Müller was still there, beaming behind the reception desk, when Miles walked in, stamping his feet on the plastic mat and brushing the snow from his shoulders.

He sounded surprised to hear that Miles was going to Brugg in the morning. He told him there was a train from Wintertal at 8.30 arriving at Grundsee at 8.40 and Brugg fifteen minutes later. Unless he would like to order a taxi? It was only fifty francs to Brugg and back. Miles said the train would be fine.

317

Herr Müller looked anxious. 'It is practice day for the race tomorrow, you know?' he said.

Miles said he expected to be back by lunchtime.

'You are not racing.' It was a statement more than a question.

Miles held up his hands. Herr Müller nodded sympathetically and handed Miles his key.

There was only one picture in Room 24. It was on the wall next to the bed. A large framed picture of Totenkopf. An enlargement of an old black-and-white postcard, by the look of it. Taken on a beautiful summer's day, probably from Schwarzegg. Miles peered at it. Something was inscribed in white across the bottom. TOTENKOPF. EIGERHUBEL. 3,005 m. BERNER OBERLAND, SCHWEIZ. 1936. Those were the days before the cable car had been installed and the panoramic restaurant had broken up the outline of the summit, but otherwise it all looked much as he remembered it. Apart from the snow, of course.

And yet there was *something* different about it. Something that didn't quite fit in with his memory of it. He stood there, staring at it for a long time, trying to puzzle it out, but he was tired and his brain had stopped working. He undressed, brushed his teeth and went to bed.

He was woken from a deep and dreamless sleep by a lot of shouting and clattering of metal. It sounded as if an army manoeuvre was in progress. It was still dark. He turned on his bedside light and squinted at his watch. Six o'clock. He got out of bed, went across to the window and drew back the curtain. A train had just arrived at the station and from every door skiers were climbing down the metal steps – boot clips flapping, skis clacking – and shuffling and clumping and clattering their way along the platform and across the shadowy, snow-filled square, their skis at the slope, their boots squeaking, towards the funicular station. From time to time a group would have to stop and wait while a car – skis strapped to its roof, chains chinking, headlights stabbing the grey gloom of the street lights – headed for the big parking lot at the bottom of the Winterberg cable car further up the valley.

Miles stood there for a while watching the pre-dawn invasion. Ten years ago he'd have happily been in the midst of them, arms and legs

318

shaky with nervous anticipation, mouth dry with excitement, head spinning with adrenalin. Now, even a funeral seemed a more attractive proposition.

He got back into bed, pulled the covers up over his ears and slept until the curtains glowed with the morning light.

Wintertal still looked like the centre of the skiing universe but now, two hours later, the view from his window had burst from dull sepia into dazzling technicolor, as though a heavy filter had been removed from the lens. Everything seemed bowed beneath the weight of new snow, from the village rooftops to the branches of the mountain pines, iced by a huge and generous hand. And, soaring above it all, the peaks of the Blumenhorn range gleamed against the pale blue canopy of the sky.

Staring out of the carriage window just below Wintertal where the train follows the east bank of the rushing Winterfluhe, watching the non-stop procession of cars and jeeps, a-bristle with skis, snaking their way up between the trees on the far side, Miles was beginning to wish he was going with them. And when, a little later, at Grundsee, they passed a train packed with grinning skiers going in the opposite direction, Miles felt decidedly envious.

Brugg was looking like all Alpine towns are meant to look in the middle of winter and rarely do. The sun shone, the snow sparkled, the mountains towered magnificently, there wasn't a cloud in the sky. It was a winter wonderland. It certainly wasn't the day or the place for a funeral.

Miles sat by the window in the Buffet de la Gare and drank a hot chocolate and wished he'd brought his camera. On the short drive to the crematorium, the taxi driver asked him if he was on holiday. Business, Miles told him firmly, and the driver didn't speak again except to tell him that the fare was seven francs fifty.

The Brugg crematorium was like crematoria the world over: a long, low, red-brick building with a tall chimney. Inoffensive, undramatic, unmemorable.

The nine-o'clock party was viewing the floral tributes in a side colonnade when Miles arrived. Behind a pair of glass doors there was a small lobby which led into the room where the service took place. On either side of the door there was a white plaster plinth topped by

319

a tasteful flower arrangement. Five men in black suits, white shirts and black ties were standing to one side of the lobby, talking in hushed tones. As Miles entered, the smallest of them glided forward. He had tinted glasses and a small droopy moustache.

'Urs Stäger,' he murmured, and extended a sympathetic hand.

Miles shook it and walked through.

The coffin was already there. So was Anna. She was the only person in the room – a dignified figure in a black coat and black fur hat, upright and motionless in the front row. Miles walked round the outside of the chairs and along her row. As he sat down next to her, she turned and looked at him. Her face was pale and grave. A faint smile crossed her features, like a summer's breeze across a cornfield, and disappeared. She turned her head away and looked at the coffin. Miles very gently took her right hand in his left. She made no response, but nor did she attempt to draw away.

A priest appeared silently through a door to the right. He wore a plain black stole over his surplice and a biretta. As he took his place, there was a sound from the back of the room. Miles turned his head in time to see Stäger ushering a big man with a grey-flecked beard and a black overcoat into the back row.

The service was short and there was no address. Anna showed no sign of emotion, until the moment when the coffin began to move off through the curtains and Miles heard her utter a faint sigh and felt a slight pressure on his hand.

Afterwards the priest sidled up to them and murmured something reassuring in German before retiring through his door.

'Are you all right?' Miles asked her.

'Yes,' she said, her voice calm and low. 'I'm fine. Thanks.'

The place was empty as they left. Urs Stäger was waiting for them in the lobby. He bowed over Anna's hand and murmured more condolences.

'You have my address in Eigerhubel,' Anna said.

'Of course,' said Stäger. 'As soon as I have prepared my account ...'

'And the ashes?'

'I could arrange for them to be delivered first thing tomorrow morning.'

'At the house of Willi Graf, the carpenter, if you would be so kind.'

'As you say,' murmured Stäger.

He was still bowing as they stepped out into the brilliance of the winter morning.

Anna turned to Miles. She gave him a long, steady look. 'Thank you for coming,' she said. 'I hoped that by leaving as I did you might be discouraged. That's why I didn't tell Ina where I was going. But she guessed and I thought you probably would, too. You're almost as stubborn as I am.'

Miles returned her solemn look. 'I thought about it for a long time,' he said. 'You must be as aware as I am of the risk you're taking by coming back here. It'll only be a matter of time before Smith catches up with you. He can't afford to have you running around knowing what you know.'

'Or you,' she said.

Miles looked up the valley towards Eigerhubel. Even from that distance the Blumenhorn dominated the skyline like some Old Testament prophet.

'Unfinished business,' he said. Then he turned back to her and grinned. 'And if you honestly thought I was going to let you finish it alone after all we …'

Anna looked at him and shook her head slowly. 'You should never have left the Army,' she said.

Miles put his arms round her and they clung together, silent and motionless in the still, cold air.

The crunch of the tyres on the snow made them both start. The black Mercedes seemed to have appeared from nowhere. It drew up beside them, polished bodywork brushing Anna's coat, engine throbbing as if with pleasure at the gentle caress.

'Miss Rogers?'

His silent approach from behind startled them for a second time. He had put on a fur hat since leaving the crematorium. With the fur hat and the beard he looked like a bear dressed up.

'Yes?'

'Inspector Muoth. Berne Police.' He looked at Miles and raised an enquiring eyebrow.

Anna said, 'This is …'

321

'Parker,' said Miles. 'Noel Parker. I am an old family friend of Miss Rogers.'

The inspector did not look convinced, but neither did he challenge it. He nodded and turned his attention to Anna.

'I have seen the voluntary statement you made to the Eigerhubel police on Tuesday. You took a long time coming forward. More than a month.'

'As I said, I was away on holiday. I knew nothing of my father's ... what had happened.'

The inspector gave a little grunt. 'It was an odd time to choose to go away, wasn't it? While your father was on holiday here?'

'As I explained in my statement, we had been out of touch. He arrived without warning. I found him a place to stay, but I had already made my plans. It was impossible to change them. The regular nurse was due back the next morning, so I left as soon as I had finished my duty. I didn't expect my father to come to the surgery. If I had known ...'

'We tried to contact you in Paris. That was the only address we had for you. Whoever answered the phone did not know where you were.'

'They are old friends. I stay with them sometimes. They allow me to use them as an accommodation address.'

'So when did you learn of your father's death?'

'When I returned to London last Saturday. I came out here as soon as I could. Had I known, of course ...' Her eyes were moist. She put one gloved hand over her mouth and reached into her pocket for a handkerchief.

Miles said, 'Unless you have any other questions ...?'

'Just one more,' said the inspector.

'Oh, really!'

'May I give you both a lift anywhere?'

He dropped them at Brugg station. He would probably have taken them to Wintertal if they had asked, but it might have led to more questions. Besides, Miles needed time to be alone with Anna.

'We don't like tourists being murdered in our country,' the inspector told them through the open car window. 'It's bad for business. And we certainly don't like having unsolved crimes on our files. If

322

you think of anything that might help – either of you – you have my card. And my genuine condolences.'

The window slid upwards and the car hissed away through the fast-melting snow.

* * *

The next train to Wintertal was not due for another twenty minutes. They went into the Buffet de la Gare and ordered coffee and brandy.

'Do you think he believed a word of it?' Anna asked.

'Good Lord, no,' said Miles. 'But if he'd asked me, I could have told him who did it and how and why, and he wouldn't have believed that either.'

'I know who,' said Anna, 'and I know how, but you still haven't told me why.'

So Miles did. He told her about the badge and gave her a brief history of the SS and the British Free Corps, and described his conversations with Anne Crosthwaite and Paul Weekley and General Hollies, and outlined the activities of the War Crimes Investigation Unit. And then he told her the story of Archie Lambourn and gave a graphic account of his visit to West Keating.

Anna sat for the most part in silence, her eyes fixed on the table, her fingers playing with her brandy glass. From time to time she would interrupt with a question. Miles had an answer for most of them, but not all.

'I suspect Archie was killed because he had threatened to reveal something to the *Daily Mail*,' he said. 'Something to do with the Diabolo Project, almost certainly. As yet, I've no idea what prompted him.'

'Whatever the Diabolo Project is,' she said.

'At the time I was more interested in the photographs. And the badge, of course. More's the pity.'

'What about this Kananga business?' she said.

'Archie was a passionate man,' said Miles. 'Passionate about politics, passionate about wildlife. The thought that an obscure species of monkey might be sacrificed on the altar of one man's self-aggrandisement would have been intolerable to him.'

'Perhaps that was what killed him?'

'You mean, it had nothing to do with any of this?'

'I mean, we don't even know if he was murdered. And, if he was, how it was engineered. And by whom. Bishop?'

'Perhaps,' said Miles. 'Perhaps it was just an accident after all.'

'Two accidents in two weeks?'

'That's not such a high rate of strike the way my luck's been running lately,' said Miles with a wry grin.

At that moment, the train arrived and speculation was suspended while they settled themselves into an empty banquette at the far end of a compartment. Then Miles launched into a long and detailed account of the life of Bill Gordon, his involvement in the Normandy Massacre and the events at Chestnut Grove.

'So Bill Gordon and Walter Grobius are the same person?'

'According to Peter Franklin. I have no reason to doubt him. The information was quite unprompted.'

'The same Grobius as in Ina's letter?'

'What do *you* think?'

'The letter never mentioned the Amber Room by name. It could have been wishful thinking on her part.'

'I might agree with you if I wasn't so certain it was Walter Grobius who took the Room from Königsberg.'

'Grobius?' she said. 'What on earth makes you think Grobius took it?'

He told her what Franklin had told him. The only thing he left out were the names of the two Russian officers.

Anna waited till he'd finished; then she said, 'It's a good story.'

'You don't sound convinced.'

She shrugged. 'What is there to be convinced about? So these SS men hijacked some lorries outside Königsberg. Who's to say what was in them? It doesn't prove anything. Like Ina, I think the Amber Room still exists, and I think the key to the secret could well be here in Eigerhubel. Maybe the Room itself is here. Maybe this mystery man Grobius brought it here at the end of the war and it's been here ever since. But I'll only believe that when I see it.'

'There's no mystery about Grobius. He may have changed his name but he's as real now as he was then.'

324

'Not to me,' she said. 'To me he's just a name in a letter. A character in a story. A figment.'

'What if I told you he's here?'

'Here?'

'Bill Gordon. He's here. In Eigerhubel. I rang his home before I came out.'

'OK,' she said, 'so maybe the Diabolo Club is a hotbed of right-wing hooray shits, and maybe they're laying on something specially right-wing and hooray and shitty to celebrate their seventy-fifth anniversary, but what's that got to do with me? Or you, for that matter? I thought you'd come out here to help me look for the Amber Room. But all you seem to be interested in is whether this man Gordon might or might not once have been a war criminal called Grobius. Well, I tell you what. Why don't you go and look for your war criminal and I'll go and look for my Room?' She turned and glared out of the window.

Miles rested his elbow on his knees and cupped his hands over his mouth. He stared at the floor for a bit without speaking. Finally he looked up. 'I wasn't going to tell you this,' he said in a soft voice. 'I reckoned you were upset enough already. But the fact is, when I told you about Grobius and the lorries, I left out one small but important detail.'

Anna was still looking out of the window when he finished speaking. She didn't say anything but, when she finally turned and looked at him, her eyes were rimmed with red. She took out a handkerchief and blew her nose. Then she fumbled in her handbag and brought out a compact and repaired the damage to her cheeks. She snapped it shut, dropped it back into her bag and took a deep breath.

'It's no good asking you if it's true,' she said.

Miles shook his head.

'In that case,' she said, 'let's find this man Gordon and ask him.'

'Good idea,' said Miles.

30

The roofs of Wintertal were dripping fast as the midday sun rose above the mountain peaks, and the snow in the square looked like over-cooked meringue on top of a lemon pie. Miles and Anna fought their way through the straggling procession of skiers that clumped towards the bottom of the funicular.

The Hotel Gummi was the only building in Wintertal that managed to appear diminished by brilliant sunlight.

'Are you planning to stay on here?' Anna asked Miles.

'Where else?'

'Why not stay with me at Willi Graf's?'

'With you?'

'The other room's free. The one my father used.'

'In that case ...'

Herr Müller wasn't pleased when Miles broke the news, though he cheered up a bit when Miles promised to mention him in his next article.

They arrived at the bottom of the funicular in time to see the 12.15 grinding and wheezing its way skywards. There was a narrow waiting room on one side of the hall, with a big glass window along the front. Lined up along the back wall was a series of framed posters advertising the various highlights of the region. There were two for Eigerhubel: one was the standard overall view of the village under snow, and the other a spectacular helicopter shot of Totenkopf, taken from a much greater height than usual and from a slightly different angle. But it was not the composition of the picture that interested Miles.

'I *knew* there was something!' he exclaimed.

'What?'

'It's the clubhouse.'

'What about it?'

'It's in a different place.' Miles pointed at the poster. 'Look, there, do you see? Snuggling up against the rock face. Almost as if it were attached to it. In 1936 it stood out over there on its own, quite a long way away. There was an old pre-war photograph of it in my room. I knew it wasn't quite as I'd remembered it, but I couldn't work out why. It was larger, too. More chalet-like.'

'So? They rebuilt it. What's so extraordinary about that?'

'Nothing at all. But why make it smaller? When people rebuild things like clubhouses, it's usually because they need more space, not less. And why jam it up against the mountain like that? It was in a perfect position before. The view's nothing like so good from back there.'

'How do you know?'

'I did a bit of snooping that first morning. I was doing it when your father nearly ran me down. I didn't have time to see much. A roof piled high with snow and a man shouting on a terrace.' Miles continued to stare up at the poster. 'I wonder when it was rebuilt,' he murmured. 'And why.'

'Willi Graf will know,' she said. 'His father probably worked on it.'

The arrival of the next funicular coincided with that of another trainload of passengers from across the road. They surged aboard and the old wooden frame heaved its way upwards. Crushed against the window by pale-faced Swiss with strong accents and even stronger breath, Miles and Anna decided that some museum pieces were better off in museums.

After a while, a *frisson* of excitement ran through the stepped compartments as the woods were suddenly filled with helmeted skiers: dozens of them, one after another, hurtling down the steep fall-line on a path no wider than a garden path, checking, twisting, dodging in and out of tight trees, bending below overhanging branches, legs pumping, hips swivelling, shoulders working like boxers on a bag, hands reaching forward, knees burning with pain as the edges of the racing skis fought for control on hidden patches of ice, never pausing for a second as they snaked their way down to the finishing line at Wintertal.

'And that's just a small part of the course,' said Miles.

At Grützi there was an unseemly rush for the Eigerhubel train. Miles didn't know which was more grating: the clattering of skis on the concrete platform or the non-stop din of Schwyzer Deutsch being hawked up and down the carriages.

Being boot-less and ski-less, Miles and Anna were able to push ahead of the crowd and find seats in the front compartment facing out over the valley.

After about half a mile, a line of flags appeared out of a small clump of trees on the upper slope. It ran for a while alongside the railway track before disappearing under a little bridge and dropping further down the slope, where it turned sharp left and ran back in a long traverse towards Grützi. Not that anyone good enough to enter the Diabolo could possibly go the wrong way, but, since the turn was only twenty yards or so from where sheer rock face met steep wooded slopes, a low net and a barrier had been erected, just in case. Miles's palms pricked with sweat.

The hands of the station clock registered precisely 1.15 as the little brown-and-yellow train pulled into Eigerhubel station. Miles and Anna jostled their way up the stairs and out into the square in front of the Hotel des Alpes. There was a moment or two of milling about in the street outside while everyone got their bearings and gathered up their skis before forming a rudimentary procession and stumping off down the main street towards the Schwarzegg cable car. It looked like Alpine Day in Lourdes.

Willi Graf's house was at the far edge of the village, hidden away at the end of a narrow path, overhung with the eaves of neighbouring chalets. Willi and his wife Alice had just finished lunch. Willi wore a green apron and smoked a bent cherrywood pipe. He was younger than Miles had expected and smaller. He had tufty red hair that stuck out in all directions and a long beard which covered his chin but not his upper lip. His mouth turned upwards at the corners in a constant smile and his eyes shone like brown M & Ms. He looked like a small boy dressed up in an elf outfit for the school pantomime.

While Frau Graf bustled off to make coffee, Anna explained to Willi in brisk German that Miles was an old friend who had turned up out of the blue and without a reservation and needed a bed for two

328

nights. Willi nodded and smiled and said that Miles was welcome but the bed was very small. Anna was surprised and said that her father had slept very well in it. Willi scratched his head and said that surely her father had slept in his own bed. Then it was Anna's turn to scratch her head and ask him what he was talking about, at which Willi went bright red and everyone realised that he had misread the situation, and then Willi went even redder and there was an awkward pause, and suddenly everyone saw the funny side of it, so that by the time Frau Graf returned with the coffee she found all three of them cackling and coughing, and Willi nodding and beaming and lighting his pipe, and Anna and Miles exchanging looks. And when she asked what was happening, they laughed all the more and Willi told her he would explain later.

As they drank their coffee, Anna asked them when the Diabolo clubhouse had been rebuilt. But for all their eagerness to supply an answer and despite much animated discussion and calculation and speculation, it was evident that theirs was a part of the village where tourism barely impinged and where the various attractions on which the economy of the village survived were as foreign as the thousands of visitors who enjoyed them.

'We'll try the museum,' Anna told him.

'There's a museum?' said Miles.

'Closed now,' said Willi. 'Open again at two.'

It was not yet 1.30 and the eaves were still dripping, but already the sun was beginning to dip towards the mountains away to the west. In another hour, the air temperature would start to drop and, an hour after that, the top of the Blumenhorn would turn pink, the sun would be off the village and everything would be freezing again. Miles pulled on a T-shirt and a pair of long johns under his polo-neck ski shirt, pullover and heavy green cords. He zipped up his calf-length, fur-lined snow boots, heaved himself into his faithful old anorak, tucked his wallet, a small notebook and a pencil into his inside pocket, picked up his battered Gamet ski gloves and his woollen bonnet, and banged on Anna's door.

Eigerhubel was at its quietest between half past one and two. The beginners' classes had revived their energies with *Rösti mit Eier* and Blumenburgers and chips and were already back on the nursery slopes

329

practising their snow-plough turns. Some of the outdoor café tables were still occupied by off-duty ski-school instructors and holiday skiers lingering over glasses of *digestif*; but the main street of Eigerhubel was pretty well deserted, except for a few locals – a couple of gnarled road men in bright-yellow jackets with big shovels on their shoulders and pipes jammed between their teeth, a young woman in a fur coat pulling her small child on a plastic sledge, non-skiers enjoying a stroll in the last of the warm sunshine.

Miles looked at each person in turn for signs of recognition. No one would remember him – certainly not with his new beard – but Anna had once been part of the community, albeit briefly, and even in her dark glasses and with her hair piled up under her fur hat, there was always a chance someone might spot her and call out.

The Eigerhubel Museum was located in the middle of the village, between the Union de Banques Suisse and the Lunnenberg Hotel and opposite Peter Seiler's ski shop. As Miles and Anna came level with the Lunnenberg, two men appeared from a side-street on the left about a hundred yards ahead and walked towards them. One was tall and thin and stooped under the weight of a sheepskin jacket; the other was fat, with a purple face and a drinker's stomach. At first Miles paid no attention to them but, as they came nearer, he saw the tall man's golf-club-secretary moustache and the long grinning teeth below ...

'Fancy a coffee?' said Miles. He grabbed Anna by the upper arm and steered her to the right and through the front door of the Lunnenberg.

'What *are* you talking about?' she said, looking round at the deserted lobby and the empty bar and dining room beyond.

'Wait,' he hissed. 'Look.' The two men passed the front door. 'That's Bill Gordon. The tall thin one. The other one's called Johnny Cunningham-Walker. Leading light in the Lambourn Set and long-standing Diabolo member.'

'So *that's* Gordon,' Anna murmured. 'He looks so ... I don't know ... suburban.'

'Himmler looked like a bank clerk, out of uniform.'

'Just seeing him like that ... Suddenly ... I should be feeling something, but ... I don't know ... He's so ... I can't ...'

'Just as well,' said Miles briskly. 'We've got things to do. Look, why don't *you* go to the museum? It'll be open in a minute. Find out what you can about the clubhouse. There might be more pictures … plans even … Tell them you're writing a piece about the race. They'll put themselves out a bit if they think there might be a bit of publicity in it.'

'What are you going to do?'

'Snoop,' said Miles. 'Meet you back at Willi's at …' He glanced at his watch. 'Make it five.'

'Five?'

'You never know …' said Miles.

The two men were almost out of sight round the bend in the street when he and Anna left the Lunnenberg. Miles walked quickly. When he was about fifty yards behind them he slowed to their pace. They didn't seem to be in any great hurry as they strolled into the Schwarzegg cable-car station.

A group of thirty or so was waiting by the turnstile that led out on to the embarkation platform: skiers mainly, plus a few sightseers lured by the prospect of seeing Totenkopf at its best. But there was no sign of Gordon or Cunningham-Walker. Miles frowned and looked quickly round the low, grey, concrete hall. Where could they have gone? There were no shops, no cafés: just the ticket office and a big empty concourse. The wires were beginning to twang now as the big red cable car slowed and eased its way between the two guide rails.

It suddenly occurred to him that they might be going in the opposite direction, down to the valley. In which case … He jogged across to the far side of the concourse where the old Winterberg lift ferried car passengers up and down between the big parking area in the valley and the Eigerhubel ski slopes a thousand feet above.

The waiting area was empty.

Behind him a bell announced the final arrival of the Schwarzegg cable car. Miles turned and walked back across the concourse. The cabin had disgorged one lot of passengers and was swallowing up the next. Miles watched as the last skier pushed through the turnstile. The uniformed conductor turned and looked at Miles, then began to walk out on to the platform. Miles was turning away when he caught sight of them, standing next to the window at the back of the cabin.

The conductor was closing the sliding glass door that led on to the platform. Miles made it just in time and squeezed through. He strolled into the cabin and stood there for a while, hands in pockets, looking at the floor. The guard stepped aboard, carefully closed the door and locked it, pressed a button, waited for the bell to ring, then pressed another, whereupon the cable car lifted out of its cradle and swung into space. Miles glanced across at the two men. They were deep in conversation.

When the cabin had cleared the lower slopes, Miles eased his way casually towards the rear. There was a space by the window just to the left of the two men. Last time he'd travelled up, everything had been blanketed in thick fog. He'd guessed the view of the village and the valley beyond must be pretty good from that height and that angle, but could never have imagined how good.

'Everything's going very well,' Gordon was saying. He sounded like a vicar at a church fête trying to cheer a harassed helper on the home-made cake stall.

'I wish I had your confidence,' Cunningham-Walker moaned.

'Oh, for God's sake, Johnny, do stop wittering. You always were a terrible worrier. Why do you think you're the size you are?'

Cunningham-Walker gave a small, not very convinced, grunt. 'What time are we on parade?' he murmured.

'They're due to land at eleven. It's all right, they *are* expected. I've cleared it with all the right people.'

'As long as we don't have any more last-minute hiccups.'

'I don't see why we should.'

'That's what you said before, and look what happened.'

'That was unfortunate, I'll admit.'

'Unfortunate? It was a complete bloody balls-up.' Cunningham-Walker's voice rose slightly. Gordon shot him a look and it dropped again. 'Every bloody paper. Front page. Inside page. Double-page spreads. Pompous pieces by every known scientist and conservationist. I'm surprised there weren't questions in the House.'

'Better that than the one we'd have finished up with if ...'

'Yes, yes, OK. Point taken.'

'Obviously if I'd known he was going to go about it the way he did, I'd have thought twice about it.'

'Typical bloody Kraut.' Cunningham-Walker spat the words out. Gordon raised an eyebrow but didn't say anything. 'Anyone else would have fixed the brakes, or the booze, or the ... I don't know ... kept it simple anyway. But not him. God preserve me from perfectionists.'

'Look. Forget it, OK?' muttered Gordon. His mouth was drawn back in a rictus of irritation. 'We had to do something. We did it. It could have been a disaster, but it wasn't. It's finished, over, done with. Kindly don't mention it again.'

There was a long silence. Miles continued to enjoy the view. The cable car was fast approaching the Schwarzegg station. It seemed almost to be climbing up the sheer rock face ahead.

'I wouldn't care if there were no more monkeys in the world,' Cunningham-Walker said. 'I hate monkeys. They remind me of my first wife.'

Miles walked ahead of them to the Totenkopf cable car. At least, he assumed he was ahead of them. He hoped that in his efforts to be anonymous he hadn't lost them altogether. But when he got to the end of the building, they were still behind him. He turned off into the men's room and, when he joined the back of the queue a few minutes later, they were far enough ahead of him not to pay him any attention. He was relieved to see they were no longer talking, and that he wasn't missing anything.

The Totenkopf cable car is half the size of the one to Schwarzegg, and for a moment he was afraid he wasn't going to get on. But the conductor waved him through, and with a bit of pushing he was able to acquire a modicum of space next to the door. He looked round at the other passengers. Through the forest of skis and poles he could see Gordon and Cunningham-Walker at the front end. But they were hemmed in on all sides, and didn't speak.

At Totenkopf, the non-skiers headed for the panoramic restaurant. Miles hung back for a few moments, then followed the last of the skiers down the iron staircase that led out to the start of the Totenkopf run.

By the time he got to the bottom, Gordon and Cunningham-Walker had vanished. He presumed they'd made straight for the clubhouse. He stood around for a while watching the latest carload

333

getting ready for the descent. Most of them were holiday-makers, pleased to find that their week coincided with the Diabolo celebrations, and looking forward to watching some of them the following day, but happy in the knowledge that they would not be required to push their skiing skills to the limit. For them, to get down the first steep face at the top of Totenkopf with some degree of style and without falling over was challenge enough in itself. The snow was still soft after a day of hot sunshine, but it was already half past two and they were keen to get in one last run before the surface hardened.

Since everyone else was heading off to the right, Miles was afraid that he might have left it too late; that the race practice might be over, and that he would not be able to get near the clubhouse without looking conspicuous. He was relieved, therefore, when a handful of earnest-looking skiers suddenly appeared at the bottom of the stairs, pulled on helmets and headed off down the left-hand path.

The start – a cheerful riot of banners and tapes and red flags and poles – was located a hundred yards or so below the clubhouse. The surface had been flattened and hardened by hundreds of boots and skis. Miles sauntered across. Some fifty skiers were waiting nervously for the starter, stopwatch in hand, microphone strapped to his head, to summon them to the gate, make sure their knees were up against the electronic breaker, and send them on their way: not down the racecourse itself – that had been lovingly prepared and preserved for the big day – but down a piste that ran parallel to it.

Behind him, the terrace of the Diabolo was crowded with members. Most were seated at two long pine tables that flanked the central door; some were lazing in soft cushions on large white deckchairs, drinks at their side, dark glasses glinting in the afternoon sun. The distinctive shapes of Gordon and Cunningham-Walker were leaning over the balcony at the far end. Unlike the majority of their fellow members, their interest was focused not on the proceedings below, but on a flat, empty area away to their left that had been marked out with little flags, like a large cricket square. From time to time Gordon would point towards the north, then cup his hand and point the fingers downwards in a series of short movements. Miles wondered if perhaps the event was to be marked with some sort of stunt: a skydiver perhaps, trailing red and white smoke. He observed the two men for

334

a while, then turned his attention to the racing. He walked forwards until he was standing at what he judged to be a discreet distance, but a large man with a brown face and a walkie-talkie spotted him and started waving at him in an officious way.

'Nein, nein. Keine Zuschauer. Spectateurs interdits. Nur eingeschreibene Skifahrer. Seulement compétiteurs,' he shouted. 'Allez. Go, please. Away.'

Miles waved his acknowledgment and turned. As he did so, a low booming sound filled the air. Officials and skiers looked up and pointed. Some of them started to ski away to the right, one or two ran, but most stayed where they were, looking up, frozen to the spot. The boom became a roar and the snow below Miles's feet trembled. He looked up. A huge slab of snow had come loose from the peak and was sliding straight down towards the clubhouse roof, pulling off more snow from lower down. It seemed as if the whole building was about to be engulfed. But then the avalanche seemed to shift direction in mid-fall and the thousands of tons of snow thundered on to the slope on the far side, like the waters at the bottom of Niagara Falls, throwing up a cloud of powder that floated up into the sky and hung there, a stroke of white from a painter's brush against the dark blue, before drifting off down the valley. The avalanche thundered onwards, out of sight, and, as it went, the noise faded, and in no time all was still and silent, as if nothing had happened.

But something had. Something that few, apart from Miles, would even have noticed, let alone commented on. For, as it swept past the clubhouse roof, the avalanche had removed a mass of snow at the back, thereby proving what Miles had suspected all along: that the clubhouse was attached to the side of the mountain. Indeed, it seemed to grow out of the rock face, like an excrescence on an old man's cheek.

* * *

'Quick. Come in.'

Anna closed the door behind him and locked it.

'I was right,' said Miles. 'There *is* something going on up there.'

335

'What?'

'I wish I knew.'

'Well, I really have found out something. The original clubhouse was built in 1925 – that's the year after the club was founded. Apparently it was nothing more than a glorified wooden shed. It lasted them for eight years but in the end it became so decrepit they had to pull it down. The new building was put up in time for the 1934/35 season, so it was barely a year old in that photograph in the hotel bedroom.'

'It looked it.'

'The club appeared to flourish for the next four seasons, but its activities were suspended during the war and the clubhouse was closed. It was reopened in the winter of 1945. The race wasn't run until the following season, in other words January 1947, but there was quite a bit of activity – club races, dinners, parties and so on. And then, in the spring of the following year, they pulled the clubhouse down and built the one that's up there now.'

'Whatever for?'

'No one knows.'

'Not even the people in the museum?'

She shook her head. 'It's not as if there's a shortage of material on the club: history, races, characters, dinner menus, press cuttings, you name it. But there's no mention anywhere of the new clubhouse.'

Miles frowned. 'How very odd. The old one was bound to have suffered a bit after being closed for six years, but to pull it down and build a whole new one … It doesn't make any sense. I wonder whose idea it was. And who paid for it.'

'I bet there were a lot of members who weren't feeling very flush just after the war. They can't have been pleased to come back to the old place after all those years only to be asked to put their hands in their pockets.'

'Unless they weren't, of course.'

'What do you mean?'

'If one of the members was so keen to move it that he was prepared to stand the whole cost himself. Or a small group of them.'

'Say that again.'

'I said, "If one of the members was so keen to move it that – " '

'That's it,' said Anna, her eyes wide. 'That's the point. Whoever was responsible didn't go to all that trouble and expense because they wanted to rebuild the clubhouse. They did it because they wanted to *move* it. It didn't need rebuilding; it needed to be in a different position. Not a hundred yards down the slope, but right next to the side of the mountain.'

'Attached to the mountain,' said Miles.

'What?'

'I'd suspected it from the time I first saw it, but there was so much snow piled up on the roof that it was impossible to see where the mountain ended and the building began. But this afternoon there was an avalanche.'

'Oh no …!' She covered her mouth with her hands.

Miles smiled. 'It's all right. I wasn't anywhere near it this time. But half the snow on the north-east face of Totenkopf fell off in one big slab. By some miracle it missed the clubhouse, but it dragged a whole lot of snow off the roof as it went, and suddenly you could see that it had been built right into the mountainside. As if it were part of it. And, if my memory of the photograph in the Gummi is correct, the rock face has been hollowed out specially to accommodate it. God knows why, though. Didn't anyone have any ideas in the museum?'

Anna took her hands away very slowly. Her mouth was slightly open and her eyes were narrowed. 'No,' she said, her voice almost a whisper. 'But *I* do.'

She walked across to where her overcoat was hanging on the back of the door. She put her hand into the inside pocket and pulled out a piece of paper. It had been folded into a shape that would fit into a manila envelope. It looked like a well-thumbed will.

'Close the curtains,' she said. 'Quick.'

'Why?' said Miles. 'What is it? What's going on?'

'Do as I ask, please.'

She switched on the bedside lamp and placed it on the chest of drawers. She placed the paper next to it and then very slowly and very carefully opened it out. The folds were worn through in places and there were holes at the corners.

337

On the left of the page was a drawing of Totenkopf, as seen from the north-east, dated 1895; on the right, a cross-sectional diagram of the peak, showing the various rock layers and formations, with explanatory notes written in a tiny hand down the side. It was a beautiful piece of work. If it had been the map of Treasure Island, Miles could not have been more astounded.

'Where did you get this?' he said.

'Where do you think?'

'Not from the museum, surely?'

She nodded and bit her lower lip, like a small child.

'You mean, they let you take it away, just like that?'

'Of course not,' she said.

'You didn't ...?'

'They had files full of them. Drawings, diagrams, photographs, sketches. They'll never miss one. I'll put it back first thing in the morning.'

Miles bent over it. 'It's wonderfully detailed,' he murmured. 'Look.' He pointed at the drawing. 'That's where the clubhouse is. See? The rock face comes straight down at that point. But not now. It goes in just there, and the building's tucked right into it. I wonder ...' He looked across at the diagram. 'If this corresponds to the drawing, then the clubhouse must be there.' He stabbed a finger at it. 'In which case, what on earth ...?'

'I know,' she said. 'Odd, isn't it? I thought you'd be interested.'

'What are they?'

Anna pulled the table lamp closer. 'They look to me like two parallel lines.'

'I can see that, but why have they been put there? What do they mean? They don't lead anywhere. Look, they start just inside the mountain, there, and go there, and then just peter out.'

'Your guess is as good as mine.'

'There are more here, do you see?' said Miles. 'And here. And there. The inside of Totenkopf seems to be crisscrossed with them. And what's that, in the middle there?'

'A square.'

'But what's it for? It must mean something. What does it mean?'

'It looks like a puzzle. A maze. You have to find your way to the box in the middle in the quickest time possible and without taking the same route twice.'

Miles turned and grabbed her by the shoulders. 'That's *exactly* what it is!' he shouted. 'Of course! A maze! That's why they built it there. Because that's where the maze started. And that's the quickest route to the box. Of course. *Of course!*'

He threw his arms round her and hugged her. She stood there for a moment, her body stiff and awkward. Then she pulled away.

'Are you making fun of me?'

'Making fun of you? *Of course not.* You've solved the mystery. Why on earth should I make fun of you?'

Anna frowned at him. 'What are you talking about? Solved what mystery?'

'It was something that Franklin said, when we first arrived. "The mountains are riddled with tunnels and caves. Some of them are big enough to be converted into aircraft hangars." '

'You don't mean there's an aircraft hangar inside Totenkopf?'

'No, not literally. But there could be a cave. A very big one. That's what that square is meant to indicate. And the parallel lines are tunnels.'

'But the one that starts from where you say the clubhouse is doesn't reach that far.'

'It may not have done in 1895, but I bet it does now. I bet it has done ever since 1948.'

Anna sat on the edge of the bed. She looked down at her hands. Then she looked up. 'You don't honestly think ...?'

'Why not? There could be casefuls of treasure hidden away in there, not just the amber panels. It's the perfect hiding place. Who would ever think of looking up there? Think of the millions of skiers and sightseers who have been up there over the years. How many of them could ever have imagined that they were standing a few hundred feet away from one of the world's greatest treasures?'

Anna said, 'And how many of the hundreds of innocent people you've interviewed over the years could ever have imagined that they were standing a few feet away from one of the world's greatest loonies.'

'You're right,' said Miles.

339

'What are we going to do?' Anna asked.

'Treat ourselves to a good dinner,' he said.

* * *

The word *racler* in French means to scrape, and a *raclette* is a dish of melted cheese scrapings. It is a great Alpine speciality.

A special type of cheese, looking like the wheel of a 1920s car, is sliced in half across the middle, and the cut side is placed against what looks like an upended electric fire. When the cheese is melted, a man takes a knife and scrapes the melted cheese on to a plate. The resulting *raclette* is eaten with small boiled potatoes and gherkins and washed down with a light white wine. When the plate is empty, it is taken away and another *raclette* is scraped on to it. This process continues until the customer, bloated and exhausted, throws in the napkin and slumps back in his seat, feeling he never wants to eat anything else ever again. Inexperienced *raclettiers* who sit down feeling they could eat the whole restaurant are often astonished to discover they are unable to manage more than half a dozen helpings. Old hands have been known to consume fifteen and still have room for dessert.

The down side to eating *raclettes* is the inevitable after-effects. Not only does one feel like the Michelin Man for hours afterwards but the whole of that night is spent lying awake with a thirst that even those who have crossed the Empty Quarter without camels have never known. All one craves is a large bucket of cold water, but this is quite out of the question since the melted cheese takes ages to digest, and cold water can turn it into something the size and the consistency of an ice-hockey puck – sometimes with fatal consequences.

Berni's Restaurant in Eigerhubel is world-renowned for its *raclettes*, and on the eve of the Diabolo Miles and Anna were lucky to get a corner table for two. Berni and his staff kept the *raclettes* coming by the hundred that evening and the noise level made Concorde sound like a Hoover. At least there was no chance of being overheard.

' "They're due to land at eleven." That's what Gordon said, right? Whoever "they" are.' Anna ran a finger round the top of her squat green wineglass. ' "On parade". What kind of parade?'

340

'It's just an expression army people use. It means being up and ready to get started. Nothing more than that.'

'If you say so.'

'I'm more intrigued by what Gordon said about them being "expected". "I've cleared it with all the right people", he said. As if they're getting special treatment. At the airport perhaps? The VIP lounge? A car on the tarmac?'

'Perhaps you're reading far too much into all this,' said Anna. 'Perhaps they were just talking about a group of friends coming out for the festivities and someone's meeting them at the airport.'

'Why was Cunningham-Walker so twitchy in that case? Why was he so concerned about last-minute hitches? And why did he start talking about Archie Lambourn? Whatever it was that Archie did, or was planning to do, and almost certainly got killed for, it was obviously more serious than a plane coming in late.'

'Such as a monkey?'

'Such as a monkey,' said Miles.

Anna ate seven *raclettes* and Miles nine before finally conceding defeat. The stove, the remains of the cheese and the boiled potatoes were taken away. Miles struggled bravely with a small wedge of *tarte aux pommes* and they both had a couple of *digestifs* before tottering back down the village street towards Willi Graf's. The village was *en fête* that night and, though the serious racers were already in bed, building up their strength for the following day, there were plenty who were there just to watch and enjoy themselves.

As they turned up the narrow alleyway between the cowsheds, Anna hooked her arm in Miles's. 'You're determined to get into that place, aren't you?' she said softly.

'You bet,' he said.

'How are you going to do it?' she asked.

Miles said, 'Someone once listed the essential requirements for being a journalist. Amongst them was ratlike cunning.'

'For all their cunning, rats get caught in traps,' she said.

'They try not to think about it,' said Miles.

Willi was up waiting for them when they came in. He wasn't smiling, though. 'Your brother,' he told Anna. 'He was here.'

'My brother?' Anna was very pale suddenly. 'What did he want?'

341

'He said that he would wait in your room.'

Anna was first through the door. Miles wasn't far behind. It could have been worse, but it was bad enough. Drawers had been pulled out. Clothes were scattered everywhere. Make-up tipped all over the floor. The window was hanging open. Willi stood in the doorway and shook his head.

Anna walked quickly across to the bed and felt under the mattress. After a while she straightened up. 'It's gone,' she said. 'The plan. He's taken it!'

Miles turned to Willi. 'What did he look like? Can you describe him?'

'Middle-aged, grey hair, face like stone,' said Willi.

'So they're here,' said Miles.

'Looks like it,' said Anna.

'Bloody hell,' said Miles.

31

Anna was still in her nightdress when she opened her door to Miles at 7.15 the next morning.

'Dress as if for skiing,' Miles told her. 'Only competitors are allowed anywhere near the start, and today that will almost certainly include the area round the clubhouse. We'll pick up skis and boots from Peter Seiler on the way. We'll need helmets, too. And race numbers.'

'Surely the entry list must be closed by now?'

'I'm sure it is.'

They breakfasted off croissants and coffee in the Café Pini next to the Lunnenberg, and by eight they were stamping their feet on the doorstep of Peter Seiler's ski shop.

Seiler's selection of equipment for hire was surprisingly good. Miles chose black Raichle RX787 boots and K2 Extremes. Anna took a pair of the Raichle in white and a pair of Rossignol DV7s Seiler assured her that in the current snow conditions the new version would give her better holding on hard snow and more stability at high speeds. He picked them out some good Scott poles, straight with adjustable straps, and a couple of race helmets in reasonable condition. He couldn't have been more helpful or enthusiastic. Miles would never have dared tell him they were never going to be used.

From there they went up to the ski school. A large crowd was trying to fight its way through the door. It looked like a New York bank at the height of the Wall Street Crash.

'Where do we get our race numbers?' Miles asked the blonde ski instructress when he'd finally managed to fight his way to the front.

'At the Schwarzegg cable car,' she said, looking straight past him, ready to field the next enquiry.

343

A small tented booth had been set up just outside the lift station. It was manned by two leather-faced officials. The first one was ticking off the names of entrants as they announced themselves and calling out their numbers, which the second one then picked out from a pile of what looked like little red sun-tops. As the competitors moved forward to join the queue, they looped them over their heads and tied the tapes at the side.

Anna looked at Miles and raised her eyebrows.

'You go ahead,' Miles murmured. 'I'll join you in a moment.'

She was well inside the building by the time Miles was at the booth.

'Name? Nom?'

Miles took a step forward and then seemed to stumble and lose his footing. He put a hand on the edge of the table to steady himself, but moments later there was a clatter of skis and he was on the ground amidst a jumble of race numbers.

'What happened?' Anna enquired when he joined her a few moments later.

'Nothing,' said Miles. 'Just a little confusion over our numbers.' He unzipped the front of his anorak. There was a flash of red and he quickly zipped it up again. 'We'll put them on later,' he said.

They managed to squeeze on to the 8.45 lift. It was crammed with racers. Most of them were Swiss Germans, though the odd French word fought its way through the twisted vowels and throaty aspirates, and he would have laid odds that the two young men with spotted handkerchiefs round their necks were English.

Anna's eyes darted suspiciously round the cabin.

'How did he know where you were staying?' Miles asked her.

'Who?'

'Alex. How did he find out you were at Willi Graf's?'

'It's a small village. It wouldn't have taken much.'

'I suppose so,' said Miles. 'I wonder what he was looking for.'

'Clues. Anything that might give him a lead. What I know. What I'm up to. Anything. Perhaps he thinks I've got the rose.'

'He couldn't have believed his luck, finding the map like that,' Miles said.

'Perhaps.'

344

'Why "perhaps"?'

Anna shrugged. 'I doubt if it'll mean a thing to him. Why should it? A few lines on a piece of paper. They could be anything. You're only guessing, after all.'

'Any fool can recognise the Totenkopf, though. He's bound to be up there sooner or later, nosing around. As long as doesn't get there before we do.'

Anna looked round. 'He's not on this car,' she said. 'I'd be surprised if he'd caught an earlier one.'

'Nothing would surprise me any more,' said Miles.

The lift nudged the last few feet up to Schwarzegg, but the people standing next to the far window were looking elsewhere, and pointing. Miles ducked his head and peered out. A helicopter was buzzing across the valley away to the right. It crossed the Gun Barrel and disappeared in the direction of Totenkopf.

'That's one way of getting up there,' Anna remarked.

'What time is it?' Miles asked, his voice suddenly urgent.

She looked at her watch. 'Five past nine. Why?'

'They're due to land at eleven.'

'Who?'

'I'm mad,' he said. 'I actually stood there yesterday and listened to Gordon explaining the whole thing to Cunningham-Walker. Where they're coming from. Where they'll be landing. Everything.'

'What are you talking about?' she muttered.

' "They're due to land at eleven", Gordon said. I naturally assumed he meant at Zürich or Geneva. But that's a three-hour journey away, at least. So, whoever they were, they obviously weren't coming for the race. By the time they got here it would be over. Land a helicopter up there this morning, on the other hand, and no one would take a blind bit of notice. They'd be far too riveted by the race. They'd take it for granted. All part of the proceedings. Typical Diabolo behaviour. "They *are* expected." Of course, but not at an airport. "I've cleared it with all the right people." He'd need to, obviously. Air-traffic control, the police, the mayor, the commune ... How could I have been *so bloody thick!*'

'Who *are* these people, though?' Anna said. 'Why the big deal?'

'I don't know,' said Miles. 'But I reckon they're bigger fish than I'd imagined. Bloody hell, we should be up there now. Hanging about, keeping our eyes open, doing something. Instead of which …'

It was another three or four minutes before the cable car docked, and another five by the time everyone had disembarked. Twenty more in a long queue for the Totenkopf cable car, twenty to get on, get up and get out, so that it was nearly ten o'clock by the time they stepped off the bottom of the iron staircase and followed the crowd to the start.

In their helmets and goggles, with 826 and 827 across their chests and a slight sinking feeling in the bowels, Miles could almost have believed that the two of them were genuine competitors and that, in the next hour or so, they would be launching themselves into the longest and most fearsome downhill ski course in the world.

Their strictly recreational skiwear was somewhat at odds with the sleeker, tighter-fitting, more obviously aerodynamic racing gear worn by the vast majority of competitors milling round them. However, no odd looks were thrown in their direction: the Diabolo was open to all-comers, and that always included a certain number of intrepid amateur enthusiasts. Not everyone makes it to the bottom in fourteen minutes. Not everyone makes it to the bottom.

The Diabolo clubhouse nudged into view round the side of the mountain. Bunting had been strung along the front of the building, bunches of balloons were hung from the corners of the windows, a champagne bar was doing brisk business at one end of the terrace and, at the other, the Diabolo devil flapped languidly on a tall white pole.

The air was loud with the honk of cocktail-party chatter. The occasional well-bred guffaw rose above the crowd like a hydrogen bubble before bursting in the cold air and floating away into the blue. From time to time a group would set off, full glasses in hands, down the wooden steps at the front, and join the crowd of competitors thronging nervously round the starting gate. Outbursts of laughter would be followed by raucous shouts of encouragement as the next two skiers – fellow members, presumably – launched themselves out of the starting gate, skating and poling furiously in their efforts to build up speed. Then the noise would die down and the group would return to the safety of the terrace and the serious business of drinking.

346

Anna and Miles made their way casually across the hard-packed surface, pitted now by the heels of hundreds of ski boots, until they were close enough to the terrace to be able to observe the celebrations at close quarters but not so close that their presence might attract unwelcome attention. Standing there while the racers strode past them on either side in a steady stream, they felt like sightseers on London Bridge at the height of the morning rush hour.

'No women,' said Anna after a while.

'The devil is traditionally a male animal,' said Miles.

'And therefore traditionally up to no good.'

'You'd hardly think so, looking at that lot. We could be observing any Sunday-morning drinks party anywhere in the Home Counties.'

'No foreigners, then?'

'One or two have slipped under the wire. Sanguinetti the car man, Von Mencken, a couple of Greek shipping types. But they're so rich that nobody minds. John Paul Getty II is an honorary knight, remember.'

'Do you know any of them?' Anna asked.

'I know who one or two of them are. That's Gerald Deighton over there in the pink pullover. And that one talking to him is called Eperon. Harry Eperon. Cunningham-Walker was around, but he seems to have disappeared. No sign of Bill Gordon. That man over there in the ski suit and dark glasses looks familiar.'

'The good-looking one with the fair hair?'

Miles nodded. 'What time is it?' he asked.

'Ten o'clock, give or take.'

'Another hour to go.'

'Right,' said Anna, 'let's just think this through. Supposing you're right. Supposing, against all likelihood, Totenkopf is like a lump of Emmental. And supposing the map is an accurate representation of the mountain's inner geography. That would presuppose that the map-maker had actually been inside the mountain. If I understand your scenario, Grobius and his friends carved out an entrance and stuck the new Diabolo clubhouse over the front. OK, so how did the artist get in there in the first place? Are there several ways in and out? There are in a piece of Emmental, of course.'

'You could be right,' said Miles. 'But how do we start looking for

347

them? Dig holes in the snow? Tap on the rock face and see if it sounds hollow?'

'What about those doors we passed on the way through from the cable car?'

'What about them?'

'One of them wasn't marked. Did you notice?'

'Perhaps we should go to the ticket office and ask if we can borrow the key. This thing … event … arrival … whatever it is, is due to take place an hour from now. We don't have time to go hunting for secret doors. We only have one option and that's to get inside the clubhouse.'

Anna threw up her hands. 'Fine. Go ahead. I don't know why I bother to say anything. You've decided what you're going to do and that's it. Fine. Do it. I'll stand here and watch you as you go up the steps and through the door. I won't have time to do much else, because you'll be booted straight out again: with luck, in one piece.'

Miles stabbed at the snow with the point of one of his ski poles. 'Well,' he said, 'thank you for your wholehearted support.'

'For God's sake,' snapped Anna, 'I thought we were in this thing together. You go on as if you are the only person in the world who wants to find this room. Some of of us have devoted most of our lives to it.'

She glared at him defiantly. But there were tears in the corner of her eyes and she bit her lower lip. Miles pulled an apologetic face and began to put an arm round her. But she stepped back.

'I'm sorry,' said Miles. 'I wasn't thinking.'

She sniffed hard. 'Perhaps you think too much,' she said.

Miles nodded. 'Perhaps you're right. Look. I've got an idea …'

Even as he explained it, he had his doubts. However much he tried to doll it up in the language of military tactics, it was a *Boy's Own Paper* stunt, badly thought out and fraught with risk, and he knew it. But time was running short. Circumstances demanded action; so did Anna; and in Miles's book, action was infinitely preferable to reaction.

'Right,' he said. 'Skis on, then.'

They banged the hard-packed snow from the bottom of their boots

348

with their ski poles and stepped into their bindings. They clipped together the chin-guards of their helmets and pulled down their goggles. They adjusted the handle straps on their poles.

Anna took a deep breath and said, 'So, we ski across as if we're heading for the starting gate. I make a turn in the deep snow and fall. I pretend I've twisted my knee. You call out to the terrace for help. Being gents, they rush to my aid. In the confusion, you ask if you can use their telephone to call for help. Bingo, you're in.'

'Simple diversionary ploy,' said Miles airily. 'Ready?'

'Oh, my God!'

'What?'

'Over there. Coming down the steps. In the white polo-neck.'

'Hell,' said Miles. 'And he's still wearing his plaster. And he's going down to the Start. We'll have to wait. Damn and blast.'

'I've waited long enough,' said Anna. She dug her ski poles into the snow, pushed hard and set off across the slope.

'For God's sake, Anna!' Miles shouted after her. 'Not now!'

But she wasn't listening. Anger had stopped up her ears and blotted out reason. The man who had killed her father was blithely strolling in the morning sun only a hundred yards away, as if he hadn't a care in the world. No amount of reasoning was going to persuade her to stand there and watch him walk away.

Miles cursed and pointed his skis after her.

'*Bitte schön.*'

The hand that clamped itself on to his right shoulder was the size of a meat plate and encased in a black leather glove.

Miles turned. The man stood about six foot three in his Salomon Integral Equipe boots. The woman wasn't much shorter. They were each holding a pair of Dynastar Vertical Extremes and the sun glinted off their skintight racing suits. The material defined every muscle, lump and bump. It looked as if it had been sprayed on. They had identical blond hair and faces that gleamed with health and high-altitude cream. They showed identical sets of perfect white teeth, but neither was smiling.

'Yes?'

'You have my number.' He stabbed a leather finger at Miles's chest. 'That is my number. Eight two six. You give it to me, please.'

Miles said, 'Look, can you wait a minute?' and turned away.

Anna was heading straight towards the man with the wrist in plaster. He appeared to be quite unaware of her. She hit him from behind, and at high speed. He went face first into the snow and she piled in on top of him. She beat at his head and neck with the moulded handles of her ski poles. He struggled to get out from underneath her, but his legs were pinned down by her skis. He tried to fight back but he needed his hands to protect himself. She was screaming at him now. Miles couldn't hear what she was saying but he could guess. He shouted out to her to stop, but he could have saved his breath. Everywhere people were turning and looking. Up on the terrace, members were pointing and crowding towards the rail. Half a dozen of them were already running down the steps and across the snow.

Miles shrugged off the huge gloved hand, but the man grabbed at the material of his ski jacket.

'For Christ's sake!' Miles shouted at him. 'Can't you see she's in trouble? I've got to go and help! Let go!'

'You give me my number!' the man roared.

Miles swung round, elbow jutting, and caught him hard in the midriff. The man grunted and took a step backwards. His fist let go of the material and he drew it back and swung. Miles ducked and the blow went over his head. As the man tried to regain his balance, Miles jabbed both poles into the snow and pushed hard. The man grabbed at him but missed. As Miles slipped out of reach, the man lost his balance completely, stumbled and fell forward into the deep snow. His skis clattered down beside him. As they fell, they came apart. One landed, sole down, and began to slide away down the slope. It quickly gathered speed and disappeared over the brow. The man roared in impotent fury.

Miles reached Anna ahead of the rescue party from the terrace. She was still screaming at the man that he was a bloody murderer and that she was going to kill him. Miles reached down and grabbed at her jacket. The man's hair was thick with snow and there were traces of blood at the base of his skull. A bruise was coming up under his right eye.

Miles tugged hard at the jacket and managed to pull her to one

350

side. The man twisted free and scrambled to his knees. His face was white with fury.

'Bitch!' He spat the word out and with his right hand reached across into his left sleeve.

'Look out!' Miles shouted.

Something glinted at the end of the plaster. It was about six inches long and wickedly thin. Miles struck at it with his ski pole but it hit the plaster and bounced off. He swung again and missed. The man narrowed his eyes and drew back his left arm.

'*Claus! Nein! Nicht hier!*'

The voice came from behind Miles's left shoulder. Harsh, urgent, used to giving orders and having them obeyed.

It was as if a frame in a film had been frozen. For a moment, nobody moved, nothing happened. The blade hovered in the air. Then, as if the film had started up again in slow motion, the arm was lowered, blade upwards. The right hand came across and the fingers encircled the left wrist. They gave a faint squeeze and the blade slid back out of sight. Anna slumped on to her side, breathing hard.

'That is better.' The voice was calm now. Almost gentle. As if dealing with a difficult child.

Miles had heard that voice before. He lowered his ski pole and turned.

They were standing in a semicircle, half a dozen of them, motionless and without expression. One of them wore a ski suit and his hair was unusually blond. He stepped forward and removed his dark glasses.

'Charlie Bishop,' said Miles.

Bishop gave a small nod of acknowledgment, then gestured towards the other man who had scrambled to his feet and was now brushing the snow from his head and shoulders. 'I believe you have already met, although you have not been formally introduced. This is my younger brother, Claus Bischof.'

32

Looking back on it later, Miles wondered if he could have made a run for it while he had the chance; skied down to Eigerhubel; got help. It would have been the easiest thing in the world. One step to the side, point the skis downhill and away. No one could have stopped him. With a gun possibly, but not with all those people around. Charlie had a ski outfit on, but he'd never have got his boots and skis on in time to catch him up. The standard run down to the village was long but pretty straightforward for someone of Miles's ability. On the other hand, they'd still have had Anna, and, by a terrible irony, she had genuinely twisted her knee in the collision.

The small party made its slow way back up the hill, Anna limping between two Diabolo members. Miles was carrying both pairs of skis on his shoulder. He paused to readjust them. Charlie waited.

'Oh, while I have the chance,' he said, 'I want you to know how sorry I was that your visit to West Keating turned out the way it did. It was unforgivable.' The German accent was more marked than before.

'All's well that ends well,' said Miles cheerfully. 'Thank you for apologising, anyway.'

Charlie laughed. 'Oh, I wasn't apologising. I was furious that the Sumatran didn't kill you before that stupid keeper arrived. *That* was the unforgivable thing.'

'Ah well,' Miles said pleasantly. 'You can rarely pull the same trick twice, I find.'

Charlie nodded. 'It was easier the first time, I must admit. Lambourn was still drunk from a party the night before. He was sleeping it off in the hall. I made up some story about one of the females not looking well. I knew he'd come straight away.

Unfortunately, I forgot to mention that she was pregnant. Stupid of me. Pregnant tigresses can be very unpredictable.'

'So nature took its course,' said Miles.

Bishop shrugged. 'Accidents happen.'

'So I've noticed.'

They could have been two old friends coming in for a drink after a good morning on the slopes.

'All right,' said Miles, 'so now I know *how* you did it – more or less, anyway. What I still don't know is *why*.'

'Because of that bloody monkey, of course,' said Charlie. 'You must have seen the file. It was with the others in the drawer in the library.'

'Oh, I saw it all right,' said Miles. 'Some rare species was being threatened somewhere in Africa. There were a lot of cuttings.'

'Rigaud's Monkey,' said Charlie. 'A pretty little thing, with a furry face and a very long tail. There are thought to be only a few hundred left.'

'And they're all in Kananga.'

'Exactly so.'

'Just where the president wants to build his palace.'

'How did you guess?'

'Destroying its natural habitat and cutting off access to its normal diet.'

'Something like that.'

'I can understand Archie Lambourn getting hot under the collar about it. He was a passionate conservationist, and a genuine animal lover. But so are you. So why didn't you get hot under the collar about it too? Why did you kill him?'

Charlie said, 'Let's just call it a conflict of interest.'

'What the hell's that supposed to mean?'

'One story at a time, Mr Maltby,' said Charlie. 'You can leave your skis here.'

Miles planted them in the snow and followed Anna up the steps.

The little procession crossed the terrace. No one paid it the slightest attention. After the brilliance of the day, it took a moment or two to adjust to the gloomy light indoors. Given the amount of money at its members' disposal, the clubroom was surprisingly modest: drab, almost. It looked like a cross between a masters' common room in an old-fashioned country prep school and a student hostel.

Facing the door was the fireplace that featured in Archie's photograph and, over it, the obscene figure of the devil, forked tongue lolling, ski poles brandished above his head, and the painted scroll bearing the club motto: THE DEVIL TAKE THE HINDMOST. Arranged in front of it in a haphazard way were a number of antediluvian and unhygienic-looking leather armchairs. To the left were a dozen or so small wooden tables covered with red check cloths, and a lot of very uncomfortable wooden chairs. Most of the right-hand side of the room was occupied by a large mahogany billiard table with a moth-eaten cloth. On the far side of that there was a small bar.

On either side of the fireplace, set back slightly, there were two doors. The one by the restaurant had an open serving hatch next to it and presumably led into a small kitchen. The one next to it had the word HON. SECRETARY painted on it in white letters. On the other side, the door nearest to the bar had a grotesque cartoon pinned up on it showing some dogs, dressed up in a variety of unlikely outfits and standing on their hind legs, peeing against a wall. Between that and the fireplace there was a fourth door. It was unmarked. Miles wondered if that was the one that led to the tunnel. There appeared to be no other way through.

'Extraordinary,' Miles murmured.

'So glad you approve.'

One of the armchairs creaked and a face turned towards Miles. It looked about the same vintage as the chair and in much the same condition. Except the chair didn't have a big golf-club-secretary moustache and long teeth and a crocodile smile.

Bill Gordon heaved himself upright. 'Welcome to the Diabolo Club,' he said. 'Please make yourselves comfortable. May I introduce some of our more distinguished members?'

Now Miles could see that other armchairs were similarly occupied.

'Dr Claud Austin – Emeritus Fellow of Brandeston College, Oxford? The Bishop of Tenterden? The senior partner of Letellier's? Lord Aldringham? You may know him better as our erstwhile Secretary of State for the Environment.'

354

As each name was called out, its owner leaned sideways out of his chair and nodded in Miles's direction.

'Gentlemen, this is Major Maltby, late of the Royal Hampshire Fusiliers, holder of the Military Cross, a brave and distinguished officer and a gentleman. A man we are pleased and proud to welcome as a guest to our club.'

Gordon drew his moustache back and showed his teeth in a gesture of blatant insincerity. Miles clenched his fists. Never in his life had he experienced such a feeling of total revulsion for a man. His instinct was to shove Gordon's teeth down his throat. But this wasn't the moment. A wrong move now – a show of anger, a hint of a threat, a contradiction – would be to risk not seeing what he had come to see and not being told what he wanted to know. Gordon had killed men before in cold blood – Anna's uncle among them – and Miles didn't doubt he would do so again. The crocodile smile had crocodile teeth. For the moment, Miles knew he must bite his tongue and go along with this absurd charade of hospitality.

'And this charming young lady over here is Miss Anna Rogers, the youngest granddaughter of Her Imperial Highness the Grand Duchess Irina Romanova. The only lady to be invited as a guest here – apart of course from the charming princess who kindly honoured us with her presence earlier this season.'

This time the old men struggled from their chairs and gave creaky bows, then fell back amidst the crumbling leather and bursting innards.

'But you must think me very rude,' said Gordon. 'Here am I welcoming you as our guest and I haven't even offered you a drink. What can I get you? A glass of champagne? Some beer? Something a little stronger perhaps? We have a particularly good single malt.'

Anna made no response.

'No? Major Maltby? Nothing for you either? What a pity. I'd hoped you might help us to celebrate. As you may know, it is seventy-five years to the day since this club was founded. In that time we have known many great men, seen many great events, but none greater than the one we are to witness today. I am aware that you have shown great interest in our enterprise in recent weeks. May I ask why?'

Miles shrugged. 'Curiosity,' he said casually. 'I'm a journalist. I was

355

out here writing one story and I stumbled on another. I followed it up, and here I am. I was just doing my job.'

'I see,' said Gordon. 'And Miss Rogers? Is she part of your story? Your research assistant perhaps? Isn't that what everyone has these days? Or is your interest more personal, like hers? You seem to have dedicated yourself to this project with an enthusiasm that far exceeds the normal call of a journalist's duty. Hardly a day has gone by without my hearing news of you: here in Eigerhubel, then in London, in East Anglia, in Copenhagen. And now here you are back again, at the height of our festivities. And yet, after all your efforts, you do not feel able to celebrate with us. I can hardly believe it. In my experience, journalists may not recognise the truth when they see it, but they can certainly recognise a free drink when it's offered. Are you quite sure?'

The eyes were as unforgiving as an open grave; the smile as dead as the smile on the face of the Totenkopf. A sudden chill had descended over the room, and for a moment Miles was afraid that their refusal might trigger some violent reaction in the old man. But the moment passed. Miles shivered.

'Never mind,' said Gordon. 'I'm sure our other guests will want to enter into the spirit of the proceedings.' He looked at his watch. 'Good heavens, is that the time? They'll be here any minute. We must get ready to welcome them. I'm afraid I'm going to have to leave you now, but Charlie will show you where you can wait until our business has been completed and they have departed. We'll talk again later. I am sorry I cannot invite you to join us. However, I hope it will be some consolation to you to know that you have been as close as any outsider could possibly be to what I believe will be seen in years to come as one of the great turning points of modern history. Gentlemen, shall we …?'

The four old men struggled to their feet and followed Gordon out into the warm sunshine. Claus stood in front of the doorway with his arms folded. Nobody spoke.

'I wouldn't mind a pee,' said Miles and set off in the direction of the unmarked door.

There was a sound of footsteps behind him. Miles was aware of Anna's voice shouting out his name, and then there was an explosion inside his head and the sun went out …

When he came to, everything was still black. There was a dull, throbbing pain at the base of his skull. He seemed to be lying on his side, though in the dark he couldn't be certain. He tried to sit up but his hands had been tied to his ankles.

'Hell's bloody bells,' he said.

'I never thought words could sound so sweet.'

'Anna?'

'Why, were you expecting someone else?'

'Are you all right?'

'I'm OK. How about you?'

'Don't worry about me. I'm used to being hit on the head. Where the hell are we?'

'In a cupboard. Beyond that, I'm as much in the dark as you are. No joke intended.'

'A cupboard, did you say? What cupboard? Where?'

'The one you were trying to get into when Charlie hit you.'

Miles groaned. 'Was that a cupboard? Oh hell. I thought it was the entrance to the tunnel. So where is it?'

'It's no good asking me,' she said. 'They tied me up and pushed me in straight after you. I saw no more than you did.'

'Where are Mutt and Jeff now?'

'No idea. I told you, they shut me in here.'

'How long have we been here?'

'Hard to say. Fifteen minutes. Twenty perhaps. Not more.'

'So the helicopter must have landed by now.'

'Sounded like it. Anyway, a whole lot of people came in. I could hear them talking and laughing and walking about, and then nothing.'

'What do you mean, nothing?'

'Just that. One minute there was all this noise and then silence.'

'You mean the voices faded away somewhere?'

'No. They just stopped. As if a radio had been switched off.'

'And you've heard nothing since?'

'Apart from your bad language, no.'

'It's got to be one of the other doors, then. They must all be in there now. We've got to get out of here, otherwise we'll miss the whole thing.'

'What whole thing?'

357

'I've no idea, but whatever it is we're going to miss it if we sit around in here much longer. Can you move at all?'

'I've tried, but I haven't got very far. I feel like a pig on its way to market.'

'Same here.'

'I managed to reach as far as my ankles but I couldn't feel any knots.'

'They're probably round our wrists somewhere. If you can get yourself over here facing me, I might be able to do something with my fingers.'

'Right,' said Anna. 'Don't go away.'

There was a lot of scuffling, accompanied by several grunts and groans.

'Where are you? I can't see a thing.' Anna's voice came from somewhere in the area of his knee.

'Not down there, anyway. Try moving further up this way.'

In different circumstances, the instructions and contrivances of the next few minutes might have had the makings of a good adult party game. But neither of them was in party mood that morning. They manoeuvred themselves until they were facing each other, only to discover that the knots had been tied in such a way that neither of them could even reach the other's, let alone untie them.

Miles rolled away on to his back, breathing hard and cursing. 'There might be something in here we can use,' he said. 'Something with a sharp edge. If I could find the light switch …'

But Charlie Bishop knew all there was to know about restraining animals with ropes, and, though Miles struggled and strained and sweated and swore, he couldn't even get to his knees.

'It's no good,' he said. 'We've had it. There's no way we're going to get out of here. We are well and truly snookered.'

'Ssh.'

'Sorry. I'm rather upset.'

'No, listen.'

Someone was moving about on the other side of the door: someone wearing rubber-soled shoes – snow boots, probably – who obviously didn't want anyone to know he was there and who shouldn't have been there. So not a member, then …

Miles was still making up his mind whether to risk shouting for help when there was a series of loud thuds, followed by the sound of splintering wood, and the door flew inwards, smashing against a row of shelves. A tall, black, cut-out shape was silhouetted against the sunlight. A hand reached out and touched a switch. The room was flooded with light and the shape turned into a person: a young man in his early twenties, with long dark hair and the romantic good looks of Daniel Day-Lewis.

'Anna!'

'Andrew! What are you doing here?'

'The same as you.'

'What do you mean?'

'I'm looking for the Room, of course. That's why you're here, isn't it?' He put his hand into his pocket and brought out a Swiss Army penknife. He inserted a thumbnail under one of the blades. 'Papa gave me this for my eighteenth birthday. I always carry it with me, but this is the first time I've ever really used it.'

Anna said, 'But Alex ...'

'Alex?' He looked up sharply. He seemed surprised to hear the name.

'He must have shown you the plan. Why else are you here?'

'Plan? What plan? I don't know what you're talking about.'

'The plan of Totenkopf. The one Alex took from my room.'

'Alex is here?' His eyes were full of fear.

'You mean, you didn't know?' said Miles.

'I haven't seen Alex since that evening we came to your room. I don't want to, ever again.'

'Oh, Andrew ...'

'I went to see Ina. She told me everything. About the other Room, about our father, everything. I felt such a fool. You see, I thought he was on our side. I never realised ... To be used like that ... We only ever met in London, you know ... You must think me very naïve ...'

'Andrew ...' Her voice was soft and low, like a mother's.

'Why are you here, then?' said Miles. 'I don't understand.'

'When Ina told me about Papa finding the rose up here ... I had this feeling ... I needed to come here and see for myself. But what's all this about a plan?'

'Anna found it in the museum. We think … I think … it shows there are tunnels in the mountains leading to a cave.'

'And you think the Room might be there?'

'That's what we're about to find out.'

'What about Alex?'

'Exactly.'

Andrew finally succeeded in pinching the big blade out. It slid through the rope as easily as if it were a length of liquorice.

They stumbled into the club room.

'Where did they all go?' Anna stared round at the empty chairs.

'Shouldn't you be sitting down?' Miles said to her.

'I've spent quite enough time on my bottom today,' she said.

'But your knee …'

'There's nothing wrong with my knee. It was an act, and it worked.'

'You're incredible,' Miles told her.

'It was your idea,' she said.

'Come on,' he said. 'There's got to be a way through from here.'

They tried the three other doors along the back wall. One led into the kitchen, one into an office, and one into a washroom and lavatory. They tapped on all the walls, they opened all the cupboards, they got down on their hands and knees and examined the floors, but they found nothing. They went back into the main room.

'It's staring us in the face and we can't see it.'

Anna said, 'The only thing that's staring us in the face is that disgusting devil over the fireplace.'

'The devil he is.' Miles's voice dropped to a whisper.

He walked forward and stood staring up at it. He remained there for a long time, silent and motionless, as if the horrible creature had hypnotised him. And then he narrowed his eyes. He stepped closer and peered at the club motto just above the mantelpiece. It was carved into an imitation wooden scroll that had been stuck on to the wall between two old-fashioned skis, like a medieval banner. Whoever had done it must have had a few first because it was completely cockeyed. Miles reached up and touched the wood. It was slightly loose. He took the end that was pointing upwards and pulled it. Very slowly and carefully.

'That's straight now,' said Anna. 'Oh, now you've gone too far.'

Miles went on pulling at the scroll until it was almost vertical. 'The devil take the hindmost,' he said, and gave it one more tug. There was a dull clunk, and the fireplace and the mantel above it swung open to reveal an opening cut into the rockface the size of a large front door and, beyond it, a tunnel, illuminated along either side by electric lights fixed into the rock, stretching away into the dark heart of the mountain.

'You were right,' Anna whispered.

'I was beginning to wonder,' said Miles.

'I'm not sure I want to go in,' she said. 'There's a smell of death.'

'The air's bound to be stale.'

'I'm afraid of what I might find in there,' she said.

Miles moved back and stood close to her. 'But it could be what you have been looking for half your life,' he said gently.

'My father had been looking for it for half a century. His brother died because of it, and when he finally found it – or at least a piece of it – he died too. If every little piece of good amber has a corpse in it, a roomful is nothing but a giant cemetery.'

'I think you're letting your imagination run away with you,' Miles said. 'Now you've come this far, you must go on.'

'Papa would have wanted us to,' said Andrew.

Anna nodded. 'Yes,' she said. 'He would.'

Andrew put out his hand. Anna took it and the two walked in through the entrance like a pair of children in a fairy tale.

Miles followed them. At the mouth of the tunnel, he paused and looked back. Only a few yards away, the sun shone, the air was warm and the world was *en fête*. But though the light streamed through the open door, the atmosphere in the room was as cold as charity. Miles shivered. He turned and walked after them.

The tunnel was as wide as the entrance but not so tall, so that Miles and Andrew had to stoop slightly as they walked. Every now and then the rock brushed against their hair, as though hands were reaching out to catch them.

After a while, the tunnel curved slightly to the left and the entrance disappeared from view behind them.

'Listen.' Anna stopped. She turned her head to one side. 'Music.'

Miles could hear it too. Indistinct. A long way off.

'It could be coming from the restaurant,' he said.

'We're nowhere near the restaurant,' she said. 'Anyway, sound doesn't travel through rock that easily.'

'Then it must be up ahead somewhere.'

As they proceeded, the music got louder. A band was playing a military march. But not the sort British soldiers march to; that bands play in London parks on summer afternoons. This was German music, played by a German band. The sort that brought back memories of the Nuremberg Rallies and a chill to the stomach.

Anna stopped again. 'I'm really not sure …' she began.

'Don't worry,' said Miles. 'I'll go ahead now.' And he strode on past them.

Fifty yards ahead, the tunnel turned to the right. Beyond that point, something glowed with a dull yellow light that played on the glistening rock and coloured the dank air like a Victorian London fog.

Miles rounded the bend and took a few more steps. Then he slowed and stopped altogether. When the others caught up with him, they saw why.

Ahead of them, the tunnel opened out into a vast cave of ice, as big as a sound stage on a Hollywood film lot. The floor was a forest of frozen needles and pillars and fantastic shapes that rose halfway to the roof, which was in turn hung with thousands of icicles. The ones nearest the walls were so long that they reached right down to the floor, so that the whole of the perimeter of the cave looked as if it were covered with giant white cobwebs. Except that they weren't white, they were pale yellow. For in the middle of the cave, like a great galleon trapped for ever in an Arctic ice floe, stood the Amber Room.

Buttressed by columns of ice as thick as tree trunks, the amber panels seemed to be attached to huge transparent sheets – of heavy glass perhaps or perspex – so that, lit from inside, the whole thing glowed, as though possessed of an energy that was not quite of this world. The effect was as theatrical as anything Miles had ever seen anywhere. It was as vulgar as a fairground attraction and as extravagant as D. W. Griffith's Babylon, and utterly sensational.

To the insistent beat of the Horst Wessel tune was now added the sound of soldiers marching. Hundreds of them, thousands, a whole

362

army. And out of the crunch of the jackboots there arose another sound, barely discernible at first, but mounting in volume until it drowned out the music and the marching and filled the cave so that the very rock seemed to be straining to contain it: the sound of men shouting in unison. 'SIEG HEIL. SIEG HEIL. SIEG HEIL.'

Anna turned to Miles, her eyes huge with fear.

'Look,' said Miles, pointing.

Running down the side of the wall, almost from top to bottom, were several long strips of plain crystal glass, about nine inches wide, through which the light shone more brightly and intensely than through the surrounding amber.

'Those must be the mirrors,' said Anna.

'Come on,' said Miles. And before she had a chance to protest, he had grabbed her by the hand and the two of them were stumbling and slipping across the uneven surface.

All three of them were breathing hard as they leaned forward and peered through the glass. The Room looked identical to the one Miles had seen in Jurmala, but the age of the amber gave it a depth and an intensity that no copy, however accurate and however well crafted, could hope to replicate. Illuminated by the dancing flames of dozens of tall flambeaux, the fruit and the flowers and the horns and the shells seemed to move about on the panels as if they were living organisms.

'I don't believe what I'm seeing,' breathed Anna.

But it wasn't the Room she was talking about. She meant what was taking place within it.

For hanging from huge poles between the torches were rows of Nazi flags, their black swastikas clearly visible amongst the folds of red. Beneath them, in two blocks, divided by a central aisle, stood the ranks of the Diabolo Club, variously dressed in skiing jackets and sports jackets and overcoats and pullovers, but all with a swastika armband. Shoulders pulled back, chests pushed out, hands raised in the Nazi salute, mouths open, they roared out those two short, simple words that the world had hoped never to hear again: 'SIEG HEIL. SIEG HEIL. SIEG HEIL.'

Facing them at the far end was a wooden platform on which stood a row of seven men: the four that Miles had met earlier in the clubhouse, Bill Gordon, and two others. One of these was a giant of a black man in a black Homburg hat and a black overcoat, with a huge, broad-featured face that beamed and gleamed in the torchlight. Miles had never seen him before in his life. But he knew the dapper little man standing beside him. He'd known him for many years. He'd stayed in his house on countless occasions and drunk his whisky and eaten at his table and, God help him, he had very nearly become his son-in-law. And because Miles had loved the man's daughter and still did, and because he thought of the man's wife as a second mother, and because the man had once been Deputy Commander-in-Chief NATO Forces in Europe and a soldier he admired and trusted, he had confided everything in him.

Along with anger and disbelief and helpless incomprehensibility, Miles felt a sense of deep disappointment in his own naïvety. How was it possible that he had never once suspected the man? He'd realised that General Hollies had been the only person who knew he was going to West Keating that day, but he'd never given it another thought. He'd spotted him in the photograph he'd found in Archie Lambourn's drawer, but had failed to recognise him. He'd told Lydia he was going to Copenhagen, but even when he'd run into Claus Bischof at the airport he hadn't put two and two together. Perhaps he hadn't wanted to.

Even now, seeing the general standing up there, smiling and nodding and approving of the very things against which he'd once fought, Miles found himself casting round for excuses: the old boy had gone prematurely senile; he was labouring under a misplaced sense of national pride; he was a double agent working for the security services ...

Miles had never been so angry with himself. But, more than anything else, he was frightened: not of the general, but of the thought that, after this, he might never see Elizabeth again.

'Who are all those men?' Andrew whispered.

'That one at the end is a bishop,' Miles whispered back. 'Next to him is an ex-cabinet minister and peer of the realm. The two on the far side are an Oxford don and a respected City stockbroker. The little man with the big head is a very senior general. I don't know who the black man is.'

364

'And the other one? The one in the middle. The one with the moustache.'

Miles said, 'He's a war criminal who calls himself Captain Bill Gordon, but his real name is Walter Grobius.'

'So that's Grobius.' Andrew thought for a bit. Then he said, 'He isn't much to look at, is he?'

'No,' said Miles. 'But then people like him never are.'

33

Bill Gordon and his distinguished guests seemed happy to bask in the roar of victory for as long as the assembled company were prepared to go on pumping it out. Chests puffed out, heads held high, self-satisfied smiles on their faces, they reminded Miles of a trio of sea lions enjoying the plaudits of the spectators at the end of a performance in the pool. It was a wonder they weren't joining in, slapping their flippers together in self-congratulation.

'I can't take any more of this,' Anna whispered. She turned and began to walk away towards the tunnel.

'Where are you going?' Miles snapped.

'To get some fresh air. This place stinks.'

'But you can't leave now,' he said in a low voice. 'Not now you've come this far. You've got to see this thing through. We all have.'

She stopped and turned. 'What's the point?' she whispered back. 'There's nothing we can do about it. We've found the Room, but we'll never get it back. I realise now, the great owners in history have never been more than curators, and the world's great possessions are permanently on loan. We should count ourselves lucky we had it for as long as we did.'

She turned away. Andrew stood there awkwardly, torn between brotherly duty and appalled fascination at the scene being played out in front of him.

'Go with her,' Miles told him. 'She needs you. I'll meet you later. I'll tell you everything then. Go on. Go.'

Andrew gave a quick smile, nodded and walked away. As he did so, the shouting stopped. The music continued for a few more bars, then that was switched off too. The ensuing silence was palpable.

Miles moved to the side of the glass and peered in. Gordon's arm was bent upwards at the elbow and his hand held outwards at shoulder level in a grotesque parody of a Hitlerian salute. His moustache was drawn back over his teeth in a equally grotesque parody of a smile. He took a step forward.

'Gentlemen,' he said. 'Fellow members of the Diabolo. This is a great day, not only in the history of our club, but in the history of the world. A turning point, when a dream becomes reality.'

Anna and Andrew tiptoed back and stood next to Miles, gazing through the glass.

'The smallest amongst us can dream the biggest dreams, but only a great man can make a really big dream come true. President Ben-Moulassa is a great man and, thanks to his generosity, our movement can now move forward in the sure knowledge that, when our moment of destiny comes, we shall be ready to seize it.'

'Who the hell's he?' Anna whispered.

'The President of Kananga. A fellow mass-murderer, tin-pot dictator and architect of one of the biggest monuments to greed and self-aggrandisement the world has ever seen.'

'Not the one who's building that palace?'

'Exactly. Thereby depriving his people of the most basic necessities of life and Rigaud's Monkey of its natural habitat and continued survival as a species. He's the reason Archie Lambourn was murdered.'

'Archie died for a monkey?'

'At least he died for something.'

Now Bill Gordon was warming to his task. 'The world is in the biggest mess it has known for more than half a century,' he was saying. 'Civil wars are raging, millions are starving, any day now the entire economic system will come crashing down about our ears ...'

'I don't understand,' whispered Anna. 'What's this Moulassa doing here?'

'Fear and uncertainty stalk the earth, and no one knows how to avert the catastrophe that must inevitably ensue. Why? Because we have no leaders ...'

Miles murmured, 'Like many of the world's dictators he's a great supporter of the neo-Nazi movement in Europe. He's also vastly rich.'

'... People are crying out for strong leadership. They *need* strong

367

leadership. It creates confidence. With a strong leader at the helm, they know where they are. They can see a future for themselves, and their children, and their children's children. Never has there been a time in history when the nations of the world have cried out louder for a strong leader to stand up and show them the way forward ...'

'The only reason neo-Nazism has not made greater advances since the collapse of Communism is lack of funds,' Miles whispered. 'Moulassa will be only too happy to part with some of his ill-gotten millions knowing they are going to a good cause. Especially when he thinks what he's getting in return.'

'... The time has come for a new generation to scale once again the heights of history and see once more the immortal lights – the lights of sacrifice and high endeavour, summoning the soul of humanity to the sublime and the eternal ...'

Anna put her hand up over her mouth. Her eyes stared blindly ahead. 'No,' she breathed. 'I don't believe it. It's not possible. Oh, my God. He couldn't.'

'It'll set his palace off a treat. And bring in the tourists.'

' ... There are only two alternatives: courage or oblivion. The moment of decision is upon us, the moment of destiny. Can we doubt which path to choose ...?'

'We've got to stop him,' Anna hissed. 'We must *do* something.'

'Yes, but *what*? What do you suggest?'

'There must be something.' Anna looked around wildly. 'Anything's better than just standing here, doing nothing.'

The voice at the end of the room droned on. 'All over Europe our members are poised to seize the moment. But to carry the standard forward we need the money to pay for it. And now we have that money. Thanks to President Moulassa, Europe can rise again. And in return, he has one of the greatest treasures in history. No one deserves it more –'

'No!'

The voice seemed to come out of nowhere, like a vengeful spirit from hell. It echoed through the cave. Gordon had stopped talking and was peering towards the back of the room, one hand shielded above his eyes. Miles spun round. The man was standing in the mouth of the tunnel. He was wearing a heavy blue storm jacket and jeans tucked inside black fur boots. At first Miles couldn't make out who it was; and then he saw the grey fox-fur hat.

'Alex!'

The stocky figure strode across the cave floor towards them. Andrew stepped back, obviously terrified. Anna remained where she was, staring at him. But Alex didn't even seem to notice any of them. His eyes were fixed straight ahead of him, like a sleepwalker.

Gordon's voice called from inside the room, 'Is there someone out there? Who is it? Go and see, would you?'

As Alex drew level, Miles saw the pistol dangling from his right hand. He had made quite a study of small arms from around the world. It looked like a Walther PPK, or a Makarov, except that it was a bit too large for a Makarov. A machine pistol, perhaps, but what? Not a Mexican Trejo. The barrel was too long. And then he remembered that after the war the Russians had produced a 9mm machine pistol called a Stetchkin. It had been standard equipment for border guards in places like Afghanistan, but was rarely seen outside the Soviet Union. As a full automatic its usable range was little more than twenty-five yards, but at 750 rounds a minute it could still make a nasty mess of a roomful of people in a very short time.

'Alex! No!' Miles's voice was low and urgent.

A door was outlined in the wall in thin parallel strips of light. Alex stopped in front of it, legs planted wide, body braced.

'Alex! Don't! It won't do any good!' shouted Andrew.

There was hubbub now inside the room. Voices were raised. Feet scuffled. Something wooden scraped against the floor. Gordon shouted, 'Get them out! Fast!' Someone else shouted, 'The back way! Use the back way!' There was more shouting, more noise, more confusion. And then the door opened and two men stood there, silhouetted against the glow of the torches. The Bischof brothers. Claus was standing slightly ahead of Charlie, his hands at his sides. He was smiling slightly, as if enjoying a private joke. Behind them, members jostled as they strained to see what was happening. Alex and Claus stood looking at each other.

Finally Claus said, very quietly, 'This meeting is private.'

Alex narrowed his eyes at him and made to step forward. Something glinted by Claus's left hand.

'Please go,' Claus said.

Alex laughed and brought the automatic up. It was barely at hip level when Claus struck. The blade went in just below Alex's rib cage. It was so fast that even Alex couldn't believe it had happened. He looked down at the little hole where the blade had pierced his jacket. He raised the gun and fired a quick burst straight into Claus's chest. It made a noise something between a football rattle and a workman's drill. Claus catapulted backwards into the crowd, blood pumping through the ragged holes of his white polo-neck.

Alex shouted, 'Anyone else ...?' He raised the gun above their heads.

Anna screamed, 'Alex, no!' She went to grab his arm, but Miles caught hold of her and pulled her backwards.

'Hold on to her!' Miles told Andrew. 'Don't let her move!'

Alex squeezed the trigger again. The burst lasted no more than a couple of seconds, but it seemed like as many hours as bullets sprayed one whole side of the Room, shattering the glass in the mirrors, chipping stones out of the Florentine mosaics, gouging holes in the amber panels.

And then, as suddenly as the terrible noise had started, it stopped. A fearful hush descended over the Room. One last fragment of glass fell to the ground and smashed. No one moved. There was a click at the far end of the Room. Miles looked quickly around. Six of the seven men who had been standing on the platform had vanished. Only Bill Gordon was still there.

He stepped back from the tall double doors at the far end of the room and turned, and as Alex walked towards him, he opened his arms wide and smiled his crocodile smile.

'That was a terrible thing you just did, my friend,' he said. Miles felt some admiration for his self-control. 'But luckily it is none of our concern. The Room does not belong to us any more. It is the property of President Moulassa of Kananga. He won't be at all pleased when he finds that his goods have been damaged. But he can afford to have it repaired. I don't think he'll ask us for a refund.'

Alex paused and looked at him with a puzzled expression, as if he was hearing the words but not understanding them. His knees buckled and for a moment it looked as if they were about to give way under

370

him, but he recovered and pulled himself upright and walked on as if Gordon had not spoken.

Painfully, slowly, and with an enormous effort of will, he managed to climb up on to the platform. He turned and faced the room. A large, dark, shiny stain was spreading across the front of his jacket.

'No one is having this room.' Alex's voice was thick and slurred, as if he had been drinking heavily. 'It does not exist.'

'What are you talking about?' Gordon sneered. He was standing beside him now. 'Of course it exists. Thanks to me the Amber Room has existed for nearly three hundred years, and it will exist for hundreds more.'

Alex turned his head and tried to focus his eyes on him, but it was an effort. 'Perhaps you are right,' he said. 'Perhaps it will. But not in the African jungle. In a real palace. In Russia. Where it belongs. Where it has always belonged.' He moved quickly to one side and snatched one of the flambeaux from its metal holder. He held it aloft, as if in salute. 'There can only be one Amber Room in this world,' he said.

Then he walked calmly towards the nearest banner and plunged the torch into its folds.

'No!' Anna's voice was barely above a whisper.

The red-and-black material, dry with age, caught fire at once. Within seconds the flames were rushing upwards, so that the banner itself became a huge torch which set alight the gilded *boiserie* work above. And, because the wood was varnished, the moment the flames touched it they seized hold and raced across the surface like water.

A terrible cry ripped through the horrified silence and Bill Gordon rushed forward, hands stretched out in mute supplication. He tried to seize the wooden pole and pull it away from the wall, but the flames had already worked their way downwards. All he could do was stand there helplessly, like everyone else, and watch with disbelief what was happening.

And while the full horror of the situation sank in, and limbs at last began to react and move, Alex set fire to two more banners.

'Stop him!' someone shouted.

'Kill the bastard!' yelled someone else.

And then suddenly everyone was shouting and rushing forward in

371

their eagerness to get their hands on him. But they were denied the satisfaction of revenge, for, as the banners burned, Alex turned, raised the torch aloft one last time and crumpled to the floor.

Someone – Miles couldn't see who – pushed through the crowd, knelt over him, and seemed to be examining the body.

Someone else shouted, 'Never mind about him!'

Now people were running back and forth, shouting instructions at one another. Countermanding them. Arguing. Groaning. Swearing.

Cunningham-Walker's school-prefect voice boomed above the rest.

'We've got to stop it spreading!'

'How, for Christ's sake?' some junior wanted to know.

'Get some water from somewhere! We need water!'

'Where the hell do we get water from?'

'From the bar, where else?'

'We'll never get there and back in time!'

'Do it!'

Then another voice from the far corner. 'Are you all right, Bill?'

'What good's water without a hose? We need a hose. How do we get water up there without a hose?'

'Bill!'

'Use the banners!'

'Good idea. Smother the flames with the banners!'

'Don't be bloody silly! They'll just catch fire!'

Gerald Deighton stood up, his face distraught, his hair dishevelled. 'Someone come and help! Bill Gordon's collapsed!'

'For Christ's sake, someone do something!' Cunningham-Walker's attention was still on the room.

'Do what? What can we do?'

'I don't know. Something! Anything!'

Deighton crouched down again next to Bill Gordon. 'He's in a bad way,' he called out.

'Can't you deal with it? We're busy.'

'I think he's had a heart attack!'

'What?'

'Can someone come over here and help?'

'For God's sake ...!'

372

'I think he may be dead!'

'We'll all be dead if we don't do something soon!'

By now, one whole section of panelling was on fire and already the flames were reaching out greedily towards the corner. As they did so, they caught the tops of the banners below, which in turn set fire to the wood above. Soon the flames were rushing along the right-hand wall.

Anna stood very close to Miles. 'Does amber burn?' she said quietly.

'Yes,' said Miles.

'We've lost it, then.'

'I'm afraid so.'

'I'm glad,' she said. 'I wouldn't have wanted it to survive. Not tainted like that.'

'At least we saw it,' said Miles.

'I suppose so,' she said. Her face was wet with tears.

Miles put an arm round her shoulder and the two of them stood there in silence, watching. There was nothing anybody could do to save it now. It would be only a minute or two before the fire spread to the other walls and the whole thing went up. Then the members would stop rushing around and shouting and screaming, and look for someone to vent their rage on. Miles didn't intend to be around when that happened; neither did Anna and Andrew.

The room was quickly beginning to fill up with acrid smoke from the varnished wood; but now, mixed in with it, there was another smell: a smell of pine, rich and aromatic, with a bitterness that stung the eyes and rasped the throat and took away the breath. It was the smell of burning amber.

Miles seized Anna by the arm. 'Let's get out of here,' he said.

'Jesus Christ!' She pulled away.

'Now, or we'll choke to death.'

'Look! Up there!'

'Forget it. It's over. Let's get the hell out of here. Now!'

'Look!'

'What is it?'

'The amber! Look what's happening to the amber!'

'Good God!'

The amber was melting and running down the walls, coating the decorations below – not in liquid honey, as Miles had imagined, but in what looked like hot, glutinous tar. Through a gap in the crowd, he could see Bill Gordon's body lying on the far side next to the wall. As it melted, the amber dripped on to him. Given time it would cover him altogether. A black fly in black amber.

34

'Come on!'

Miles grabbed her arm for a second time and the three of them stumbled towards the tunnel. They were almost at the entrance when there was a cry from Anna as she slipped on a patch of ice and fell heavily. Miles turned and started to haul her to her feet.

Gunfire echoed once more through the cave. Bullets cracked and smacked and zinged off the rocks like a swarm of mad maybugs. At first Miles couldn't make out where they were coming from. Then he saw him. He was standing, silhouetted in the doorway of the Room, his blond hair orange under the flames, legs bent, ski-suited body crouched as he steadied the gun in both hands.

'Charlie Bishop!' shouted Miles. 'He's got Alex's gun! Come on, move!'

They had a twenty-second start on him, if that.

The first stretch was short and they were round the left-hand bend and out of sight in no time. But from then on, the tunnel ran straight most of the way until it curved round to the right again and into the home stretch. The lighting, though adequate for their purposes, was far from ideal for someone trying to hit a moving target at over a hundred feet with an automatic weapon.

'When we get round the bend, don't run in a straight line,' Miles told them. 'Keep zigzagging. And keep low. And for Christ's sake, keep going!'

There was no sign of Bishop by the time they reached the end of the straight section. Perhaps something had happened to him in the cave: someone had tried to stop him, or he'd gone back to help or he'd slipped on the ice. Ducking low, they rounded the bend. Miles was afraid the fireplace might have closed after they'd gone.

He'd never been so glad to see light at the end of a tunnel.

They made their way cautiously into the clubhouse, but it was as silent and deserted as when they'd left it. Miles tried to swing the fireplace shut, but it seemed to be locked open. If there was a release lever, they didn't have time to look for it now.

Anna and Andrew were already out on the terrace, blinking against the unaccustomed glare. Miles ran out and slammed the door behind him. He grabbed the end of one of the heavy tables and pulled it across the doorway.

'Now what?' Anna asked.

'Andrew, you run like hell to the cable car. Go straight to Willi Graf's and wait for us there. Go!'

Andrew grabbed the hand-rails beside the steps, swung himself down on to the snow and disappeared out of sight round the side of the building.

'Us?' said Anna. 'What are *we* going to do?'

'Put your boots on! Quick!'

They were next to the door where Charlie had put them, hinged wide open like baby birds waiting to be fed. Their helmets lay beside them.

'Why?'

'Do as I say. And your helmet.'

It took only a few seconds to kick off their moccasins, step into their Raichles and snap them shut.

'Come on! The skis are just down here.' Miles grabbed her hand and pulled her towards the steps.

'But the Totenkopf run starts from way over there. We'll never get there in time.' She pointed across the hillside to where the figure of Andrew could be seen scrambling his way along the path towards the cable car.

'Who said anything about the Totenkopf?' said Miles.

It suddenly dawned on her what he was saying. 'The Diabolo? You must be joking.'

'We don't have to go down it,' he said. 'Just pretend. We'll ski down to the start and mingle with the crowd. Bishop'll never recognise us in our helmets and goggles. With our numbers we'll look just like any other racers. Come on! Let's go!'

They stumbled down the steps, threw their skis flat on the ground and stamped into them. They pulled their goggles down and looked round for their poles.

'Gloves,' said Anna.

'Damn! They must be still in the clubhouse. Never mind.'

Miles grabbed his poles, pushed his hand through the straps, jumped his skis round and pushed off. Anna was only seconds behind.

There was a large crowd milling around near the start. Some were doing last-minute exercises: deep knee bends, swivelling their trunks with a pole held behind their necks, lifting their legs up and down. Others were crouching, eyes shut, hands moving in front of their faces as they travelled the course in their imaginations. Most were just standing about, shuffling their skis on the snow, waiting for the starter to announce their number over the tannoy.

Miles looked back up the hill. Bishop was already out on the terrace, grasping the rail and scanning the slopes.

'He's up there,' said Miles. 'Follow me! Don't look round!'

Taking care not to tread on other people's skis, they manoeuvred their way through the crowd until they found a small space near the announcer's table. Miles glanced up. Bishop was still there. Then people started stumbling out on to the terrace behind him – in ones and two at first, but then in a steady stream. Soon there were dozens of them out there, hands on knees, coughing and gulping in mouthfuls of fresh air.

'Why should he want to kill us?' Anna said. 'We're not the ones who killed his brother, or set fire to the Room. What's the point? It's all over.'

'In Bishop's mind, we're as guilty as Alex. If it hadn't been for us, Alex would never have found the Room. God knows how many millions this'll cost the movement. And, of course, Bishop knows perfectly well that the first thing I'll do when I get to a telephone is ring my newspaper. If I were him, I'd want to kill me.'

'*Fünf ... vier ... drei ... zwei ... eins ... los!*'

With a shout of encouragement from the waiting competitors and a clang of cowbells, the next pair set off down the first straight.

The tannoy crackled: '*Achthundertundzwanzig. Achthunderteinundzwanzig.*'

'Eight twenty and eight twenty-one,' said Anna. 'Four more to go till they get to us. What are we going to do?'

'I'll go and tell them we're not feeling well. Stay here.'

'Hurry!' She looked nervously up at the terrace. 'Miles, wait! He's not there!'

'What?'

'He's not on the terrace any more. He's disappeared!'

'He's probably gone inside. Perhaps he's gone back to help people out of the tunnel. Stop worrying. We're safe as long as we stay here.'

'What if he's gone after Andrew?'

'He won't have.'

'How do you know?'

'It's us he's after. He wouldn't know Andrew if he saw him.'

'*Achthundert und zweiundzwanzig. Achthundertunddreiundzwanzig.*'

'English bastard!'

The German racer loomed out of the crowd, blue eyes blazing, jaw thrust forward, closely followed by his tall, blonde companion. He seemed to have acquired another pair of skis since their last meeting, though not a new race number.

'Saved by the bell!' said Miles.

He had untied the tapes at his side and almost had the thing over his head when the man grabbed him by the front of his anorak.

'Wait! I'm just giving it to you, you silly sod,' Miles told him.

'My ski!' the man shouted. 'You pay!'

'Oh, for God's sake!' snapped Miles. 'You've got insurance cover, haven't you?'

'*Achthundertundvierundzwanzig. Achthundertundfünfundzwanzig.*'

'Look, I'll sort it out with you later,' said Miles. 'Take the numbers and go. You'll miss your turn.'

'Miles!'

'What?'

'He's coming!'

'Who?'

'Charlie Bishop!'

'Oh, for God's sake! Let go of me, you stupid man! Take your bloody numbers and go! Go on! Go away!'

'He's on skis!'

378

'What the hell's he doing on skis?'

'Skiing. What do you think?'

'I meant …'

'You pay!' the man roared again. 'My ski! Very expensive!'

'He's coming this way.'

'Stand still! Don't move!'

'For God's sake, Miles!'

'*Achthundertundsechsundzwanzig. Achthundertundsiebenundzwanzig.*'

'Those are our numbers,' Anna wailed.

'Go and tell them we've scratched,' Miles told her.

Anna began to push her way towards the starting officials. The German assumed the worst.

'But that is my wife's number! She cannot race!'

'She's not racing. Don't you understand?' Miles shouted at him. 'Neither of us is. She's just going to tell them. Take your number and go, for God's sake, or you'll miss your turn!'

But the man's English wasn't up to all that detailed explanation. As far as he understood the situation, he'd been pushed out of the race; on top of which he'd lost a ski and there was no doubt in his mind who was going to pay for it all.

Holding Miles's anorak with one huge fist, he brought the other back and swung. Miles saw it coming a mile off and ducked. He didn't have time to let go of his poles, so he put a left and a right into the man's stomach while still holding them. The effect was extremely satisfying.

The man doubled up, winded.

His wife ran forward and put an arm round him. She looked up at Miles, her face drawn with hatred.

'English bastard!' she screamed.

Miles looked across at Charlie Bishop. He was standing at the edge of the crowd, peering across at the absurd little drama that was being played out near the starting gate. He started to push his way towards them.

'Come on, Anna. Quick!'

'Where?'

'They've called our number!'

'We can't possibly!' she said.

379

'We've got to!' said Miles.

'I don't believe this is happening!' said Anna, as she slid after him.

Somehow they managed to scramble through the gap in the ropes in time and into the starting stalls.

'*Fünf ... vier ... drei ... zwei ... eins ... los!*'

'Ski in my tracks,' Miles called out to her as they came out of the gate. 'Make the same turns I make. I won't go too fast. You won't come to any harm.'

'English bastard!'

The roar followed them down the valley, like the frustrated bellow of a mythical monster when a victim escapes its clutches.

The Diabolo course begins easily enough with a long, straight *schüss*, followed by a high-banked, left-hand turn leading out on to a wide, steep valley. An expert would take it straight, but it allows the amateur plenty of room for short, swinging turns down the fall-line.

Miles hadn't put on skis since the day of the avalanche, and Anna looked rusty too, but the snow at the top was soft and lightly pisted, flattering their techniques and making every turn a pleasure: especially so, given the numbers of spectators in their big scarves and heavy overcoats and fur-lined boots who watched them from behind the orange ropes at the top.

Having negotiated the steep face of the valley, Miles checked and slowed and called over his shoulder.

'You all right?'

'Fine,' she shouted. 'Except I can't feel my hands.'

'They'll warm up.'

'I hope I do.'

She had nothing to apologise for. Miles wished now he hadn't said anything about following in his tracks. She was perfectly capable of making her own.

The bottom of the valley gradually levelled out and the course swung in a big, gentle S before straightening out into another long *Schüss* down to a narrow path that curved to the right, following the contour of the hill. The two skiers ahead of them looked like insects crossing a white eiderdown.

As he carved his way round the first bend of the S, Miles looked back up the valley, expecting to see the next pair behind them, crossing the ridge. As amateurs who hadn't even entered, they were both skiing strongly and well; but the Diabolo traditionally attracted a large, daredevil element that only slowed and turned when it was absolutely necessary, and if he was going to be overtaken by a couple of local speed merchants Miles wanted to be prepared for it. It didn't surprise him, then, to see that the first one to come over the top was taking the valley straight. The odd thing was that there was only one.

'What is it?' Anna called out.

'Nothing,' Miles called back. 'We're doing well.'

He looked up again as he swung right. The solitary skier was in a low crouching position, with both poles tucked under his armpits, and moving very fast. He straightened slightly and Miles recognised the pale-blue ski suit. It wasn't carrying a race number.

'He's right behind us!' Miles shouted, 'We're going to have to get moving!'

'Well, move then!' Anna shouted back.

Miles tucked low. The K2s' reputation for gliding was well deserved. The *schüss* was pretty badly rutted by this stage in the race and Miles was wary of catching an edge, yet the skis moved beautifully over the uneven surface and held their line effortlessly the whole way, barely slowing when the path rose slightly at the end.

'We can probably stay ahead of him if we keep this up.'

They were both breathing hard by the time they'd skated across the little col where the Schwarzegg run joins from the right, and Miles's thigh muscles were beginning to feel the strain. He'd also lost all feeling in his hands. His palms looked like two slices of raw meat. He'd have given anything to stop for a moment to ease the burning in his legs and rub some circulation back into his hands. He looked across at Anna but she showed no signs of flagging.

'Are you all right?' he called back.

'You don't have to keep asking!' she yelled.

Hundreds of spectators lined the hill below the Schwarzegg lift. None of them could possibly have known that, of the fifteen hundred skiers who were to barrel past them that morning, there were two who

381

were skiing, literally, for their lives. One careless slip, one badly caught edge, one moment off-balance and it would be the last run of the day. Or any other day.

From here, the Diabolo course followed the long traverse above the Stockli drag lift that led to the Gun Barrel. Miles remembered it very well. It was the way he had come down from Pauli's restaurant that afternoon. He was hardly likely to forget it. More of a worry to him now, though, was the fact that ahead was the longest stretch of the course that was out of the range of spectators. If Bishop caught up with them here ...

Glancing over his shoulder, it looked to Miles as if they had made up a bit of ground since the bottom of the valley. They had almost reached the end of the traverse by the time Bishop crossed the col.

'We're doing fine,' Miles shouted as they powered their way through the half-powder, half-cut-piste of the Lion's Teeth Ridge.

The entrance to the Gun Barrel came quicker than he had expected. He remembered there was a bend to the right at the top of the steep path that zigzagged down below the pass, but he had been skiing well within himself that afternoon. Today, there was a certain degree of recklessness in his skiing, engendered by a euphoric, and quite unjustified, feeling of invulnerability. Experience should have taught him to recognise the danger signs.

The bend took him completely by surprise. He saw the little row of flags. He checked hard, throwing a cloud of snow out over the valley, but he'd left it just too late. The momentum threw him sideways. He fought desperately to recover his balance, swayed a couple of times and then toppled head first over the edge.

The slope below was only a few degrees off the vertical. He threw his arms out in front of him, but there was no way he could stop himself sliding towards the path thirty feet below. He tried to swing his legs round in the hope of getting some purchase with his skis, but they had become tangled, and in that position there was nothing he could do about it. It was a situation in which he knew only too well that anything can happen. If his bindings didn't come undone soon, he'd be lucky to get out with anything less than a twisted knee. The new snow helped to slow his progress but, even so, he was bound to come down hard on the path, and his wrists and arms were going to take the brunt of the impact.

He was almost on top of the path when he felt the bindings release. Miraculously, both feet came out at the same time. He jammed the balls of his hands deep into the snow and at the same time threw the lower part of his body sideways and downwards. The path rushed up to meet him.

'Hell's bloody teeth!' he shouted.

He wasn't in a completely upright position when he met the path, but he was upright enough to be able to use his knees to absorb most of the shock before pitching sideways into the soft snow at the side.

He lay there for a moment, dazed and winded. He could hear Anna's voice calling down.

'Are you all right?'

'Fine,' he groaned.

Seconds later she was bending over him anxiously.

'I'm all right, honestly,' he said. 'Where are the skis?'

They had come to rest, tips down, in the soft snow just above the path. Using their poles, they managed to hook them out and drag them down on to the path. Miles brushed the bindings clean and, placing one hand on Anna's shoulder, banged the snow from his boots. They were seconds well spent. He couldn't risk them releasing in the middle of a turn further down.

Anna led the way down the hairpins. Though still very shaky, he managed to make the turns without mishap, and soon the rhythm started to return and the speed built up again. Check, compression, extension, and round. Check, compression, extension, and round. Even so, it came as no surprise that, by the time they'd reached the last bend and the safety of the open gully that led to the Blumen Saddle, Bishop was already halfway down the hairpins.

The Diabolo is one of only two downhill races in the world that include a section of uphill skiing, and the scramble over the Saddle tests tired leg muscles more than anything else on the course.

Bishop was *schüss*-ing fast down the gully as they herring-boned the last few steps to the ridge. But he was no longer crouching with his ski poles under his armpits: he was skiing upright and trailing both poles in his left hand. In his right was the Stechkin.

Out of doors it hardly made any sound at all, and if it hadn't been for the puffs of snow around their heels they might not even have realised that he was firing it.

'Christ!' croaked Miles through a throat that ached from hard breathing. 'We're like sitting ducks up here!'

'Why didn't we take the Blumen run? The village is only two minutes from here.'

'He'd have seen us,' said Miles. 'We've got to go on a bit. Find a place where we'll be out of sight and our tracks won't be spotted. There are woods just below Niederwald. We'll try and lose him there.'

The thought had not escaped his mind that the last time he had strayed from a marked piste and tried to beat his own path home it had ended in disaster. Nor that there was a good outside chance that it might happen again, and that this time there would be no last-minute reprieve.

A long easy traverse took them to a point halfway down the Niederwald run. Cheered on by a sprinkling of spectators, they carved a couple of long turns down the prettiest section of the blue run, then swung right, took the short, knee-pounding bumps of Molly's Meadow pretty well straight and, after dodging through a narrow strip of wood, emerged next to the Eigerhubel–Grützi railway line.

Now the course was lined two or three deep with spectators, waving and yodelling and clanking cowbells, urging the racers to even greater speeds and more daring deeds.

Miles didn't think he could keep going much longer. The strength was draining from his legs by the second. Every turn now was an effort and he must have bruised a rib in the fall because, every time he breathed in, he felt a sharp stabbing pain in his left side that took his breath away before it was halfway into his lungs.

Blood was running down his ski poles.

Here would be as good a place to leave the course as any. They could disappear round the back of the crowds without Bishop realising. He might just assume they had made ground, and ski on. Miles looked to his right for possible gaps in the lines of spectators. But the path suddenly began to steepen, his speed built up again, and no sooner had he spotted a gap than it was gone. To stand any chance of escape, he would need to slow his speed drastically. Now. Just thinking about it had lost him valuable seconds. Glancing over his shoulder, he realised that Bishop was less than fifty yards behind them and closing fast. The crowd, in the hope of witnessing a brief moment of drama, cheered them on to greater efforts.

'Faster!' Miles yelled to Anna.

'I can't!' she yelled back.

'Try!'

'I *am* trying!'

And then a small child walked across in front of them. She wore a tiny white ski suit and a pink bonnet tied under the chin with a ribbon, and pink woolly mittens, and pink snow boots. She looked like the Easter Bunny. Having appeared from nowhere about twenty yards ahead and taken a few steps, she stood there uncertainly in the middle of the track. Had she remained there Miles could have gone round her, but she suddenly lurched to the right. Miles shouted, 'Look out!' and veered to his left. The child's mother chose that moment to make a daring rescue bid. Somehow Miles managed to squeeze through the gap between the mother and the line of spectators, but, skiing immediately behind him, Anna's view had been partially blocked. She had no time to react. The mother had bent down and was scooping the child up when she saw her. Anna swerved to the left and in her anxiety to avoid hitting her she caught an edge and went hard down on to her left side. She slid helplessly for another ten or twelve yards before a ski tip caught one of the marker poles and she spun round and finished up lying on her back, in the middle of the track, with her skis lodged amongst the spectators' feet.

Miles edged hard left and right and side-slipped to a stop. He stood there, leaning on his poles, fighting for breath, powerless to do a thing, watching as Bishop skied straight at her. Knees bent, head low, poles jutting out behind him, he seemed to be aiming his ski tips straight at Anna's head.

Miles dredged up his last reserves of breath and let out a single high-pitched yell. 'No-o-o!'

It was enough to break Bishop's concentration. He looked up and at that moment his skis wandered to the left: perhaps only by a few inches, but it was enough. There was a faint click as his right boot clipped Anna's helmet, but his eyes never wavered for a second from the figure of the man standing in the middle of the course in front of him. The man who knew too much and would tell all. The man who had to die if the movement was to live.

Miles swivelled his skis round, pointed them down the fall-line and pushed as hard as he could, and again, and again. But, by the time his K2s were running, Bishop's tips were almost overlapping his backs and he could practically feel the man's breath in the gap under his helmet. He could hear the sound of a pocket being unzipped as Bishop reached for the gun.

But the crowds were thick all the way to Niederwald, and beyond. Miles gambled that he would hold his fire until they came to a stretch of the course below the railway, out of the spectators' range.

There was less than a second between them as they turned sharp right and plunged through the little tunnel under the line. Miles heard a metallic scrape and a curse and guessed Bishop had misjudged the width and caught the edge of a binding against the side.

Then he was through and out and zig-zagging his way steeply down between deep moguls.

Miles was skiing on automatic pilot. If he'd thought for a second about what lay below him, fatigue and despair would have overwhelmed him and a bullet in the back might have come as a relief. But he didn't think. He just skied.

He was halfway down the mogul field when he remembered where he was. It was the section of the course he'd spotted coming up on the train the previous morning. The bit where it turned sharp left to Grützi. Where his palms had started sweating ...

Now he could see the flags marking the route, and the stretch of red netting. A race marshal in an orange anorak had been positioned at the side of the track to wave people through, just in case ...

Bishop was still at the top of the mogul field when he saw Miles turning to the right and the official running after him, shouting and trying to beckon him back. He skied the field fast, poles clenched in one hand, gun in the other. As he approached the turn, the official ran forward, his arms spread wide, shepherding him in the other direction. Bishop fired a short burst and the official's head exploded against the Blumenhorn.

Miles glanced quickly down to his left. It looked like a perfect

386

deep-powder slope: except he knew that, just beyond it, just out of sight, the powder ran out … He wondered if Bishop knew it too. He thought probably not.

He sat back on his skis and let the tips ride free. The snow was so deep and so cold, it flew over his shoulders. And then he saw where the snow ended. It was less than fifty yards away. He glanced back. Bishop was closing fast. And then Miles realised. It wasn't because he was a good powder skier; precisely the opposite. On the piste he was as fast and technically proficient as any good amateur, but like many good piste-bashers he couldn't cope with the deep stuff. The technique wasn't there. He was one of those who just kept going and hoping for the best.

Bishop fired another burst, but again the shots went wide.

Miles was desperately close to the edge now. The far side of the valley was almost in view, but he showed no sign of slowing. Neither did Bishop. Now Miles could feel the snow giving slightly under his skis. He was less than ten yards from the edge when he made his turn. Technically speaking, it should have been impossible. But Miles was due for a spot of good luck, and Bishop wasn't. By the time he realised his mistake, it was already far too late. Sailing out into space, his despairing cry mingled with the croaking of the crows as they wheeled and glided like black undertakers against the brilliant white of the Blumenhorn.

35

'Where the hell have you been?'

'Switzerland.'

'Again? More free skiing?'

'Actually, Neville …'

'I thought you were supposed to be going to Kentish Town, to talk to Lambourn's ex-missis.'

'Didn't you get my article? I faxed it to you ages ago.'

'Oh, that. I was going to run it the following Monday, but the *Sunday Times* came up with a long piece that covered much the same ground. Don't worry. You'll get paid. But, listen, I'm still quite interested in an interview with Boozy Camilla …'

'Forget Boozy Camilla,' said Miles. 'Forget the Lambourn Set. I've got a story that'll really knock your socks off.'

'Not another.' The voice was heavy with boredom.

'Have you ever heard of the Amber Room?'

'No.'

'How about President Moulassa of Kananga?'

'Ask me another.'

'The Diabolo Club?'

'Ah, now that rings a bell. Wasn't Archie Lambourn something to do with the Diabolo Club? Now that might put a nice spin on the ball.'

* * *

'I do hope this isn't the end of our friendship.' Irina screwed another cigarette carefully into her holder and set fire to it with the Zippo. 'You may not always want to see me, but I shall always be happy to see you.'

Miles put a hand over hers and smiled.

She looked up at him from her chair. 'Anna may not be back for some time,' she said. 'She and Andrew have decided to stay on in Paris. They need time to get to know each other again. She feels she's neglected him in recent years. She has a strong sense of duty.'

'I know.'

'You'll miss her, I expect.'

'Yes,' said Miles. 'We became very close. But it was a thing of its time. It couldn't have lasted.'

Irina nodded. 'What does?' she said. Then she turned sideways and picked up the amber rose from the little table next to her chair. She held it up between her thumb and forefinger. The outlines of the insect were etched sharp against the morning light. 'This little chap's turned out to be quite a survivor, though,' she said.

'Perhaps for some of us there is life after death,' said Miles.

'One can always hope,' said Irina. 'Hope is the only thing that gets us through. My dreams are over, but you still have many to come. If ever you feel your spirits flagging, perhaps this will help to freshen your resolve.' She smiled and held the rose out to him.

He shook his head. 'I couldn't possibly,' he said.

'Please,' she said. 'For me. To remind you what might have been.' Her eyes were dark in her long, pale face.

* * *

Miles started writing his story. No newspaper was ever going to publish it. But he did it anyway. For himself. For his children and grandchildren, if ever he had any. And for Elizabeth. From time to time he picked up the rose and gazed into it, and wondered if he would ever see her again.

And then, a week later, Lydia Hollies rang. There'd been an accident. The general had been out after pigeons. He was climbing over a stile. His foot must have slipped. He was so meticulous about things like safety catches. She couldn't understand it.

Miles drove down that afternoon. Lydia met him at the front door. She had been crying. She looked at him and shook her head. Miles put his arms round her and held her.

'Does she know?' he asked softly.

He felt her head nodding against his chest.

Elizabeth was in the drawing room. She was sitting on the floor in front of the fire. The labrador was lying next to her, his head resting in her lap. Miles sat down beside her and took her hand and opened it out palm upwards. He took the rose out of his pocket and placed it in her palm. She looked at it for a while. Her eyes shone in the firelight. Then with her other hand she took it and held it out against the flames. Her eyes reflected the honey glow.

For a long time she didn't move, and then she turned and looked at him. Her face was very grave. And then her eyes narrowed with concentration and her lips began to move.

'Beautiful,' she said.

And she held the rose out towards him, but he couldn't really see it because his eyes were too full of tears.

* * *

On 2nd March, Neville rang.

'This Amber Room in Russia there's been all the hoo-ha about,' he said. 'The one they've unearthed. Was it you who mentioned something about it the other day?'

Miles said, 'I asked if you'd ever heard of it, and you hadn't.'

'I shouldn't think there's anyone in the world who hasn't heard of it now,' he said in a tone that was almost accusing. 'The amount of coverage it's getting, anyone would think they'd discovered the lost world of Atlantis.'

Miles said, 'To the Russians, it's not far short.'

'It's in some palace near St Petersburg, apparently,' Neville told him. 'They've reconstructed it just as it was before the war.'

'Yes.'

'They're opening it to the public next week. You seem to know quite a lot about it. You'd better go and take a look. Try and keep it to twelve hundred words. Usual fee and expenses. OK?'

'OK,' said Miles.

* * *

The great palace glowed blue in the winter sunshine. The trees in the park bent under the weight of the snow and the fountains in the formal garden were frozen into weird ice sculptures.

The queue stretched down the front steps and across the forecourt as far as Rastrelli's gilded gates. The temperature inside the house was only slightly lower than in the Temperate House in Kew Gardens. Even so, Miles wondered if he would ever feel his toes and fingers again.

He deposited his overcoat, and the black fur hat he'd bought that morning in the hotel shop, at the compulsory cloakroom and rejoined the procession. The heavy-faced attendants ensured that it kept moving at a steady pace.

'Human breath can dull the patina,' an American voice behind him stated authoritatively.

A large woman in a dark-blue suit with a face like a boiled ham launched into a loud, monotonous commentary as they shuffled in. 'This is the famous Amber Room,' she announced. 'Originally made for King Friedrich the First of Prussia, it was presented in 1716 to Tsar Peter the Great to symbolise the military alliance between Prussia and Russia. For many years it was in the Winter Palace in St Petersburg, until the Empress Catherine brought it here to Tsarskoe Selo in 1755 ...'

'It's incredible,' said the American, his voice hushed with awe. 'When you think ...'

Miles looked at him and smiled.

'Isn't it incredible?' the American said.

'Incredible,' said Miles, and followed the procession obediently into the Picture Hall.